811

W9-BXY-834

Family Tree

Also by Barbara Delinsky

THE WOMAN NEXT DOOR
COAST ROAD
THREE WISHES
FOR MY DAUGHTERS
MORE THAN FRIENDS

DOUBLEDAY LARGE PRINT HOME LIBRARY EDITION

Doubleday

New York   London   Toronto   Sydney   Auckland

Family Tree

Barbara Delinsky

This Large Print Edition, prepared especially for Doubleday Large Print Home Library, contains the complete, unabridged text of the original Publisher's Edition.

PUBLISHED BY DOUBLEDAY

ISBN 978-0-7394-7784-7

PRINTED IN THE UNITED STATES OF AMERICA

This Large Print Book carries the Seal of Approval of N.A.V.H.

For Cassandra,
a precious gift

Family Tree

Chapter 1

Something woke her mid-dream. She didn't know whether it was the baby kicking, a gust of sea air tumbling in over the sill, surf breaking on the rocks, or even her mother's voice, liquid in the waves, but as she lay there open-eyed in bed in the dark, the dream remained vivid. It was an old dream, and no less embarrassing to her for knowing the script. She was out in public, for all the world to see, lacking a vital piece of clothing. In this instance, it was her blouse. She had left home without it and now stood on the steps of her high school—her *high school*—wearing only a bra, and an old one at that. It didn't matter that she was sixteen years past graduation and knew none of the people on the steps. She was exposed and thoroughly mortified. And then—this was a first—there was her *mother-in-law*, standing off to the side, wearing a look of dismay and carrying—bizarre—the blouse.

Dana might have laughed at the absurdity of it, if, at that very moment, something else hadn't diverted her thoughts. It was the sudden rush of fluid between her legs, like nothing she had ever felt before.

Afraid to move, she whispered her husband's name. When he didn't reply, she reached out, shook his arm, and said in full voice, "Hugh?"

He managed a gut-low "Mm?"

"We have to get up."

She felt him turn and stretch.

"My water just broke."

He sat up with a start. Leaning over her, his deep voice higher than normal, he asked, "Are you sure?"

"It keeps coming. But I'm not due for two weeks."

"That's okay," he reassured her, "that's okay. The baby is seven-plus pounds—right in the middle of the full-term range. What time is it?"

"One-ten."

"Don't move. I'll get towels." He rolled away and off the bed.

She obeyed him, partly because Hugh had studied every aspect of childbirth and knew what to do, and partly to avoid spreading the mess. As soon as he returned, though, she supported her belly and pushed herself up. Squinting against the sudden light of the lamp, she took one of the towels, slipped it between her legs, and shuffled into the bathroom.

Hugh appeared seconds later, wide-eyed and pale in the vanity lights. "What do you see?" he asked.

"No blood. But it's definitely the baby and not me."

"Do you feel anything?"

"Like terror?" She was dead serious. As prepared as they were—they had read dozens of books, talked with innumerable friends, grilled the doctor *and* her partners *and* her nurse-practitioner *and* the hospital personnel during a pre-admission tour—the reality of the moment was something else. With childbirth suddenly and irrevocably imminent, Dana was scared.

"Like contractions," Hugh replied dryly.

"No. Just a funny feeling. Maybe a vague tightening."

"What does 'vague' mean?"

"Subtle."

"Is it a contraction?"

"I don't know."

"Does it come and go?"

"I don't *know*, Hugh. Really. I just woke up and then there was a gush—" She broke off, feeling something. "A cramp." She held her breath, let it out, met his eyes. "Very mild."

"Cramp or contraction?"

"Contraction," she decided, starting to tremble. They had waited so long for this. They were as ready as they would ever be.

"Are you okay while I call the doctor?" he asked.

She nodded, knowing that if she hadn't he would have brought the phone into the bathroom. But she wasn't helpless. As doting as Hugh had been lately, she was an independent sort, and by design. She knew what it was to be wholly dependent on someone and then have her taken away. It didn't get much worse.

So, while he phoned the doctor, she fit her big belly into her newest, largest warm-up suit, now lined with a pad from her post-delivery stash to catch amniotic fluid that continued to leak, and went down the hall to the baby's room. She had barely turned on the light when he called.

"*Dee?*"

"In here!"

Buttoning jeans, he appeared at the door. His dark hair was mussed, his eyes concerned. "If those pains are less than ten minutes apart, we're supposed to head to the hospital. Are you okay?"

She nodded. "Just want a last look."

"It's perfect, honey," he said as he stretched into an old navy tee shirt. "All set?"

"I don't think they're less than ten minutes apart."

"They will be by the time we're halfway there."

"This is our first," she argued. "First babies take longer."

"That may be the norm, but every norm has exceptions. Indulge me on this, please?"

Taking his hand, she kissed his palm and pressed it to her neck. She needed another minute.

She felt safe here, sheltered, happy. Of all the nurseries she had decorated for clients, this was her best—four walls of a panoramic meadow, laced with flowers, tall grasses, sun-tipped trees. Everything was white, soft orange, and green, myriad shades of each highlighted with a splotch of blue in a flower or the sky. The feeling was one of a perfect world, gentle, harmonious, and safe.

Self-sufficient she might be, but she had dreamed of a world like this from the moment she had dared to dream again.

Hugh had grown up in a world like this. His childhood had been sheltered, his adolescence rich. His family had come to America on the *Mayflower* and been prominent players ever since. Four centuries of success had bred stability. Hugh might downplay the connection, but he was a direct beneficiary of it.

"Your parents expected pastel balloons on the wall," she remarked, releasing his hand. "I'm afraid I've disappointed them."

"Not you," he answered, "we, but it's a moot point. This isn't my parents' baby." He made for the door. "I need shoes."

Moving aside knitting needles that held the top half of a moss green sleepsack, Dana carefully lowered herself into the Boston rocker. She had dragged it down from the attic, where Hugh hid most of his heirloom pieces, and while she had rescued others, now dispersed through the house, this was her favorite. Purchased in the 1840s by his great-great-grandfather, the eventual Civil War general, it had a spindle back and three-section rolled seat that was strikingly comfortable for something so old. Months ago, even before they had put the meadow on the walls, Dana had sanded the rocker's chipped paint and restored it to gleaming perfection. And Hugh had let her. He knew that she valued family history all the more for having lived without it.

That said, everything else was new, a family history that began here. The crib and its matching dresser were imported, but the rest, from the changing pad on top, to the hand-painted fabric framing the windows, to the mural, were custom done by her roster of artists. That roster, which included top-notch painters, carpenters, carpet and window people, also included her grandmother and herself. There was a throw over one end of the crib, made by her grandmother and mirroring the meadow mural; a cashmere rabbit that Dana had knitted in every shade of orange; a bunting, two sweaters, numerous hats, and a stack of carriage blankets—and that didn't count the winter wool bunting in progress, which was mounded in a wicker basket at the foot of her chair, or the sleepsack she held in her hand. They had definitely gone overboard.

Rocking slowly, she smiled as she remembered what had been here eight months before. Her pregnancy had just been confirmed, when she had come home from work to find the room blanketed with tulips. Purple, yellow, white—all were fresh enough to last for days. Hugh had planned this surprise with sheer pleasure, and Dana believed it had set the tone.

There was magic in this room. There was warmth and love. There was security. Their baby would be happy here, she knew it would.

Opening a hand on her stomach, she caressed the mound that was absurdly large in proportion to the rest of her. She couldn't feel the baby move—the poor little thing didn't have room to do much more than wiggle a finger or toe—but Dana felt the tightening of muscles that would push her child into the world.

Breathe slowly . . . Hugh's soothing baritone came back from their Lamaze classes. She was still breathing deeply well after the end of what was definitely another contraction when the slap of flip-flops announced his return.

She grinned. "I'm picturing the baby in this room."

But he was observant to a fault. "That was another contraction, wasn't it? Are you timing them?"

"Not yet. They're too far apart. I'm trying to distract myself by thinking happy thoughts. Remember the first time I saw your house?"

It was the right question. Smiling, he leaned against the doorjamb. "Sure do. You were wearing neon green."

"It wasn't neon, it was lime, and you didn't know what the piece was."

"I knew what it was. I just didn't know what it was called."

"It was called a sweater."

His eyes held hers. "Laugh if you want— you do every time—but that sweater was more angular and asymmetrical than anything I'd ever seen."

"Modular."

"Modular," he repeated, pushing off from the jamb. "Knit in cashmere and silk—all of which comes easily to me now, but back then, what did I know?" He put both hands on the arms of the rocker and bent down. "I interviewed three designers. The others were out of the running the minute you walked in my door. I didn't know about yarn, didn't know about color, didn't know about whether you were any kind of decorator, except that David loved what you did for his house. But we're playing with fire, dear heart. David will kill me if I don't get you to the hospital in time. I'm sure he's seen the lights."

David Johnson lived next door. He was an orthopedic surgeon and divorced. Dana was always trying to set him up, but he always complained, saying that none of the women were *her*.

"David won't see the lights," she insisted now. "He'll be asleep."

Placing her knitting on the basket, Hugh hoisted her—gently—to her feet. "How do you feel?"

"Excited. You?"

"Antsy." He slid an arm around her waist, or thereabouts, but when he saw from her face that another contraction had begun, he said, "Definitely less than ten minutes. What, barely five?"

She didn't argue, just concentrated on

slowly exhaling until the pain passed. "There," she said. "Okay—boy or girl—last chance to guess."

"Either one is great, but we can't just hang out here, Dee," he warned. "We have to get to the hospital." He tried to steer her toward the hall.

"I'm not ready."

"After nine months?"

Fearful, she put her hand on his chest. "What if something goes wrong?"

He grinned and covered her hand. "Nothing will go wrong. This is my lucky tee shirt. I've worn it through every Super Bowl the Patriots have won *and* through the World Series with the Red Sox."

"I'm serious."

"So am I," he said, all confidence. "We've had tests. The baby's healthy. You're healthy. The baby's the perfect birth size. It's in the right position. We have the best obstetrician and the best hospital—"

"I mean later. What if there's a problem, like when the baby is three? Or seven? Or when it's a teenager, you know, like the problems the Millers have with their son?"

"We aren't the Millers."

"But it's the *big* picture, Hugh." She was

thinking of the dream she'd had prior to waking up. No mystery, that dream. It was about her fear of being found lacking. "What if we aren't as good at parenting as we think we'll be?"

"Now, *there's* a moot point. A little late to be thinking of it."

"Do you realize what we're getting into?"

"Of course not," he said. "But we want this baby. Come on, sweetie. We have to leave."

Dana insisted on returning to the master bath, where she quickly washed her face, rinsed her mouth, and brushed her hair. Turning sideways for a last look, she studied her body's profile. Yes, she preferred being slim—yes, she was tired of hauling around thirty extra pounds—yes, she was dying to wear jeans and a tee shirt again. But being pregnant was special.

"Dana," Hugh said impatiently. "Please."

She let him guide her down the hall, past the nursery again and toward the stairs. In architectural circles, the house was considered a Newport cottage, though "cottage" downplayed its grandness. Built in a U that faced the sea, with multiple pairs of French doors opening to a canopied patio, a large swath of soft grass, and a border of beach roses that overlooked the surf, it was a vision of corbels, columns, white trim and shingles gently grayed by the salt air. One wing held the living room, dining room, and library; the other, the kitchen and family room. The master bedroom and nursery were in one wing of the second floor, with two additional bedrooms in the other. The dormered attic housed an office, complete with a balcony. Every room in the house, with the sole exception of the first-floor powder room, had a window facing the sea.

It was Dana's dream house. She had fallen in love with it on sight. More than once, she had told Hugh that even if he had turned into a frog with their first kiss, she would have married him for the house.

Now, approaching the nearer of two staircases that descended symmetrically to the front hall, she asked, "What if it's a girl?"

"I'll love a girl."

"But you want a boy deep down, I know you do, Hugh. It's that family name. You want a little Hugh Ames Clarke."

"I'd be just as happy with Elizabeth Ames Clarke, as long as I don't have to deliver her myself. Careful here," he said as they started down the stairs, but Dana had to stop at the first turn. The contraction was stronger this time.

She was prepared for pain, but the fact of it was something else. "Can I do this?" she asked, shaking noticeably as she clung to his arm.

He held her more tightly. "You? In a *minute*."

Hugh had trusted her right from the start. It was one of the things she loved. He hadn't hesitated when she suggested barnboard for the floor of his otherwise modern kitchen or, later, when she insisted that he hang his family portraits—large, dark oil paintings of Clarkes with broad brows, square jaws, and straight lips—in the living room, though he would have gladly left them packed away in the attic.

He took his heritage for granted. No, it was more than that. He rebelled against his father's obsession with heritage, said that it *embarrassed* him.

Dana must have convinced him that he was a successful figure in his own right, because he had let her hang the oils. They gave the room visual height and historical depth. She had splashed the large leather furniture with wildly textured pillows, and Hugh liked that, too. He had said he wanted comfort, not stuffiness. Butter-soft leather and a riot of nubby silk and chenille offered that. He had also said he did not like the settee that had belonged to his great-grandfather because it was stern, but he gave her wiggle room there, too. She had the oak of that settee restored, the seat re-caned, and cushions and a throw designed to soften the look.

Not that she saw *any* of it now. She focused on one step after the other, thinking that if these contractions were just the beginning, labor might be pretty bad, and if there were any other way to get this baby out, she would opt for it now.

They were barely at the bottom when she gasped. "I forgot my pillow."

"They have pillows at the hospital."

"I need my own. Please, Hugh?"

Settling her on the bottom step, he ran up the stairs and was back with the pillow under his arm in less than a minute.

"And water," she reminded him.

He disappeared again, this time into the kitchen, and returned seconds later with a pair of bottles. "What else?"

"Cell phone? BlackBerry? Omigod, Hugh, I was supposed to have a preliminary meeting with the Cunninghams today."

"Looks like you'll miss it."

"It's a huge job."

"Think maternity leave."

"This was supposed to bridge it. I promised them that I'd make schematic drawings right after the baby was born."

"The Cunninghams will understand. I'll call them from the hospital." He patted his pockets. "Cell phone, BlackBerry, what else?"

"Call list. Camera."

"In your case." He scooped the bag from the closet, staring in dismay at the yarn that spilled from the half-zippered top. "Dana, you promised."

"It isn't much," she said quickly, "just something small to work on, you know, if things are slow."

"Small?" he asked as he tucked in the yarn. "What are there, eight balls here?"

"Six, but it's heavy worsted, which means not much yardage, and I didn't want to risk running out. Don't be impatient, Hugh. Knitting comforts me."

He shot a do-tell look at the closet. There

were bags of yarn on the shelf above, the floor below. Most closets in the house were the same.

"My stash is not as big as some," she reasoned. "Besides, what harm is there in making the most of my time at the hospital? Gram wants this pattern for the fall season, and what if there's down time *after* the baby's born? Some women bring books or magazines. This is *my* thing."

"How long did they say you would be in the hospital?" he asked. They both knew that, barring complications, she would be home the next day.

"You're not a knitter. You wouldn't understand."

"No argument there." Squeezing the water bottles into the bag, he zipped it, put the strap on his shoulder, and helped her out the front door. They crossed the porch to the cobblestone drive where Hugh's car was parked.

Rather than think about how she was trembling or, worse, when the next pain would hit, Dana thought about the little cotton onesies in that bag. They were store-bought, but everything else was home-made. Hugh thought she had packed too much, but how to choose between those tiny knitted caps and booties, all cotton for August and exquisitely done? They took up no space. Her baby deserved choices.

Of course, her in-laws hadn't been any wilder about these items than they had about the nursery décor. They had provided a layette from Neiman Marcus, and didn't understand why the baby wouldn't be wearing those things home.

Dana let it pass. To explain would have offended them. Hand-knit to her meant memories of her mother, the love of her grandmother, and the caring of a surrogate family of yarn-store friends. Hand-knit was personal in ways her husband's family couldn't understand. The Clarkes knew their place in society, and much as Dana loved being Hugh's wife, much as she admired the Clarke confidence and envied their past, she couldn't forget who she was.

"Doin' okay?" Hugh asked as he eased her into the car.

"Doin' okay," she managed.

She adjusted the seat belt so that the baby wouldn't be hurt if they stopped short, though there was little chance of that. For an antsy man, Hugh drove with care, so much so that as time passed and the contractions grew more intense, she wished he would go faster.

But he knew what he was doing. Hugh always knew what he was doing. Moreover, there were few other cars on the road, and they had green lights all the way.

Having pre-registered at the hospital, he had barely given their name when they were admitted. In no time flat, Dana was in a hospital gown, with a fetal monitor strapped around her middle and the resident-on-call examining her. The contractions were coming every three minutes, then every two minutes, literally taking her breath.

The next few hours passed in a blur, though more than once, when the progress slowed, she wondered if the baby was having a final qualm itself. She knit for a while until the strength of the contractions zapped her, at which point Hugh became her sole source of comfort. He massaged her neck and her back and peeled her hair from her face, and all the while, he told her how beautiful she was.

Beautiful? Her insides were a mass of pain, her skin wet, her hair matted. Beautiful? She was a mess! But she clung to her husband, trying to believe every word he said.

All in all, their baby came relatively quickly. Less than six hours after Dana's water had broken, the nurse declared her fully dilated and they relocated to the delivery room. Hugh took pictures—Dana thought she remembered that, though the memory may well have been created later by the pictures themselves. She pushed for what seemed forever but was considerably shorter, so much so that her obstetrician nearly missed the baby's birth. The woman had barely arrived when the baby emerged.

Hugh cut the cord and, within seconds, placed the wailing baby on her stomach— the most beautiful, perfectly formed little girl she had ever seen. Dana didn't know whether to laugh at the baby's high-pitched crying or gasp in amazement at little fingers and toes. She seemed to have dark hair— Dana immediately imagined a head of fine, dark-brown Clarke hair—though it was hard to see with traces of milky-white film on her body.

"Who does she look like?" Dana asked, unable to see through her tears.

"No one *I've* ever seen," he remarked

with a delighted laugh and took several more pictures before the nurse stole the infant away, "but she's beautiful." He smiled teasingly. "You did want a girl."

"I did," Dana confessed. "I wanted someone to take my mother's name." Incredibly—and later she did remember this with utter clarity—she pictured her mother as she had last seen her, vibrant and alive that sunny afternoon at the beach. Dana had always imagined that mother and daughter would have grown to be best of friends, in which case Elizabeth Joseph would have been there in the delivery room with them. Of the many occasions in Dana's life when she desperately missed her mother, this was a big one. That was one reason why naming the baby after her meant so much. "It's a little like being given her back."

"Elizabeth."

"Lizzie. She looks like a Lizzie, doesn't she?"

Hugh was still smiling, holding Dana's hand to his mouth. "Hard to tell yet. But 'Elizabeth' is an elegant name."

"Next one'll be a boy," Dana promised, craning her neck to see the baby. "What are they doing to her?"

Hugh rose off the stool to see. "Suctioning," he reported. "Drying her off. Putting on an ID band."

"Your parents wanted a boy."

"It's not my parents' baby."

"Call them, Hugh. They'll be so excited. And call my grandmother. And the others."

"Soon," Hugh said. He focused on Dana, so intent that she started crying again. "I love you," he whispered.

Unable to answer, she just wrapped her arms around his neck and held on tightly.

"Here she is," came a kindly voice, and suddenly the baby was in Dana's arms, clean and lightly swaddled.

Dana knew she was probably imagining it—infants couldn't really focus—but she could have sworn the baby was looking at her as if she knew that Dana was her mother, would love her forever, would guard her with her *life*.

The baby had a delicate little nose and pink mouth, and an every-bit-as-delicate chin. Dana peered under the pink cap. The baby's hair was still damp, but it was definitely dark—with wispy little curls, *lots* of little curls, which was a surprise. Both she and Hugh had straight hair.

"Where did she get these?"

"Beats me," Hugh said, sounding suddenly alarmed. "But look at her skin."

"It's so smooth."

"It's so *dark*." He raised fear-filled eyes toward the doctor. "Is she all right? I think she's turning blue."

Dana's heart nearly stopped. She hadn't seen any blue, but given the speed with which the baby was snatched from them and checked, she barely breathed herself until the staff pediatrician had done a thorough exam, given the baby a resoundingly high Apgar score, and pronounced her a hearty, healthy seven pounds.

No, her skin wasn't blue, Dana decided when Lizzie was back in her arms. Nor, though, was it the pale pink she had expected. Her face had a coppery tint that was as lovely as it was puzzling. Curious, she eased the blanket aside to uncover a tiny arm. The skin there was the same light brown, all the more marked in contrast to the pale white nails at the tips of her fingers.

"Who *does* she look like?" Dana murmured, mystified.

"Not a Clarke," Hugh said. "Not a Joseph.

Maybe someone on your father's side of the family?"

Dana couldn't say. She knew her father's name, but little else.

"She looks healthy," she reasoned.

"I didn't read anything about skin being darker at birth."

"Me, neither. She looks tanned."

"More than tanned. Look at her palms, Dee. They're lighter, like her fingernails."

"She looks Mediterranean."

"No. Not Mediterranean."

"Indian?"

"Not that, either. Dana, she looks *black*."

Chapter 2

Hugh hoped he was being facetious. He and Dana were white. Their baby couldn't be black.

Still, standing there in the delivery room, scrutinizing the infant in Dana's arms, he felt a tremor of fear. Lizzie's skin was a whole lot darker than any other Clarke baby he had ever seen, and he had seen plenty of those. Clarkes took pride in their offspring, as evidenced by the flood of holiday pictures from relatives each year. His brother had four children, all of the pale white Anglo-Saxon type, their first cousins had upward of sixteen. Not a one was dark.

Hugh was a lawyer. He spent his days arguing facts, and, in this case, there were none to suggest that his baby should be anything but Caucasian. He had to be imagining it—had to be blowing things out of proportion. And who could blame him? He was tired. He had been late coming to bed after watching the Sox play Oakland, then awake an hour later and keyed up ever since. But boy, he wouldn't have missed a minute of that delivery. Watching the baby come out—cutting the cord—it didn't get much better than that. Talk about emotional highs!

Now, though, he felt oddly deflated. This was his child—his family, his genes. She was supposed to look familiar.

He had read about what babies went through getting out of the womb, and had been prepared to see a pointy head, blotchy skin, or even bruises. This baby's head was round and her skin perfect.

But she didn't have the fine, straight hair or widow's peak that marked the Clarke babies, or Dana's blond coloring and blue eyes.

She looked like a stranger.

Maybe this was a natural letdown after months of buildup. Maybe it was what the books meant about not always loving your baby on sight. She was an individual. She would grow to have her own likes and dislikes, her own strengths, her own temperament, all of which might be totally different from Dana's and his.

He did love her. She was his child. She just didn't look it.

That said, she was his responsibility. So he followed the nurse when she took the baby to the nursery, and he watched through the window while the staff put drops in her eyes and gave her a real sponge bath.

Her skin still seemed coppery. If anything, juxtaposed with a pale pink blanket and hat, it was more marked than before.

The nurses seemed oblivious to the skin tone. Biracial marriages were common. These women didn't know that Hugh's wife was white. Moreover, there were far darker infants in the nursery. By comparison to some, Elizabeth Ames Clarke was light-skinned.

Clinging to that thought, he returned to Dana's room and began making calls. She was right about his parents' wanting a boy—having had two boys themselves, they were partial to children who passed on the name—but they were excited by his news, as was his brother, and by the time he called Dana's grandmother, he was feeling better.

Eleanor Joseph was a remarkable woman.

After losing her daughter and her husband in tragic accidents four years apart, she had raised her granddaughter alone, and through it all she built a thriving business. Its official name was The Stitchery, though no one ever called it anything but Ellie Jo's.

Prior to meeting Dana, Hugh knew next to nothing about yarn, much less the people who used it. He still couldn't even remember what SKP was, though Dana had explained it to him more than once. But he could appreciate the warmth of his favorite alpaca scarf, which she had hand-knit and which was more handsome than anything he had seen in a store—and he could feel the appeal of the yarn shop. During these final weeks of Dana's pregnancy, as she cut back on her own work, she spent more time there. He dropped in often, ostensibly to check on his pregnant wife, but also to enjoy the calm atmosphere. When a client was lying to him, or an associate botched a brief, or a judge ruled against him, he found that the yarn store offered a respite.

Maybe it was the locale. What could be better than overlooking an apple orchard? More likely, though, Hugh sensed, it was the people. Dana didn't need her husband checking up on her when she was at the shop. The place was a haven for women who cared. Many of those women had been through childbirth themselves. And they showed their feelings. He had walked in on conversations having to do with sex, and it struck him that knitting was an excuse. These women gave each other something that was missing from their lives.

And Ellie Jo led the way. Genuine to the extreme, she was delighted when he told her they had a girl, and began to cry when he told her the name. Tara Saxe, Dana's best friend, did the same.

He called his two law partners—the Calli and Kohn of Calli, Kohn, and Clarke—and called his secretary, who promised to pass the news on to the associates. He called David, their neighbor. He called a handful of other friends, called his brother and the two Clarke cousins with whom he was closest.

Then Dana was wheeled back to the room, wanting to know what the baby was doing and when she could have her back. She wanted to talk herself with her grandmother and Tara, though both were already on their way.

Hugh's parents arrived first. Though it

was barely nine in the morning, they were impeccably dressed, his father in a navy blazer and rep tie, his mother in Chanel. Hugh had never seen either of them looking disheveled.

They brought a large vase filled with hydrangea. "From the yard," his mother said unnecessarily, since hydrangea was her gift for any occasion that occurred from midsummer to first frost. Chattering on about the *good* fortune that this year's batch contained more whites than blues, for a girl, she passed Hugh the vase and offered her cheek for a kiss, then did the same to Dana. Hugh's father gave them both surprisingly vigorous hugs before looking expectantly around.

With his mother still marveling about the speed of the delivery and the many advances in obstetric care from when *her* children were born, Hugh led them down the hall to the nursery. His father immediately spotted the name on a crib at the window, and said, "There she is."

At that point, Hugh hoped for excited exclamations on the sweetness and beauty of his daughter. He wanted his parents to tell him that she looked like his mother's favorite great-aunt or his father's second cousin or, simply, that she was strikingly unique.

But his parents stood silent until his father said gravely, "This can't be her."

His mother was frowning, trying to read names on other cribs. "It's the only Clarke."

"This baby can't be Hugh's."

"Eaton, it says Baby Girl Clarke."

"Then it's mismarked," Eaton reasoned. A historian by occupation, both teacher and author, he was as reliant on fact as Hugh was.

"She has an ID band," Dorothy noted, "but you never know about those. Oprah had a pair of parents on whose babies were mislabeled. Go ask, Hugh. This doesn't look like your child."

"It's her," Hugh said, trying to sound surprised by their doubt.

Dorothy was confused. "But she doesn't look anything like you."

"Do I look like you?" he asked. "No. I look like Dad. Well, this baby is half Dana, too."

"But she doesn't look like Dana, either."

Another couple came down the hall and pressed their faces to the window.

Eaton lowered his voice. "I'd check this out, Hugh. Mix-ups happen."

Dorothy added, "The newspaper just ran a story about a woman who gave birth to twins from someone else's vial, and you can almost understand it—how can they *possibly* keep all those microscopic things apart?"

"Dorothy, that was in vitro."

"Maybe. But that doesn't mean there aren't mix-ups. Besides, how one becomes pregnant isn't something sons would necessarily share with their *mothers*." She shot Hugh a sheepish look.

"No, Mom," Hugh said. "This wasn't in vitro. Forget mix-ups. I was in the delivery room. This was the child I saw born. I cut the cord."

Eaton remained doubtful. "And you're *sure* it was this child?"

"Positive."

"Well," Dorothy said quietly, "what we see here doesn't resemble you or anyone else in our family. This baby has to look like Dana's family. Her grandmother rarely talks about relatives—what, were there *three* Josephs all told at the wedding, counting the bride?—but the grandmother must have family, and then there's Dana's father, who is a *bigger* mystery. Does Dana even know his name?"

"She knows his name," Hugh said and met his father's eyes. He knew what Eaton was thinking. His parents were nothing if not consistent. Pedigree mattered.

"We discussed this three years ago, Hugh," the older man reminded him, low but edgy. "I told you to have him investigated."

"And I said I wouldn't. There was no point."

"You would have known what you were marrying."

"I didn't marry a 'what.' " Hugh argued, "I married a 'who.' I thought we beat this issue to death back then. I married Dana. I didn't marry her father."

"You can't always separate the two," Eaton countered. "I'd say this is a case in point."

Hugh was saved a reply by the nurse, who waved at him and wheeled the crib toward the door.

This baby was his child. He had helped conceive her, had helped bring her into the world. He had cut the cord tying her to her mother. There was symbolism in that. Dana wasn't her sole caretaker anymore. He had a part to play now and for years to come. It was an awesome thought under even the most ordinary of circumstances, and these didn't feel ordinary in the least.

"Are either of you pleased?" he asked. "At the very least, happy for me? This is my baby."

"Is it?" Eaton asked.

Hugh was a minute following—initially thinking that it was simply a stupid remark—then he was furious. But the nurse was wheeling the crib toward him. He held out his wrist for her to match the baby's band with his. "Are these the grandparents?" she asked with a smile.

"Sure are," Hugh said.

"Congratulations, then. She's precious." She turned to him. "Is your wife planning to breast-feed?"

"Yes."

"I'll send someone down to help her start." The door to the nursery closed, ending Hugh's show of brightness.

He turned on his father. "Are you saying Dana had an affair?"

"Stranger things have happened," said his mother.

"Not to me," Hugh declared. When she shot him a warning look, he lowered his voice. "And not to my marriage. Why do you think I waited so long? Why do you think I refused to marry those girls *you* two loved? Because *then* there would have been affairs, and on my side. They were boring women with boring lifestyles. Dana is different."

"Obviously," remarked one of his parents. It didn't matter which. Both faces bore the accusation.

"Does that mean you won't be calling all Clarkes to tell them about my baby?"

"Hugh," said Eaton.

"What about the country club?" Hugh asked. "Think she'll be welcomed there? Will you take her from table to table on Grill Night to show her off to your friends, like you do with Robert's kids?"

"If I were you," Eaton advised, "I wouldn't worry about the country club. I'd worry about the town where you live, and the schools she'll attend, and her future."

Hugh held up a hand. "Hey, you're talking to someone whose law partners are Cuban and Jewish, whose clients are largely minorities, and whose neighbor is African American."

"Like your child," Eaton said.

Hugh took a tempering breath, to no avail. "I don't see any black skin in this nursery. I see brown, white, yellow, and everything in between. So my baby's skin is tawny. She also happens to be beautiful. Until you can say that to me—until you can say it to Dana—please—" He didn't finish, simply stared at them for a minute before wheeling the crib down the hall.

"Please what?" Eaton called, catching up in a pair of strides. He had Hugh's long legs. Or, more correctly, Hugh had Eaton's.

Please go home. Please keep your ugly thoughts to yourselves and leave me and my wife and our child alone.

Hugh said none of those things. But his parents heard. By the time he reached Dana's door, he and the baby were alone.

Chapter 3

One look at Hugh's face and Dana knew what had happened. Hadn't her excitement been shadowed by worry? Hugh's parents were good people. They gave generously to their favorite charities, not the least of which was the church, and they paid their fair share of taxes. But they liked their life as it was. Change of any kind was a threat. Dana had had to bite her tongue over the uproar wreaked when the senior Clarkes' South Shore town voted to allow in a fast-food franchise, over the objections of Eaton, Dorothy, and other high-enders who wouldn't eat a Big Mac if their lives depended on it.

Dana loved Big Macs. She had long ago accepted that her in-laws didn't.

No. She didn't care what Hugh's parents thought. But she did care what Hugh thought. Much as he was his own man, his parents could ruin his mood.

That had clearly happened. He was distracted, seeming angry at a time when he should have been laughing, hugging her, telling her he loved her, like he had done at the instant of the baby's birth.

Dana needed that. But if her mind registered dismay, she was too emotionally numb to feel it. He had the baby with him, and Dana wanted to hold her. She felt an instinctive need to protect her, even from her own father, if need be.

She started to sit up, but Hugh gestured her back. His hands appeared absurdly large under the baby. She cradled the infant, savoring her warmth. Other than remnants of ointment in her eyes, her face was clean and smooth. Dana was enthralled.

"Look at her cheeks," she whispered. "And her mouth. Everything is so small. So delicate." Even the color. Light brown? Fawn?

Carefully fishing out a little hand, she watched the baby's fingers explore the air before curling around one of hers. "Did your parents hold her?"

"Not this time."

"They're upset."

"You could say."

Dana shot him a glance. His eyes stayed on the baby.

"Where are they now?" she asked.

"Gone home, I assume."

"They're blaming me, aren't they?"

"That's a lousy word, Dee."

"But it fits. I know your parents. Our baby has dark skin, and they know it isn't from your family, so it's from mine."

He raised his eyes. "Is it?"

"It could be," Dana said easily. She had grown up on questions without answers. "I have one picture of my father. You've seen it. He's as white-skinned as you. But do any of us really know what happened two or three generations ago?"

"I do."

Yes, Dana acknowledged silently. Clarkes did know these things. Unfortunately, Josephs did not. "So your parents blame me. They expected one thing and got another. They're not happy with our daughter, and they blame me for it. Do you?"

" 'Blame' is the wrong word. It implies something bad."

Dana looked down at the baby, who was looking right back at her. She was peaceful and content. Elizabeth Ames Clarke had something special, and if that came from genes they hadn't expected, so be it. There was nothing bad about her. She was absolutely perfect.

"This is our baby," Dana pleaded softly. "Is skin color any different from eye color or intelligence or temperament?"

"In this country, in this world, yes."

"I won't accept that."

"Then you're being naïve." He let out a breath. Looking exhausted, he pushed a hand through his hair, but the few short spikes that habitually shadowed his brow fell right back down. When his eyes met hers, they were bleak. "My clients come from every minority group, and, consistently, the African Americans say it's tougher. It's gotten better—and it'll continue to get better, but it isn't going away completely—at least, not in our lifetime."

Dana let it go. Hugh was one of the most accepting people she knew. His would be a statement of fact, not bias.

So maybe she *was* being naïve. This baby was already familiar, though Dana would have been hard-pressed to single out any one feature that was Hugh's or her own.

She was mulling that when the door

opened, and Dana's grandmother peered in. Seeing her face, Dana forgot everything but the exhilaration of the moment. "Come see her, Gram!" she cried. Her eyes filled with tears as the one woman she trusted more than any other came to her side.

Handsome at seventy-four, Ellie Jo had thick gray hair, secured at the top of her head with a pair of bamboo needles, soft skin, and a spine still strong enough to hold her tall. She looked as if she had lived a stress-free life, but her appearance was deceptive. She had become a master at survival, largely by crafting for herself—and for Dana—a meaningful, productive, reverent life.

She was all smiles as she approached. Her hand shook against the pale pink blanket. She caught in a breath and exhaled with awe. "Oh *my*, Dana Jo. She is just the most precious thing I've ever *seen*."

Dana burst into tears. She wrapped an arm around her grandmother's neck and held on, sobbing for reasons she didn't understand. Ellie Jo held Dana with one arm and the baby with the other until the tears slowed.

Sniffling, Dana took a tissue. "I don't know what's wrong."

"Hormones," Ellie Jo stated, wiping under Dana's eyes with a knowing thumb. "How do you feel?"

"Sore."

"Ice, Hugh," Ellie Jo ordered. "Dana needs to sit on something cold. See what you can get?"

Dana watched Hugh leave. The door had barely shut when her eyes flew to her grandmother's. "What do you think?"

"Your daughter is exquisite."

"What do you think of her color?"

Ellie Jo didn't try to deny what they could both so clearly see. "I think her color is part of her beauty, but if you're asking where it came from, I can't tell you. When your mother was pregnant with you, she used to joke that she had no idea what would come out."

"Was there a question on your side of the family?"

"Question?"

"Unknown roots, like an adoption?"

"No. I knew where I was from. Same with my Earl. But your mother knew so little about your father." As she spoke, she peeked under the edge of the tiny pink cap and whispered a delighted "Look at those curls."

"My father didn't have curls," Dana said. "He didn't look African American."

"Neither did Adam Clayton Powell," her grandmother replied. "Many black groups shunned him because he looked so white."

"And did whites accept him as an equal?"

"In most instances."

But not all, Dana concluded. "Hugh's upset."

"Hugh? Or his parents?"

"His parents, but it spread to him." Dana's eyes filled with tears again. "I want him to be excited. This is *our baby*."

Ellie Jo soothed her for a minute before saying, "He *is* excited. But he's trying to deal with what he sees. We might have known to expect the unexpected. *He's* been primed to see the newest Ames Clarke."

"He'll want answers," Dana predicted. "Hugh is dogged that way. He won't rest until he finds the source of Lizzie's looks, and that means going over *every inch* of our family tree. Do I want him to do that? Do I *want* to find my father after all this time?"

"Hey!" came a delighted cry from the door.

Tara Saxe had been Dana's best friend since they were three. Together they had suffered through their mothers' deaths, what seemed like endless years of school, the scourge of teenage boys, and not knowing what they wanted to be. Married straight from college to a pianist who was content to live in her childhood home, Tara had three children under eight, an accounting degree she had earned at night, and a part-time job she hated but without whose pay she and her husband couldn't live. The only thing ever ruffled about her was her light brown hair, which was chin length, wavy, and rarely combed. Otherwise, she was a perfectionist, juggling the minutiae of her life with aplomb.

She was also a knitter and, in that, Dana's partner in copying other designers' new styles. At the start of each season, they scoped out the most exclusive women's clothing stores in Boston, taking notes. Then, though both of them had other jobs and *no* time for this, Dana designed patterns, which, between them, they knitted— occasionally the same sweater multiple times, each with variations of color or proportion. Tara's reaction to the process told Dana—and more important, Ellie Jo— whether the pattern would work in the shop.

Now Tara hugged her and oohed over the baby much as Ellie Jo had done. Only Dana didn't have to ask Tara what she thought. Tara was forthright as only a best friend could be. "Whoa," she said, "look at that skin. Where did you say you got this baby, Dana Jo?"

"I assume she's a relic of my unknown past," Dana replied, relieved to joke. "Hugh's upset."

"Why? Because he can't say she's the spitting image of his great-grandfather or his great-*great*-grandfather? Where is he, anyway?"

"Gram sent him for ice."

"Ah. I'll bet you're starting to need it. Oh, and look at this baby, rooting around. She's hungry."

Dana's breasts were larger than they had been pre-pregnancy, though no larger now than last week or the week before. "Do I do it this early?"

"Oh yeah. She isn't starving for milk yet, and you have colostrum."

Dana opened her gown. Tara showed her how to hold the baby so that she could latch on, but it took several minutes of manipulating Dana's nipple before they finally managed, and then, Dana was stunned by the strength of the sucking. "How *does* she know what to do?"

Tara didn't answer, because Hugh had returned, and what with her hugging him and Ellie Jo trying to position the ice, the question was forgotten. All too soon, though, Dana's two favorite women left to go to work, and she was alone again with Hugh.

"Is she drinking?" he asked, looking on with interest, and for a minute, Dana imagined that he had moved past his parents' ill will.

"She's going through the motions. I don't know how much she's getting."

"She's getting what she needs," came a voice behind Hugh. It was the lactation specialist, introducing herself and looking on, then pulling and pushing at Dana's breast. She asked a few questions, made a few suggestions, and left.

Dana put the baby to her shoulder and rubbed her back. When she didn't hear a burp, she tried patting. She peered down at her daughter's face, saw nothing to signal distress, and returned to rubbing.

"So," Hugh asked with undue nonchalance, "what did Ellie Jo say?"

It was an innocent question, but there were other things he might have said. Discouraged and suddenly excruciatingly tired, Dana said, "She's as startled as we are."

"Does she have any idea where the color is from?"

"She isn't a geneticist."

"No suspicions?"

"None."

"Suggestions?"

Dana wanted to cry. "About what? How to lighten the baby's skin?"

Hugh looked away and sighed wearily. "It'd be easier if we had a few answers."

"Easier to explain to your parents?" Dana asked, knowing she sounded bitter. There was a . . . not a wall, exactly, but something separating them. Before, they had always been in sync.

His eyes were dark and, yes, distant. "Easier to explain to your friends?" Dana asked. "Easier for your parents to explain to *their* friends?"

"All of the above," he admitted. "Listen.

Here are the facts. White couple has black baby. It isn't your average, run-of-the-mill event. People will ask questions."

"Do we have to give them answers? Let them think what they want."

"Oh, they will. Their first thought will be my mother's—that there was a mix-up in the lab."

"What lab?"

"Right. I told her that, even though it was none of her business. But she won't be the last to wonder."

"Would it matter if we'd had help conceiving?"

"That's not the point. I just don't like people speculating about my personal life, and they will as long as there's reason to speculate. So." He raised three fingers. "First guess is in vitro." He folded a finger. "Second is a relative with African roots." Another finger lowered. "Know what the third is?" He dropped his hand. "She isn't mine."

"Excuse me?"

"She isn't mine."

Dana nearly laughed. "That's ridiculous. No one will think that."

"My parents did."

Her jaw dropped. "Are you kidding?"

"No. And don't knock that one, either. It's a logical possibility."

"*Logical?* Your parents thought I had an *affair*?" She was appalled. "For *God's* sake, Hugh."

"If my parents thought it, other people will."

Dana was livid. "Only people who don't know us. People who do, know that we're happily married. They know we're together every free minute."

"They also know I was in Philly for a month nine months ago trying a case."

Dana was stunned. "Whoa!"

The baby whimpered in response.

"Not *me*, Dee," Hugh said, but his eyes remained dark. "Not me. I'm only playing devil's advocate. *They'll* wonder, particularly since the baby came two weeks early."

"And you'll tell them there isn't a chance," Dana stated.

"Do I know what happened while I was away in Philly?"

"You sure know what happened the weekends in between."

"You could have done both."

Dana was beside herself. "I can't believe you're *saying* this."

"I'm only saying what *other* people will."

Dana peered at the baby's face. It was scrunched up, ready to cry. Lifting her off her shoulder, she tried rocking her, but all the while she was growing more dismayed. "Would I be so *dumb* as to have an affair with an African American and try to pass his baby off as yours?"

"Maybe you weren't sure whose baby it was."

"Wait. That's assuming I cheated on you."

The baby's cries grew louder.

"Why's she crying?" Hugh asked.

"I don't know." Dana tried holding her closer, but it didn't help. "Maybe she senses that I'm upset."

"Maybe she's hungry."

"I just fed her."

"Your milk isn't in yet. Maybe she needs formula."

"Hugh, I'll have milk. I'll have plenty of milk."

"Okay. Maybe she's wet."

That was a possibility. Dana looked around. "I don't have anything. There must be something here."

"Where?"

"I don't know. Call the nurse."

"I'll *get* the nurse," Hugh said. "She should be here, anyway. Hell, if we wanted to do this alone, we would have checked into the Ritz." He went out the door.

Given the speed with which he returned, Dana suspected the nurse had been on her way. Soft-spoken and reassuring, she took the baby and set her in the crib. Opening one drawer after another underneath, she pointed out Pampers, ointment, baby wipes, burp pads, and other goodies.

The baby cried louder when her bottom was bared, but the nurse calmly showed them how to clean, apply ointment, and re-diaper her. She showed them how to support the baby's head and talked about care of the umbilical cord.

When the nurse left, Hugh stood at the crib, his back straight in a way that had CLARKE written all over it. Unfortunately, Dana was a Joseph. And this tiny, helpless baby, who was she?

Chapter 4

Hugh stared at the baby for the longest time. He had always loved the fact that Dana bore no resemblance to his family, yet he was desperately searching for a familiar feature in his child. So was this his comeuppance for devaluing familial traits—fathering a baby who didn't have any one of those traits?

Feeling a helpless tug, he leaned down over the infant. "Hey," he whispered. "Hey," he said again, this time with a smile.

Lizzie didn't blink. She had remarkable eyes, Hugh decided—deep brown irises, delicate lids, long dark lashes. Her nose was small and perfectly formed. And, yes, she had the softest, smoothest skin. She really was a breathtakingly beautiful child. Reaching for his camera, he took a picture. Then he glanced at Dana.

Hugh loved his wife. He truly did. He loved her for many things, not the least being that she was genuinely laid-back. She didn't get mired down in details the way he did. She didn't have his compulsive need for order or logic or precedent. She went with the flow, could adapt to change with a smile and move on. He admired her for that.

At least, he always had. Now, as he looked at the baby again, Dana's nonchalance suddenly seemed irresponsible. She should have made it her business to know who her father was. It would have made things a whole lot easier.

He started to say something to her, but saw that her eyes were closed. Choosing to believe she had fallen asleep, he left the room and took the elevator to the ground floor. He was looking around for a quiet place to use his phone when someone called his name.

David Johnson strode toward him, lab coat open over deep blue scrubs, shaved head gleaming. David wasn't only a neighbor; he was a close friend. They had first met five years ago, when the acre of waterfront land Hugh bought was nothing but clumps of beach grass and heather. David's house had become Hugh's emergency outpost during a long year of building, with ac-

cess to beer in the fridge and a list of resources that had saved Hugh inestimable
effort and time.

One of those resources was Dana. If
Hugh owed David for any one thing, it was
that.

"Hey, man," David exclaimed now, grinning broadly as he clapped Hugh on the
back. "How's the new dad?"

Hugh shook his hand. "Shell-shocked."

"Quick delivery, Hugh. Can't complain
about that. Is the little one adorable?"

"Absolutely. Hey," Hugh said, needing
David's help again, "are you coming or
going?"

"Coming from OR, going to office. I have
three minutes to run up and take a peek.
How about you?" David asked with a glance
at the opening elevator.

"I have to get messages and make some
calls. Will you be around later?"

"I'm done at six, but I have meetings at
Harvard after that, so it's either see your
girls now or tomorrow."

"See them now," said Hugh. "Dana'll
appreciate it."

David moved into the elevator seconds
before the door closed. He turned and shot

Hugh a smile. Bright white, it lit his hand-some dark face.

Oh, yeah, they had to talk. David would understand the problem. Not only had he grown up black, but after marrying a white woman, he had fathered a daughter whose skin was the same shade as Lizzie's.

David's daughter was well adjusted. She was happy. Holding tight to that thought, Hugh found a quiet corner near the hospital's front entrance and accessed his phone messages.

From his law partner Jim Calli came an exuberant "Great news about the baby, Hugh. Rita and I want to stop over as soon as they get home. And don't worry about things here. Julian and I will cover."

From Melissa Dubin, one of the associates who worked for him, came a victorious "Congratulations, Hugh! One baby and one legal coup! The prosecutor of the Hassler case just called to say he's dropping the worst three charges against our man. He made it clear that the misdemeanor charge still stands, but we all know Hassler won't do time for that. This is *good*."

The next message wasn't as happy. "Hey, man," said Henderson Walker in a low, urgent tone, "we gotta talk. There's guys here lookin' to hurt me. I already got two threats. And don't tell me to tell it to a guard, because the guards are in on it. I need to be transferred. You gotta tell them that."

Hugh had known trouble was brewing with Henderson, and while he wasn't sure that the danger was as great as Henderson feared, he had been planning to stop at the jail that afternoon. Using his BlackBerry, he e-mailed the associate who worked with him. "HW feels threatened. Call him."

The next message was from his brother. Three years Hugh's junior, Robert was an executive vice-president in the company begun with a single hotel six generations earlier. One hotel had become six, then a dozen. Succeeding generations of Clarkes had expanded the business into banking, venture capitalism, and entertainment. The conglomerate was successful enough to regularly replenish the family wealth. It was currently headed by Hugh's uncle, the eighth Bradley Clarke.

Never eager to branch out as Hugh and his father had done, Robert was a blunt-talking businessman. "Dad's incoherent," was his message. "Gimme a call."

With a feeling of dread, Hugh tapped in his brother's private line. "Incoherent how?" he asked without preamble.

"Hold on." Robert's voice faded. "Can we finish up later? Great. Close the door on your way out, will you?" There was a pause, a distant click. Hugh pictured Robert swiveling in his high-back chair to look out floor-to-ceiling windows at the Boston skyline. When he spoke again, his voice was clear. "Dad says the baby is black. What's he talking about?"

"Her skin isn't exactly white."

"What color is it?"

"Light brown."

"That's impossible," Robert argued. "She has two white parents."

"One of us must have an African ancestor."

"Well, it isn't you, so it has to be Dana. Does she have a clue who it is?"

"I wish she did. It'd shut Dad up."

"He's saying she may have kept it a secret from you."

"She doesn't *know*."

"Dad says that if she doesn't have an African-American relative, she had an affair."

Hugh felt a headache starting. Closing his eyes, he pinched the bridge of his nose.

"Did she?" Robert asked.

"Hell, no."

"Are you sure?"

Hugh opened his eyes. "Dana is my *wife*. I *know* her. Come on, Rob, support me in this. Dana did not have an affair. Tell Dad that. I don't want him starting rumors."

"Then you'd better find Dana's relative. See, as far as Dad's concerned, of the two possibilities—a black relative or infidelity—infidelity is the more palatable to him."

Hugh could guess why. "Does he dislike Dana that much?"

"He always felt you married beneath you, but there's another reason he'd prefer infidelity. If the baby isn't yours, Dad can say it isn't his grandchild."

Hugh was sick. "That's pathetic."

"He is who he is."

"Yeah? So who *is* he? To read his books, you'd take him for a man who thinks minorities have been wrongly victimized for years. But now he doesn't want to be related to one? What does that say about *him*?"

"It says he's a closet bigot," Robert replied calmly. "Want to know what else he says?"

Hugh didn't have to reply. He knew nothing would keep Robert from telling him. Robert had competed with him from the time they were kids. He still loved one-upping Hugh, knowing something Hugh didn't.

What was amazing, Hugh realized, was that even though his brother was now more important than Hugh, if power and money were the measure, Robert still felt that competitive childhood need.

"He believes that you either truly didn't know she had an affair, or that you did know but refuse to admit how wrong you were in marrying her. He says that there certainly won't be any big baptism, not with so many questions about the parentage of this child."

"The baptism isn't his affair. It's Dana's and mine."

"One word from him, and half the guests will stay away."

"Let them," Hugh declared, but he had heard enough. "Hey, Robert, I have to go. Do me a favor, though? Call Dad and tell him he's wrong about Dana. She didn't have an affair, and if he raises the subject with his buddies at the club, he'll end up with egg on his face. Dana and I will sort things out, but we'll do it in our own good time."

"He thinks it was your neighbor, by the way."

"David?"

"He's African American."

"He's one of my closest friends! You're nuts."

"Not me. Dad. But you may want to check it out. I know a good detective—"

"Got my own, thanks," Hugh said and quickly ended the call. He did have his own detective and would be calling him to try to track down Dana's father. First, though, he wanted to contact the geneticist who did most of his DNA work.

He tried to call her, but she wasn't there, so he bought a cup of coffee and walked outside to the patio. He was just sitting down on a bench when his phone rang. His partner's cell phone number appeared.

"Hey, Julian."

"I have to be at the courthouse on the Ryan case, but it shouldn't take more than an hour. I thought I'd drive by the house afterward and get Deb. She wants to see the baby. Is Dana up for a visit?"

Julian was one of Hugh's closest friends. They had met in law school, drawn to each other by a shared vision of the kind of lawyer each wanted to be. Julian was as open-minded and caring as anyone Hugh knew, but he still hesitated.

"I don't know, Julian. She's pretty wiped. Neither of us got much sleep, and she's starting to hurt. It might be better to wait until we're home."

"But she's okay, isn't she?"

"She's fine. Just exhausted."

"Then we'll take a quick peek at the baby and leave."

"If you drive all the way down here, Dana will want to visit. Really, Julian. Give her a day to recoup."

"Deb'll be disappointed. But I hear you. Will you let me know if I can do anything at the office?"

Hugh ended the call feeling like a fool. He couldn't *hide* the baby. Today, tomorrow, the day after—it wouldn't make any difference when Julian saw her—Lizzie's skin would still have a copper tint. Julian wouldn't care. Nor would Deb. But they would ask questions.

As he sat there with cooling coffee, staring blindly at a bird that had perched on the end of his bench, his thoughts were interrupted by a high-pitched voice on the far side of the hedge bordering the patio.

He ignored it. He had problems of his own. He didn't need to hear someone else's. But when that distressed voice rose again, he couldn't help but listen.

"I tried!" she cried. "I can't get *through*." There was a pause, then a desperate "How am I supposed to *do* that? He won't take my *calls!*" When she continued, her voice was lower, though still easily heard. "There's this first surgery and he's stuck in a body cast for six weeks. And they keep talking about growth plates, which'll mean more operations. I don't have the money for that." She paused. "Do *you* have insurance? It isn't just me." She added with a sob, "I didn't *ask* for that car to hit him, Mama. I was right there in the yard. The car came out of nowhere and swerved onto the sidewalk."

Hugh was intrigued despite himself.

"I just *told* you," she argued. "He won't

take my calls, and I know he's in Washington. He was on the news the other night talking about some big Senate vote. He just doesn't want to admit Jay is his."

Hugh smiled. He knew congressmen. He knew power brokers of other ilks as well. As a group, they were arrogant SOBs.

"I didn't plan on getting pregnant either," the girl continued, "but I didn't do it alone. Doesn't he have a responsibility to help?"

Yes, he did, Hugh thought silently. If a man sired a child, he did have a responsibility.

There were a few diminishing sobs, then, "Mama? Please don't hang up. Mama?"

Not his business, Hugh told himself. Especially not now.

Tossing the last of his coffee into the bushes, he rose from the bench. Rather than heading back into the hospital, though, he rounded the hedge and entered the garden.

The woman was doubled over on a bench similar to the one he had been sitting on. He could see denim legs, the back of a slim-fitting tee shirt, and an unruly mass of auburn hair. A pair of stubbed cigarette butts lay in front of her sneakers.

"Excuse me?" he said.

Startled, she lifted her head. Her left eye strayed, but her right held his. Both were red.

Gently, he said, "I was sitting on the other side of the bushes and overheard your call. I may be able to help."

She wiped her eyes with fingers that shook. "By hitting on me?"

He smiled. "No. I'm married. My wife just had a baby. But I'm a lawyer. It sounds to me like you have a father who is denying paternity of his child."

"You had no right to listen in on my call."

"You weren't exactly whispering. That father does have a legal responsibility. I know. I've handled paternity cases."

She gave him a dismissive once-over. "You don't look like a lawyer."

"Like I said, my wife just had a baby. Literally. We've been up all night. I don't look like this when I'm going to court."

She choked out a humorless laugh. "If I can't pay my boy's medical bills, how can I pay a lawyer?"

"When I find a worthy case, I don't charge."

"Oh, yeah." She stood. She was tall—five

nine, he guessed—and that one direct eye leveled him a cynical look. "Right." She stuffed her phone in the small pocket at the front of her jeans and turned to retrieve a worn canvas pouch.

Taking his wallet from his own jeans, he pulled out a business card.

She didn't take it.

Undaunted, he said, "I know Washington. I have a large network of contacts there."

"Not for this. You can't help."

"He's that high?"

She didn't confirm or deny. Nor did she turn and run.

"How old is your son?" he asked.

She raised her chin. "Four."

"Hit by a car?"

"Yes. Two days ago. His spine is messed up. And his leg."

"Is the father a senator?"

Staring at him, she put the strap of her bag on her shoulder.

"And he won't take your calls?" Hugh persisted. "I can get through to him."

"Yeah. Right. If he won't talk to me, why would he talk to a *lawyer*?" She said the word like lawyers were scum.

"He'll be frightened of the publicity if he

doesn't," he said. "Bring a lawyer into the picture, and he'll want things settled quickly and quietly. Trust me. I know these guys. They think they can do anything they want while they're out there on the campaign trail."

"He wasn't campaigning. He was hunting."

"Around here?"

"In New Hampshire. He had dinner at the restaurant where I work. I waited on him."

Hugh could picture it. Neither the mess of her hair, nor her pallor, nor that wandering eye could hide the fact that she was very attractive. "Is that where he's from—New Hampshire?"

"No. He was someone's guest."

"Are you from New Hampshire?" If so, the case would be out of his jurisdiction.

"Massachusetts," she said. "Just over the line."

It was a go. "Can you prove you were together?"

"No."

"Did anyone see you?" When she didn't reply, he added a goading "And you're sure it happened the way you say?"

"I took the motel room," she snapped.

"The clerk saw me. But I don't know if he saw the man I was with." She looked down to rummage in her bag.

"Did you talk with him after that night?"

"I called to tell him Jay was born." She took out a cigarette.

"And you got through?"

"No. I said it was personal. They put me through to someone who said it was always personal with women like me."

"I take it he said the boy wasn't his boss's."

"Oh, yeah." She tossed the cigarette back in her bag.

"Are you sure he is?"

"Jay looks just like him."

"Looks can deceive," Hugh said. "Did he pay you?"

"I don't need this," she muttered, starting to walk away.

"Wait. I'm sorry, but these are lawyer questions. If I don't ask them, someone else will."

"Not if I don't do anything," she replied sweetly.

"You have to do something. There's your boy to consider. He needs care, and you have no insurance. What about the driver of the car?"

"He died."

"The accident was that bad?"

"No. He had a heart attack," she offered in a measured way. "That's what caused the accident. He was, like, eighty. He didn't even have a license."

"Which means he was uninsured."

"Correct."

"And your mother can't help. Father? Boyfriend?"

She gave a slow headshake.

"Which leaves our man in Washington," Hugh concluded. "He owes you." There was a case here—and he was glad for the distraction. "Look, your son needs help. I'm offering it to you free of charge. Most mothers would jump at that." He held out the card again. "Take it. If you call, you call. If you don't, you don't."

She looked at the card, finally took it. Her hand still shook. Hugh wondered when she had last had a meal and might have offered her money for that, if he hadn't suspected she would refuse it.

She read the printing. "How do I know

you're not from him, trying to get me a lousy deal?"

"I don't even know who he is."

"How do I know you're not lying?"

"Check me out. You have the name there. Call another lawyer in town. Or Google me. You'll see the kind of cases I handle. I'd like to handle this one."

"Why?"

"Because it resonates. Because I don't think men should father children and then deny responsibility for them. I told you that at the start."

Her eyes narrowed. "Do you have a personal gripe—like, your father did that to your mother?"

"No. But I've known men who've done it. I know how their minds work. They'll try to get away with as much as they can, until they're cornered. Then they back down fast. I'm telling you—you have a case." And he wanted it. He liked helping powerless people. There were laws on the books to protect them—laws that, like his family, went back hundreds of years.

She remained torn, but that was okay. He had had clients who blabbed their stories to strangers—worse, to the press—at the first provocation. They were trouble.

Cautious clients were good clients. And cautious, she was. "How do I know you won't come up with hidden charges for me to pay? How do I know you won't sue *me* for that money?"

"We sign a contract, and I waive my right to a fee."

"Yeah. Right. And I'm supposed to believe you'll really fight for me when you're not being paid?"

He had to hand it to her. She wasn't dumb. "Yes, you're supposed to believe that," he said. "It's called *pro bono* work. Any lawyer with an ounce of humanity does it. In my case, I also have a reputation to protect."

"So how do I know you don't just want the publicity?"

"If I wanted publicity, I'd go somewhere else. A case like this will settle quietly. Sometimes, all it takes is letting the guy know he'll be taken to court. Right now, he thinks you'll do nothing. That's his arrogance. One call from your lawyer, and he'll see you differently."

Her defiance crumbled. "All I want is to be able to take care of my son."

"What, exactly, do the doctors say?"

"He has a fractured spine. A chunk of bone got into the spinal canal, so they did emergency surgery, but they're worried about the growth plate, which means that Jay could grow crooked, and if that happens, he'll need more surgery. Only these doctors won't do it—they say I'll need a specialist, and the best one, they say, is in St. Louis. I'd need a place to live, and I'll lose my job. Even aside from the medical costs, how'm I going to pay for all that?"

He touched her shoulder. "I can get you money for treatment."

She shrugged off his hand. "What if you can't? What if he refuses? Where'll that leave me?"

"Same place you are now. Think about it. What do you have to lose?"

"Is it a power trip for you?"

"A personal one," he admitted. He did want to handle a case he thought he could win, especially now, when he was feeling powerless to do anything about his daughter. A case like this would make up for the qualms he had about Lizzie. "But, hey," he said, backing off, "I don't badger. You have my card. You have my name. I don't know yours and suspect you're not ready to tell me. If you do decide to give it a shot, I'll know you as the garden mom."

That said, he headed back into the hospital.

Chapter 5

Tired as Dana was, she had only to look at Lizzie and her spirits soared. She called friends to share the news—Elizabeth Ames Clarke, seven pounds, nineteen inches, born at 7:23 a.m. She knitted between calls, nursed the baby again, had toast and tea, then stood over the crib until her legs wobbled, before crawling back into bed.

Sleep when the baby sleeps, Ellie Jo had advised more than once in the last few weeks, and Dana had read the same thing in books. More than sleep, though, she needed Hugh. That need kept her awake, worrying. She put a hand on her stomach, which was almost flat again. It was striking, the difference a few hours made.

Her insides tightened. Her uterus contracting? Possibly. More likely it was fear and, with Hugh absent, a whisper of loss.

Dana knew loss. It was a paramount theme of her early life. She had been five when her mother was "lost," but it was another three years before she could say the word "dead" and several more after that before she could grasp what it meant.

"Lost" was a gentler word. Her grandmother used it repeatedly in the days after the sea had swept Elizabeth away. Dana had never seen her mother lifeless. They had been wading, and while Dana continued to play in the shallows, her mother swam out beyond the surf. Dana hadn't seen her pulled away by the undertow. Nor did she see the wave that hit her own body and knocked her senseless. By the time she woke up in the hospital, ten days had passed, and the funeral was done. She never even saw her mother's casket.

"Lost" meant that her mother could still be found. To that end, Dana spent hours in the yarn store with her eyes on the door, waiting, fearing that her world would positively fall apart if her mother didn't come home.

The fear eased with time. The yarn shop was her port and Ellie Jo her anchor. But part of her always felt that little hole inside. Then she met Hugh, and the hole shrank.

Her eyes opened at the sound of the

door. Trying to gauge Hugh's mood, she watched him approach the bed. His focus was on Lizzie, sleeping now in the crook of her arm. His expression softened.

He did love this child. Dana knew he did. He had to. He was that kind of man.

"Did you see David?" he asked after a bit.

"Sure did," Dana said lightly. "He was very sweet."

"What did he say?"

She didn't go into David's praise of the baby. That wasn't what Hugh wanted to hear. "He said that one of us has African roots. He says it explains why he's always felt connected to us."

Hugh snorted. When Dana sent him a questioning look, he said, "I'm glad we're connected. He'll be able to tell us what we can expect down the road, his Ali being biracial and all."

"She's arriving this week. She'll be here until school starts."

Hugh nodded. After a minute, he said, "Ali's a sweetie. I love seeing her." After another silence, he looked down at the baby. "Can I hold her?"

Heartened, Dana carefully transferred her to Hugh's arms. Lizzie didn't wake.

He studied her. "She seems like an easy baby. Will this last?"

"I just asked the nurse the same question. She said maybe yes, maybe no. Did you get something to eat?"

He nodded and glanced at the tray on the bedstand. "You?"

"Some. Did you make more calls?"

"Accessed messages, mostly. I talked with Robert. Dad's in a stew."

"Then it's good that this isn't Dad's baby," Dana remarked, mimicking Hugh. When he didn't reply, she added, "Did you talk with him directly?"

"No."

"Maybe you should. Get it out in the open."

"I'm not ready. My parents are . . . my parents."

"They're elitist," Dana said.

"That's unfair."

"Does it fit?"

"No," he replied, but not quickly enough.

"Then it's only the surprise that's the problem," said Dana. "They'll get over this, Hugh. It isn't a tragedy."

Shifting the baby in his arms, he turned and sat on the edge of the bed.

"It isn't," Dana insisted. "Tragedy is when a baby is born with a heart defect or a degenerative disease. Our baby is healthy. She's responsive. She's beautiful."

"She just isn't *us*," Hugh said, sounding bewildered.

"Isn't us? Or just isn't the us we know?"

"Is there a difference?"

"Yes. Babies are born all the time with features from earlier generations. It just takes a little digging to learn the source." When Hugh didn't answer, Dana added, "Look at it this way. Having a baby of color will boost your image as the rebel lawyer." When Hugh snorted again, she teased, "You did want to be different, didn't you?" He didn't reply. "Come on, Hugh," she pleaded. "Smile?"

The smile came only when he looked at the baby again. "She is special, that's for sure."

"Have you taken any good pictures?"

He glanced toward his camera, which lay in the folds of her bag by the wall, and said with a brief burst of enthusiasm, even wonder, "Y'know, I have." Securing the baby in his left arm, he retrieved the camera and turned it on. With the ease of intimacy, he sat close beside Dana and scrolled through the shots with her. In that split-second of closeness, everything was right.

"Omigod, look," she cried. "She's what there—seconds old?"

"And this one of you holding her for the first time."

"I look awful!"

He chuckled. "It wasn't like you'd just been to a picnic." He pulled up another shot. "Look at those eyes. She's remarkable. So aware from the start. And wait." He scrolled farther. "Here."

Dana caught her breath. "Amazing you got that. She's looking at me with total intelligence. Can you crop me out?"

"Why would I want to? This is an incredible mother-daughter shot."

"For the announcement. We want one just of her."

Hugh scrolled through several more pictures. "Here's a nice one. I'll print these up tonight and put them in the album you got at the shower."

"How about the announcement?" Dana said again. "We need a picture for that. The stationery store promised they'd have them ready to go in a week once we give them everything."

Hugh was focused on the monitor, scrolling forward and back. "I'm not sure any of these is perfect."

"Even that first one? I love it because she isn't all swaddled. Her hands are so delicate."

"She's still messed up from the birth in that one."

"Which gives it an immediacy," Dana coaxed. "But you can take more now."

"She's sleeping now."

Dana thought Lizzie's features were as striking in sleep as when she was awake. "Oh, Hugh. I don't want to wait. The envelopes are all addressed and stamped. There are so many people we want to tell."

"Most of them will know anyway," he said with sudden sharpness. "In fact, I'm not sure why we're even sending announcements."

Startled, Dana said, "But you were after me for weeks to make an appointment with the stationer. You insisted on coming. *You* chose the photo announcement and insisted you could get a good shot to use."

He didn't move, stayed close, yet she felt

a chill seeping in. A moment later, he rose, put his camera away, and gently set the baby in the crib.

"Hugh?"

When his eyes finally met hers, they were troubled. "I'm not sure we should include a picture with the announcement."

Dana sank into her pillow. "You don't want people to see her. But they will eventually. We can't keep her in the house under wraps."

"I know. But sending a picture out now is only going to provoke questions." He took a quick breath. "Do we need to put ourselves on display? Word'll spread about the baby anyway. People love to talk."

"So?"

"So do we have to *fuel* the gossip? It'd be one thing if I could say that my wife's grandfather was black."

"Why does it *matter*?" Dana cried. She didn't care if her grandfather was black. She didn't care if her *father* was black. It wouldn't change who she was.

Unfortunately, Hugh cared. "We need to locate your father."

Dana was immediately defensive. "I suggested doing it before I was ever pregnant, and you said it didn't matter. I *said* what if there was a medical problem, and you said you didn't want to know and that if something arose we'd deal with it."

"That's exactly what we're doing. Dealing with it means tracking down your dad now. My man can do that."

His man was Lakey McElroy. A computer nerd from a family of Irish cops, Lakey was socially inept, but very smart. Where his brothers knew the streets, he knew the hidden alleys. He also knew his way around the Web. On more than one occasion, he had found information that Hugh had given up on. If anyone could find Dana's father, Lakey could.

Dana felt the old ambivalence—wanting to know, not wanting to know. Perhaps Hugh was right to insist. This wasn't only about her anymore. It was about Lizzie, too.

"We don't have much to go on," she reminded him.

"We have a name, and a picture. We have a place, a month, and a year."

"Roughly," she cautioned, because she had thought about this far more than he had. "My mother never said exactly when they were together, so it's fine to count backward from the day I was born, but if she delivered me early or late, we could be wrong."

"You never asked?"

"I was five when she died."

"Ellie Jo must know."

"She says no."

"What about your mom's friends? Wouldn't she have confided in them?"

"I've asked before. I could ask again."

"Sooner rather than later, please."

It was the *please* that bothered her—like this was a business matter, and she had let him down. She told herself it was only the Clarke seeping out through a crack in his otherwise human veneer, but tears filled her eyes. "I can't do it now," she said. "I just had a baby."

"I'm not saying now." His cell phone vibrated. He looked at the ID panel. "Let me take this. It may help."

Genevieve Falk was a geneticist whom Hugh had found years before when he needed a DNA expert for a case. She was intelligent and down-to-earth.

Now, standing at the window with the phone to his ear, he said a grateful, "Genevieve. Thanks for calling back."

"We're on Nantucket, but you said it was urgent."

"I need your help. Here's the scenario. A very white couple gives birth to a baby that has the skin and hair of an African American. Neither parents nor grandparents have remotely brown skin or curly hair. The assumption is that there's an African-American connection further back—mabe a great-grandparent. Is this possible?"

"Great-grandparent, singular? On only one side of the baby's family? That's not as probable as if there were such a relative on both sides."

"There isn't. The baby's father's family is thoroughly documented."

"Was the mother adopted?"

"No, but her father is an unknown quantity. In the one picture we have, he looks very blond."

"Looks don't count, Hugh. Miscegenation has created generations of people with mixed blood. Some say that only ten percent of all African Americans today are genetically pure. If the other ninety percent have genetic material that is even partly white, and that material is further diluted with each level of procreation, not only would their features be white, but suddenly producing a child with African traits would be improbable."

"I don't need to know what's probable, only what's possible," he said. "Is it *possible* for racial traits to lie dormant for several generations before reappearing? *Can* a light-skinned, blond-haired woman produce a child with non-Caucasian features?"

Genevieve sounded doubtful. "She can, but the odds are slim, especially if those several generations before were filled with blond-haired ancestors."

Hugh tried again. "If, say, the baby's grandfather was one-quarter black but passing for white, and the baby's mother had no African-American features at all, could the baby inherit dark skin and tight curly hair?"

"It would be rare."

"What are the odds?"

"I can't tell you, any more than we know the odds of a redhead appearing after several generations without."

"Okay. Then at what point would it become impossible?"

" 'Impossible' is not a word I like to use. Genetic flukes happen. Suffice it to say that the further back you have to look, the less probable your scenario becomes. Does the mom know of *no* black relatives?"

"None."

"Then I'd suspect hanky-panky," Genevieve concluded bluntly. "Someone had an affair, and clearly it wasn't the dad. Have your client do a DNA test to prove paternity. That would be the first and easiest line of attack. By the way, how's your wife? Isn't she due soon?"

Dana listened to Hugh's half of the conversation with her eyes closed. She opened them the instant he ended the call. He looked so grim that her stomach began knotting. "Is it not possible?"

"It is if your father has a healthy dose of African-American blood. The smaller that dose is, the more remote the chances."

"But it is possible," Dana repeated. "It has to be. I refuse to believe that if my father was first- or second-generation racially mixed, my mother wouldn't have known. According to Gram Ellie, she truly didn't know. Unless she was hiding it from everyone."

Hugh stretched his neck, first to one side, then the other. "What Genevieve suggested," he said, "and this is a quote, is hanky-panky."

"Like the wife had an affair? Well, of course she suggested that. She's used to working with you when you're representing a client, and your clients aren't saints. She would never have suggested it if she'd known you were talking about us. Why didn't you tell her?"

"Because it's none of her business," he said. "And because I wanted an objective opinion."

"If you'd told her it was us, she might have been able to give an *informed* opinion."

He made a sputtering sound. "They just don't know the odds." Turning back to the window, he muttered, "I half wish you'd had an affair. At least, then, there'd be an explanation."

"So do I," Dana lashed back. "I'd like an

explanation for why my mother died when I was five, or why my father never wanted to know about me, or why Gram Ellie's Earl, who was the kindest, most loving person on earth, didn't live to see me get married, but some of us don't get explanations. Most of us aren't privileged like you, Hugh."

"It's just that this is all so bizarre. It'd be nice to have something concrete."

"Well, we don't."

He shot her a glance. "We will. If you talk to anyone who might have information on your father, even the slightest idea of where he was from, I'll get Lakey on it. Will you ask? This is important, Dana. It isn't idle curiosity. Promise me you will?"

Dana felt a stab of resentment. "I'm not blind. I *see* how important this is to you."

"It should be just as important to you," he shot back. "We wouldn't be in this situation if you'd tracked your father down when you were young."

"And if I had found him and learned he was even the slightest bit black, would you have married me? Is there a racial limit to your love?"

"No. There is not. I love this child."

"Love is a word, Hugh. But do you *feel* it? I need to know, both for Lizzie *and* for me."

"I can't believe you're asking me this."

"I can't believe it either," Dana said. She could see him closing up before her eyes. Suddenly, he was a Clarke to the core.

"You're tired," he said coolly and headed for the door. "So am I."

She might have called him back, might have apologized, might have *begged*. Her sense of loss was larger than ever.

Desperate to blunt it, she took her knitting from the bedside table and sank her fingers into the wool—a blend of alpaca and silk, actually. It was a deep teal color with a thread of turquoise, just enough to lend movement without muting the cables, popcorns, and vines she would incorporate into the piece.

She began working stitches from one needle to the next, doing row after row, cables and all, with the kind of steadiness that had kept her afloat for longer than she could recall. She couldn't have said what size needle she was using, whether it was time for a popcorn, or if she was achieving the desired drape. She simply inserted the needle into a stitch, wrapped yarn around it, and pulled it through, again and again and again.

She needed to sleep, but she needed this more. Knitting restored her balance. She wished she was home, but not in the house overlooking the ocean. She wanted to take her baby to the one overlooking the orchard. It was at the end of a tree-lined lane, a stone path away from the yarn shop. Cradling Lizzie, she would sit with her feet up on the wicker lounger on Ellie Jo's back porch, drinking fresh-squeezed limeade, eating warm-from-the-oven brownies, patting Veronica, Ellie Jo's cat. Then she would take the baby down that short stone path—and, oh, the need was intense. Dana was desperate to sit at the long wood table with its bowl of apples in the middle. She longed to hear the whirr of the ceiling fan, the rhythmic tap-tap of needles, the soft conversation of friends.

If she had any history at all—any place where she was loved unconditionally—that was it.

Chapter 6

The arrival of new yarn at The Stitchery was always an event. New colors from Manos, textures from Filatura di Crosa, blends from Debbie Bliss and Berroco—once a box was open, word spread through the knitting community with astonishing speed, bringing the mildly curious, the seriously interested, the addicted. In the days following shipments, particularly as a new season approached, Ellie Jo knew to expect an increase in visitors. She also knew who would like what, who would buy what, and who would admire a new arrival but buy an older favorite.

Ellie Jo was as eager for new yarn as any of her customers. Rarely did she put skeins in a bin without holding one out. Her excuse, a perfectly legitimate one, was the need to swatch a sample to tack to the bin, so that customers could see how the yarn would look knit up. What that did, of course, was to let Ellie Jo sample the yarn, herself. If she liked the feel of it as she knit and the way it came out, she ordered skeins for herself.

Today, as she returned from visiting Dana and the baby, she wanted to stop at her house first. But the UPS truck was parking in front of The Stitchery, and, with the store still ten minutes shy of opening, someone had to let the man in.

So she stopped beside him in the small pebbled lot, unlocked the door, and showed him where to put the boxes. He had barely left when her manager, Olivia McGinn, arrived wanting to know all about Dana, again distracting Ellie Jo from her chores at the house. Other customers arrived, and the shop was abuzz.

There was excited talk about the baby, excited talk about Dana, excited talk about the boxes. Ellie Jo wasn't sure she would have been able to concentrate enough to actually sell yarn. Fortunately, Olivia could do that. Indeed, at that very moment, she was waiting on a mother and her twenty-something daughter who were just learning to knit and wanted novelty yarns for fall scarves.

Customers like these were good for sales; novelty yarn was expensive and quickly worked, which meant that if the customer enjoyed herself, she would soon be back for more. One scarf could lead to a hat, then a throw, then a sweater. If that sweater was cashmere at upwards of forty dollars a skein, with eight or more skeins needed, depending on size and style, the sale could be hefty. Moreover, a year from now, this mother or her daughter might be one of those to rush to the shop when there was word new yarns had arrived.

That was how business worked. Ellie Jo had learned through trial and error, after her initial resistance to selling these same pricey items. Natural fibers remained her favorites, but if novelty yarns brought in trend-seekers who subsidized the shop's more organic tastes, who was she to complain? In recent years, she had developed the utmost respect for innovation.

That was why, putting off her return to the house a bit longer, she took a box-cutter and opened the first of the new boxes. This was no novelty yarn. A blend of cashmere and wool, the skeins included the golds, oranges, deep rusts, and dark browns that would be big for fall. The line was a new one for The Stitchery, but from Ellie Jo's first view of it at the knitting show in April, she had known it would sell.

The front door dinged yet again, and Gillian Kline excitedly called her name. Gillian taught English at the nearby community college, an occupation whose hours were flexible enough to allow for frequent visits to the shop. She was fifty-six, of modest height and a weight that had her forever dieting, but her most marked feature was a head of red waves that had neither faded in color nor thinned with age.

Now, with that hair caught up in a fuchsia clasp that only Gillian would dare wear, and a bouquet of pink roses in her hand, she went straight to Ellie Jo and gave her a long hug. Gillian had been one of Elizabeth's closest friends, and in the years since her death had been a surrogate daughter. Neither gave voice to the fact that Elizabeth should have been here to welcome her granddaughter.

"For you, Great-Gram Ellie," said Gillian. "Your Lizzie is *perfect*."

Ellie Jo lit up. "You've seen her?" She

took the flowers, which were taken from her seconds later and put in water.

"Just now," Gillian said and rummaged in the satchel that hung from her shoulder. "Hours old, and I wouldn't have missed it for the world." In no time, she had a picture of Dana and the baby on the monitor of her digital camera, for the other women to admire.

Ellie Jo was relieved. Dana looked tired but happy and totally comfortable holding the baby. It was hard to see if Lizzie looked any different from expected; Dana was so washed out that, by comparison, any child would look dark—not that the coloring bothered Ellie Jo one whit. She just wasn't up for questions.

"She's so sweet!" cried one.

"She has Hugh's mouth," decided another.

"Zoom it in," ordered a third, and Gillian complied.

Juliette Irving, a friend of Dana's and herself a young mother, with year-old twins asleep in a stroller by the door, remarked, "Look at her! Is that Dana's nose? When will they be home?"

"Tomorrow," Gillian said.

"Elizabeth Ames Clarke," announced Nancy Russell, clearly touched by the name. A florist whose latest passion was knitting flowers, felting them, and sewing them on shawls, sweaters, and purses, she was a contemporary of Gillian's, another childhood friend of the first Elizabeth.

"It's a long one," Gillian warned. "Can we do it overnight?"

"It" was a hand-knit quilt, with the baby's full name and date of birth worked into designated squares. The women had already made squares in yellow, white, and pale green. Now, with the sex of the child known, the remaining squares would incorporate pink. Each piece would be eight inches square, in a fiber and shade of the knitter's choosing, with those closest to Dana and Ellie Jo doing the lettered squares.

"We'll need them by noon tomorrow, so that we can stitch them together," Nancy advised. "Juliette, can you call Jamie and Tara? I'll call Trudy. Gillian, want to call Joan, Saundra, and Lydia?"

One of the women, Corinne James, had taken the camera from Gillian and was viewing the picture close up. Corinne James was Dana's age. Tall and slim, she had stylish shoulder-length hair, wore fine linen pants, an equally fine camisole top, and a diamond-studded wedding band. Although her friendship with the knitters hadn't spread beyond the shop, she was there often.

"What an interesting-looking baby," she observed. "Her skin is dark."

"Not dark," argued another, "tan."

"Who in the family has that coloring, Ellie Jo?" Corinne asked.

Ellie Jo was suddenly warm.

"We're trying to figure that out," Gillian answered for her and caught Nancy's eye. "What do we know of Jack Jones?"

"Not much," replied Nancy.

"Jack Jones?" Corinne echoed.

"Dana's father."

"Does he live around here?"

"Lord, no. He was never here. Elizabeth knew him in Wisconsin. She went to college there."

"Were they married?"

"No."

"Was he South American?"

"No."

"Is 'Jack Jones' his real name?"

Ellie Jo fanned herself with the invoice

from the yarn box. "Why wouldn't it be?" she asked Corinne, not that she was surprised by the question. Corinne James had a curious mind and, surprising for a woman her age, something to say on most every topic.

The younger woman smiled calmly. " 'Jones' is a good alias."

"Like 'James'?" Gillian asked pointedly.

"No, Corinne. 'Jack Jones' is his real name. Or was. We have no idea if he's still alive."

"Doesn't Dana know?"

"No. They're not in touch."

"So where is the dark skin from?" Corinne persisted, as though involved in a great intellectual dilemma. "Hugh's side?"

Gillian chuckled. "Hardly. Hugh's family is your basic white-bread America."

"Then your husband, Ellie Jo?"

Ellie gave a quick headshake.

"Earl Joseph was ruddy-cheeked," Gillian told Corinne, "and the kindest man you'd ever want to meet. He was a legend around here. Everyone knew him."

"He was soft-spoken and considerate," added Nancy, "and he adored Ellie Jo. *And* Dana. He would have been beside himself with excitement about the baby."

"How long has he been gone?" Corinne asked.

Gillian turned to Ellie Jo. "How long has it been?"

"Twenty-five years," Ellie Jo answered, fingering the new wool. Yarn was warmth and homespun goodness. It was color when days were bleak and softness when times were hard. It was always there, a cushion in the finest sense.

Kindly, Corinne asked, "How did he die?"

Ellie Jo felt Gillian's look, but the accident was no secret. "He was away on business when he fell in his hotel room and hit his head. He suffered severe brain trauma. By the time help arrived, he was dead."

"Oh my. I'm *so* sorry. That must have been difficult for you. Something like that happened to my dad—a freak accident."

"Your dad?" Ellie Jo asked.

"Yes. He was the head of an investment company that he started with a group of friends from business school. He was on the corporate jet with two of his partners when it went down. My brother and I were in our twenties. We still think it was sabotage."

"*Sabotage?*" Juliette asked.

"We were skeptical, too," Corinne confessed intelligently, "until things got weird.
The company didn't want an investigation.
They said it would hurt business, and sure
enough, the FAA investigated, blamed the
accident on faulty maintenance, and the
business tanked. My dad was made out to
be responsible. And *then*—"

Ellie Jo had heard enough. She raised a
hand. "While Corinne tells her story, I have
to run to the house. I'll be right back, Olivia,"
she called, heading for the door just as the
bell dinged.

Jaclyn Chace, who worked part-time at
the shop, came in, eyes alight. "Congratulations on the baby, Ellie Jo! Have you seen
her?"

"I have," Ellie Jo said as she passed.
"There's another new box on the table.
Open it for me, like a good girl?"

With the door closing behind her, she
went down the stone path to the house.
Over one hundred years old, it had dove
gray shutters and a veranda front to back.
Now, climbing two wood steps, she crossed
the back porch and entered the kitchen. Her
tabby, Veronica, was sprawled on a sill in
the sun. Ellie Jo went on into the front hall

and up the stairs, through the rising heat, to her bedroom.

The windows were open here, too, sheer curtains letting in only the slightest movement of air. Ellie Jo ignored the heat. Taking a scrapbook from a shelf in the rolltop desk, she opened it and looked at the faded black-and-white snapshots. There was Earl, in a shot taken soon after they met. He had been a Fuller Brush salesman, shown up at her door intent on charming her into a sale, and, yes, she did buy several brushes. She smiled at the memory of those happy days. Her smile faded when she turned to the loose papers tucked behind the photos. She took out several.

Closing the scrapbook, she put it back on the shelf. Holding to her heart what she had removed, she went down the hall to Elizabeth's old room. It still held the bed, dresser, and nightstand Elizabeth had used. The closet was another story. The clothes were long gone. The closet now held yarn.

Sliding the center stack of boxes out of the way, Ellie Jo pulled on the cord to unfold the attic ladder. Grasping its frame, she climbed up. The air was still, the heat intense. Little here was worth noting—a carton filled with chipped china from the earliest days of her marriage to Earl, a hatbox holding her short wedding veil, the old steamer chair that Earl had loved. Of Elizabeth's things, there was a single box of books from her last semester of college.

Should Dana come looking up here, she wouldn't stay long. Given the heat in summer, the chill in winter, and the absense of anything useful, she wouldn't think to bend over and go to the very edge of the eave, as Ellie Jo did now, or to remove a section of the pink insulation that had been added only a handful of years before in a futile effort to modulate heat and cold. Fitting the papers between two joists, Ellie Jo replaced the insulation, went slowly back down the ladder, refolded it, and closed the hatch.

She had read these papers often, and she still could, but no one else would see them. They would remain under the eaves until either fire, a wrecker's ball, or sheer age consumed the house, at which point there would be no one left who had known Earl, no one to think less of him for what he had done. He would forever be a good man in the eyes of the town, which was how it should be.

The Eaton Clarkes lived in a seaside community forty minutes south of Boston. Their elegant Georgian Colonial stood amid other similarly elegant brick homes, on a tree-lined street that was the envy of the town. Sightseers were few, inevitably choosing to drive along the water, and that suited the residents of Old Burgess Way perfectly. They liked their privacy. They liked the fact that their groundskeepers could easily spot a car that didn't belong.

Spread in a graceful arc on a ridge, Old Burgess stood higher than even the seaside homes on the bluff. Indeed, had it not been for dense maples, oaks, and pines, and lavish clusters of ornamental shrubs, its residents might have had a view of the ocean, not a bad thing in and of itself. Unfortunately, though, that would have meant also seeing the overly large houses that new money had built at the expense of the more quaint summer cottages, now mostly gone. The residents of Old Burgess had no use for the nouveaux riches, hence the cultivation of their leafy shield.

They were dignified people. Most had either lived long enough in their homes to have raised a generation of children, or were that second generation themselves, raising the third. When they held parties, loud music ended at eleven.

Eaton and Dorothy had lived on Old Burgess Way for thirty-five years. Their brick home had white columns and shutters, black doors and wrought-iron detail, five bedrooms, six bathrooms, and a saltwater pool. Though there were times in recent years when the place echoed, they wouldn't have dreamed of selling.

Eaton liked being with those who shared his values. He wasn't the richest or most prominent on the street, but he didn't have to be. A historian and best-selling author, he much preferred to blend in. Book signings were difficult for him in that regard, comprised as they were of total strangers. The class he taught at the university was another matter. Here were serious, talented students, mostly seniors as intent on gaining behind-the-scene tips on writing about history as they were into history itself. Blessed with a love of the past and a faultless memory, Eaton could talk spontaneously about most any time period in American life.

As for the behind-the-scene tips, this was easy, too. It was his life. Granted, connections opened doors, and he had them, as most of these students did not. His forebears had played a role at every stage of American history. Indeed, each of his books included the cameo appearance of at least one of them. That was the single common element in his body of work, eight books to date. And the ninth, due out in five short weeks? In it, Clarkes played the lead. *One Man's Line* traced the history of the family as it wove among luminaries, gaining in prominence and wealth with each successive generation. The focus was history. This was, after all, what Eaton was known for. But the time span was greater than that, say, of his book on the demise of the League of Nations. And the personal element was strong, offering intimate details of the lives of his early ancestors.

"The printer just delivered a sample of the book-party invitation," Dorothy reported, coming toward him from the library door. "I don't think it's right, Eaton. It doesn't have the dignified feel I want."

She put it down on the desk. Sitting forward, Eaton immediately saw the problem. "The ink color is wrong. This is blue-gray. We want green-gray."

Dorothy frowned at the sample. "Well, if that's all, it isn't as bad as it could be. Still, they'll have to send this back and have it redone, and if the envelope liners match this blue-gray, they'll have to be reordered, too. By the time they get it right and print them up, we'll be at the deadline for mailing. There's no more room for error."

Eaton didn't want to hear that. "We should have let my publisher do it."

"But they did an *awful* job last time. These invitations go to people whose opinions we value. Would you show up at the University Club wearing a bargain-basement suit? Absolutely not. You like presenting yourself a certain way, and the invitation to your event is no different. This is the start of your tour, it's on your home turf, and it's important. Did you call Hugh?"

In a measured way, Eaton asked, "Did Hugh call me?"

It was a rhetorical question. The phone had been ringing since they walked in the door. If any of the callers had been Hugh,

Dorothy wouldn't have asked. No, the calls would have been from people hearing of the birth of Hugh's child. Thinking about that put Eaton on edge.

He had two sons. While Robert was traditional, agreeable, and, Lord knew, successful, Hugh was the one most like Eaton, and not only in looks. Both were athletic. Both were intellectually creative. Both had chosen fields outside the family field and excelled.

If Eaton had a soft spot, Hugh occupied it.

"Where is Mark?" he barked.

"You sent him home," Dorothy answered quickly, defensively. "You left him a note before we went to the hospital, don't you recall? You said we were celebrating a new baby, so there wouldn't be work today, and I'm not sure what work there is now, anyway, Eaton. He's your researcher, and the book is done."

"He's my assistant," Eaton corrected, "and, yes, there *is* work still to do—interviews to complete, speeches to outline. It used to be that all you had to do when you toured was sign your name to books. Now they want a speech. They want entertainment. Did I give Mark a *paid* day off?"

"I don't know, but if you did, it's done, and it was not my doing, so please don't yell at me."

Eaton quieted. He couldn't be angry at Dorothy. Hugh's folly wasn't her fault.

"Did you call him?" she repeated, albeit with deference.

Eaton didn't reply. Rather, he sat back in his tall leather chair and looked at the books that surrounded him, floor to ceiling, shelf upon shelf. Like his neighbors, these books were his friends. The books he had authored himself sat together on a side shelf, clearly visible, though in no way singled out. While Eaton was proud of each one, they wouldn't have existed without those that had come before.

One generation led to the next. Wasn't that the theme of *One Man's Line*? Early reviews were calling it "eminently readable," "engrossing," "an American saga," and while Eaton wouldn't have used the word "saga"—too commercial—he agreed with the gist. Ancestral charts appeared at various points in the book, growing more elaborate with the years. They were impressive and exact.

"Eaton?"

"No. I haven't called."

"Don't you think you should? He's your son. Your approval means the world to him."

"If that were true," Eaton remarked, "he wouldn't have married the woman he did."

"But did you see how pale and tired he looked? Yes, I know he was up all night, but he didn't plan for this to happen. They had no indication that her father was African American, and maybe he isn't. Maybe it came through the grandmother's side. Call him, Eaton."

"I'll see," Eaton said dismissively.

But she was dogged, stronger now. "I know what that means, it means you won't, but this is about a child, Eaton. She's a living, breathing human being, and she has at least some of our genes."

"Does she?"

"Yes, she does."

"You're too soft."

"Maybe, but I love my son. I don't wish him hurt, not by her and not by you."

"Dorothy, he basically told me to jump off a cliff."

"He did not."

"He did. It was right there in his eyes. You weren't close enough. You couldn't see."

"He was upset. Goodness, if *we* were upset seeing that child, after all the months looking forward to it and now fearing that something's amiss and not knowing what to think, imagine what *he's* feeling."

"*What about us?* We *were* looking forward to this baby. Every single one of our friends knew how much. So. Tell me who called."

Dorothy brightened. "Alfred called. And Sylvia. And Porter and Dusty—they were on two extensions, talking at the same time, so I could hardly hear.

"How much do they know?"

Her brightness faded. "Only that it's a girl. And Bradley. Bradley called."

Eaton's head buzzed. "And how did Brad know? Robert." He let out a breath. "Does that boy know the meaning of discretion?"

"Oh, Eaton," Dorothy said with resignation. "If not from Robert, Brad would have heard it from someone else. This won't remain a secret for long."

Eaton knew that and was annoyed. "What did Hugh *expect* marrying her? I said this back then, and I say it again now—she may well have married him for his money."

"Oh, I don't think—"

"Of course you don't. You don't want to admit Hugh made a mistake and, besides, she knit you the afghan you wanted, which you interpret as a sign of affection, though it may not be at all. The thing about marrying someone so different is that you never know what drives them."

"If it's only about money, why does she work? She could be lunching with friends, or spending the day at the spa, for God's sake. If it's only about money, why does she make the effort she does?"

Eaton snorted. "Effort? Please. What she does isn't work. She drives from house to house visiting people who are either lazy or lack taste, and then she trots off to the Design Center, likely as an excuse to buy things for her own house. She certainly doesn't work like Hugh does."

"But she earns money. And she isn't the only wife who works. Look at Rebecca Boyd. Look at Amanda Parker."

"Look at Andrew Smith's daughter and

the Harding girls," Eaton countered. "They *don't* work. Dana could be doing things to help Hugh in his career. She could be doing charity work. She could make important contacts for him through that."

"But he represents criminals."

Eaton sighed. "No, Dorothy," he explained with the patience of one accustomed to dealing with ill-informed students, "he represents people who are *accused* of being criminals. Jack Hoffmeister is the president of a bank. He was accused of fraud by one of his vice-presidents, after he fired the man for incompetence, but the accusation was entirely false, as Hugh proved. He earned a good fee and several referrals from that one, and whose contact was Jack? Yours. You met him through the Friends Committee at the hospital. Hugh's wife should be involved with groups like that. I've told him that dozens of times, but he doesn't seem to hear."

"What has happened now is different. You need to talk with him."

But Eaton wasn't groveling. "If he wants me to talk to him, an apology is in order. I have my pride."

"I know that, dear. It explains his."

Eaton was unsettled. "Are you taking his side?"

"There are no sides. This is our son."

He pointed a finger at her. "You'll stand behind me in this, Dorothy. You'll stand behind me in this."

Chapter 7

Hugh headed home to shower and change, but his cell phone kept ringing as he drove, friends calling to congratulate him, promising to be over soon to visit, and if it wasn't the phone, it was his BlackBerry.

Can't wait to see the baby!

Looking forward to seeing the baby.

When can we see the baby?

Everyone wanted to *see* her, and that should have been a tribute to Dana and him, proof that their friends cared. Hugh should have been ecstatic.

He didn't know why he wasn't—why there was a rock in his gut when he thought about the baby. He kept hearing Dana's disappointment in his reaction, and he didn't know what to do. Their love had come so easily. They had married within eight months of first meeting, and had never looked back. And he wasn't doing it now. It sounded, though, like she was.

Is there a racial limit to your love?

There was not, and he resented her asking. He had no prejudice. She had only to look at his work for proof of that.

Is there a racial limit to your love?

The question came again, louder now and sounding like a dare. Had he been playing devil's advocate, he might have said she was creating a diversion or, worse, a cover-up.

Hugh didn't want to believe that. He didn't believe she had been unfaithful. She loved him too much to cause him that kind of pain—and it would be excruciatingly painful, if it were true.

But there was the baby, with her beautiful brown skin, and no explanation for its source. Didn't he have a right to ask questions? Didn't it make perfectly good sense to choose one of a *dozen* other birth announcements that didn't have a picture on the front?

He walked in the kitchen door and picked up the phone. The pulsing tone told him that there were messages, but he didn't access them. Rather, he called the office.

His secretary was not happy to hear from him. "You aren't supposed to be working," she scolded. "You're supposed to be with Dana and the baby. I've been given orders not to talk shop."

Hugh humored her. "Then just a yes or a no, please. Did Alex get in touch with Henderson Walker?"

"Yes."

"Is he going over to the jail?"

"No."

"The situation is defused?"

"Yes."

"Did we get a continuance on the Paquette case?"

"Yes."

"Did I get a call from someone calling herself 'the garden mom'?"

"No."

"Okay. That's it. And, Sheila, if the latter does call, I want the message ASAP. Don't give it to anyone else. There's a personal connection here."

He hung up the phone feeling marginally better, but picked it up again seconds later and punched in another number.

"Hammond Security," came a familiar voice, deep and mildly accented.

"Hey, Yunus. It's Hugh. How are you?"

"I'm fine, my friend. We haven't talked in a very long time."

"My fault. Life is too busy. But I think about you often. How is the job going?"

Yunus El-Sabwi, born and raised in Iraq, had fled his homeland in his early twenties, taking his young wife and two daughters to America to ensure them a better life. After becoming an American citizen, he enrolled in the police academy, graduated at the head of his class, and, at a time when community policing encouraged the hiring of minorities, won a spot in the Boston Police Department. In the course of eight years, he was cited numerous times for his work. Then came September 11, and everything changed. He was marginalized within the department, widely distrusted for the links he kept to relatives in Iraq. One rumor held that the money he sent monthly to his parents was earmarked for terrorists, another that he was transmitting sensitive security information in code. When the federal government refused to bring charges, deciding that it feared the ACLU more than it feared Yunus, the local authorities charged him with drug possession.

Hugh defended him on that charge,

agreeing with Yunus's contention that he had been framed. A jury agreed with it, too, and so the case ended. No one was ever charged for planting drugs in Yunus's locker, and though Yunus was reinstated to the force, his life was made so unpleasant that he finally resigned. He now worked in the private security force of a company owned by Hugh's family.

"It's going well," Yunus replied. "I got a fine one-year review."

"And a raise, I hope."

"And a raise. They knew if I didn't they would have to answer to you. Thank you, my friend."

"Don't thank me. You're the one who's doing the work. How are Azhar and the girls?"

"*Hamdel lah*, they are well. Siba will be a senior this year. And she has decided to be a doctor. She wants to go to Harvard."

"That's a fine choice, Yunus."

"Well, she has to get in. But she was given an interview, and her grades are good."

And her connections, Hugh thought, making a mental note to call the head of admissions, a Clarke family friend.

"And tell me," said Yunus, "how is your wife? Did she have her baby?"

"She did. A little girl."

"*Hamdel lah ala al salama!* Such good news! Azhar will be happy to hear it. Perhaps we can visit them soon?"

"I'd like that."

Hugh was smiling when he hung up the phone. He had been appointed by the court to represent Yunus after three separate lawyers opted out, and in taking the case he had had to buck the will of the police department, the local district attorney, and the FBI. He hadn't received money other than reimbursement for court costs, but the emotional reward had been huge. Yunus El-Sabwi was hardworking and focused. Not only would he give his life for his family, but his loyalty to friends was absolute. Hugh had become a beneficiary of that.

Feeling better, Hugh went upstairs to shower and shave. Revived, he pulled on clean jeans and a fresh tee shirt, put the dirty sheets in the washer and fresh sheets on the bed, then set off for the hospital again. Along the way, he stopped at the flower shop for a balloon bouquet, at a local boutique for an absurdly expensive tie-dyed pink onesie, and at Rosie's, Dana's favorite café, for a grilled chicken salad.

Dana was feeding the baby when he arrived. Still buoyed, he smiled, admired the flowers sent by friends, asked how she was feeling, whether the doctor had been in, when she could go home. He traded her the salad for the baby, and managed to change his first diaper.

He didn't mention the birth announcement, didn't mention Dana's father, didn't mention ancestry. His mood deflated some when his uncle called and harassed him about Lizzie's coloring. But Hugh was firm. It wasn't an issue, he said, and proceeded to talk about the miracle of the birth.

Dana appreciated his enthusiasm. She smiled. She answered his questions. But her focus was on the baby, even while she ate her salad. He sensed she was holding back where he was concerned.

And later, as he drove home, *that* was what he obsessed about—not Lizzie's color, his uncle's rudeness, or the fact that neither of his parents had called. All he could think about was that if Dana was holding back, it was because she had something to hide.

Late the next morning, Dana was discharged. She dressed the baby in the pink tie-dyed onesie, which took some doing. Four adult hands—make that four *inexperienced* adult hands—kept getting in each other's way. But they managed, and when Hugh brought the car around, they had no trouble securing her in the car seat.

Hugh had waited for this, had imagined it so many times—driving his wife and child home—and it was good at first, the same euphoria he had felt earlier. Dana was beside him in the front, looking back at the baby every few minutes, clearly excited.

Then the baby started to fuss. Hugh pulled over; Dana got into the back; he resumed driving. Lizzie continued to cry.

"What's wrong?" he asked, glancing worriedly in the rearview mirror. He couldn't see much; the baby was directly behind him and facing toward the rear of the car.

"I don't know," Dana said. She took a pacifier from her bag. That did the trick, but only for several more miles. Then Lizzie began crying again.

"Is she wet?" he asked.

"If she is, there can't be much. I changed her right before we left."

"Then, hungry?"

"I think she's just fussy. I wish I could take her out and hold her, but that'd be totally dangerous."

"Not to mention illegal," Hugh said. "Want me to pull over?"

"No. Let's just try to get home."

He drove to the sound of sporadic crying. When they were five minutes from the house, Lizzie finally fell asleep.

Ellie Jo and Gillian Kline were at the house when they pulled up, and Hugh was as relieved to see them as Dana was delighted. These two experienced mothers knew why babies cried. Moreover, with Hugh's parents nowhere in sight on what should have been a special family day, their presence was particularly welcome.

They changed the baby, gave her to Dana to feed, murmured soft words of encouragement when it took a while to get her to nurse. *Totally normal*, they said more than once, then *She'll catch on*, and *There she goes, look, that's good*. Hugh watched from the door, drawing comfort from their calm.

When Lizzie was asleep and he suggested taking her up to her crib, Dana opted instead for the family room.

They settled the baby in a bassinet there, settled Dana on the sofa nearby, then produced a bag from the local deli and made lunch, something Hugh hadn't thought of but welcomed. When they finished eating, the guard changed. Ellie Jo and Gillian were replaced by Tara and Juliette, and a while later by two of Ellie Jo's friends, and a while after that by two neighbors from down the street. All brought willing hands, intimate knowledge of babies, and foil-covered pans containing dinners enough for a week.

Hugh found himself leaning against the doorjamb while others took care of the baby. He was a third wheel, relegated to the status of observer, so much so that he was tempted to go to the office, where he would feel useful at least. If he had done that, though, he wouldn't have heard the talk.

Everyone thought Lizzie was a beauty and that she had a sweet temperament. A few tried to see resemblances—*Hugh, I think she has your mouth*, or, *That is definitely Dana's nose*—none of which Hugh saw. They remarked on her skin and her hair, praising both features—*Her coloring is elegant*, or, *What I would give for curls like these.* And, of course, there were questions about their source, with more than one teasing glance at Hugh. *So, Hugh, where did you say you were nine months ago?*

Hugh laughed the first time and smiled the second, but when the question came a third time, he said a blunt "Philadelphia," which brought laughter from the questioner and a quick explanation from Dana. The next time he said the same thing, she shot him an annoyed look. But he felt no remorse. He had warned her that there would be questions, and he was tired of being the sole butt of the joke.

By five in the afternoon, it was Hugh's friends who began appearing. There were several from his office bearing flowers and gifts, and their remarks about Lizzie were enthusiastic and kind; but then came Hugh's family friends, young men with whom he had grown up. Clearly, they had been told about Lizzie and wanted to see her for themselves. There was an intensity to their curiosity. They said nothing aloud about the baby's parentage, not so much as an acknowledgment of her color, which was a statement in and of itself.

His basketball buddies weren't as restrained. They appeared shortly after six, four big guys en route to their weekly game. They carried roses for Dana and a Celtics onesie for Lizzie, and the silence when they saw her was comical.

Hugh, my man, who is this?

Dana, you little minx. Working with a client, you say? We've heard that one before.

So, I guess we're all cleared, except for Denny. Where is Denny, anyway?

Denny, the only African American in the group, was singing that night—as he did with a group from his church once a month. David was another matter. Just as the basketball group was getting ready to leave, the man strode through the front door. Granted, the door was wide open. Granted, David strode everywhere. Granted, he was a physical guy who had never been stingy with hugs. Hugh watched him swoop down to kiss Dana, then lean over the bassinet to stare at a baby who looked so much like his own that it would have taken a saint not to think twice.

Out on the front walk minutes later, Hugh's basketball buddy Tom said, "What's the story with that guy?"

"Story?"

"His relationship with Dana. Is it on the up-and-up?"

"Totally," Hugh said, but he was suddenly angry—angry at Tom, at his parents, at David. David was such a good friend that Hugh had never before considered his skin color. Now, all that was changed.

And *then*, with the basketball foursome pulling away from the curb, Hugh turned back to the house only to hear his name called. Looking down the street, he saw his neighbor jogging toward him. Monica French was one of the women who had visited earlier. In her midforties, she was married to a man who was rarely seen, but she had two teenagers and three dogs who made up for it. The dogs were with her now, three big Akitas, all crowding around her so eagerly that as she attempted to stop she almost fell.

"Hugh," she said then. "There's something I have to say, and I know it may not be appropriate, but it really is a matter of conscience. Is David a friend?"

"The best," Hugh replied, because he knew where this was headed. Monica was a busybody who walked her dogs three times a day and had no problem stopping along the way to point out, for the benefit of the ignorant homeowner, a dead shrub in the garden, a blown bulb above the garage door, or the swarm of bees by a shutter.

"If that's true," she said, "then you have nothing to worry about, because a best friend wouldn't do what I'm suggesting. But I looked at that little baby earlier and kept asking myself where her color was from, and I have to tell you, David is around a lot."

"So?" Hugh asked.

"So, he's black."

"I think I noticed that."

"I've seen him inside with Dana when you're not home."

"Yes. She tells me—not that you saw her, but that David stops by."

"He's sometimes there for an *hour*."

"Sixty minutes? Not forty-five or ninety?"

Monica stared. "Make fun of me if you want, but I think David is in love with your wife."

"I'm sure he is," Hugh said, sounding calmer than he felt, "but that doesn't mean he'd ever get her in bed. My wife loves *me*, Monica."

"But there's love-sex and there's sex-sex. David is one sexy guy."

"Ah. That explains your keeping track of his comings and goings. Have the hots for him, do you?"

She stared up at him for another minute, then said, "Forget I mentioned it."

Tugging at the dogs, she let them pull her back home, and just in time. Had she stayed a minute longer, she would have seen the black sedan that came down the street. Hugh's brother, Robert, emerged and turned back to help his uncle climb out.

Bradley Clarke was five years older than Eaton, which put him at seventy-four, give or take. He wasn't as tall or good-looking as his brother, though the Clarke jaw and broad brow were marked, but what he lacked in physical stature he made up for in business acumen. There were older living Clarkes, a cluster of cousins in their nineties, but Bradley was the one who feathered the family nest and, in so doing, was perceived as being the patriarch.

Hugh admired his uncle. He was grateful

that the family interests were in such capable hands.

That said, he had never liked the man. He found him arrogant, curt, and devoid of warmth. Robert, who worked with him on a regular basis—and who now went on into the house while Bradley stood with Hugh at the curb—claimed to have seen the warmth many times. Hugh had to take it on faith.

That faith was tested the minute the older man opened his mouth. "What in the hell did you say to your father? He's in a lousy mood."

"I'm sorry if he's taken it out on you," Hugh said with due deference, though he refused to cower. "He said some ugly things about my child."

"Is it yours?"

"Yes."

"Did you figure out yet where its coloring is from?"

"It's a she, and we assume one of Dana's ancestors was African American."

"Then Dana is black."

"So's your chauffeur," Hugh said lightly, and ducked his head to smile at Caleb. Hugh had passed many an otherwise unbearably boring family event standing outside on the drive by the car, talking with Caleb. "Maybe he'd like to come take a look at my daughter?"

Bradley said, "No need for that, but I would." He was halfway up the stairs when David came from the house and innocently extended his hand.

"Mr. Clarke. David Johnson. Good to see you again."

Bradley's face was stony. His hand met David's in a perfunctory shake. Then he went on inside.

Hugh swore softly and rubbed the aching back of his neck.

"Trouble?" David asked.

Hugh snorted. "At least he didn't see you sprawled all over her."

David made a face. "Huh?"

"Oh, come on. I can only laugh up to a point."

"Can you explain that?"

"They think you're the father."

David drew in his chin. "They do? Wow. I'm flattered."

"Yeah, and while you're flattered, I'm humiliated. Dana's my wife. It's all well and good that you think she's great, but do you have to march into my house like you own the place?"

David took a step back and held up a hand. "No harm meant."

But the dike had burst. Hugh couldn't stop. "Where's your common *sense*, man? Hell, we can pretend we don't see her coloring, but there's this baby who looks like *you*, and there you are, head over heels in love with my wife—"

"Hold it, Hugh. Your wife is my *friend*."

"You knew her before I did," Hugh realized with some discomfort. "Was there something going on between you two back then? A secret you agreed not to share?"

"No."

"But you date white women all the time. You were married to one. In my field, that's called precedent."

"You're outta line."

"Don't tell me I'm outta line," Hugh shouted, "she's my wife!"

"Hugh," said Robert, opening the screen.

Hugh turned and glared at his brother and uncle. He felt like he was being cornered, pushed toward something he loathed but was helpless to stop.

Eyes on Hugh, David held up a cautioning

hand. Then he turned and went down the stairs.

"What was that about?" Bradley asked in an imperial tone.

Hugh lashed out, "Did you see my daughter?"

"Yes."

"Do you think she's my daughter?"

"She's definitely a Joseph baby."

"And the father?" Hugh asked. "Who do you think that is?"

"Who do *you* think?" Bradley shot back.

"I thought it was me, until you all started looking at *him*," he said, nodding toward David's house, "but there's a way to find out. Know how many DNA tests I've arranged for my clients? I know how it's done and who does it best." He strode past them and into the house.

❦

Dana was tired. Her bottom ached and her breasts were starting to harden. She loved seeing friends, loved seeing David, but she could have done without Hugh's brother and uncle. Robert had made a brief show of affection; his uncle hadn't even tried. And now Hugh, saying . . . *what*?

"I want DNA tests done. There's been one remark too many."

"DNA tests?" she asked, unable to grasp it.

"To prove I'm Lizzie's father."

"What are you talking about?"

"I'm talking," he said grimly, "about David. His name keeps coming up. I want it decided."

Dana was incredulous. "*Decided*?"

The baby started to cry. Pushing herself up from the sofa, Dana retrieved Lizzie from the bassinet. She rocked her from side to side, but she kept crying. So Dana propped herself on the cushions, raised her tee shirt, opened her bra, and brushed the baby's mouth with her nipple. Lizzie didn't latch on at first. She rooted and searched and cried. Dana was starting to think that something had to be wrong, because hadn't Tara said babies were born knowing how to suck, and Lizzie had done this now— what—ten, twenty, *thirty* times?—when it finally worked.

"Decided," Hugh said.

Dana's eyes met his and stayed only long

enough to see that he was serious, before focusing on the baby again. "If you actually believe, for one instant, that this is David's child—if you actually *believe* I would be interested in any man but you—if you actually believe I would *be* with someone other than my *husband*—something's wrong with us, worse, with our marriage." Her voice shook. "I thought you trusted me."

"I do."

"But you're accusing me of having an affair with David," she said, keeping her eyes on Lizzie so that she wouldn't lose it completely, "and don't tell me you're playing devil's advocate, because that doesn't work in this case. This is about trust." Tears threatened. She managed to hold them off, but her voice shrank in the process. She did raise her eyes then. "What's happening to us, Hugh?"

Hugh pushed a forearm over his brow, then put his hands on his hips.

Dana's heart was breaking. This was her husband, her *husband*, so distant from her now. Quietly, she asked, "Do you honestly think she's David's?"

"She doesn't have my coloring."

"Or mine, but neither one of us knows for

sure about the coloring of every single one of our ancestors." She quickly nodded. "Okay. Uh-huh. *You* do. So one of *my* relatives came from Africa. I don't have a problem with that. Do you? I mean, what's the big deal here? You're not a bigot, Hugh."

"Don't confuse the issues. Infidelity has nothing to do with bigotry."

She was beside herself with—what? Disbelief? Anger? Hurt? "You *do* think I've had an affair. If you'd been honest with your geneticist, she might have reassured you. Shouldn't we be looking for my father?"

Hugh raised his eyes to the window and looked out at the sea. When he looked back, her heart sank. She needed warmth, but there was none. He was the lawyer on a quest.

"First a DNA test," he said. "That'll prove I'm the father."

Dana bowed her head over the baby and began to cry. She would have never, never, never in a million years imagined it would come to this.

"*Prove*, Dana," he said. "This is about damage control. You don't care what other people say—we've established that—but I do. You're not up to searching for your father yet and that could be like looking for a needle in a haystack. This is the quickest way to rule out one possibility."

In a burst of fury, she looked up. "While you're at it, why not ask David to take the test?"

"If we ask David, we offend him. If we call my geneticist, who then tells me to *do* the test, we embarrass me."

"What about me?" Dana whispered into the baby's short curls.

"I can't hear you."

Obviously, she thought, rocking gently.

"And there's another thing," Hugh charged, forceful again. "You feed the baby. Ellie Jo rocks the baby. Gillian or Tara or Juliette changes the baby. If I'm the father, what's my job?"

He was feeling left out. Dana wondered if that was what this was about. It would be a bizarre explanation, but at least it would be something. The rest didn't make sense.

So she finished feeding Lizzie and handed her to Hugh, then slowly went up the stairs, showered, and, needing an escape, picked up her knitting. Only it was suddenly all wrong—yarn, pattern, *every- thing*. In a fit of dissatisfaction, she pulled the stitches off the needles and ripped out her work, which dissolved like nothing more than another illusion when she gave it a tug. Stuffing the mess of yarn into her bag, she opened the window, eased into bed, and listened to the surf, desperate to hear her mother's voice. But there were no words of comfort coming in on the tide, only this great lump in her throat. Bizarre explanations notwithstanding, Hugh had said things that cut to the core.

Dropped stitches could be picked up, an ill-fitting sweater could be reknit, a bad skein of yarn exchanged. Words were something else. Once said, they couldn't be taken back.

Chapter 8

Dana knew what a DNA test entailed. She also knew that there were different kinds of DNA tests, ranging from those that used blood, hair, or bone marrow, to those that analyzed the saliva in a wad of chewing gum. Hugh had used DNA evidence increasingly when trying cases, and had spoken often of it with her. She knew that for the results of a DNA test to be admissible in court, strict standards were required. But she flat-out rejected anything invasive, such as drawing blood from the baby. She had told Hugh—dead serious—that he would have to take her to court for that.

He was satisfied using buccal swabs, a method in which small applicators collected cells from the inside of the cheek. And he wasted no time. On Thursday morning, a courier arrived at the house with the three test kits.

"Three?" Dana asked, eyeing the kits with distaste.

"One for each of us," Hugh replied patiently.

"Why me? We know I'm her mother," she said with a glimmer of challenge.

"You're our baseline," he explained. "Since the maternity of the baby isn't in doubt, the lab starts by comparing your DNA to Lizzie's. Whatever genetic components don't match up between you two have to come from the father. They then test my DNA for those components."

Dana glanced at the courier, who stood in the kitchen waiting. "Is he your witness that I won't try to switch your sample with a sample from David?"

Hugh asked the courier to wait outside. When the man had left, he said, "That was unnecessary."

"Why? It's all a matter of trust."

"You're not making this any easier on me."

Dana was livid. "The last forty-eight hours should have been the happiest of my life, but you've made them miserable. Truly, Hugh, in my world right now, it's not all about you." She shot a resentful look at the kits. "Can we get this done, please?"

It didn't take long. Hugh swabbed the baby's cheek, then Dana's. She forced herself to watch while he did his own, then sealed the kits and delivered them to the courier. By the time he returned to the house, she was upstairs, showering again herself, then sponging the baby head-to-toe on the changing table. She felt dirty after the procedure. She had to clean them both.

Dressing Lizzie in a new onesie, she put her in her crib and covered her with the blanket Gram Ellie had knit. For a few minutes, while the baby settled in to sleep, she watched, astonished, still, at her daughter's perfection. Then she looked around the nursery. It was to have embodied contentment and joy. As idylls went, it was perfect in every physical regard, which went to show how deceptive appearances could be.

Dana might have cried at the unfairness of it had she not been so tired. Curling sideways in the rocker, she closed her eyes and dozed. The doorbell rang; she ignored it. Same with the phone.

Shortly before noon, she tried feeding Lizzie again. Her milk was coming in, and her swollen breasts made it hard for Lizzie to nurse. Or maybe it was the milk. Dana went through all the possibilities until Lizzie finally latched on, but it was one more thing to worry about.

"Want me to burp her?" Hugh asked from the door.

Startled, Dana looked up. "You're still here."

"Where else would I be?"

"The office," she said, hating the whiny sound of her voice.

"You knew I was taking time off after the baby was born," he reasoned.

Oh yes, and these days together were supposed to have been wonderful. Taking the baby from her breast, she put her to her shoulder and rubbed her back.

"Gillian called. I didn't want to wake you."

Dana nodded.

"And some gifts arrived, really cute stuff," he said, still from the door.

She might have asked about them. She was curious, but Hugh's presence put a damper on her excitement.

"You're still angry," he concluded.

She glanced at Lizzie's face, lightly patted her back.

"Talk to me, Dana."

She sent him a look of despair. "What do you want me to say? That I understand? That I agree with what you've done? I'm sorry. I can't do that."

Lizzie's lips opened for a tiny bubble of air.

The sound made Dana smile in spite of herself. "Good girl," she cooed and, using her fingers to support the baby's head, held her up. Eyes the color of warm chocolate smiled back at her. "You're my sweet little girl, just two days old. Would you like more milk? Just a little more? Let's see." She put her to the other breast, and again it took the baby a minute to get her lips around the nipple. Hugh might have said something during the process, but Dana ignored him. When Lizzie was finally nursing again, she sat back in the rocker and closed her eyes.

"Is she okay?" he asked.

"Yes."

"What was that about?"

"She's learning. So am I."

He was silent for several minutes. Then he asked, "Can I do something? Do you need diapers or cream or anything? Maybe lunch from Rosie's?"

"No. Thank you."

"Want me to make you lunch from what's here already?"

"My grandmother's bringing sandwiches."

"Oh. Okay. So, what about a pharmacy run?"

"Tara's bringing a tub of A&D later. That's all I need. You could go get another Diaper Genie. I'd like to keep one in the laundry room for times when I change her down-stairs."

"I can do that." He paused, then, "About the announcements—"

Dana cut him off. "You were right," she said, opening her eyes and staring at him. "We don't need to send announcements. Especially since we don't really know if you're her father."

He sighed. "Dana."

"What?" she asked. "I shouldn't be angry that you think I had an affair? And why would you think it? Because I was born out of wedlock? Because our baby doesn't happen to look like *you*? Actually, Hugh, she does look like you. She has your mouth."

"I don't see it."

"That's because you're fixated on her color. But if you watch her really closely, you'll see that she has the same little quirk at the corners of her mouth that you do. Not all the time, just when she's *studying* something. It's a pensive little Hugh mouth. Isn't that ironic?"

Hugh didn't say anything.

Closing her eyes again, Dana let Lizzie nurse until the sucking slowed. Then she propped her on her knee with a hand braced under her chin, and rubbed her back.

"Want me to do that?"

Dana almost said, *I don't need your help.* But she hated the sound of bitterness, too much of which had already come from her mouth. So she carefully passed him the baby, then took an armful of dirty things from the hamper and carried them down to the laundry room. She made herself a cup of tea and was drinking it when Ellie Jo arrived.

Dana immediately felt better. Her grandmother was a survivor. She was proof that bad things would pass.

While Ellie Jo took Lizzie to her room, Dana returned to her own. Desperate for normalcy, she pulled out a pair of prepregnancy denim shorts. Though it took a little work, the zipper went up. Cheered, she put on a hot pink cropped tee shirt, stepped into canvas slides, and brushed her hair up into a knot.

A short time later, she was with her grandmother on the patio. Having finished their sandwiches, they were stretched out on lounges under the canopy, knitting while the baby slept in the carriage nearby. Though the late-August sun was warm on the grass, the sea breeze moderated its heat. It was in this spirit that Dana alternately knitted a row, purled a row, briskly adding inches to the moss green sleepsack that Lizzie would need come fall.

Barefoot, she crossed her ankles and inhaled. She loved the ocean, always had—which was odd, given how her mother had died. But Ellie Jo had taken Dana right back into the water the summer after Elizabeth's drowning, and as frightened as Dana had been, once she was swimming, the ocean actually soothed her. Elizabeth loved the sea. Dana fancied that her soul was out in the waves. She felt at peace.

And so, with the smell of the salt air soothing her senses and her knitting needles working hypnotically, she felt herself start to unwind.

Her mother had died, and life went on. So life went on now, too.

After a minute, she set aside her knitting and went to the edge of the lawn. The last of the beach roses were sparse splashes of pink in a sea of green. She knelt, cradled one in her hand, touched its petal. Like the smell of the sea, this gave her comfort.

"Dana! Hi, Dana! Dana! Over here! It's me, Ali!"

Dana looked toward David's yard and, sure enough, there was Ali. Seven years old and wiry, she was jumping up and down as she waved. An explosion of hair bobbed around her face.

Grinning broadly, Dana waved back. She rose and started toward the little girl. There was no fence or hedge. Though David's house was a contemporary Cape and quite different from theirs, the landscaping was the same blend of grass and seaside shrubs.

Ali threw herself into Dana's arms. "Daddy says I'm not supposed to bother you, so I was hoping you'd be outside, and then there you were! Daddy says you have a new baby. I wanna see, can I see?"

"First, let me look at you," Dana said. Setting the child down, she took Ali's chin in her hand.

"Radiant" was the word that came to mind, because Ali's tawny skin positively glowed in the sun. Her eyes were brown and excited, her mouth set in a wide grin that showed off her little white teeth and a head of hair streaked a dozen shades of brown.

Dana had always loved Ali—had always been drawn to the child's joyful approach to life. She gave her another hug and stood back for a look. "You are taller and more beautiful than before. How can that *be*?"

"I'm getting old. I'll be eight pretty soon, and I played soccer for most of the summer, so Mommy says my legs are stretching. Can I see the baby?"

"Alissa!" David called from the back door. "I told you not to bother the Clarkes!"

Another time, Dana might have taken the remark as an innocent directive, but anything "innocent" seemed to have gone the way of her husband's suspicion. "It's no bother," she called to him. "Hugh's gone for

a couple of hours, so it's just my grandmother and me. Oops," she added comi-
cally, refocusing on Ali, "and the baby. She's
still so new I forget, and of *course*, you can
see her. Run on over and take a peek, and
say hi to Gram Ellie while you're there."

She watched the child race off, arms and
legs wheeling. Gram Ellie looked up and
joined her at the carriage.

Dana was wondering if Ali would notice
the baby's complexion, when David approached. He wore a polo shirt and khakis,
clearly taking time off from work now that
his daughter had come.

"This could be awkward," he said. "Ali is
going to want to spend time over there with
you, but your husband won't be happy."

With customary ease, Dana gave his arm
a fond shake. "Hugh adores Ali."

"He did once, but then he liked me, too.
You know he thinks that's my baby, don't
you?"

"Did he say that?" Dana asked, embarrassed. "I'm sorry. He's not himself."

"Maybe he is," David charged. "Maybe
what we see now is the real Hugh—and that
wouldn't be the exception to the rule. Know
how many people believe in racial equality

until an African-American family wants to move in next door? Know how many people believe in affirmative action until their kid gets rejected by the same college that accepts a black kid with lower scores?"

"David—"

His tone softened. "Know how often I wished you were my wife? Maybe Hugh sensed that, but you and I both know I never touched you." His face crumbled. "Christ, you *never* looked at me the way you look at him. What's he *thinking*?"

"He's not," Dana said, and, for a split second, wondered if David was either. *Know how often I wished you were my wife?* She didn't want to hear that, so she focused on what David had said about Hugh, and wondered if it was true. She had always believed Hugh to be a man of conviction, but if that was so, she didn't know how to explain his reaction to Lizzie's birth.

"Is he taking it out on you?" David asked.

Dana didn't mention the paternity test. It was too humiliating. Instead, she looked out over the water and sighed. "I'm not sure who's doing what to whom. We're still living in two-hour shifts, and between tiredness and newness, things are weird."

"Is he helping? I would, Dana. For all else that I did wrong in my marriage, I did help with Ali."

Dana looked at him. "What did you do wrong?"

"I put my work ahead of my wife's. I put Ali before her. I treated her like a maid."

"Deliberately?"

"No," he said with a wry twist of his lips. "Was it subconscious? Maybe. My mother's mother was a maid. My mother was a teacher, but she did all the housework at home. So was I thinking that it would be fair turnaround if my white wife cleaned toilets?" He shrugged. "Truly, she just had more time than I did."

"Were you faithful?" Dana asked. It was something Hugh would be wondering.

David glanced over at Ali. She was moving the carriage forward and back under the guidance of Ellie Jo. "Is Ali going to wake the baby?"

"No. She's fine. Were you, David?"

He was a minute in answering. "I was faithful right up until the end. By that time, Ali was about the only thing Susan and I shared. I was way too busy and way too lonely. There was a one-night thing. Susan found out. That was it. She filed for divorce the next day. It was like she was just waiting for an excuse. Infidelity was more acceptable than racial incompatibility."

"Racial incompatibility?" Dana asked. "Explain."

"I think she had second thoughts."

"About marrying an African American? Was that really it?"

"Maybe not," he conceded. "Maybe it was my imagination. I was a surgeon, she was a nurse. She kept telling people—kept *joking*—that she married up. But she said it one too many times. Her friends—our friends—were mostly white. I got to feeling that she needed to explain to people why she had agreed to marry me."

"That sounds like *your* insecurity."

"Maybe."

"What about Ali? Does your wife apologize for her?"

"No. She thinks Ali is the best kid on the block—smartest, prettiest—and she doesn't hesitate to brag. So is that overcompensation, too?"

"No. She *is* the best," Dana said, knowing she was biased. "You're being hypersensitive, David."

"Well, in any case, they live in Manhattan. Half the kids in her school are non-Caucasian, so it isn't an issue."

"Will she notice Lizzie's color?"

"Probably not. Color isn't high on her list of priorities. She doesn't feel different in any way."

"Do you worry she will?"

He took a tempering breath. "Yeah, I worry. If she falls for a white guy, his parents may not be thrilled. My wife's parents weren't thrilled." He cleared his throat. "We played up the surgeon part for them."

"Are they close to Ali?"

"Yes. They could see their daughter in her right from the start. Give your in-laws time, Dana. Right now, Lizzie's a thing. All infants are. Once she develops a personality, they'll fall for her. They won't be able to help themselves."

"You mean, they'll love her in spite of themselves?" Dana said dryly. "Just because she doesn't look like a Clarke—"

"It isn't that," he broke in. "There wouldn't be a problem if she looked exactly like you. The problem," he said, "is her color."

Dana hated the sound of that. "Is this what her life will be like—that color is the first thing people see? What happened to political correctness?"

"It's an ideal. But hell, it's pretty stupid when a guy robs a bank and the cops say they're looking for someone six-one, dark hair, lanky build, last seen wearing jeans and a red jacket. Shouldn't skin color be included? Isn't that part of the physical description? And don't tell me the bank teller didn't notice." His voice rose in passion. "It's such an obvious exclusion, that the motive speaks for itself. So, yeah, color's the first thing people see. It's always the first thing they see. Anyone who says he doesn't is lying."

"You're upset. Hugh did this."

"No, Dana. I'm telling you what it's about."

"For your daughter? For mine?"

"For both. It's always there in the wings."

"I've never heard that from you before," she said.

"We've never discussed this before."

Dana realized it was true. David had always been just David. "Was there a time in your life when you weren't aware of color?" she asked.

"As a discriminatory thing? Sure. When I

was little. My father was white. One of my brothers looked exactly like him. So in our house, skin color was like hair color, just another physical trait."

"When did it change?"

"When I was four. Kids can be cruel at a playground. I had no idea what the names meant. My parents explained."

"How? What did they say?"

"That people gravitate toward those who are like them—that they're threatened by people who are different—that, as differences go, skin color is the toughest because it can't be hidden. I worked twice as hard in med school, and I still do it now, as a doctor. Even after all this time, do you think I can just sit back and relax? Think again." He pointed to his face. "When things go wrong, this is the first thing they cite."

"For you?" she asked skeptically.

"Believe it, Dana. Look what's happening here—with you, with your baby. He thinks it's mine? What is he, *nuts*?"

"It's his family—"

"Whoa," David cut in, eyes wide and angry again. "Hugh's, what, forty years old? Don't blame his family. He has a mouth."

"And he's used it, trust me, but that family is a way of life."

"How can you defend them?"

"I can't. They live in such a rarefied world that they're half a century behind in some things."

"Well, they're wrong."

"Of course they're wrong," said Dana. "I can't believe the rest of the world is as bad—or, let's say, I don't want to believe it. Your Ali is happy. She accepts her color, like she accepts her hair and her smile. I want Lizzie to be that way."

"Then work on your husband," David advised.

"Daddy," Ali cried, running up, "I just saw Baby E-lizabeth. Dana, Dana, she is so *lit-tle*." Shoulders scrunched up, she tapped her thumb and forefinger together right in front of her face. "Her nose is lit-tle and her mouth and her eyes. How can she be so *lit-tle*?"

Dana put an affectionate hand on Ali's head. "She's just two days old. Isn't it amazing?"

Ali grabbed Dana's hand. "I want to hold her. Gram Ellie said I had to ask you. Can I, Dana?"

"She has to wake up first."

"Can I take her for a walk? Can I wheel the carriage? Gram Ellie says maybe you would let me—"

"Can't do, pumpkin," said David. "We have to go meet the swimming teacher in a little while."

"I'm taking lessons at the town pool," Ali told Dana, turning back to her father. "Then later?" she begged. "We have *all* afternoon and *all* night."

"No, we don't," David replied. "We have to shop for things to take camping, then we have to pack. We're leaving tomorrow at dawn."

Pressing close to Dana, Ali said an excited, "I'm getting a sleeping bag and a flashlight and a backpack. Gram Ellie's making Baby E-lizabeth a sweater. I want to make one for her, too. Can I, Dana?"

"A sweater?" Dana teased. "When did you learn how to knit?"

"I haven't learned yet, but last time I was here, you promised you'd teach me, so I want to learn now."

"Aren't you a little young?" David asked.

"No, I am not. Dana was seven. I'm almost eight."

David sighed. "That may be true. But this isn't a good time. Dana just had a baby."

Slipping an arm around Dana's waist, Ali said, "I can take care of the baby while she teaches me." She looked up from Dana's side. "Can we do it at the yarn store?"

"Ali," David warned, but Dana touched his arm.

"I'd love it, David. You're back from camping on Sunday night, right? How about Monday?"

"I wouldn't make promises, if I were you," he advised. *Think of Hugh*, his eyes added.

"I can do what I want," she said firmly. "I would love to teach Ali to knit, and I'd love to do it next Monday."

Chapter 9

The garden mom was Crystal Kostas, though her last name came only when Hugh met her face to face. When she called his office late Thursday afternoon, she only said "Crystal" and refused to leave her phone number. Fortunately, his secretary, Sheila, sensed the girl's nervousness and, on the spot, set a meeting for Friday morning.

Crystal arrived at the office wearing a long skirt with her tee shirt. Her auburn hair was anchored by a barrette at her nape in a way that downplayed the plum streaks. But her sandals were worn, and her face even more drawn than when he had seen her last.

He guided her down the hall from the reception desk and, once in his office, closed the door. He gestured her to one of the leather chairs, then, because she looked so nervous, said, "Would you rather I have an associate in here with us?"

She shook her head and looked around,

first at the diplomas on the wall, then at the picture of Dana on the credenza, then at some bronze bookends that had been made by an artist on Martha's Vineyard. His parents still owned the house in Menemsha, but he and Dana had only made it there once this summer.

"Can I get you a cup of coffee?" he asked.

She shook her head.

He put an ashtray on the side table in her arm's reach, and took a seat.

Now she was looking at the pictures on the wall. Framed in wood, they were the standard charity-event shots, in which Hugh stood shoulder to shoulder with celebs. She would be impressed. Most of his clients were. Wasn't that the point?

He leaned forward and put his elbows on his knees. "Do I look more like a lawyer today?" He wore a pair of tan slacks, an open-neck shirt, and a navy blazer.

She shot him a glance. "Yes."

"How's your son?" he asked.

"Not good."

"Is he stable?"

She nodded.

"Tell me more, Crystal."

She chewed on a corner of her mouth. Finally, seeming resigned, she said, "He's healing okay from the surgery. He's in a body cast, and a cast for the broken leg. But at least the pain and the numbness are gone. And the paralysis."

"Paralysis?"

"Of, um," she waved an unsure hand, "um, they called it saddle something. Anesthesia." She looked up, the left eye still drifting left. "Saddle anesthesia. He couldn't control his bladder. The operation fixed that."

"When can he go home?"

"Soon." Her expression told him this was not a good thing. "I don't know how I'll get him up and down the stairs with all that plaster on him. And it'll be a while before we know about the growth plates."

"How long is a while?"

"Maybe in six weeks when we go back for a smaller cast. Or it could be another two years. They don't want Jay growing lopsided. More surgeries would prevent that." She grew agitated. "They keep talking about this doctor at Washington University, like he's the only one they'd trust to do the surgery if Jay were *their* kid, but that's in St.

Louis, like I have money to travel. And then I'm sitting there helping Jay eat, and a lady from the hospital comes to talk about finances, because it's like the hospital was willing to do the surgery when they thought I had no money at all, but now they're looking at the paperwork, and they say I earn too much. I earn twenty-eight thousand a year. Do you know how *little* that is when you're trying to raise a child?"

Hugh had done the math with other clients. "You still want to go ahead with this?"

"I can't pay you," she said pointedly.

"I said I wouldn't charge you, and I promised you we'd put it in writing. Give me your full name, and that's the first thing I'll do." He took paper and pen from the desk. "It's Crystal, then?"

"I checked you out," she said. "No one's suing you."

"No."

"And you win a lot."

"I try."

"And your wife did just have a baby."

"How'd you check that?" he asked with gentle suspicion. "Hospital records are private."

Her chin came up, a touch of satisfaction there. "After we talked, I went to the information desk and said I was visiting the Clarkes. They told me what room. I just wanted to be sure you weren't lying."

"I don't lie," Hugh said, and waited. She knew what was needed if they were to proceed. "Let's start with a name. Three, actually—yours, his, and the boy's."

She began with her own. "It's Kostas." She spelled it out as he wrote. "And my son is Jay Liam Kostas."

"And the father?"

"J. Stanton . . ." She hesitated.

J. Stanton. There was only one in Congress. "Are you talking about *Hutchinson*?"

She pressed her lips together.

"Stan Hutchinson fathered your child?" he asked in amazement.

"You don't believe me," she said, gathering her pouch. "I shouldn't have come."

He caught her wrist. "I do believe you. I know his reputation." He released her wrist. "Please. Sit."

She swallowed, sat, and said bleakly, "Reputation? To hear him talk on TV, you wouldn't know there was anything bad."

"Of course not. He preaches morals with

the best of them, but I hate to tell you this . . ." He stopped. Many women believed they were the one who would win a man away from his wife. He wondered if Crystal Kostas had harbored such hopes.

But she said, quite dispassionately, "You're going to say I'm not the first, but his man said that when I called. The guy laughed this horrible laugh and said women are *always* trying to pin things on the senator and that I'd have to get in line. He said it'd be a waste of time, since everyone *knows* the senator is married and that he does *not* believe in cheating. Well, I don't *want* the senator," she said with distaste. "I just want the best medical care for my son—for *his* son."

"Hutchinson. This will be a good case."

"Can I win?"

"Assuming we can find corroborating evidence that you were with him at the time of the boy's conception. It's what I told you at the hospital on Tuesday. Hutchinson won't want publicity from this. Two of his major issues are family values and health care for the uninsured. Your son makes a mockery of his words on both counts."

"But all those other women—know how *cheap* that made me feel?"

Hugh might have pointed out that she had slept with a married man. But it wasn't his job to judge, only to represent the rights of his client.

"The irony," he said, "is that the senator has had so many women that his chief of staff can get away with making them all feel cheap." Hugh sat back and grinned. "Apparently, none of those other women had the resources to take him on. I do." He pulled up his pad. "How old are you?"

"Twenty-nine."

"And the boy is four?"

"Yes."

"Where do you live?"

Once he had the address on paper, he tore off the sheet and phoned Melissa Dubin. A male associate might resonate better with Hutchinson's man, but Melissa would be better with Crystal, and Crystal was key at this stage. Without corroborative evidence, there would be nothing to compel Hutchinson to take a DNA test. And a DNA test was the single piece of evidence that would prove, beyond a doubt, the paternity of a child.

Hugh thought of Dana, and felt uneasy. She was really angry. He didn't want to think she had slept with David, but how well did he know David? How well did he know *Dana*?

"Tell me more about you," he invited Crystal.

She fished in her bag and took out a cigarette, but made no move to light it. "You ask."

"Did you grow up in Pepperell?"

"Yes."

"With parents?"

"My father died when I was ten. Lung cancer."

It was all Hugh could do not to look at the cigarette in her hand. But he wasn't a doctor, and he sure as hell wasn't a judge. "Do you have any siblings?"

"A brother in the Air Force. We don't see him often."

"So you live alone?"

"With Jay."

"Do you date?"

"I used to." She frowned. "Not since Jay, but why does this matter?"

Hugh set down his pen. "If you make a claim that Stan Hutchinson is the father of your child, the first thing his people will do is to try to show a pattern of promiscuity on your part. A DNA test will determine Jay's parentage, but they won't want it done. If you have a history of one-night stands, or a history of problems that may be on record somewhere, I need to know. Is there *anything* about you and men I should know about?"

"No."

A soft knock came at the door, and Melissa slipped in. Hugh introduced her to Crystal, gave her the sheet of paper he'd torn off, and asked her to draw up the agreement.

As soon as she left, he faced Crystal again. "I'll want to talk with your son's doctors. Are you okay with that?"

"Isn't my word good enough?" she asked.

"It is for me. But it won't be for Hutchinson or for a judge. The more people we have vouching for you and your situation, the better. Jay is at a good hospital. His doctors' word will be crucial in establishing the seriousness of his condition. Among other things, we'll need to know how much money will be needed in the next couple of years."

Crystal put the cigarette to her lips and rummaged in her bag for a match.

Hugh gave her this time. From everything he had seen in her up to that point, she would reach the right decision.

"Fine," she said at last. "His doctor's name is Howe. Steven, I think."

Hugh knew the name. Steven Howe was top-notch. This would help. He wrote the name on his pad and flipped to a new page. "Tell me about your work."

"I'm a waitress."

"Always?"

"Yes. I started weekends when I was sixteen. If you're waiting for me to say I wanted to go to college, don't. I did lousy in high school. I hate studying."

"Then tell me about your job. Where do you work?"

She drew on the cigarette. Exhaling a ribbon of smoke, she said, "It's a bar and grill. Lots of beef and chicken. Lots of regulars who leave lots of tips. And booze. Lots of that. The booze makes the biggest profit for my boss and for me."

"Who's your boss?"

She looked down at her hands, turned the cigarette, took another draw.

"I'll have to know," Hugh explained gently. "He's the one who'll have to vouch for Hutchinson being in his place on a night you were working."

"Todd MacKenzie," she murmured. "Mac's Bar and Grille. He's the owner."

Hugh wrote it down. "How long have you worked there?"

"Eight years, less the two months after Jay was born."

"You worked right up until the birth?" Hugh asked in surprise.

"I didn't gain much weight. Besides," she added with a half-smile, "the regular guys liked me. They were kind of protective, y'know?"

Hugh suspected more than a few were turned on. He had already established that Crystal was attractive.

"Does Todd know who fathered your baby?"

"He guessed. I didn't say he was wrong."

"Did he see you leave with Hutchinson?"

"I didn't leave with him. He was outside in his car when I finished work."

"Was he alone?"

"Yes."

"Was it a rental car?"

"I don't know."

"Color? Make?"

"I can't remember."

"Who approached whom?"

"I went to the car. He was just waiting, and there was no one else left. He asked if there was a place we could go. I told him to follow me."

"Why?"

"He didn't know the way."

"I mean, why did you want to be with him? You said you don't sleep around."

She put the cigarette to her mouth, inhaled. "I was feeling lonely. He was there, and he was handsome."

"Did you know he was married?"

"Not then."

"Okay. So you went to the motel. Name?"

"The Exit Inn. It's in an out-of-the-way place."

Hugh wrote it down. "And you took the room?"

"Yes. He gave me cash."

"Do you know the name of the clerk?"

"No."

"Let's back up a little. Was Hutchinson wearing a suit?"

"No. A plaid shirt and pants."

"Flannel shirt? A hunting shirt?"

"Yes."

"What color?"

"I don't remember."

"Did you flirt with him much in the restaurant?"

"Not with words. There was this . . . thing when he looked at me."

Hugh didn't have to ask what that "thing" was. Hutchinson was a ladies' man. He could be talking in a room filled with people, but when his eye passed over a woman, he made her feel she was the only one there.

"Did anyone else notice it? Your boss, maybe?"

"I don't know."

"Did Hutchinson talk with any of the other patrons?"

"I don't remember."

"Did he pay for his dinner by credit card?" Hugh asked. A receipt would be proof he was there.

"He didn't pay. The guy with him paid."

"Do you remember the date?"

"October seventeenth."

"No pause there," Hugh remarked.

"It was my birthday," she explained. "No one else was remembering my birthday, not that he did. But it was something for me that night." She stubbed out the cigarette. "Jay was the best birthday gift I ever got. Just so you know, I've never regretted having him. He's the best thing in my life. His father was just . . ." her upper lip curled, ". . . just a way for me to get Jay. Except for the accident, I wouldn't go near him again."

As reassuring as Hugh found her certainty, it raised another issue. "Did you plan it?" he asked. "Did you want to get pregnant?" That would muddy the works.

"No," she said in an emphatic two-syllable *no-wa*. "I made him use a condom. It didn't work."

"So, if you didn't want anything to do with him afterward," Hugh said, trying to trip her up, which was exactly what Hutchinson's lawyer would do when he took a deposition, "why did you call him when Jay was born?"

"Just to tell him he had a son."

Hugh was thinking that Stan Hutchinson had two other sons and three daughters, not to mention several grandchildren, when Crystal said, "I thought maybe he'd want to *know* his son. Silly me. Well, I learned. I didn't call again. And I wouldn't be wanting money from him now if Jay weren't sick. You say he won't want this made public because of his image, well, what about me? Think it's fun for me to have to go after someone who thinks I'm dirt?"

"No. I can't imagine it is."

"It isn't," she said with some force. "I don't need rich people. I think they're shallow and unfeeling and greedy. They use people and throw them away when they're done."

"I'm rich," Hugh said. *Shallow and unfeeling?* No. His own DNA test was simply to answer his parents' questions and his friends' jokes.

Melissa Dubin returned with the attorney-client agreement. Hugh looked it over and passed it to Crystal.

She read through once, then a second time. "What's the catch?"

"The catch is that once you sign it, you have to do your part. You have to search your memory—I mean, really search and pull out every possible detail of your time with Hutchinson. Anything you can remember about him will help, whether he wore a watch, anything unusual about his manner, his clothes, his body. We'll be talking with the doctors and with your boss, but you're the one who was with the man himself that night. Tell me he has a mole on the back of his thigh, and, assuming the tabloids haven't printed it, we have him in a compromising position."

She looked disgusted.

"I can't do it without you," he warned. "I'm offering my services for free, but I'm not looking to fail, which is what'll happen if I don't have your full cooperation. Are you with me?"

She hesitated a minute, but she did sign. Hugh signed after her, folded one copy, put it in an envelope, and gave it to her. "You'll do that thinking for me?"

"Right now?" she asked meekly.

He went to the credenza, took a small notebook from inside, added a pen, and handed her both. "As soon as you can. Start writing things down. Try reliving the entire night. I want to know what you were wearing, what time you left work, what time you got to the motel, what time you left. Try to remember something about the clerk. Try to remember where you parked. Did Hutch park beside you? When he left, did he say where he was going? If you knew something about his schedule that wasn't public knowledge, it'd prove you were with him."

She was frowning at the notebook. When she looked up, she seemed cautious. " 'Hutch'? Is that a nickname?"

"Uh, yuh."

"I never heard that on TV."

"Actually, I know him," Hugh admitted. "He owns a summer house not far from ours."

"If you're his neighbor," Crystal cried in dismay, "why would you ever go after him?"

Hugh might have cited the man's self-righteousness, or his propensity for playing dirty. He might have said that Hutch would speak at any charity event but never open his wallet or that he had snubbed Eaton by refusing to be interviewed for *One Man's Line*. He might have added the guy insisted on manning the grill, but overcooked his burgers, charred his hot dogs, and cooked his sweet corn until the kernels were hard, none of which was the point.

"Because," Hugh said briefly, "he's wrong."

Chapter 10

At the same time that Hugh was questioning Crystal, Dana set off for the yarn store on a similar quest, but she was at a distinct disadvantage. For one thing, her mother, who had known the man in question, was dead. For another, the affair had taken place thirty-four years ago.

Oh, and the man's name was Jack Jones. There had to be dozens of Jack Joneses in or around Madison, Wisconsin, at the time Dana was conceived. Finding the right one might be next to impossible. But she could almost understand why Hugh was desperate to know.

"Hi, Lizzie, how's my Lizzie?" Dana called into the back seat. Ironic, how the catalyst for a disagreement could be the sole comfort against it.

Disagreement? It was more than that, and it was eating at Dana. She tried to find calm in the reminder that she had a career, but when she phoned the Cunninghams about rescheduling, no one was home. The same was true with her contact for the North Shore Designers' Showhouse, a project she saw as her professional post-baby debut. And when she called to check on the status of the few pieces of furniture still on order for current clients, she learned nothing more than when she had called the week before.

All in all, it was a relief to be out of the house. As tentative as her body still felt, Dana relished the control that came from having her foot on the gas. Gram Ellie had it right. She said that life was like raw wool, filled with slubs and catches that required diligent spinning to smooth.

Diligent spinning. That was all. Dana would be fine. She *would* be fine.

Turning into The Stitchery's drive, she saw her grandmother's car parked beside the verandaed house. Passing it, she went on to the shop. She climbed from the driver's seat and opened Lizzie's door. "Hi, sweetie," she said, leaning in with a bright smile. "Wanna see where Mommy grew up? Want to see where Mommy's *mommy* used to spend time?" Her voice caught, so she busied herself unlatching the baby carrier from its base.

"You look very pretty in green," she told Lizzie, admiring the baby's onesie and matching cap. Seconds later, though, she removed the cap and tossed it back in the car. "We do not need this." She fluffed Lizzie's curls and kissed the child's forehead. "Or this," she said, leaving the receiving blanket in the car.

She had barely opened the screen door when Gillian was at her side. In the space of a breath, Tara, Olivia, Corinne, and Nancy surrounded her, all oohing and aahing over the baby.

Laughing, Dana set her bags on a bench by the door. Ellie Jo, who was leaning against the long oak table watching, opened her arms to Dana. "You shouldn't have driven," she scolded. "It's too soon."

"The doctor didn't say no. I feel fine, Gram, really I do."

"You look tired."

"So do you. I have an excuse. What's yours?"

Ellie Jo smiled. "Worry." Linking her elbow with Dana's, she drew her away from the girls. "How's Hugh?"

"The same." Dana looked around the shop. She loved the wild colors, raised her face to the ceiling fan, breathed in the essence of early McIntosh apples. "Ahh," she said. "Better." She turned back to the baby.

Gillian was holding Lizzie, with the others hovering around her. "We need a picture," Dana said.

Corinne took Gillian's camera and began shooting.

Dana directed. "There." The flash went off. "Now Gillian and Lizzie alone. Oh, that's *perf*ect." Another flash. "Ellie Jo, you join them now." When someone suggested that Dana get in the picture, she did it happily, thinking that this was what having a new baby was about.

Gillian insisted on showing Lizzie the cradle that the group had bought for her.

"I *love* it," Dana cried, but, with her hands covering her mouth, she was looking at the knitted quilt that was artfully arranged over its side. It had the baby's name and the date of her birth, and was so beautiful that Dana burst into tears. She hugged everyone, then insisted on taking the quilt and draping it around Lizzie. Corinne took pictures of that, too.

The baby fussed.

"Too warm," said one of the many mothers.

"Or hungry," said another.

Using the quilt as a cushion, Dana settled into one of the chairs to nurse. The speed with which Lizzie latched on—a first, really—spoke of either her hunger or the comforting atmosphere in the yarn shop. Convinced it was the latter, Dana was glad she had come. Drawing strength from her friends, she broached the issue of her father.

"I have to find him," she said softly.

"That's a tall order, sweetie," Gillian told her. "Looking at Lizzie, I've been trying to remember what I know, and it's next to nothing. I grew up with your mom. We were best friends, and the only time we were apart was during college. We saw each other at Christmas and during the summer, but calling on the phone was really expensive back then. My understanding is that Liz met your father during spring break, then got involved in term papers and finals. By the time she came home for the summer, she knew she was pregnant."

This was consistent with what Dana had already found out. "Was he a student there?"

"I don't know. Your mom wouldn't talk about it. All she said was that it was over, that she wanted you, and that she wasn't going back to school."

"Why wouldn't she talk about it?"

"Likely because it was painful."

"Because she didn't want it to end?"

Gillian smiled sadly. "I'm guessing yes. Every woman dreams that her hero will show up and whisk her away. Well," she caught herself, "back then, we dreamed it."

Dana didn't think times had changed so much. With only a tiny edit or two, Gillian's scenario described her own experience with Hugh.

Getting back to her father, she asked, "Did he know about me?"

"My impression is that he took off before Liz ever knew she was pregnant."

"The picture I have was taken when they were at a bar. Who took it?"

Gillian shook her head. "A friend? Maybe her roommate?"

"Do you remember the names of any of her friends there?"

"Some names. There was a Judy and a Carol. Last names? No."

"The roommate was Carol," Ellie Jo said. "I don't recall her last name."

"Would their names be in a yearbook?" Tara asked.

But Dana knew the answer to that one. "If so, we don't have it. Mom didn't graduate. She dropped out after junior year to have me, and, besides, even if we got our hands on the yearbook, can you imagine how many Carols and Judys there are in a school of, what, twenty thousand students?" She turned back to Gillian. "Would she have confided in anyone else? Maybe her doctor?"

"Her doctor was Tom Milton, right here in town, but he's been dead for years."

"Then we're back to the roommate," said Dana. "There must be a name somewhere. Maybe in the box in the attic?"

"Textbooks," Ellie Jo replied. "They're only textbooks, and not many at that. Elizabeth wasn't nostalgic about school. Come the end of exams, she sold the books she was done with. She hadn't gotten around to selling these."

"Why do you keep them?" Tara asked.

Ellie Jo thought for a minute before she said, "Because they were hers."

And, oh, Dana knew about that. Hadn't she kept boxes of her mother's knitting—wool that had never been worked, patterns never followed, odd-ball remnants?

"Maybe there's something in the textbooks," she asked, "a scribble in a margin that might mean something?"

"I've searched every one of those books, and there's nothing," her grandmother insisted. "Don't waste your time. You have a baby to take care of."

Propping Lizzie on her lap, Dana rubbed her back.

Corinne walked over and joined them. "Her skin is just beautiful, Dana. Oliver and I have a good friend whose great-grandmother was visibly African American. Our friend has blond hair and blue eyes. I've always thought she would look much more distinct if she had some of those earlier traits."

Distinct. Dana liked the sound of that word. "Distinct" could mean unique, as in special, which was how Dana saw the baby. Or it could mean having immediately recognizable traits, which was how the Clarkes saw it. "Does your friend identify with her great-grandmother at all?"

"Identify? Perhaps privately. Acknowledge? Not publicly. Her life is very white."

Dana winced. "Why does that remark jar me?"

"It's blunt," Gillian said.

"Blunt," confirmed Corinne, "but not inaccurate. Black people 'pass' all the time."

Dana liked that remark even less. "How do you define 'black'?" she asked.

"This country adheres to the one-drop rule," Corinne said smoothly. "That's why my friend is quiet about her history. She and I were in the same dorm at Yale. Soon after Oliver and I started dating, she began seeing a friend of Oliver's who was noticeably African American. Her mother had a fit when she found out. The experience brought us closer. I respect who she is and understand what she does. We serve together on the board of the museum."

"Then is the difference between races a socioeconomic one?" Dana asked.

But Corinne was glancing at her Rolex.

"Speaking of the board, I have to run. We're in the final countdown for our major fundraiser. The baby really is adorable, Dana. Enjoy her."

Dana watched Corinne glide to the table, slip her knitting in a project bag, and head for the door. Annoyed by the conversation, she said a little bitterly, "How can Corinne wear linen and never wrinkle?" Her own blouse looked slept in. Granted, there had been a baby beneath it minutes before. Still, "I *look* at linen, and it wrinkles."

"Starch," Tara said. "She's that kind of woman."

Dana agreed. Prior to talking with Corinne, she had actually been feeling good about herself.

She lifted Lizzie, and looked at her face. "Corinne is odd."

The baby burped. Dana and Tara laughed.

"She always buys the cheapest yarn," Dana went on. "Have you ever noticed? She'll admire a skein of pure cashmere and talk about how much of it she needs for a particular sweater, then she'll say something like 'I'm buying that yarn right after I finish this scarf.' It's always scarves now. It used to be sweaters."

"Scarves are fashionable."

"The ones she makes use a single skein of sock-weight wool for a total of five bucks."

"She does a beautiful job," Ellie Jo said in Corinne's defense. "Not all women can."

"But she never does buy the expensive yarn, does she?"

Ellie Jo nodded. "She does. Just last week, she bought a skein of Jade Sapphire 2-ply. That's thirty-five dollars."

"*A* skein? One?"

"That's all the pattern called for. She's making a beret."

"Okay," Dana said, offering Lizzie the other breast, "maybe I'm wrong about that, but forget buying yarn. She's just too smooth to be real. Nothing ruffles her."

"That's a good thing," argued Ellie Jo. "I wouldn't ridicule it."

"I'm not," Dana said, struggling to verbalize what she felt. "It's just that she's *so* calm. I mean, she's told stories about her mother running off to be part of a religious cult and her husband surviving childhood leukemia and the guy who renovated their house bilking them of hundreds of thousands of dollars. It's like her life has a gazillion traumas, but she doesn't blink."

"You missed the one about her father dying in a plane crash," Gillian murmured.

"Her father?" Dana asked in disbelief.

"She's convinced it was sabotage."

Dana looked from one face to another. "See? That's what I'm saying. How can one have all of these awful experiences, and still be even-tempered?"

"She's rich," Tara remarked. "That helps."

Technically, as Mrs. Hugh Clarke, Dana was rich, too. That didn't keep her from suffering emotional ups and downs. And now Corinne mentioned the one-drop rule? Dana didn't feel black. How could she look in the mirror, at pale skin and blond hair, and feel African American? Was that how the Clarkes were seeing her? No, she didn't feel black. But she was starting to feel exposed.

"Maybe Cousin Emma knows something," Dana suggested. "She always claimed she was close to Mom."

"Do *not* call Emma," Ellie Jo said. "She knows *nothing*."

Dana was startled by her grandmother's

force. "Don't you think, even for Lizzie's sake—"

"I don't. Your father had no part in raising you. He doesn't even know you exist. He spent a week with your mother and never bothered to call her afterward. That was neither caring nor responsible."

"What if he wasn't a student but was just passing through?" Gillian asked. "What if he *did* try to reach her afterward, only she was already gone? There could be any number of innocent explanations."

But Ellie Jo's mind was made up. With uncharacteristic vehemence, she said, "Do not look for the man, Dana. It will only cause you grief."

Silence followed her outburst. Dana was as mystified as the others. Talk about calm characters, Ellie Jo topped the list. The only explanation now was that she felt threatened by the possibility of Dana's father reappearing and vying for her affection.

Ellie Jo stood. "I'm going back to the house for a bit."

"Are you feeling all right?" Gillian asked.

"I'm fine. I'm *fine*. There is absolutely nothing wrong with me. I have a right to be seventy-four, don't I?"

"Gram?" Dana called, sharing Gillian's concern.

But Ellie Jo didn't stop. The screen door dinged open and slapped shut.

Chapter 11

Dana stared after her. When the door dinged again a few seconds later, she thought it was Ellie Jo regretting her brusque departure, but it was Saundra Belisle, looking behind her, probably puzzled that Ellie Jo hadn't stopped to speak.

Saundra was an elegant African American, tall, slim, and stylish. She wore her gray hair cropped close to her head and today was dressed in white pants and a burgundy blouse. Neither had a designer label. Saundra was far from wealthy, but she did have class.

A retired nurse, she had only been frequenting the shop for the last few years, but she was a lifelong knitter. That made her the first to tackle complex patterns, which she was happy to teach to others.

Dana caught Saundra's eye and gestured her over. Taking the baby from her breast, she put her to her shoulder and patted her back. But when she glanced at the door again, Saundra hadn't moved. Her large dark eyes were on the baby. She seemed unsure.

"I'll send her over," Gillian said as she rose. "I have to leave anyway." She kissed Dana, then the baby. "I'll have the pictures printed. Lotsa copies. Keep an eye on Ellie Jo, okay?"

"I will," Dana said, "and thank you for the quilt. You know what it means to me."

Gillian smiled and went to Saundra, who approached with her eyes on the baby. She went behind Dana's chair and bent down to better see Lizzie's face. She touched the child's head with a trembling hand.

"I heard about this little one," she said ever so softly. "Hello, Elizabeth." She stroked Lizzie's head, then, still softly, asked Dana, "May I hold her?"

Dana transferred Lizzie to unquestionably able arms.

"Oh *my*," Saundra cooed. She had one hand under the baby's head, one under her bottom. "Look at this. *Look* at this."

"Didn't expect it, did ya?" Dana quipped.

"No, ma'am, I surely did not," Saundra said with a drawl not usually heard in her voice. "She is clearly a face from the past. This is quite stunning."

Dana liked that word. "It's also mystifying. We had no idea I had a relative who was African American."

"It isn't something that people of color who have lost that color often discuss."

"But you saw it right away."

"Oh yes," Saundra said with the arch of a brow. "She is not Hispanic. My, my, my," she sang to the baby.

Dana studied Saundra's features. Her lips were full, but her nose didn't have the breadth it would have had if she'd been of pure African descent.

"You're part white, aren't you?"

"I am," Saundra said, still singing to the baby. "My mama was black and my daddy white." With the utmost care, she put the baby to her shoulder. Holding her there as though she were delicate crystal, she drew slow circles on Lizzie's back with the flat of long, red-tipped fingers.

"Did you worry about having children yourself?" Dana asked. They had never before discussed race; as with David, it had always been irrelevant.

"I never had children," Saundra reminded her.

"Because of this?"

"Because there were too many others to care for. But if it's color you're asking about, no, I wouldn't have worried. I'm comfortable in my skin. I'd have been comfortable with theirs."

Tara joined the conversation. "Do you have siblings?"

"Not now. I did, though. A brother. He died several years back. He was much older."

"What did he look like?" Dana asked.

Saundra smiled crookedly. "Even more gray and wrinkled than me."

"You are not wrinkled," Dana said, because other than a few crow's feet, Saundra's skin was remarkably tight. "And, besides, that's not what I mean."

"I know," she said, relenting. "In his youth, my brother was a handsome devil. He was tall, lean, and lighter than me."

"Did he ever have children?"

"Oh yes," she enunciated clearly, "*quite* a few."

"Huh," Tara mused. "He spread it around."

"I would have put it more delicately," Saundra said. "But yes."

"What did the children look like?" Dana asked.

"He preferred white women, so the children were white."

"Very white?" Dana wanted to know how many generations it took for color to vanish. It might give her a hint as to how far back to look.

"Some were very white. Others looked like this sweet one here."

"Why did he prefer white women?" Tara asked.

Putting her cheek to the baby's head, swaying now from side to side, Saundra said softly, "I guess he thought white had more status than black."

"Do you?" Dana asked.

Saundra shrugged. "I think higher percentages of poor people are uneducated and criminally disposed, and more poor people are black than white. I don't necessarily buy into the stereotype, but I understand its source."

Dana was unsettled. "Do you see me as superior to you because my skin is white? I must have some mixed blood."

Saundra snorted. "You're not black."

"I am," Dana insisted. "The one-drop rule says I'm black." But she felt like an impostor.

Saundra rolled her eyes as if to say, *Spare me.* "I don't see you as superior to me, because you've never acted that way. You relate to me as you relate to your own grandmother, and Ellie Jo and I are alike. We both came from upwardly mobile families and have solid enough nest eggs to live comfortably." She frowned. "Is Ellie Jo all right, by the way? She seemed disturbed when I passed her."

"She was," Dana said with another look at the door. "I don't know what's the matter. She hasn't come back yet."

"Should I go over and check on her?" Tara asked.

"No. If she's not back in a few more minutes, I'll go. That nest egg, Saundra—were you just prudent all those years?"

"Some. I also inherited a bit." She smiled. "I don't feel inferior now. It was different when I was young. I used to dwell on it then. For years, I was a maid."

"I thought you were a nurse," Tara said with a frown.

"From the time I was sixteen to the time I got that degree, I cleaned toilets and washed clothes. I didn't feel superior to anyone then, but would it have been any different if I'd been white and doing those things? Being a maid brings with it a certain mind-set, regardless of color. The one advantage a white maid has over a black maid is that going back and forth on the bus, no one guesses the truth of what she does." She tipped her head and peered at Lizzie. "I think this angel is sleeping," she whispered.

Tara lit up. "Put her in the cradle, Dana. Let her sleep there. I want to see what you've done on the sweater."

With an exquisitely tender expression, Saundra held the baby in front of her for another minute before returning her to Dana.

Lizzie's eyes were closed, mouth puckered as she nursed in her dreams. Then her lips parted—and there was Hugh again in the corners.

With a rush of feeling, Dana put her cheek to Lizzie's. "One minute she's so real, the next I can't believe she's here." She held her for another minute until the wave of emotion passed. Then she lowered her into the cradle and reached back for the quilt. "Did you see this?" she asked Saundra.

"I surely did," Saundra said, smiling broadly.

"You did some of it, didn't you? Which part? Wait. I know." Spreading out the quilt, Dana pointed to a yellow square, then a pale blue one, displaying a star and a seahorse, each in the same color as its field but set apart by contrasting stitches, in Saundra's inimitable style. Dana hugged her. "I adore this, Saundra. Thank you. My baby is so loved." Since the baby didn't need the quilt for warmth, she folded it over the foot of the cradle.

"How's your husband doing with her?" Saundra asked when Tara was gone.

"Great," Dana enthused. "He changes diapers, burps her, walks her when she cries. He had a meeting in the office, so I thought I'd bring her here."

"What does he think of her color?"

"He's surprised."

"Upset?"

"Oh, I don't think Hugh's upset about her color," she said, giving him the benefit of the doubt. "He's upset with me for not knowing my background. But he loves Lizzie."

"He should," Saundra said. "She's his child."

Dana glanced toward the door. "No sign of my grandmother. I think I'd like to check on her while the baby's sleeping. Will you be sitting here?"

Saundra smiled. "I won't move."

Walking at a clip, Dana went down the path and climbed the back steps of the house. "Ellie Jo?"

There was no response from her grandmother, only from the cat, who was meowing halfway up the stairs. The tabby didn't scoot down the steps in her usual haste to rub Dana's leg, but continued to meow. Something was wrong.

"Gram?" Dana called, frightened. Preceded by the cat, she ran up the stairs. *"Gram?"*

Veronica led her down the hall to Elizabeth's bedroom, where Ellie Jo sat on the floor at the base of the attic ladder. Her face was ash-pale, her breathing shallow and fast. Books were scattered around her, a half-empty carton on its side.

Dana ran over and crouched down. "What happened?"

"I was coming down."

"Carrying this box? And you fell. Does anything hurt?"

"My foot."

Dana was already reaching for the phone. She quickly punched in the line to the store. Trying to sound calm, she said, "Olivia, it's me. I'm at the house. Would you send Saundra and Tara?"

"No need for that," Ellie Jo said as soon as she'd hung up. "I'm all right." She tried to rise, but Dana held her down.

"Saundra's a nurse. Indulge me, please. Are those the textbooks you mentioned?"

"There's nothing else up there."

"*Dana?*" Tara called from downstairs.

"*In my mother's room.*"

Seconds later there were sounds on the stairs, then the two women appeared, with Lizzie in Saundra's arms. By the time Saundra determined that the only serious damage done by Ellie Jo's fall was to her ankle, Ellie Jo was breathing more evenly. When she refused an ambulance, Dana insisted on driving.

Between the three of them, they got Ellie Jo to her feet and managed to get her downstairs. But when Tara offered to take

her to the hospital, Dana refused. "I'm taking her."

"What about the baby?"

"I have everything she needs, and I can
nurse her when she's hungry. Really, I won't
be comfortable staying here. Besides, you
have to get home for the kids."

Tara tried to argue, but Dana was firm.
When Saundra offered to ride along with
Ellie Jo, it was settled.

Lizzie must have known that her great-
grandmother was hurt, because she slept
through much of the drive and, once inside
the hospital, continued sleeping in the sling,
snug to Dana's body.

Ellie Jo's broken ankle was a simple one.
She was fitted with a walking cast and
crutches, which she was told to use for the
first several days.

Relieved, Dana brought the car around to
the front door of the hospital. She had no
sooner settled her grandmother inside than
she saw Hugh. He stood on the far side of
the entrance, with his hand on the shoulder
of an attractive auburn-haired woman. They
were deep in conversation.

Dana had no idea who the woman was or
why he was with her, but she was shaken by

the sight of him. She couldn't just climb into the car and drive off.

"Be right back," she told Ellie Jo, and quickly crossed the main lobby. She hadn't quite reached Hugh when he looked up, caught sight of her, and went pale.

Chapter 12

Hugh's first thought when he spotted Dana was that something was wrong with the baby. "Where's Lizzie?"

"In the car," Dana said, and quickly added, "with Saundra. My grandmother fell and broke her ankle. It's been set. I was just about to take her home."

Not the baby, then. He felt a wave of relief, followed by another concern. He liked Ellie Jo. She had never treated him as anything less than a grandson, and she wasn't as young as she had once been. "Is she all right?" When Dana nodded, he said, "You should have called. I'd have helped."

"You were at the office. I didn't want to bother you." Her eyes sent a more poignant message.

Unable to go there, he said, "Dana, this is Crystal Kostas. I'll be representing her. Her son is upstairs recovering from surgery. Crystal, my wife, Dana," he said. Then, wanting to talk to Dana, he said to Crystal, "I think we're set for now. Call as soon as you've written stuff in that notebook. You have my home number?" When Crystal nodded, he took Dana's arm and started back toward the car. "How did Ellie Jo fall?"

"She was getting something in the attic and lost her footing coming back down the ladder. What's wrong with that woman's son?"

"He was hit by a car. He's four."

"Is he badly hurt?"

"Badly enough that without more surgeries, he may not walk again."

Dana stopped. "That certainly puts things in perspective."

"You don't know the half," he went on, thinking that Dana liked hearing about his work. "The boy's father—who refuses to acknowledge him—is Stan Hutchinson."

Her eyes widened. "The senator?"

"The senator. And Crystal has no health insurance."

"Huh-uh. There's your case. Does your father know?"

"No." He looked out toward the street. "I can't get myself to call."

"Anger? Pride? Fear?"

"Anger," Hugh said. It wasn't the whole truth, but it would do.

"Anger lingers," she remarked.

"Yes." Hugh continued walking toward the car. "Has Lizzie been okay?"

"Perfect. She's the easiest baby."

"Spoken by one who's had a slew," he teased, and opened Ellie Jo's door. "That's quite a wad of a foot, Ellie Jo. Is it hurting?"

"A little," said Ellie Jo.

"Hugh," Dana called from inside the driver's side. With a knee on the seat, she gestured toward the back. "Have you met Saundra Belisle?"

Hugh extended a hand. "I think I've seen you at the shop." He remembered her. She had a certain authority.

Saundra put her hand in his. "It's my pleasure. Congratulations on the birth of your baby. She's a marvelous little being."

Hugh believed her. Feeling better, he tried to see Lizzie, but couldn't from where he was. He closed Ellie Jo's door, rounded the car, and opened the one by the baby.

"Hey, you," he said softly.

She closed her eyes, shutting him out. Apparently, she hadn't liked the DNA test any more than Dana had. He wished he could make her understand that he was only building their case. He wished he could make Dana understand it, too.

"I have to get Ellie Jo home," Dana said. She was speaking pleasantly enough, but there was little warmth in her eyes. She was angry, still. And the longer the anger lingered, the more it worried him. This wasn't the Dana he knew.

He wanted to talk about it, but this wasn't the time. So he leaned in to kiss Lizzie, then straightened and closed the door. "When will you be home?"

"That depends on what I find at the shop. I have to talk with Olivia and the part-timers to make sure one of us is there every day to open and close."

"One of *us*?" he asked quietly. "You just had a baby."

"Lizzie loves the shop," Dana said with enthusiasm. "You should see the cradle there, and the women made *the* most beautiful quilt. The shop is a perfect place for her. It's quiet, and there's always someone around to help."

Hugh could imagine. "Is that a dig?" he whispered.

She didn't deny it. But her eyes did

soften. "I have to go, Hugh," she said and slipped into the car.

He closed the door and stood back. She hadn't asked when he would be home, he realized, and wondered if she was preoccupied, or if she just didn't care.

🍂

He was well out of the city when he put in a call to his father. He wasn't surprised when his mother answered. She was the gatekeeper while Eaton was at work.

"Hi, Mom."

There was a skipped beat, then a relieved "Hugh." She spoke softly. "I'm glad *you* had the good sense to call, at least. Your father's been impossible. I've been after him, but he's too stubborn for his own good. How is the baby?"

"She's fine."

"I'd like to get over to see her, but it's difficult with Eaton right here. Do something about this, Hugh. He thinks that you have mortally offended him."

"*Me?*"

"You said something while we were at the hospital."

"*I* did? *You* two stood there suggesting I wasn't Lizzie's father!"

"Eaton was upset."

"Hold it, Mom," he said, because much as he hated attacking his mother, she wasn't innocent in this. "You didn't say he was wrong. What was it you said? 'Stranger things have happened'?"

"Well, they have, but I was just making an observation. Anyway, it's during times like these that we have to stick together. We have to support each other, not refuse to talk."

"Stick together, as in you, me, and Dad against my wife and child?"

"That's not what I mean."

"Do you have a problem with Lizzie's color?" he asked bluntly.

"I don't," she protested. "You *know* I don't. Wasn't I the first one over at the Parkers' to greet that little grandson who was adopted from Korea? Wasn't I the first to suggest that the hospital auxiliary honor Leila Cummings, one of our *brilliant* African-American doctors? I was even the first to encourage your Uncle Bradley to set up a college fund for the children of minority employees. How can you call me a bigot?"

"I haven't called you a bigot. But Lizzie is one of *us*. Why haven't you been over to see her, even without Dad?"

"Because your *father* is set against my going, because *you* offended him, and he won't get . . . off . . . his . . . *duff* until you apologize."

"Fine," Hugh said. "Is he there?"

"Yes," she snapped. "You can be as unpleasant as he is. Hold the phone."

Hugh held. He was in the middle lane of the highway, being passed right and left. Had someone honked to speed him up, he might well have made a rude gesture.

A minute passed. Clearly, Eaton didn't want to talk. Hugh was beginning to wonder at what point he would simply hang up—when there was a click, then Eaton's voice, all business.

"Yes, Hugh."

Suddenly not quite sure that he wanted to hear what his father would say, he decided to start casually. "What's happening with the book?"

"Not the book. The tour. The publicist just faxed me the schedule to date, and I've been on the phone with her ever since. They have me booked into supermarkets. *Super-*

markets, for Pete's sake. It used to be that a book tour was a dignified thing."

"Don't you have a say?"

"Yes," Eaton drawled, "but they have the stats on their side. People *are* buying their books in warehouses. Do the salespeople in those warehouses make personal recommendations? Do the salespeople in those warehouses *read*?" He grew resigned. "But maybe it's just as well. I don't know about this book. It may have errors."

"What kind of errors?"

"The kind that can derail my career."

"I don't believe that," Hugh said. "You're very careful. Not so your friend Hutch."

Eaton snorted. "Friend?"

"I'm representing a woman whose child he allegedly fathered."

There was a pause, then a cautious "Can she prove it?"

"We're working on that."

"The proof better be good," Eaton warned, "else he'll accuse you of going after him because I was ticked off. What's she want—money?"

Hugh put his palm to the horn when a car cut into his lane immediately in front of him. "Not for herself. The boy was hit by a car and has serious needs. She tried to get through to Hutch when the boy was born, but she was told to get in line behind all the other women trying to hit him up with claims."

"Hutch is no altar boy."

"No. None of us is, I guess." It seemed the time. "If I offended you at the hospital, I'm sorry."

There was a scalding "If? Do you doubt it?"

"Dad, I was under pressure," Hugh said, feeling about ten years old. "You said something totally offensive."

"But perhaps not totally off the mark," Eaton countered. "Brad told me you're doing a paternity test. That says you have your own doubts."

"No. It says I was pressured by my family to get solid proof that the baby is mine. A DNA test is the only way I know of doing that."

"So? What'd the lab say?"

"They'll say it's my baby. But I won't have the formal results for another few days."

"And you don't have any doubts, given your next-door neighbor?"

"No more than I have about you living all these years beside a man Mom dated before she started seeing you."

"Now, there's another offensive remark," Eaton charged.

"Dad," Hugh pleaded with a frustrated laugh, "why is it offensive when I say it, and not offensive when you do?"

"I've been married to your mother for more than forty years. *And* she never had anyone's baby but mine."

It was one too many digs. "Are you sure?" Hugh asked. "You and I look alike, but what about Robert? He doesn't look like you."

"I'm hanging up now," Eaton advised.

"No, don't," Hugh relented. "Please. I really want to talk."

"About who fathered your brother?"

"About why my daughter's color matters. You champion minorities in your books. I champion them in court. Is it all an ego trip? Or do we truly believe in equality? Because if we do, my daughter's skin color shouldn't matter."

"Does it matter to you?"

"Yes," Hugh confessed. "It does, and I don't know why."

"Why do you think?"

"I don't *know*. If I did, I wouldn't be asking. Maybe it matters to me because it matters to my family. Dana's racial makeup doesn't change who she is."

"Not for you."

"For you?" Hugh asked, and honked long and hard when another car cut him off. "Why should it? She's the woman I've chosen. Would it matter if she's *purple*?"

"Not to other purple people."

"For *God's* sake, Dad."

"I'm sorry, Hugh, but people gravitate to their own. It's a fact of life."

"Lizzie *is* our own."

"We'll talk about this more once you have the results of that test."

"And if it proves I'm her father?"

"I don't want to discuss this now."

But Hugh did. "What *then*? Will you accept Lizzie as your legitimate grandchild? Will you accept *Dana*?"

"Not . . . now!" Eaton ground out with a sternness Hugh rarely heard. "The timing of this could *not* be worse. I have too much else on my plate right now."

"Fine," Hugh said, then added lightly, "Okay. Talk soon. Bye."

It was dusk before Dana returned home to find Hugh's car in the driveway. She was glad he was there. Beyond that, though, she was too tired to feel much beside discouragement. After settling Ellie Jo in, she had gone to the foot of the attic ladder, picked up the scattered books, and returned them to their carton. In the process, she had searched each one for something her mother might have left—a letter tucked into the crease or a note in a margin—anything that might give a clue to the identity of Dana's father or the name of a roommate or friend. Since these books were from her mother's last months in school, it stood to reason that if Elizabeth had doodled anything pertinent it might be there.

She had continued leafing through the books until Ellie Jo called out needing help to get to the bathroom, which raised a whole other worry. Ellie Jo couldn't stay alone.

Dana thought of moving in to help. That would serve Hugh right. But she couldn't imagine getting up every few hours to feed Lizzie and again to help Ellie Jo.

One solution was to hire a nurse for Ellie Jo, but her grandmother flat-out refused. She insisted that she had only called for help because Dana was there and that she could manage just fine if she was alone. She showed Dana this by returning to bed on her own.

Dana gave up the fight. She was too tired to do anything else.

Now she pulled in beside Hugh's car. He was at the open front door before she could lift the baby from the car. He didn't offer to help, just stood there and watched.

She could have used his brawn, but would be damned if she would say it. His expression was stoically Clarke, his mood unreadable. It was only when she was inside that he finally took the carrier from her arm. Without a word, she returned to the car for the rest of her things.

By the time she was back in the house, he had unbuckled Lizzie and lifted her out. She was crying in short little spurts, and his holding her didn't improve her spirits.

"What's wrong?" he asked Dana.

"She's hungry. I'll feed her." Dropping her

bags at the foot of the stairs, she took the baby and lowered herself to the sofa in the family room.

"You look beat," he said, mildly accusatory. "Have you been on your feet all afternoon?"

"No. I rested at Gram's."

"Not long enough. Ellie Jo may be sidelined, but you have to take care of yourself. Especially nursing. If you get run-down, it won't be good for Lizzie."

"I know that," Dana said. She held down the swollen part of her breast so that she could watch the baby nurse.

Hugh settled into a leather chair cattycorner and put his elbows on his knees. His tone was surprisingly accommodating. "Talk to me, Dana. This silence isn't like you. It isn't who we are."

She made a discouraged sound. "Do you know who we are? If you do, clue me in, because I sure as hell don't know."

"I'll rephrase that," he said. "This isn't who we were before the baby was born."

No. It wasn't. The fact of that was so sad that Dana choked up.

"Talk to me," he repeated.

She swallowed and raised her eyes. "What would you have me say?"

"That you understand. That you realize that what I did was for the best."

"I don't," she said simply and held his gaze. Once, she would have lost herself in it, but not now.

"Come on," he coaxed. "Say what you're feeling."

"It's about trust," she blurted. "Trust has always been a big thing for me—trusting that a person would be there, would *always* be there, like my mother wasn't. I never wanted to lose anyone again. Then you came along, and I thought I could trust that you'd always be there, but I can't. I can't trust that you're in my corner. I can't trust that you'll love me if my father turns out to have mixed blood. I feel dirty. I feel like you cheated on me."

He frowned. "Are you talking about the DNA tests, or about today?"

"Today?" She didn't follow.

"My being with Crystal."

"Crystal? Your client?" It took her a minute to follow, then she was dismayed. "You mean, did I wonder if she was *more* than that? Of *course* not, Hugh. You're my husband. Besides, you're with women all the time. It's part of your job."

"Some wives would have been uneasy."

"I wasn't." Lizzie lost the nipple and frantically turned her head from side to side until Dana guided her back. "I trust you when it comes to women," she said without looking up. "It's the other stuff that's the problem. It's your lack of trusting me."

"I do trust you."

"Not enough," she said with a warning look—and was grateful when he spared her the bit about wanting solid proof for his family. "See, I keep thinking this is the first test of our marriage, and we've failed. By the way, I'm getting nowhere looking for my father. I've talked with my grandmother and my mother's friends, and I went through some of my mother's things, but I haven't found anything that could even remotely tell me where my father is. My best hope is finding my mother's college roommate. Her first name was Carol, but that's all I know. The college doesn't have a record of who she is, and even if they did, she might not remember anything."

"Lakey may be able to get the roommate's last name."

"Fine," Dana said and reeled off the facts. "My mother was Elizabeth Joseph; she entered the University of Wisconsin in 1968; she dropped out after her junior year to have me. I don't know the name of her dorm. She was an art history major, but she also took English, Spanish, and math. She was lousy at math. I found some of her tests today. She got C-minuses."

"I'll give Lakey what you have."

"I want you to know, Hugh, that if our baby had come out white, I would not be looking for this man. If she'd been born with *red* curls, would you have said I needed to find him? Of course not. So why am I doing this? Why is it so important to know? Do I really *care* where my great-great-great-grandfather was from? And if I find my father," she raced on, "will I feel differently about myself?"

Hugh didn't answer.

And that annoyed her. He was the one who had wanted to talk. "So let's talk about this," she ordered. "We're all for minorities—civil rights, affirmative action, equality in the workplace—but *we* only want to be white. Are we hypocrites?"

"We?"

"You. First and foremost, you think of yourself as a Clarke. I think of myself as Dana. Isn't that telling?"

"If your family had the history mine did, you would understand."

"If yours had the history mine has, *you* would understand." She took a deep breath. "But it isn't just you and your family, or me and mine. It's wondering what our daughter is going to face growing up and whether she and I will be facing it alone."

"I'll be there."

"Will you?"

"I've been here, haven't I? You're the one who's been gone."

She took the baby from her breast, put her to her shoulder, and patted her back. Wearily, she asked, "How did things go so wrong so fast?"

"They haven't gone so wrong."

"They *have*. *Look* at us, Hugh."

"It'll pass. A couple more days and we'll have the lab results."

Dana wanted to scream. "That's not the *point*. I'm talking about *trust*."

He sighed. "Oh, come on. It was only a *cheek swab*, Dana."

Dana was beside herself. Responding to

a tiny, responsible voice in her head, she slid her feet to the floor and prepared to take Lizzie upstairs.

"What about this weekend?" Hugh asked.

"What about it?"

"Will you be at your grandmother's?"

"Some of the time."

"Julian and Deb want to come over. And Jim and Rita."

"That's fine."

"Will it be awkward?"

Awkward? Given the weekend that they might have had, it would be *totally* awkward. "Not for me," she said, suddenly furious. "I think our baby is perfect. You're the one with the problem. Maybe if you tell them about my grandmother's medical problem they'll wait a while."

"I don't think I can put them off."

"Then you're the one who has to worry about awkwardness. Are you going to let them know you aren't sure she's your child?"

"Of course not."

"Then you'll pretend she is. Ah. Another show. Think you can pull it off?"

They stared at each other for the longest

time, Dana standing, Hugh in his chair. She refused to take back the words.

Finally, he said, "Is that cynicism or fatigue?"

Quickly remorseful, she took a breath and said gently, "I suspect it's both. I'm going to bed."

Chapter 13

Eaton Clarke had heartburn. He suspected it was the Mexican food they had had Friday night. The restaurant was new and well reviewed. He had been the one to suggest that they try it, and the two couples with them were game. But he'd had a bad feeling about the place from the minute they walked in. The tables were too close together and the waiter too familiar.

The dinner conversation hadn't helped. Everyone wanted to talk about Hugh and his baby—or, more pointedly, Dana and her child—because Eaton's brother Brad had spread word about the question of the baby's paternity. In the course of three hours, Eaton got more advice than he wanted. It was either "Do not establish a college fund if the child isn't yours," or "Change your will," or even "It wouldn't hurt to put the Vineyard house in trust."

His chest burned all night. He felt better

when he woke up Saturday morning, but worse when he joined his partners for their weekly tennis game. They, too, had advice.

He was in a thoroughly bad mood when he called his brother on his way home from the club. "What in the hell are you doing, Brad? I can't go anywhere without people knowing about Hugh's baby. Is there some reason you're telling everyone in sight that Hugh may not be the father?"

"It's true. He may not be."

"But he *may* be, and then what? This is our *personal business*, Brad."

"Not if the child isn't Hugh's. I saw the look on his face the other afternoon. He's furious with his wife. I'm telling you, Eaton, trouble's brewing there."

Eaton didn't like his tone. "Does that please you?"

"It has nothing to do with whether it pleases me or not. We all had our questions about Dana."

"I thought you liked her."

"I did while she was faithful, but it looks like Hugh has a live one on his hands."

"Does *that* please you? Does Hugh's situation make you feel less bad about your daughter's divorce?"

"Anne's divorce has nothing to do with this," Brad shot back. "If you think I'm playing a game of tit-for-tat, you're off the mark. Not that that surprises me. You're the writer, and I'm the businessman. You're sitting around waiting for royalties, while I'm making all of us more wealthy. I don't play games, Eaton. I have more important things to do."

"That's right," Eaton concluded, "so just shut your mouth about Hugh. Don't be a petty little busybody. This isn't your business. Keep your nose *out* of it."

He ended the call knowing that he had offended his brother, but having had the last word, Eaton felt a perverse satisfaction. It vanished when Dorothy met him at the door with word that Justin Field had called no more than two minutes earlier. Justin was his longtime friend, personal lawyer, and the executor of his estate.

"What does he want?" Eaton asked, though he feared he knew.

"We talked a bit about the wedding plans for Julie. Justin and Babs are very excited. She's thirty-eight, so they'd almost given up hope, but he went on and on about how wonderful the fiancé is. Then he said he wanted to talk with you about Hugh."

Eaton stood at the rosewood hall table, sifting through the mail as he spoke. "Is it a coincidence that I just played tennis with Justin's partner?" he barked. "These men are little old ladies!"

After a single silent beat, Dorothy remarked, "So am I."

"Oh, Dot, you know what I mean. Little old ladies gossip because they have nothing else to do with their time. You have other things."

"I gossip. Only I don't see it as gossip. I see it as sharing news with friends."

He looked at her, wondering where she was headed. "Are you malicious?"

"Of course not."

"There's your difference," he decided. "My tennis friends are very happy to see me slip up. Same with Bradley. He's never gotten over the fact that I refused to follow him into the business, and as for my tennis partners, they're still smarting because I won't give them unlimited numbers of signed editions of my books. Is there some good reason why they can't go out and buy the copies that they want signed for their wife's cousin's proctologist? Am I a charity?"

"No, dear," Dorothy said. "I believe that's what Justin wants to discuss."

Eaton eyed her sharply. "My being a charity?"

"Your being treated like one by Hugh's wife in the event that his marriage falls apart. It's no different from what our friends said last night."

"Which was extremely annoying."

"They're simply acting out of concern for you."

"Have I asked for their help?"

"No, but you haven't denied it, and that is often an invitation." Her tone grew plaintive. "You don't say anything, Eaton. You just let the questions sit there. Why don't you simply tell them they're wrong? Why don't you tell them that this child is Hugh's, and that there's nothing wrong with his marriage, and that the child's coloring adds an interesting element to the family, because it does, you know. I have no problem having a grandchild of African-American descent. Do you?"

Eaton sighed. "Are you still annoyed that I won't go visit Hugh?"

"Well, he did call."

"And was no help at all. He's asking the same questions you are, at a time when I don't want to think about it. Dorothy, I have a book due out in a little over three weeks. Have you made it clear to the events coordinator that I want hors d'oeuvres *passed* at the book party?"

"Yes, dear."

"What about the invitations? Have they gone out?"

"They were mailed yesterday. I've told you these things, Eaton."

Eaton took a breath in a bid for patience. "If you've told me and I haven't heard, it's because I have other things on my mind. I've been booked to appear on national television, and you can be sure I'll be questioned about my family. They'll want me to vouch for the things I've written."

"Vouch for what things?" Dorothy scolded. "You wrote this book well before little Elizabeth was born. No one will hold it against you if she isn't listed on an ancestral chart, and there would be absolutely no need for you to include a chart of Dana's family. But forget the book," she said with the dismissive wave of a hand. "I'm not talking about the book. I'm talking about our son and his child. I want to go over and visit."

Eaton looked up in surprise. "Fine. Go."

"I want you with me. It won't be the same if I go alone. They'll think something's wrong."

Eaton said, "Something *is* wrong."

"Then *do* something about it," Dorothy cried. "Hire an investigator. Change your will. Put the Vineyard property in trust so that she can't get her hands on it. Either you accept the baby or you don't. Don't you see the damage that's being done while you vacillate?" She glared at the clock on the wall, then reached for her purse. "I have to go to the market. If we're having the Emerys here for hors d'oeuvres before the theater, I need to buy food."

Eaton stared after her as she went out the door. "Drive carefully," he finally said out of sheer habit.

❧

Dorothy kept both hands on the wheel and her lips pressed together. She didn't need Eaton telling her to drive carefully. She drove carefully all on her own—had been doing so for forty-nine years—and had a spotless record to show for it, which was more than Eaton could say. He had two accidents on his slate—one from a winter-blizzard skid, the other from a ten-car chain pile-up on the expressway. She could blame the first on the weather, but the second would have been preventable if he had left the requisite number of car lengths between his own car and the one in front of him.

No, she didn't need Eaton to tell her how to drive.

Nor, she decided, did she need him to tell her whom to call and whom not to. Taking one hand from the wheel, she flipped open her cell phone and thumbed in Hugh's number. The phone rang several times, and then Dana's recorded message came on.

With both hands on the wheel again, Dorothy negotiated the local roads to the supermarket. She put on her blinker, about to pull into the parking lot, when she had another thought and drove on past. Three minutes later, she parked in front of a local boutique that radiated yellow, orange, and pink. It was a small place, owned by two young women. She had discovered it quite by accident when she had needed a last-minute bread-and-butter gift to take along for a weekend visit to friends.

She went inside, smiled at the owner, and said firmly, "I want one of your mother-and-daughter sets for my daughter-in-law and her brand-new baby. What's the most unusual thing you have?" Dana liked bright and unusual. Dana could *wear* bright and unusual.

Soon Dorothy walked back out with a package wrapped and ribboned with the same yellow, orange, and pink that had initially drawn her to the store. Satisfied, she skipped the supermarket and pulled into the smaller lot of a gourmet cheese and wine shop. Inside, she bought a wedge of cheese, several cracker selections, and— defiant still—a dozen each of the home-cooked coconut-crusted chicken fingers and skewers of beef satay. So Eaton wouldn't get his favorite mini-quiches from the recipe she had been making for years. These other appetizers were every bit as good, without demanding an hour of her time in the kitchen. Present them on elegant serving-ware, she reasoned, and their guests wouldn't know the difference.

Satisfied for the second time in thirty minutes, she returned to the car. Spotting the bright package in the passenger's seat, she started the engine and let it idle while she tried Hugh's number again.

This time, Dana answered.

For a split second, Dorothy wavered. She didn't normally do things that she knew would upset Eaton, and it wasn't a matter of obedience, but respect. His instincts were good, and his heart was usually in the right place. The problem was, she didn't know where his heart was now.

So, boldly, she said, "Dana, this is Dorothy." She usually called herself "Mom," but Dana preferred "Dorothy," and maybe she had a point. "How are you?"

There was a pause, then a cautious "I'm fine. How are you?"

"Very well, thank you," Dorothy said as though nothing was wrong. "Tell me how the baby is."

"She's adorable," Dana said in a lighter tone. "I swear she just smiled. I know it's too early, that it's probably gas, but it did look pretty."

"How is she eating?"

"Very well. I think we've found a rhythm."

"What about sleeping?"

"Uh, still a ways to go with that. She's a little confused between day and night."

"Do you keep the light off when you're with her at night?"

"I use a nightlight."

"Good. There should be no playing, then. Let her sleep nighttimes as long as she will, but wake her every four hours during the day." Hearing her own words, she added quickly, "Actually, those are just suggestions. I had my turn, my son Robert always says when I start telling him how to handle his children."

There was a pause, then Dana said, "I'm open to suggestions. The only thing I can't change is Lizzie's color."

"Are you calling her Lizzie, then? That's very sweet for a little girl. 'Elizabeth' is just a beautiful name, and she may grow up to insist that we all call her that, but 'Lizzie' works for a baby. Funny, Robert was always a Robert, never a Bob to anyone but Hugh. How is Hugh doing, by the way? Is he helping you with the baby? Did I ever tell you that Eaton never changed a diaper? Not a one, but then, none of his friends did, either. Back then, it was really up to us moms to do things like that, because we were full-time mothers—not that there's anything wrong with *not* being a full-time mother." She paused, concerned by Dana's silence. "Are you there, dear?"

"I'm here," Dana said.

"I would like to come over," Dorothy announced. "I picked up a little something for you and Lizzie, and I'd like to see her. She's probably changed a lot, even in four days."

"Not her color, Dorothy. You need to know that."

"I know it," Dorothy acknowledged quietly. Then, because that didn't seem like enough to say on the subject, she added, "I'm not trying to deny her heritage, because I've been thinking of little else for the past few days. But that baby just happens to be my grandchild."

"There are people who aren't sure about that," Dana said, and Dorothy felt ashamed. The business at the hospital that first day would haunt her always.

"When one suffers a shock—not suffers, *experiences* a shock, it's very easy to lash out. I do believe that Lizzie is my grand-child."

"And Eaton?"

"I'm speaking for myself now."

"Does he know you've called?"

"No," Dorothy said before it occurred to her to lie, then backpedaled, "but that's nei-ther here nor there, because I want to see my grandchild. Tomorrow isn't a good day, but Monday would be." Eaton would be in his office and wouldn't be any the wiser if she told him she was going into Boston to shop. "Would that work for you?"

"I'll be at the yarn store on Monday. My grandmother broke her foot, so I'm trying to help there."

"Broke her *foot*? Oh dear. I'm sorry to hear that. I hope it isn't a bad break?"

"No, but it means she can't move around as easily as she'd like."

"But what about the baby?" Dorothy asked. "Who's with her while you're at the yarn shop? Now, that's something I could help with. I could babysit while you fill in for Eleanor."

"I need Lizzie with me since I'm nursing. We have a cradle there."

"Oh. Well, then, would Tuesday work?"

Eaton would be playing tennis again. "I take it Hugh will be back at work?"

"Yes."

"Then that's *perfect*," Dorothy crowed. She didn't care to see Hugh right now, any more than she wanted Eaton knowing what she was doing. This was between Dana, Lizzie, and her. "I could come early, as soon as Hugh left for the office, and I could even bring breakfast."

"I promised Tara I'd meet her for breakfast," said Dana.

"Is it wise to take a baby so young out to a restaurant?"

"It's a local place, just a five-minute drive from here, and the pediatrician says it's fine."

"Well, that's good," Dorothy remarked brightly, though her spirits fell. It sounded like Dana didn't want her around, which wasn't entirely unjustified. The thing was, Dorothy really did want to see the baby.

"Tuesday late morning might work," Dana said. "We should be home by ten. I wouldn't be leaving for The Stitchery until after lunch."

Dorothy perked up. "I'll bring lunch. That will be *so* nice. I know you like Rosie's. I could stop there on the way. Tell me what you'd like."

"Any kind of salad with grilled chicken—"

"No, no. Please be very specific."

"A grilled-chicken Caesar, lightly dressed."

"Then that's what you'll have."

Chapter 14

Dana didn't tell Hugh that his mother had called. Petty, she knew. And controlling. But she was feeling more vulnerable than she ever had. Lizzie's birth was forcing her to think about her own father and the issue of race. Time and again, she looked in the mirror, wondering how her life would have been different if her skin had been Lizzie's color. For one thing, she doubted she would be married to Hugh.

But she was. And that weekend was a difficult one. He was two different people—guarded with her, enthusiastic with friends. When Julian pulled out his camera and insisted on taking a family photo, Hugh was all smiles. He put his arms around Dana and held the baby and her close. Hypocritical though she thought it, his manner set the tone for their friends—which, ironically, made her point. Yes, there were questions, but once he explained that Dana had never known her father, that was the end of it. Tell people the truth and they move on, she had said. Show excitement and they show it in return.

No, the problem was when they were alone. The DNA test lay between them, tethering each to his own side of their king-size bed.

When Hugh went to the hospital Sunday morning to visit Jay Kostas, he brought a bag full of books, a remote-control toy car, and an oversize Patriots shirt. The boy was in a quad. Only two of the beds were taken, the other by a child whose parents kept the drapes drawn.

Jay wasn't a large boy. The body cast gave the impression of girth, until one looked at his arms and legs, which were extremely thin. When Hugh arrived, he was watching cartoons on an overhead TV set and Crystal was sleeping, sitting in the chair. The boy recognized him from his previous visit. His eyes lit when he saw the gifts.

"Wake up, Mommy," he whispered.

Crystal lifted her head. She was a minute focusing, which said something about the rest she wasn't getting in her own bed at home. Still, she managed a sleepy "Hi."

"How's it going?" Hugh asked.

She stretched. "Not bad."

"Whaddaya got?" Jay asked, with his eyes on the gifts.

"These are for your mom."

The boy's face fell.

Hugh laughed. "Just kidding." He put the bag of books on the tray table. "These may or may not work. I had to rely on the recommendation of a clerk. It's been a while since I was four. But the car's something else."

Jay had already reached for that, then reached for the shirt. "Does it have a number on it?"

"Sure does."

"What number?"

"Four," Hugh said, and helped unfold the shirt.

He was about to tell him that four was Vinatieri's number, when Jay said excitedly, "Can I put it on, Mommy?"

Hugh guessed that would take a little work. Crystal was already unbuttoning the pajama top. Lifting Jay forward, she removed it. The cast was like a vest with a mandarin collar, starting just under his chin, ending at his hip. "That's not so bad," Hugh remarked. "How's it feel?"

"It itches," said the boy.

"I should've brought a back scratcher."

The weight of the cast was another problem. Hugh could see how heavy it was from the way Crystal was struggling to hold the boy up and pull on the shirt at the same time. He gave her a hand.

When it was done, Jay said, "Wow. This is my *best shirt*." He reached for the control bar and began to work the car. His enthusiasm was a gift that wasn't lost on Hugh. Likewise, his smugness when he finished a particularly good run. It was J. Stan Hutchinson all the way.

He watched Crystal playing with her son, thinking that not only was she attractive but she was a good mother. Her smile told him she appreciated what he'd done.

It was nice to feel appreciated. He was thinking it would serve Dana right if he was drawn to another woman. Only he didn't *want* another woman.

"I'm working on remembering things," Crystal said, moving to his side.

"Anything you want to share?"

"Not yet." She looked past him. "Here's the doctor."

The man in white was watching Jay. "Nothing wrong with his thumbs," he remarked before extending a hand to Hugh. "Steven Howe."

"Hugh Clarke. I talked with an associate of yours the other day. He hadn't seen the release Crystal signed and didn't feel free to talk."

"I've seen it," the doctor said. "I have a few minutes now." He led the way to a small office adjacent to the nurses' station. "What do you want to know?"

"The exact nature of the injury and what needs to be done to heal it," Hugh said.

"The accident caused a compression fracture of the L-4 vertebral body," the doctor began, "with bilateral pelvic numbness. Emergent imaging studies showed retropulsed bone bulging into the spinal canal, which in turn resulted in the effacing and deforming of the thecal sac at that level."

"Translation?"

"A vertebral fracture caused bone fragments from the spine to break into the spinal canal and push on nerve roots there.

We opened the spine and removed enough of the fragments to relieve pressure on the nerve roots. Had we not done this within the first few hours, there might have been permanent neurological damage."

"No permanent damage, then?"

"Not neurological. The Risser cast will hold the fracture in a safe position until it heals. I don't anticipate any problem on that score."

"His mother mentioned growth plates."

"There's the problem. I would guess, given Jay's initial fracture and my experience with similar ones, that there has been some level of damage to the inferior and superior plates on the right side of the body. If this proves to be the case, the boy's left side grows while the right side doesn't. This would cause a scoliotic deformity."

"Meaning?"

"His torso will pitch over to the right. If this happens, his body will try to compensate, and in so doing create a whole new set of problems. We don't want those to arise, which is why we recommend early surgical intervention."

Hugh heard a "but" and dipped his head.

"It's a very specialized field," the doctor said.

"She mentioned St. Louis."

"The best man is there."

Hugh would probably have to depose him, too. For now, though, he asked, "Would you be willing to give an affidavit covering all of the above?"

"Of course." The doctor pulled out his card.

"Is the prognosis good?" Hugh asked.

"For Jay? With proper medical treatment, very good. He'd be home now if it weren't for the leg cast. We don't want him walking on it for a couple of weeks, and the Risser makes crutches difficult. We're training him on a walker. Once he can handle that, he'll be discharged. We'll see him in six weeks and get a better grasp then on the situation with the growth plates. If he gets down to St. Louis soon after that, he could be playing soccer next year."

"And if not?"

"He'll be watching from the sidelines for good."

❦

Dana was returning from the yarn shop late Sunday afternoon, carrying a sleeping Lizzie to the patio in her car seat, when David and Ali came out of their house to barbecue on the deck. David spared Dana a glance before busying himself with the grill. Ali waved and shouted, then looked at her father and was silent.

Dana was having none of that. No matter how David felt about Hugh, she didn't want Ali suffering for it. Leaving Lizzie safe in the carrier, she crossed her own yard into theirs. "Hey," she said. "You guys are back earlier than I thought you'd be. How was camping?"

As though Dana's entry into their yard was the magic key, Ali ran over to her. Her hair was a tangled mess and her tee shirt stained blue, but her cheeks were pink and her dark eyes danced. "It was *awesome*! Daddy and me walked for *hours*, then"— she began waving her hands to illustrate— "we found this little place where the trees weren't too close, and we put up a tent and collected sticks and cooked over a fire."

"What'd you cook?"

"Marshmallows."

"Marshmallows. Is that all?"

"Oh, there was other stuff, but the marsh-mallows were the best." She started moving her hands again. "First you have to get a stick, then you use this little knife to clean it off and sharpen it, and then you push marshmallows onto the stick. You have to hold the stick over the fire," she demon-strated, "and turn it all the time, or else it's gonna catch fire and get chaired—"

"Charred," David said.

"Charred." She turned to Dana. "Are we knitting tomorrow? You promised you'd teach me."

"And I will, yes, tomorrow."

"Oh, *good*. I have swimming—when do I have that, Daddy?"

"Two," David said.

"Two, so we could do it before that, maybe at eight or nine or ten." She was bouncing on her toes, looking toward the car carrier. "Is the baby in that thing?"

"She is."

"Can I see her?" she asked, taking Dana by the hand.

"Ali—" David warned.

"It's okay," Dana said. "We'll be right back." Breaking into a trot to keep up, she ran with Ali to the carrier.

Ali made a hushed sound and, kneeling on the stone, clutched the sides of the carrier. "She's sleeping again," she said, looking up at Dana. "Why is she always sleeping?"

"That's what babies do. They aren't able to do much else until they grow bigger, and in order to grow bigger, they need sleep."

"And food," Ali added, stage-whispering now. "I'll bet Baby E-lizabeth would *love* marshmallows toasted all nice and brown and gooey—" She stopped short, broke into a big grin, and stood.

Hugh had materialized at the screen door. He came out with his eyes on Ali and his head cocked to the side. He wore the teasingly skeptical expression that Dana loved. "That can't be Alissa Johnson," he said. "The one *I* remember is at least a foot shorter and nowhere near as grown-up as the young lady here. So who is *this*?"

Ali continued to grin. "It's Ali."

Hugh held up his hand for a high five. The child slapped it. When he moved it higher, she jumped to slap it again. "Atta *girl*," Hugh said.

"*Ali*," David called.

"I have to go now," Ali said. "I promised

Daddy I'd help him make dinner." She ran across the lawn.

Hugh stared after her. "Do you think David told her what's going on?"

"I think he told her not to bother us because of the new baby. I can't imagine he said anything else."

"You ought to ask him."

"I think you should."

He shot her a vexed look. "I can't."

"You'll have to apologize to him at some point."

"Yeah, well, not yet," he said, and there it was again, the paternity test coming between them in ways Dana didn't know how to prevent. Some of her pain must have shown, because he added, "It's only a technicality, Dee. You know I know I'm Lizzie's father."

They stared at each other for a minute before Hugh turned to Lizzie. He knelt, touched her tummy, which was all but lost in the fabric of the striped onesie. Her head tilted to the side, eyes closed, dark lashes splayed over the deep gold of her cheeks. "I just came from the hospital. I was visiting Jay Kostas. He's a cute little boy who faces a lot of serious operatons. It really does make you grateful for what you have. Lizzie is very healthy."

Dana took a slow breath. "Yes. She is healthy. I'm grateful for that."

"Should I carry her inside?"

"No. The fresh air is good. I think the ocean sounds soothe her."

"Soothe her or you?"

"Both," Dana admitted. "I hear my mother in the waves. Maybe Lizzie does, too."

Hugh looked up. "What does your mother say?"

Dana studied the water. "She says that what's happening between us isn't good. That we have so much going for us, that we're crazy to be letting something like this come between us. That we're being childish."

"Do you agree?"

"Yes."

He stood. "So . . . ?"

She met his gaze. "It isn't as simple as agreeing or not. Everything is relative. We had something that was *perfect*." Her voice caught on the pain of memory. "Maybe it was an illusion. But I want it back, and that's impossible."

"Nothing's impossible."

"Spoken by one who's led a charmed life."

"Come on, Dee," he chided. "Listen to your mother."

Forgive and forget? Dana thought and bristled. If Hugh didn't see that their lives were forever changed, if not by the DNA test then by the implications of Lizzie's color, he was the one who was being childish. "Do you always listen to your parents?"

"No," he conceded, but changed the subject. "Did Ali notice her color?"

"She hasn't said anything."

"Do you think she was just afraid to comment?"

"Ali, afraid to comment?" Dana asked dryly. "No. I think she just doesn't see anything out of the ordinary. Many kids don't. It's all about how they're raised."

"In other words, when the time comes, we have to make sure that whatever school Lizzie attends is multicultural."

"Which may rule out the public schools here," Dana said. David was their only African-American neighbor.

"Do you think it bothers Ali coming to this town?" Hugh asked. "Does she feel out of place?"

Dana considered that. "I don't know about her. I may not look like I'm of African descent, but apparently I am, which means I'm different from most people here. That's unsettling."

"No one sees anything different."

"So, I'm okay because I don't look black?"

"That's a loaded question."

"It's a valid one. Why should my daughter be treated any different from me? Why should Ali?"

He scratched the back of his head and left a hand on his nape. "In an ideal world, they wouldn't."

"I'm a generation closer to Africa than Lizzie is. By rights, I should feel the brunt of the prejudice more than she does."

"By rights, you should, but that's not the way it works."

"It's pretty shocking, coming all of a sudden like this," Dana said, trying to express some of what she felt. "At least Ali and Lizzie will be prepared."

❧

From the minute Dana picked Ali up Monday morning, the child was full of talk. There was a detailed summary of the movie she and David had watched the night before, an in-depth description of the blueberry pancakes that had just been made for her by the babysitter David had hired to stay with her while he worked, a blow-by-blow of the phone conversation she had had with her mother no more than an hour before.

She quieted some when they arrived at the shop. They had barely stepped foot in the place when she spotted the knitted dolls that sat together on display with a how-to book.

They were adorable dolls—Dana had herself knit several in the display—remarkably simple in design compared to dolls on sale in traditional toy stores. They were either cream, brown, or beige, knit in stockinette stitch, finished with yarn-strand hair and felt features.

Ali was intrigued. She touched a face, held a small hand, crossed a pair of floppy legs. When Dana said she could have one, her whole face lit up—and then, won over by *that* bliss, Dana said she could have *two*. But it wasn't pure indulgence on Dana's part. She couldn't think of a better beginner's project for a seven-year-old than a scarf for a doll.

Ali studied the dolls with the care of one picking a diamond. Dana had time to feed Lizzie before the choice was finally made, and then Ali appeared before her, proudly holding her prizes. When Dana said she had to name them, Ali didn't hesitate. "Cream," she said, holding out the ivory doll, then held out the brown one, "and Cocoa."

Dana hadn't been thinking of those particular names, but she couldn't argue. "Cocoa and Cream it is," she said and led the child to the odd-ball basket. It held leftovers from customers' projects, along with remnants of discontinued dye lots, all for use by beginners.

Ali wasted no time in choosing a ball of bright red wool. "This for Cream, don't you think?" she asked.

"And for Cocoa?"

Ali was longer picking this one. Finally, she came up with one that she liked. It was a dark green worsted-weight wool with a touch of mohair for added softness.

Dana took needles, sat at the table with Ali, and showed her the basic stitch. She went over it once, then twice, exaggerating the steps. When she did it a third time, she added the rhyme "In through the front door / once around the back / peek through the window / and off jumps Jack."

Ali grinned. "Do it again," she ordered, and so Dana did, remembering the day Ellie Jo had sung her the song and taught her to knit.

"Let me do it," Ali said, taking the needles. Dana showed her how to hold the yarn and guided her hands through the first several stitches, but that was all it took. Ali was a quick learner. Focused on her work, she seemed perfectly comfortable with the other women, pausing from time to time to ask questions. *What are you making? Who's it for? What if he doesn't like it? Why'd you pick that color?*

Watching as she rocked Lizzie's cradle, Dana decided that Ali's mother was definitely doing something right.

❦

Hugh was back at work, and none too soon, given the mounting backlog. He had a motion for discovery to file on a mail fraud case, a forensic pathologist to meet on a vehicular homicide one, and a meeting with a new client who was accused of perjury in a federal indictment. He also had decisions to make regarding a wrongful-termination suit, and kept drifting back to this case. His client, who sold homeowners' insurance, claimed that he had brought in more accounts than any other single agent, but that since his contacts were, demographically, among a less wealthy group, his average yield was consistently lower, hence his firing. Hugh's client—and most of that man's clients—were African American.

Hugh wanted to include racial discrimination in the suit and spent much of Monday trying to work out the logistics—only to decide against it at the end of the day. Racial discrimination would be hard to prove and might be a distraction from his client's other, more solidly documented claims. Practicing law was about picking one's fights.

Life was about picking one's fights, he realized. He might argue forever with Dana about his motive for running a DNA test, but the more pressing issue was finding her father. With so little to go on, that was posing a problem.

Tuesday morning, when Crystal Kostas called, she was a welcome diversion. He was only too happy to buy her breakfast at the hospital in exchange for her notes. She ordered a three-egg omelet with toast, home fries, and coffee, and ate hungrily while he read. Her jottings were surprisingly coherent, with headings at the top of each page.

There was a list of other patrons who had been at the restaurant at the time she had waited on the senator, with asterisks next to the names of regulars who knew her.

There were descriptions of the motel clerk—late twenties, skinny, glasses—and the car the senator had driven—a dark SUV with a roof rack and step bars of a lighter color.

She had listed the date and approximate time of the encounter, and had written out several pages of her recollection of her conversation with the senator. She listed the order of events—she had taken the room, he joined her once she was inside and left before she did. She described his tall, solid build, and the bald spot at the back of his head.

He had sucked on breath strips and had

offered her one. She didn't know what kind they were.

The last page had no heading and contained only one name.

"Dahlia?" Hugh asked.

Crystal put down her toast and wiped her mouth on a paper napkin. "He called it out."

"Called it out? When?"

"When he came."

"Came? You mean, climaxed?"

She nodded. "Is it his wife's name?"

"No, ma'am," Hugh said, but his mind was working. "Maybe a mistress."

Crystal seemed disappointed. "He'll deny it. He'll deny having lovers."

"Maybe," Hugh alleged with rising excitement, "but what if there are other women— women on that list Hutchinson's chief of staff claims exists? What if they could testify under oath that he called out the same name when they were with him?"

Chapter 15

Tuesday morning, Dana met Tara for breakfast. Three other friends joined them to celebrate Lizzie's birth with cinnamon brioche French toast, broccoli quiche, and hazelnut decaf. Returning home afterward, she had barely pulled into the drive when Ali appeared beside her car.

"Look, Dana!" she cried with glee as soon as the door opened. She was holding the tiny red scarf in her hand as though it were a ribbon of glass. "I finished! Now I want to make the one for Cocoa, but I don't know how to cast out."

"Cast *on*," Dana corrected, and looked at Ali's work. "Ali, this is fabulous! Good for you!"

"I love it. Daddy says I've found my itch."

"Niche?"

"Niche. Will you help me start the next one? And after that one, I want to make them blankets for winter." Eyes cupped, she put her face to the back window. "Why is Baby E-lizabeth crying?"

"She's hungry," Dana said. "Tell you what. See those boxes at the front door? Help me bring them in while I feed Lizzie, and I'll teach you how to cast on. You're going to have to know how to do that yourself once you're back in New York." She opened the car door to get the baby.

"I'm not going back to New York."

"You're not?" This was news. "Where are you going?"

"Nowhere. I'm staying here."

Dana emerged from the car with a whimpering Lizzie. "Since when?" David hadn't mentioned it. If Ali was going to live with him, he would be scrambling to find her a school. Her school in Manhattan didn't start until mid-September. Schools here began in less than a week.

"Since today," Ali replied. "I decided I want to stay with Daddy."

"Does he know?"

"I'm telling him tonight. He won't mind. He loves having me here." She ran toward the front door, where a stack of three boxes stood. She picked up the first just as Dana approached with the baby. "Are these all for Baby E-lizabeth?"

Dana glanced at the labels, but Lizzie's fussing allowed for no more. "Looks that way. Put them over here, sweetheart. Hugh will open them when he gets home."

Lizzie needed feeding and changing. When that was done, Dana taught Ali to cast on. Then, with Ali at her heels, she carried Lizzie up to the spare bedroom. Opening the closet door, she pulled out a carton. She gently laid the baby on the Oriental rug and opened the box.

"Oooooooh," breathed Ali. "More *yarn*."

"This yarn's special," Dana explained. "It's my mother's stash, mostly leftovers from things she knit when I was little. Look," she said, pulling out a ball of bulky wool in avocado green that Elizabeth had used for a scarf and a remnant of the yellow yarn from Dana's bunny hat. There were other skeins she didn't recognize.

Curious, she pulled out the patterns that were tucked in against the side of the box. Most were books, opened to the page her mother had worked. Dana thumbed through, finding other things Elizabeth had knit.

Then she came to the single-page patterns. They were of the custom variety that The Stitchery offered for classic crew neck, V-neck, and cardigan sweaters. The basic pattern was pre-printed, then, based on the customer's measurements and the weight of the yarn chosen, the sales clerk filled in the number of stitches to be cast on, the number of increases required, and the length for each of the sweater's parts. In the course of knitting, the customer returned whenever adjustments were needed.

Looking closer, Dana realized that the logo on these patterns wasn't from The Stitchery. They had come from a store in Madison, which meant Elizabeth's college years.

Intrigued, while Lizzie slept on the floor and Ali neatly separated the yarn by color, Dana looked through the rest of the patterns. There were ones for making Fair Isle sweaters, fisherman's knits, and a Shaker scarf. There was also one for a Faroese shawl, with a faded drawing on the front. Dana had seen new books at the shop containing patterns like these, a revival of shawls that had originated generations earlier on Denmark's Faroe Islands. That her mother had worked up this style of shawl more than thirty-five years ago was stunning to Dana—and suddenly, without looking further, she knew this would be her signature project for fall. Knit from the hem up, with a gore in the center of the back and shaping at the shoulders to ease the fit, the shawl could be designed with long ends that wound around the wearer's waist and tied out of the way. Dana's deep teal alpaca-and-silk, while heavier than some of the more lacy, mohair-type shawls made on the Faroes, would be a modern twist, perfect for women her age.

Excited, she was about to open the pattern when her cell phone rang. Taking it from her pocket, she flipped it open. "Hello?"

"Dana? Marge Cunningham. How are you doing?"

"Great, Marge. Thanks for calling back. I'm sorry I had to cancel last week. I was hoping we could set up another appointment."

"Actually," Marge said, "we've rethought this. Since you have a new baby and we have a very large house to decorate as soon as possible, we've hired Heinrich and Dunn."

Dana felt a stab of disappointment. "I'm sorry. I hadn't realized there was a rush, or I'd have met with you sooner." She might have said that Heinrich and Dunn would give the Cunninghams exactly what the firm had given their two neighbors, which was precisely what Marge had said she didn't want.

"Oh, you know," the woman breezed now, "it was one of those things where once we made the decision, we just got caught up in it and wanted to move-move-move." She ended with a little laugh. "But thanks anyway, Dana. And good luck with that little baby girl. I hear she's a winner."

Dana hung up feeling, surprisingly, no loss at all. With Ellie Jo sidelined, she had more than enough to do at the shop.

Content, she opened the pattern in her hand. Like the title on the front, it was hand-written. A note was inside.

Here are the instructions. My mom translated them into English from my grandmother's Faroese, and they may have lost something in the process. You know everything about knitting, though. If there's a mistake, you'll catch it.

We miss you here. I understand why you left, but the dorm isn't the same without you. Please think of coming back with the baby next year. He'll be gone by then, so you'll be free.

Dana reread the sentence. Heart pounding, she turned the note over to see the envelope that was affixed to it by a rusty paper clip. The sender's name was there, as was a return address.

❦

Dana had uncovered two secrets. The first was the name and address of a woman who had known her mother during those crucial pregnant days in Madison, and though the address was very old, it was a starting point.

The second was more intriguing. *He'll be gone by then, so you'll be free*—the implication being that Dana's father may not have been the one-night stand Elizabeth had led people to believe. Dana wasn't sure she liked the *you'll be free* part; it implied something controlling, even *evil* about the man. And since Dana had checked on the Web for a Jack Jones at Elizabeth's college during the years she was there, he may not have been a student at all. Still, her mother's friend might know more.

Ali left, but Dana didn't immediately act on her discoveries. Hugh wanted her father found immediately, but for her, those old ambivalent feelings were strong. And, besides, Dorothy was due to arrive.

She was tucking the envelope in the pocket of her jeans when the doorbell rang, and the next hour was truly pleasant. Dana shouldn't have been surprised. One on one, she had always enjoyed her mother-in-law. The surprise—given what had happened in the hospital the week before—was the genuine delight Dorothy found in the baby. There was no standoffishness, no handling Lizzie like she was a stranger's child, no withholding of the affection that Dana had seen her show Robert's kids. Her gift too— matching hand-painted anoraks for Dana and Lizzie—was unusually sensitive.

Dorothy insisted on holding Lizzie for all but the time the baby was nursing. It was only when she was about to leave, handing

Lizzie back to Dana but keeping a hand on the child's head as if reluctant to sever the touch, that she mentioned that day the week before.

"I want you to know," she said, "how sorry I am about what happened at the hospital. You get settled into a certain social circle and start acting a certain way, and you don't think twice about it because everyone else around you behaves exactly the same way. But it's not who I am, certainly not who I was raised to be. I wasn't born a snob. Being a Clarke for so long now, there are just certain expectations . . ." Her voice trailed off.

What could Dana say? That it was all right? That being a Clarke justified poor behavior?

Given how raw she felt on that score, all she could do was to ask, "Do you doubt that Hugh is her father?"

"Of course not," Dorothy scoffed, still touching the baby. "Even if I couldn't see it with my own two eyes, which I can, I knew deep down that you wouldn't be with anyone but Hugh. You're a good woman, Dana. A good mother. You know, I was wrong before Lizzie was born when I insisted you needed a baby nurse. That was how we did it, but I've had time to think about it, and you don't need help. You lost your own mother, so you want to be there as much as possible for your own daughter. I understand. Mothers want certain things. They dream that their family will be united and loving, and that isn't always possible. But Eaton's book party is coming up, and I desperately want everyone from the family there, especially you and Hugh. If you don't have a babysitter, then I want you to bring Lizzie with you—and I don't care *what* Eaton says."

Dana realized it was the first time since Dorothy had come that she had said her husband's name.

"Does he know you're here?"

"Oh yes," Dorothy said, then stopped short, met Dana's eyes, and raised her chin. "No. Actually, he does not. He's a stubborn man, and it's not only with you and Hugh and this little girl. He picked a fight with his brother, so they're not talking, and now Bradley is taking it out on Robert, so Robert is angry with Eaton *and* with me, because he thinks I ought to be able to talk sense into my husband. But isn't this ridiculous.

Here I am stealing out of the house to buy a gift for my newest grandchild. I charged it on my own credit card. Did you know I had one?"

Dana had to smile. "No, I didn't."

"Well, I do. I'm not a total fool."

Watching her drive away a few minutes later, Dana remembered the dream she had had moments before her water broke. In it, Dorothy had been the critic who found Dana lacking. Now Dana wondered if she had misinterpreted that. An argument could be made that Dorothy was there in the dream to help her out.

🌿

Dana had taken the phone off the hook and was napping on the family room sofa when Hugh arrived home.

"Hey," he said gently.

She bolted up, assuming Lizzie was crying. When she realized it was Hugh, hunkered down beside her, she responded with a smile. She would have touched his cheek, had she not noticed his smug expression.

"The lab faxed me the test results. No doubt about it, Lizzie's mine." He patted his shirt pocket. "This is proof, Dee. It will silence my family."

Dana sat up.

"I bought the cutest little onesie," he went on. "And these for you."

She saw a bouquet of roses, the same mix of colors he had strewn in the nursery when she had first learned she was pregnant. The memory was bittersweet.

She took a deep breath to rouse herself fully from sleep. Then she said, "Thank you."

"Now, there's enthusiasm."

Dana went over to the bassinet. The baby was still asleep. She raised her eyes to the sea and wondered what her mother would say about turning down flowers. Ungrateful? Rude?

"Is this sleep deprivation?" Hugh asked.

She looked back. "This what?"

"Bitchiness." He was still squatting and holding the cellophane-wrapped bouquet.

"Not sleep deprivation. Dismay. Am I supposed to be happy that your test proved something that was never in doubt?"

His eyes were probing. "I thought you'd be pleased to be able to put the issue to rest."

"Hugh," she said with an exasperated sigh, "the test isn't the point. It was your *doing* it."

"But I had to. Try to see it from my side." He stood up.

"No, you try to see it from my side," she countered. She didn't know if it was Dorothy's visit that gave her strength, but she refused to back off. "What we had before all this was special. Before I met you, I never dated super-rich guys, because I didn't trust them not to use and then discard me."

He made a dismissive sound. "No guy would do that."

"I grew up in this town," she argued. "I saw it happen more than once. There were the super-rich, and then there were the rest of us. We were playthings of the super-rich. Take Richie Baker. We called him The Spoiler, because his goal was to deflower virgins. As soon as he'd slept with one, he dumped her, and who's he married to now? One of the super-rich. I learned to avoid guys like you. And then suddenly all that caution didn't make sense, because everything about you—*everything*—spoke of decency and trust. Did I ever ask about women you'd dated before me? No, because they were irrelevant, because I knew that you felt differently about me."

"I did. I do."

To his credit, he looked concerned. She wanted to think he was finally hearing her.

"I know you did. You loved what was different about me. Only now you're not so sure if it was an illusion, just like my being white was apparently an illusion."

"You're confusing the issues."

"Okay. Go back to the paternity test. You needed an answer, and that was the quickest way to get one. Well, now you have the results. Will you call your dad? Your uncle? Your brother? Will you call your basketball buddies? Will you tell David he's in the clear?" She took a quick breath. "Don't you see, Hugh? Using this information now is as insulting to me as your running the test in the first place."

"Hey. Give me some credit. I won't start calling people with these test results."

"You mean you'll only tell them if they ask? Like, the next time someone makes a joke about Lizzie's color, you'll say you ran a paternity test and know that Lizzie is yours?" She raced on. "Well, if we've estab-

lished that you are Lizzie's father, that
means I'm African American. That's taking
some getting used to on my part."

Hugh didn't say anything.

She went on. "I keep wondering if this
business about David and the paternity
test was just a smokescreen, so that you
wouldn't have to face the truth. Well, your
family may be glad to know that our baby is
legitimate, but now they're going to have to
deal with my heredity. You will, too. Maybe
all of your balking has to do with that."

"Balking?"

"Doubting. My being with David. My being irresponsible in not tracking my father
sooner than this. Are you less trusting of me
because I'm not purebred white? Do you
want to stay married to me?"

"Don't be ridiculous, Dana."

"What kind of answer is that?" she asked.
"I'm talking about our marriage, Hugh. Can
we find a way to get back to where we
were?"

"Yes," he snapped, "but not until we get
to the truth. Let's find your father—"

Dana interrupted. "Where's your whiz
Lakey?"

"Working on it."

She saw his lack of success as a validation of her own. "It's not easy, is it."

"No, but we'll get there. We'll find the man and learn whether there's anything else we ought to know."

"Like what?"

"Medical conditions. That's what all this is about. Once we're fully informed, we can put this behind us and move on."

Dana wasn't appeased. "It isn't about *information*. It's about *us*!" Discouraged, she said, "For what it's worth, I have a lead. I found someone who might have known my father."

He raised a brow. "Someone here?"

"No. A friend of my mother's in Wisconsin. I found a letter she sent after I was born. It suggested that my mother was with the man for longer than a week."

"Really? Interesting. But if he was a student, 'Jack Jones' wasn't his name. Lakey did check that out."

"Then 'Jack Jones' wasn't his name," Dana concluded.

"Can you reach this woman?" Hugh asked.

"I don't know."

"Should I have Lakey try?"

"No. I'll do it." She saw the doubt in his eyes. "I'm capable, Hugh. I could have found my father years ago, could have hired my own detective, but I didn't want to find him badly enough. But you do. So I'll do it. Because I respect that you need to know."

He stared at her. "I'm the bad guy then?"

"Damn it, yes!" she cried. "I keep thinking back to the first few hours after Lizzie was born, and realizing that the experience would have been totally different if you hadn't wanted to explain away her color so that no one thought it was *your* problem. Well, it is, Hugh. Only it doesn't have to be a problem. Why can't we be proud of our daughter? Why can't we send out the birth announcement? Do you love Lizzie, or don't you? Do you love me, or don't you? That's what it's about, Hugh." She touched her heart. "It's about what's *here*."

Chapter 16

On Thursday, after two days of hesitation, Dana approached Gillian Kline at the shop. She had been close all of Dana's life. Dana trusted her judgment.

"I found a letter from an Eileen O'Donnell to my mother," she said, and waited for a sign of recognition.

But Gillian frowned. "The name isn't familiar. Who is she?"

"She was a dormmate of my mom's. Her married name is McCain. Eileen O'Donnell McCain."

"I don't recognize it."

Dana showed her the letter and waited while she read it. Then she said, "Maybe I should ignore it. How could she have been anyone important in my mother's life if you don't know her name?"

"Because," Gillian said reasonably, "your mother was in Madison for three years, and I wasn't with her. I couldn't have known all her friends. There may have been friends she chose not to mention."

"But why would she do that?"

"Maybe because they knew *him*. Liz led us all to believe that the guy was a one-night stand, but according to this letter, that wasn't so."

Dana persisted. "But who is Eileen O'Donnell, and why should I believe her?"

Gillian put an arm around her shoulders. "Because you have no one else. Besides, it's not like she wrote *you* that letter. She wrote it to your mother, assuming no one else would see it, which gives it validity."

"Then you think I should call?"

Gillian smiled sadly. "I think yes. You've come this far. You'll always wonder. That is, if you can find her phone number."

Dana let out a resigned breath. "I already have."

"Via Hugh's detective?"

"No. The Alumni Directory. It's online."

Gillian smiled in a wise way. "So, sweetie, isn't there a message in that?"

Dana made the call, but not for herself. She was still torn about wanting to know who her father was, all the more so now with the suggestion that her mother had wanted to avoid him. She didn't make the call for Hugh, either. She did it for Lizzie. The child had been born with genetic traits that were going to impact her life. In time, she would ask questions. She deserved answers.

Eileen O'Donnell McCain lived in Middleton, a Madison suburb. Dana punched in the number as she stood in the family room. The bassinet was nearby, the baby kicking her little arms and legs.

A teenaged girl answered.

"I'd like to talk with Eileen McCain, please," Dana said.

There was a half-hidden groan—the girl was clearly hoping for someone else—but a nonetheless civil "Who's calling?"

Dana took a breath. Time to commit. "It's Dana Joseph." No need to offer her married name. This was the one her mother's friend would know, and she did use it professionally. "My mother was a college friend of Mrs. McCain."

"Hold on." The receiver fell with a clatter.

After a minute, there was a wary "Hello?" This voice was more mature.

"Mrs. McCain?"

"Yes?"

"I'm Dana Joseph. I believe you knew my mother in college—Elizabeth Joseph?"

The woman's voice quickly warmed. "*Liz.* Of course. And you're the daughter. I'm so pleased you called. I heard well after the fact that your mother had died. I'm sorry. She was a wonderful person."

Dana would have loved to ask, *In what way?* She remembered so little that even in spite of all that Ellie Jo and Gillian had told her, she hungered for more. But that wasn't her first priority. "Thank you," she said simply. "I was actually going through an old knitting stash of hers and found the directions you sent for your grandmother's Faroese shawl. I'm an avid knitter like my mom, so I opened up the directions, and there was the letter you sent along with them. You implied that you knew the man who fathered me. The thing is, I've just had a baby and there's a medical situation— well, not actually medical, but a physical situation—that I want to check out, so I'd like to contact him, only I don't have a clue where to begin."

"What did your mother say about him?"

"Not much," Dana replied, feeling a touch of disloyalty at the criticism implicit in her tone, but her mother had been wrong. Certain responsibilities came with being a parent, which was precisely why Dana was making this call now. As mixed as her own feelings were, as Lizzie's parent she owed the child this. "We all had the impression that he was someone just passing through town. She told me his name was Jack Jones."

There was silence on the other end, then a sigh. "Well, that was part of his name, and it was what we called him. His full name was Jack Jones Kettyle."

Jack Jones Kettyle. Kettyle. "Did you know him?"

"It was hard not to know him. He was a year ahead of us, and a party boy of the first order—at least, until he met your mother. He was madly in love with her. She was the one who broke it off."

Dana was startled. "She was? But *why*?"

"Lots of reasons. He adored her, probably too much, and she felt smothered. She didn't love him that way. There was also his religion. He was devout."

"Devout what?"

"Catholic," Eileen said. "He was from a big family and wanted an even bigger family, and he made no bones about wanting to go back to New York, have his sons be altar boys, keep his wife at home knitting sweaters."

"She rejected him because he was *Catholic*?" Dana asked in disbelief. Catholic, not black. The irony boggled the mind.

"It wasn't the religion per se. His family was overbearing. She met them once. It was a disaster. That visit probably ended Jack's chances. But he did love Liz."

"Liz, or the image of Liz knitting?" Dana asked.

"Liz. But, yes, knitting added to the image. Liz was comforting to him. She was comforting to most of us."

Dana thought of Gillian, and of Nancy Russell and Trudy Payette. All three had known Liz growing up and said the same thing. "I was only five when she died. All I knew was that she was the center of my world."

"Of Jack's, too, for a while. He fell hard."

Struggling to grasp this, Dana was silent. "I'm sorry," she said when she collected her thoughts. "This isn't what I expected." She paused, then asked, "How can a playboy be a devout Catholic?"

"Ever hear of JFK?"

"I have a picture of my father. He wasn't as good-looking as JFK."

"Maybe not in a picture, but in person there was something about him. He had charisma. And he fought hard for your mother. For the longest time, he refused to accept that she wouldn't marry him."

He'll be gone by then, so you'll be free. That explained the letter. But there was so much more Dana wanted to learn. She didn't know if Eileen McCain had answers, but Gillian was right. Dana had no one else to ask.

"Did she learn she was pregnant before or after she broke up with him?"

"After."

"And that didn't change her mind?"

"No. She didn't love Jack. She couldn't see raising her child in the kind of family he wanted."

"Did she ever consider an abortion?"

"Lord, no. She wanted the baby. Wanted you."

"But it meant she had to drop out of school."

"Not had to. Chose to. She was happy going home. She loved her parents and knew that they would love her child."

"Did Jack Kettyle know she was pregnant?"

"Not to my knowledge. She left school before she showed."

"What excuse did she give for leaving?"

"She said she missed home and could finish her degree in Boston. Did she ever do that?"

"No. My grandmother's yarn store had just opened, and my mother wanted to work there. But please go back to Jack. If he was so in love with her, why didn't he try to reach her at home?"

Eileen didn't immediately answer. Finally, apologetically, she said, "Oh, he was hurt. He turned to his second choice, likely on the rebound, got *her* pregnant, and didn't look back."

"Did he marry her?"

"I believe he did."

"Are they still married?"

"Last I heard."

"Were there any other men? I mean, for my mother?"

"Dozens. There were some great guys who would have loved to date her. But Jack was, well, irresistible."

Dana rephrased the question. "I mean, had she slept with others? It would be humiliating, for both of us—Jack and me—if I approached him and made a false accusation. Is he definitely my father?"

"Oh." An embarrassed laugh. "I'm sorry. I misunderstood. No, she never slept with anyone else here. Jack Kettyle was the only one."

"Sounds like a gem," Dana said. "He was a playboy, but he was devout, and apparently ignorant. Didn't he know about birth control, even the *rhythm* kind? And after unprotected sex, didn't he ever wonder if she was pregnant? Did he ever call her at home after she left school?"

"I don't know the answers to those questions."

Dana leaned toward the bassinet and cupped Lizzie's cheek. More quietly, she said, "I was just venting."

"You mentioned a medical problem? Is the baby not well?"

"She's wonderful. It's just that she has certain African-American features, and we're trying to trace them back. My husband's family is well documented, so the obvious guess centers on my biological father. Think Jack Jones Kettyle is biracial?"

"No, but I can only base that on his appearance. I never saw the rest of his family. Liz did, but she never mentioned race."

"I mean, is this poetic justice or what?" Dana asked. "I'm worried that my daughter will be rejected because she's African American, and my own mother rejected someone because of his *religion*."

"It was the lifestyle she rejected, not the religion. She just didn't love him enough."

"Sad," Dana said. There seemed only one thing left to ask. "Do you know where he is now?"

"No, but the Alumni Directory will."

Dana gave a self-deprecating laugh. "Of course. That's how I got your number. It's even online."

"No need to look online. I have last year's edition right here. Hold on, please."

Dana left the baby's side, but only to get pen and paper. Minutes later, she had a name, address, and phone number. The question was what to do with them.

Chapter 17

Friday morning, thanks to the persistence of his detective, Hugh was able to move against the senator. He called Crystal first. She answered her cell phone from Jay's bedside. As pleased as she sounded with his news, she was cautious.

"How do you contact him?" she asked.

"I'll overnight a letter marked 'Personal and Confidential,' which means his chief of staff will open it. I'll say that I'm representing Crystal Kostas in connection with the paternity of her son, and that before I initiate legal proceedings, I would like the senator's lawyer to contact me."

"You think someone will actually call you back?"

"I do. They'll recognize my name and know they're not dealing with an ambulance chaser."

"Is one other witness all I need?"

"It's a solid start. That's two of you independently confirming an intimate detail about the senator."

"Was she with him for long? Did she get pregnant, too?"

"No, she didn't get pregnant, and she was only with him once. She never even called his office, which means she doesn't have an ax to grind."

"How did your detective find her?"

"She's a well-known actress."

"Were there pictures of them together?"

"Not published," Hugh said with satisfaction, "but Lakey has a source at the tabloids who showed him unpublished ones. That's the thing about being a public figure. She's an actress; it didn't bother her to be photographed with a married senator. It's the married senator who should have been more careful. Of course, it suits our purposes just fine."

"So now won't someone from his office try to buy her off?"

"I'll have a signed affidavit before they can do that. In the meanwhile, my detective is still looking for some of the senator's other women. The more we have, the faster he'll cave."

Hugh knew that the moment he posted the letter the clock was ticking. If he didn't hear from the lawyer by midweek, he would file preliminary papers with the court for a determination of paternity. Crystal didn't want public proceedings. But they had to get the senator's attention.

What Hugh didn't tell Crystal was that three other prominent women whom Lakey approached had refused to talk. One had shaken her head and quickly closed the door. A second had said, "I'm not allowed to talk with you." The third simply said, "I can't." Either the senator had bought their silence, or they feared his retribution in ways that the actress was successful enough not to.

Crystal Kostas wasn't successful, which meant that there would be no quid pro quo. To the senator, she was a nobody. But she wasn't a nobody to her son. She was all he had.

With an intimate knowledge of the Hutchinson power and wealth, Hugh was gunnin' for bear.

Dana spent much of Friday at the shop. This was where, surrounded by friends, she felt most secure. It was also where Lizzie was loved by enough people so that Dana could leave her asleep in the cradle, while she spent time with her grandmother.

Ellie Jo didn't look well. She was finally able to put weight on her walking cast, but she remained pale and unsteady, growing older right before Dana's eyes. Worse, she didn't welcome concern. Dana knew to tend to her without making a fuss. By Friday afternoon, though, Ellie Jo seemed increasingly cross.

"Is something bothering you?" Dana asked. They were at the small round table in Ellie Jo's kitchen, white plates resting on orange placemats that had been felted by Ellie Jo's friend Joan. Dana's plate was clean. Though her body continued to slim down, her appetite was voracious. Conversely, Ellie Jo had barely touched her food.

"I don't like this cast," she complained. "It slows me down."

"Is there something else? You're way too pale."

"That's what happens when you get old."

"All of a sudden? Like in one week?"

"Yes, in one week after something like this," Ellie Jo said, waving a none-too-steady hand at her foot, which rested on a chair. Veronica sat snug against the cast, less interested in the food on Ellie Jo's plate than on the cranky look on her mistress's face.

"When was the last time you had a checkup?" Dana asked.

Ellie Jo looked her in the eye. "Six months ago."

"And everything was fine?"

"Everything was fine. Give me credit, Dana. I may be old, but I'm not ready to go. I worry about you, and I worry about Lizzie. If my Earl was here, he'd be taking Lizzie out for walks and showing her off in town. He would be such a help. He was a good man, Dana. You can be proud of the kind of person he was."

Dana was proud of Earl. The man she really wanted to discuss was her father, but the last time she had mentioned the man,

Ellie Jo had stormed off and fallen on the attic stairs.

So she left without saying a word. As she drove home, she remembered what her mother had whispered to her the night before. *Tell Hugh what you learned.* But she couldn't tell Hugh. She just couldn't—which made her feel terrible—which was one of the reasons why, when she spotted David and Ali playing basketball in the driveway, she picked up Lizzie and headed their way.

David was a friend. Dana needed a friend.

Smiling, she watched him swoop Ali up so that she could dunk the ball in the basket. The instant the little girl's feet hit the ground, she ran over and threw her arms around Dana's waist. She didn't say anything, just held on, grinning broadly.

David wiped his face with the hem of his tee shirt, but it wasn't until Dana gestured him over that he joined them. "How's it going?" he asked.

"Not bad," Dana replied as Ali broke away. "Lizzie went for two four-hour stretches last night."

He smiled at the baby, who was gazing lazily at nothing in particular.

"Dana, watch this!" Ali cried, and demonstrated her dribble.

"Good girl," Dana called.

"I can teach Lizzie how to do this when she's big enough," Ali called back. When Dana turned Lizzie to face the driveway, Ali shouted, "Look, Lizzie. Watch me dribble."

The demonstration was barely done when David touched Ali's head. "Pumpkin, run in and get a couple of waters from the fridge?"

Heaving the basketball into the yard, Ali set off in an exaggerated run.

As soon as she was out of earshot, David said, "You still look tired."

"Just because Lizzie sleeps for four hours doesn't mean I do," Dana replied. "Has Ali said anything to you about Lizzie's color?"

"No, but I told you, she probably won't. Her own mother is white." He dropped his voice. "How're things at home?"

Dana shot him a sad smile and shrugged.

"He's still being an asshole," David interpreted.

"No. That's too harsh," she said, feeling a need to defend her husband. "He's good with the baby and helps out a lot. He loves her, he really does." She traced Lizzie's soft little cheek with a forefinger and cooed, "Hi, baby, how's my sweetie?" Her finger stilled. "He's still pretty pissed at me for not anticipating this."

"How in the hell could you anticipate anything without knowing your father?"

"Yeah, well, *I'm* pretty pissed that no one told me about him, but my mother's dead, my grandmother has nothing good to say about the man, and Gillian knows nothing." She sighed. "For what it's worth, I've found his real name. Hugh doesn't know yet. I should be telling him. I should be calling my father on the phone. Why am I not doing that, David?"

David ran a hand over his smooth head. "Maybe 'cause you're not sure you'll like what he has to say."

"I don't care if one of his parents was African American."

"Forget the black part," said David. "Think about why he was never involved in your life. That must have bothered you. It'd bother *me*."

Dana smiled. David knew feelings. He claimed that his divorce had forced him to confront his emotions, but Dana suspected he had always been sensitive.

"There's more," she said. "He never knew

my mother was pregnant. He married soon after she left college. What if I call, and he tells me to get the hell away before I wreck his happy home life?"

"Tell him you'll be happy to do that after he answers your questions. If you're only going to have one shot at the guy, Dana, make it count."

Lizzie chose that moment to crunch up her body and make a deposit in her diaper. Dana wondered if it was an editorial comment.

"Here, Daddy!" Ali interrupted, approaching on the run with four water bottles, plus Cream hugged to her chest. She was nearly there when she bobbled the bottles.

David caught them before they fell. "That was too big an armful."

"Well, I needed four," she told him, "one for you, one for me, one for Dana, one for Lizzie." She came right up to the baby, then wrinkled her nose. "Pew. Is that what I think it is?"

"I'm afraid so," Dana said.

"And you have to clean it up? I'm never going to have babies if I have to do that." Proudly, she held up Cream. The red scarf was wrapped neatly around her neck.

"Doesn't she look beautiful," Dana exclaimed. "And where's Cocoa?"

"Inside."

"What's she doing there?"

"Hiding."

"From what?"

The little girl shrugged. "She's safe there. Dana, can Lizzie drink water?"

"I suppose she can, only she couldn't do it from this kind of bottle."

"I can't wait until she's old enough to play with me. Can I pretend she's my sister? My mother's getting married, did you know that? She says she's doing it so I can have a sister, 'cause that's what I really want, only I don't know if I'm going to like that sister."

Dana looked at David. "I didn't know Susan was remarrying."

"Neither did I until last week," he said, but he was frowning at his daughter. "Why won't you like that sister?"

She shrugged again. "I dunno. Maybe I will." She ran off toward the house.

"Where are you going?" David called.

"I wanna watch my movie," she called back. She slipped inside just as Hugh's SUV turned onto the street.

Dana watched it approach. "Bad timing.

He loves seeing Ali. He'll hate the thought of losing out to a movie."

"The movie isn't a jerk," David muttered.

She shot him a chiding look. "Hugh isn't either. He's just unsettled."

David snorted. "Try 'unmanned.' He's always been able to pick and choose his colored folk. This time he couldn't."

"Come on, David. That's unfair. He defends African Americans in court with more vigor than he defends white guys. Besides, I've watched him with Lizzie. He just adores her, and he adores Ali."

David snorted again.

Dana sighed. "Okay. You're still angry. I think I should go home."

She turned just as Hugh got out of the car and headed their way. He looked gorgeous—she might be angry, resentful, or hurt, but she would always think that. White shirt open at the neck, blue blazer hooked over his shoulder, he walked with typical Clarke confidence. Only the look in his eyes was tentative.

"How're you doing?" he said to David, and held out a hand.

David deliberately pocketed his own, at which point Dana had had enough.

"I'm going home to deal with what's in Lizzie's diaper. I'll let you two deal with what's out here."

❦

Hugh might have laughed. Dana had always been clever with words. Yes, there was shit between David and him. Even now, David was turning and heading for the house.

"Wait. David. Hold up."

David stopped but didn't turn.

"I owe you an apology."

"Yup," David said, still without turning.

"I'm sorry."

"Easy words, man."

Hugh sighed. "I was wrong. I made accusations I shouldn't have made."

"Yup," David said again, but he turned to look at Hugh.

"I was upset. I was under pressure."

"That's life."

"Not my life. Say I'm spoiled, say I'm arrogant—say what you want, but confusion is new to me."

"And pressure? You have it at work. How do you handle that?"

"It's not personal. I never felt pressure like this, even when I married Dana—and don't call me a snob. You've been a good friend. I miss talking with you. If I ever needed your advice, it's now."

"So I'm your black resource," David said.

Hugh stared at him. "If I wanted a resource, I could call any one of the experts I use. You're my friend. I want my friend's advice. Come on, David," he said wearily, "don't you think you're overreacting?"

David didn't blink. "There's no overreacting when it comes to color. It's there, it raises hackles, and it ain't goin' away."

"Do you honestly think I'm a bigot?"

"I never thought so before. Now I'm not so sure."

Hugh didn't immediately reply. David had actually put it well. "That's two of us," he confessed, "and, let me tell you, it isn't making me feel great. I have no problem with Lizzie's heritage. She's my daughter. I don't care if her skin's darker than mine. So what is hanging me up?"

"Could be your lily-white family and friends."

Hugh might have mentioned his Cuban law partner, African-American basketball pal, and multi-cultural client base. But he got David's point. "My family is what it is. I can't change them."

"No, but you can ignore their influence. Why do you have to agree with them?"

"I don't. I've argued with every fuckin' *one* of them in the last ten days. But I do care what they think. Same with my friends."

"If they can't accept your daughter, they're not friends."

"It's not that they can't accept her, just that they ask questions. Isn't that a normal reaction? Am I wrong to want answers?"

"No."

"Dana thinks I am."

"I doubt that, but tracking down her father is more complicated for her. It isn't just a race issue."

"It isn't that for me, either."

"No? But you need to find him so people will know where Lizzie gets her color. So here's a question. If you'd had a say in it, would you have given her brown skin?"

Hugh didn't lie. "No. What about you? What would you have chosen for Ali?"

"White skin," David replied. "She'd have an easier life—unless she grows up to fall for a black devil like me, in which case her mother might have a fit."

"So where does it end?"

"Beats me."

"I'm asking for advice here. What am I supposed to do?"

"Love your little girl."

"What about my wife? She thinks I'm a racist."

"You'll have to convince her you're not."

"How?"

David held up both hands. "Hey, not my business. She's *your* wife, as you told me more than once last time we talked."

Hugh sensed an ebbing of the tension between them. "But you do love her."

"You bet I love her. She's an amazing woman. But she's married to you."

"And you don't think I'm just that little bit insecure?"

"I hadn't."

Hugh smiled dryly. "Then I'm not the only one who's learned something new."

❦

Dana was on the patio when Hugh returned. She watched him while he stood at the carriage studying Lizzie. "When you look at her like that, what are you thinking?" she finally asked.

It was a while before he said, "You can't really do much with a baby this young. She eats, she cries, she sleeps, she poops."

"You knew it'd be like this at first."

"I expected we'd never have a minute to sit still."

"Do you love her?"

"Of course I love her. She's my daughter."

"Did you love her when she was first born?" Dana asked.

He looked at her. "Did you?"

"Yes." Of all the things she didn't know, this she did.

Hugh turned back to the baby. "Mothers love. That's what they do. Fathers have to grow into the job." The surf exploded on the rocks below, sending spray higher than the beach roses. "I don't know all the answers, Dee," he said. "So, okay, I shouldn't have done a paternity test. Can we please put that behind us and move on?"

Dana wanted to. More, though, she wanted to move back and recapture what they'd had. Only she wasn't the same person she had been before the baby was born.

She tried to explain. "I keep wondering what my life would have been like if I had grown up like Lizzie will. If my skin had been dark, would I have had the same friends? The same opportunities?" She kept her eyes on him. "So then I start wondering what would have happened if Lizzie had been born with, say, kidney disease, and I'd gone looking for my father and discovered that he was African American. Would we have embraced him? Would we have told people? Kind of like, if you can't *see* it, does it matter? And that's wrong."

He was quiet. Finally, he said, "I agree."

"So what do we do about it?" she asked. "Two weeks ago, if someone had proposed this hypothetical situation and asked me how you'd react, I'd have given a different answer. That makes me wonder what I know about you and what I don't."

"Life is a work in progress," Hugh said.

Dana hated platitudes. "What does that mean?"

"Answers will come. You can't be miserable every minute until they do."

"I'm not miserable. I have Lizzie. I have my grandmother. I have my friends."

"You have me."

"Do I?" she asked sadly. "If I don't know who I am—and if who I am matters to you—how can I know that for sure?"

He didn't answer. Instead, he looked toward the surf. When he spoke, he sounded oddly vulnerable. "So where do we go now?"

The vulnerability mirrored her own feelings. Feeling connected to him in that, she reached into her hip pocket and removed a piece of paper. Unfolding it, she looked at her father's address. "Albany," she said, and held out the paper to Hugh.

Chapter 18

They set out early Wednesday morning, heading west through Massachusetts toward the border of New York. Barring traffic tie-ups, they would reach Albany in three hours. A six-hour round-trip would have been exhausting for Dana without Hugh, particularly since she would have had to stop to tend to Lizzie.

"Leave her with me," Tara had offered.

But Dana recalled David's words. "If I have only one shot at this man, I want to make it count. How can he not look at this little face and melt?"

"You want him to feel affection?" Tara asked in surprise.

"I want him to understand why I'm seeking him out. I want him to *see* why it means so much to me."

That said, Dana was prepared for the worst, a door slammed in her face, the visit over before it began. Anticipating that possibility, Hugh had suggested calling first, but she vetoed the idea. She had come this far. She at least wanted a glimpse of the man.

Hugh would be a witness, which was another reason she was glad he had come. If she got nowhere with Jack Jones Kettyle, she didn't want any questions afterward about how hard she had tried.

Besides, Hugh's presence offered emotional support. He knew she was feeling vulnerable. He had made her breakfast before they left, stopped of his own volition at Dunkin' Donuts for her favorite latte, and made a restroom stop without her having to ask.

The drive was uneventful, but Dana was wound tight by the time they reached Albany. She nearly snapped when their MapQuest directions landed them in front of a church.

"This can't be right," she cried. She would be horrified if they had come all this way for nothing.

Hugh was rechecking the directions, looking from the church to a small house tucked in behind it. He gestured at the latter. "I think it's there."

"But that's part of the church."

"It's the rectory. Maybe he rents the place."

"Maybe the address is wrong," she said. "But the Alumni Directory listed it twice, both as residence and workplace. He graduated from the College of Engineering. I just assumed he did computer work or something from home."

Hugh caught her eye. "There's only one way to find out."

They parked in one of three spaces alongside the rectory. While Hugh unbuckled Lizzie, Dana went to the back hatch and took a diaper from her bag. She changed the baby with shaky hands, but when Hugh offered to carry her, she shook her head. She needed to feel Lizzie's warmth against her body. The baby was her security, proof that she was loved.

"It'll be okay, Dee," Hugh said gently, putting an arm around her shoulder.

"Depends how you define 'okay,' " she said. "What if this is some kind of joke, and the man really lives in the graveyard out back?"

"That'll give you closure."

"You think?"

The rectory was a small, square brick

structure whose only adornment was an arch of overhanging oaks. The path was gravel, with bits of grass pushing through.

The front door was open. They rang the bell and waited at the screen until a woman came to the door. She wore beige—skirt, blouse, and espadrilles—and appeared to be forty or so, which meant that either she was an amazing-looking fifty-five, or she wasn't Dana's father's wife.

"I'm looking for Jack Kettyle," Dana said quickly.

"Well, you've come to the right place. I'm Mary West, the parish secretary." She held the screen open. "And you are?"

"Dana Clarke," Dana said, realizing that if she was the parish secretary and this was the parish house, there was still the grave-yard possibility. "This is my husband, Hugh, and our daughter, Elizabeth."

The secretary smiled at Lizzie. "She is just *beautiful*. How old?"

"Just two weeks."

"How lucky you are to have gotten her so young. Are you newly moved to town?"

Dana didn't correct the misunderstanding. "No. We're just here for the day. For the morning, actually." It was eleven.

"Well, visitors are welcome for *however* long," said Mary, and gestured them into a modestly furnished living room. "Please make yourself comfortable. Would you like a cold drink?"

Albany was well inland, and while the ocean air had begun to cool, the breezes hadn't made it this far west. Dana felt the heat, but doubted she would be able to swallow. She shook her head, to which the secretary said, "Father Jack is in his study. I'll let him know you're here." She vanished.

Dana turned wide eyes on Hugh. "Father Jack?" she whispered. "*Father* Jack?"

"Beats me," whispered Hugh.

"The man I'm looking for is married and has kids. Jack Kettyle can't be Father Jack. What if it's all been a lie?"

"Then we'll start over."

"How? This is the only name I have, and I've looked *everywhere*."

"Hello," came a voice from the door.

Dana turned. Recognition was instant. The face was more mature, the hair more silver than blond, and the black pants, black short-sleeved shirt, and white clerical collar a far cry from madras and jeans. But this was definitely the man in her picture.

His smile lingered, though he seemed puzzled. "Mary was right," he said in a kind enough voice. "You look exactly like someone I know, only she's in San Francisco. I talked with her just this morning."

Dana forced herself to speak. "I'm Dana Clarke, and I was looking for Jack Kettyle, only I don't think he's a priest."

"He is," the priest confirmed, still kindly.

"You're Jack *Jones* Kettyle?"

"Whoo. Someone's done research. That's right."

"A *priest*? But I was told you were married and had children."

"I do. Six of them. But my wife died ten years ago, and our children are all grown, so I decided to do something different with my life."

Hugh joined the conversation. "I didn't think married men could be priests."

"I'm a widower. Given the shortage of clergymen, I was accepted. Men like me have experience in marriage and parenting. That makes us an asset to a parish."

"Don't priests need a degree in theology?" Hugh asked.

"Yes. I spent four years in the seminary. Then I spent a year as a deacon, helping out on weekends. At the end of that year, I was ordained. I was fortunate," he said, smiling again. "Not all priests get their own parish right away, but my home parish was losing its priest, and since I already knew so many of the parishioners, it was a logical appointment."

His explanation did nothing to reconcile the priest with the playboy. Dana wasn't convinced she had found the right man. "Where did you go to college?" she asked.

The priest folded his arms and leaned against a high-back chair. "Undergraduate? University of Wisconsin."

"Did you know a woman named Elizabeth Joseph?"

"I sure did. She stole my heart, then up and left school."

"Why did she leave?"

"She missed home and figured she could finish up there."

"Do you know what happened to her?"

More serious now, he said, "She drowned. It was a long time ago."

"How do you know that she died?"

"I bumped into a mutual friend who had heard about it." He seemed to realize that the questions weren't idle ones.

"Did you ever try to contact her family?"

"No. Like I said, she stole my heart. But she didn't love me, so I married someone else. I realized that thinking about Liz wasn't fair to my wife. So I stopped. The choice was between pining forever over a relationship that wasn't to be, or moving on. Putting Liz behind me was the only way I could survive." Quietly, he said, "You knew her."

Dana nodded. "She was my mother."

His face brightened for a second. In the next instant, his color drained away.

Dana had had time to prepare. She wasn't shocked to be facing her father, only startled to find that he was a priest.

"How old are you?" the man asked.

"Thirty-four. I was born seven months after my mother left Wisconsin."

As he stared at her, his eyes filled.

"You really didn't know?" she asked.

He shook his head. Then he pulled himself together and turned to the baby. "She's yours?"

"Yes, and she's the reason I'm here," Dana said. "I don't want anything from you, don't *need* anything from you, so if you're thinking I've come asking for money or

something, you're wrong. I'm only here because my husband and I—"

"Hugh Clarke," Hugh said, offering his
hand, "and this is our daughter, Elizabeth."

The priest took his eyes off the child long
enough to shake hands with Hugh. Then he
looked at the baby again. "Elizabeth. I'm
glad."

"Lizzie," Dana specified, "and since she
has some obvious African-American traits,
we wanted to learn where they came from."

The priest drew back. "She isn't
adopted?"

"No, nor was there a mix-up in the lab
or an affair with a friend," Dana said to
rule out further speculation. "My husband
knows everything about his family, but I
know little about mine. Are you African
American?"

The priest blew out a puff of air and, smiling sheepishly, scratched the back of his
head. "Whoo. This will take some getting
used to. I didn't ever suspect that Liz had
a child."

Dana was impatient. "She did, and I'd like
you to answer my question."

"No. I'm not African American."

"You seem sure."

"My sister needed a bone-marrow transplant a few years back. We scoured the family for a compatible donor and finally found one in a second cousin, but in the process, we mapped out the family tree in great detail."

"Why did she need the transplant?" Dana asked, curious in spite of herself.

"Leukemia. She's fine now, a miracle of modern medicine."

Dana was glad, both for the woman and for herself. She couldn't deal with the thought of Lizzie inheriting a potentially lethal illness. "So you have no relative of African descent," she repeated. When the priest shook his head, she looked at Hugh in bewilderment. "Lizzie's bronze skin had to come from somewhere."

"Would you, uh, like to sit down?" Father Jack asked. *Father Jack*, Dana thought. Easier to think of him as a father to thousands.

"Yes," said Hugh, and nudged her toward a sofa.

She whispered, "We got our answer. We can't stay."

"We can," he said softly. "Let's make the

trip worth it." Lizzie was starting to squirm. "Want me to hold her?"

Dana shook her head, shifted the baby to her shoulder, and jogged her gently.

Hugh sat beside Dana and addressed the priest. "Has your family had any other instances of cancer?"

"No." Father Jack took the wing-back chair and leaned forward, elbows on his knees.

"Any other hereditary illnesses?" Hugh asked.

"High blood pressure, but otherwise we're a hardy bunch." He looked at Dana. "Where do you live?"

"About a mile from where I grew up."

"Did your mother ever marry?"

"She didn't live long enough."

"Then you never had siblings."

"No siblings. I was the focus of my mother's life, and after she died, the focus of my grandparents'."

"What do your children do?" Hugh asked the priest.

Father Jack smiled. "There are four boys. One's a techie, two are teachers, the last is working as a waiter in L.A. while he goes on casting calls. My older daughter—she's thirty-three—is a full-time mother. She has four kids. Her sister is studying law."

Dana shot Hugh a sharp look. She didn't want him prolonging the visit. "Lizzie's hungry. We ought to go."

Hugh shot a glance at the far end of the room. "Want to feed her there?"

Dana did not. She wasn't baring her breast in front of this man. Besides, the heat was stifling. She wanted to leave.

"Please stay a bit," the priest said. "I'd like to hear about your life."

Pressing her lips into a thin line, she shook her head. "There's no need."

"It isn't a matter of need," he said kindly—and Dana *hated* that. *Where had he been all these years—happily raising his six children until they were happily independent, so that he could become a priest?*

"It's me," she said with a definite lack of grace, but unable to help herself. "My need. I want to go home." She sent Hugh a beseeching look and rose. Mercifully, he did the same.

Lizzie quieted some with the movement as Dana walked toward the door. Hugh opened it.

"Are you sure you won't stay just for a little while?" the priest asked. "Maybe for lunch? Or we could go get a sandwich in town."

Dana turned. "And if someone came over to us and asked who we were, would you tell them?"

"Yes."

"Wouldn't it hurt your career?"

"Absolutely not. I've fathered other children."

"Illegitimate ones?" When he didn't answer, she said, "What about the legitimate ones? Will you tell them about me?"

"I'd like to, but I have to know more about you first."

"Why's that?" Dana asked sharply.

"Because they'll ask."

"Not because you yourself want to know?"

"Dana," Hugh said softly, but Father Jack held up a hand.

"She has a right to be angry," he told Hugh, then said to Dana, "and yes, I want to know more myself."

"To make sure I'm *yours*?"

"You're mine."

"How can you be sure?" she challenged.

"How do you know my mother wasn't with another man?"

The priest smiled. "Wait here," he said, backing into the house. "For one minute more. Please." He turned and went in the direction of his office.

Dana wanted to leave pretending that the man who had irresponsibly sowed his seed back in Madison was equally irresponsible now, but she didn't move. Overwhelmed and confused, she could only pass Lizzie to Hugh and brace her back with her hands.

"This is how I know," said Father Jack, returning. He was holding out a framed photograph that showed him arm in arm with a young woman wearing a cap and gown. Both were beaming. "This was taken last year at graduation in Wisconsin. That's my daughter Jennifer."

Dana glanced at the picture, then did a double take. She took the photo from him, eyes glued to his daughter's face. It might have been her own. Apparently, every feature of Dana's that hadn't come from her mother was Jack's.

For all the years Dana had wanted a sibling, all the years she had wished her family was larger, to find she had a half-sister who looked so much like her was excruciating.

Her eyes filled, but she refused to cry. Instead, she asked, "How can this be? We had different mothers."

"Yes. Only her mother looked a lot like yours." He paused, embarrassed. "Anyway, the rest of her came from my genes."

Dana stared at the picture for another minute before handing it back. "Well," she said awkwardly, "thank you. That decides it, I guess." Her throat closed up. Turning, she began walking toward the car.

"I'd like to visit," the priest called after her.

She didn't respond. She didn't have a clue as to what *she* wanted.

She was vaguely aware of Hugh strapping the baby into her seat, and knew that the child was fussing again and had to be fed. But she buckled her seat belt and waited without looking back at the priest, waited until Hugh backed around, waited until he had returned to the street and driven out of sight of the church. Then she bent over and began to weep.

Chapter 19

Hugh had no idea what to do. But he couldn't just drive, with Dana crying in the front seat and the baby crying in the back. And there wasn't a Dunkin' Donuts or McDonald's in sight. So he pulled into the parking lot of an office building, found a spot under the shade of an oak, and let the car idle.

He touched Dana's arm. When she didn't pull away, he rubbed her shoulder. He didn't speak. There was really nothing to say. He had hoped for more by way of answers from this trip. But if he was disappointed, she had to be feeling worse. So he sat, lightly massaging her neck to let her know he was there.

When the weeping finally slowed to hiccoughs, he left the driver's seat, unbuckled the baby from the back, and gave her to Dana, who silently pushed up her top and let the baby nurse. The silence was instant.

Hugh drank some water from the bottle in

his cup holder, and offered it to Dana. She took the bottle, drank, then closed her eyes and continued to let Lizzie nurse.

He didn't say anything until she shifted Lizzie from her breast to her shoulder.

"Are you okay?" he asked then.

She shook her head no. "Was that a help? Do we have any answers?"

"We do know he's your father."

She put her cheek to the baby's head and continued to rub her tiny back.

"And we know that he has no African-American heritage," he added.

"Do you believe him?"

"His story was pretty convincing."

Dana continued rubbing Lizzie's back until a tiny bubble came up. Then she wiped the baby's mouth with her bib, and put her to the other breast. "Was it a little *too* convincing?"

"You mean, designed to preclude doubt?" Hugh had considered that. "But he didn't know we were coming. Not many people can think on their feet that way."

"An incorrigible liar could."

"Do you think he's that?"

Dana raised discouraged eyes to his. "I don't know what to think. I didn't expect a priest. I didn't expect a man who would imply that he loved my mother, or one who would run for a picture of his daughter to show me how much she and I look alike. I didn't expect he would want to stay in touch."

"But all that is good, isn't it?" Hugh wouldn't mind telling his family that Dana's father was a priest. It would go a long way toward shutting them up.

Dana sighed wearily. "There's so much going on right now—the baby, us, my grandmother. She won't welcome sharing me with the man she feels hurt her daughter. And we don't have any answers, Hugh. Look at Lizzie. If she didn't get that skin from my father, where's it from?"

Ellie Jo, Hugh guessed. "We'll figure it out."

"How?"

"I don't know, but we will. Anyway, you must be hungry. Want to stop somewhere for lunch?"

"I'm not comfortable staying in Albany," she said.

"Are you hungry, though?"

"Probably."

Gently, he prodded. "Is that a yes or a no?"

"I'm not hungry, but I know I have to eat to keep producing milk."

"If you want to stop nursing, stop. I'm fine with formula."

Her eyes flew to his. "I *want* to nurse. What I meant was that I know *my* responsibility even if he didn't. If you really loved someone, wouldn't you hunger for news? Wouldn't you try and find out how she was and what she was doing?"

"I would," Hugh said. "It's called fighting for what you want."

"That's right," Dana replied in a burst of angst. "He didn't fight. He just gave up—turned off—closed up!"

"Feels kind of like what you're doing," Hugh remarked.

"Me?"

He softened the accusation by accepting blame. "I hurt you. I'm sorry for that. But your response has been to shut me out. I know that you loved me before, Dee. Where did that love go?"

Mute, she stared at him.

"What Father Jack said back there about not pining over a relationship that wasn't meant to be?" Hugh continued. "Is that how you feel about us, that we weren't meant to be?" When she didn't answer, he went on. "Because if you do, I disagree. This is a period of adjustment. That's all."

"Lizzie's skin isn't going to suddenly become white."

"Obviously," he said, "but that doesn't mean we have to be hung up on her color. You accuse me of being upset about it. 'Upset' isn't the right word. I'd like to know where it's from. Is that asking so much?"

"In that I have no *idea* where it's from, yes. In that I'm struggling to figure out who I am, *yes*. In that I've just gone through an emotional wringer and don't want to talk about this right now, *yes!*" Taking the baby from her breast, she propped her on her thigh.

When she said nothing more, he offered a quiet "There you go again, shutting me out."

"I'm struggling with this, Hugh."

"Okay." He backed off. "Okay. Let's think about lunch. One thing at a time."

And that was how they took it. When Dana finished burping Lizzie, he buckled her back into her seat. They got burgers and fries at a drive-through, and ate as they drove. By the time they hit the highway, Dana had closed her eyes.

Hugh drove on in silence. He was feeling completely useless when his cell phone rang. It was his secretary, wanting to patch through a call from Daniel Drummond. Hugh's spirits revived.

Daniel Drummond was a big-name Boston lawyer with an ego to match. He claimed to be the model for at least one lead character on every TV legal series with a local setting, and he certainly had the looks, the skill, and the flair. He was known for flamboyance, and was arrogant to a fault.

Hugh and he had worked together once, representing clients in a complex case. They had never opposed each other before.

"How are you, Hugh?" Daniel asked in a booming voice.

"Great, Dan. And you?"

"I was fine until I got a certain call." He remained collegial. "What's going on here?"

"That depends on who called."

There was a snort. "You know my client list. What's the most high-profile case you ever hope to try?"

"Well, there is one that's come down the

pike, but I have no desire to try it. We're hoping for a settlement that is quiet and quick. If this is the case you're referring to, then you and I need to meet. Cell phones aren't safe."

"*Cell* phones aren't safe?" Collegiality dissolved. "Try false accusations. Do you know how many of these calls he gets?"

"Where there's smoke . . ."

"Be real, Hugh. Do you know who you're dealing with?"

"I do."

"Then you know what he stands for. An accusation like the one you made in your letter won't go over well."

"That's not my concern. My concern is my client."

"So's mine, and my client doesn't like being threatened."

"Neither do I," Hugh said. "Look, Dan. The situation here is urgent. Either you and I meet tomorrow, or I file papers in court. My client has nothing to lose. Does yours?" They both knew he did. "There's a quiet solution to this. It starts with a meeting in my office. Tomorrow morning. Name a time."

"I'm not free until next week."

"Then your client called the wrong lawyer. Anything beyond Friday, and we file."

"Come on, Hugh. It's never *really* urgent with these women."

It was the old get-in-line ploy, which infuriated Hugh. "It is this time. We're talking about a child's health crisis. If you can't help me out, a judge will."

"Health crisis? Tell me more."

"Not here. In my office. If not tomorrow morning, then Friday." He could give an inch, but only that. "Name a time."

"I would have to do it early morning—say, seven. I hear you have a new baby. That could be hard for you."

"Seven a.m. Friday. I'll be at the door to let you in."

❧

Dana slept a good part of the way home. She felt better as they got out of the car, and when Hugh suggested he watch the baby while she drove over to talk with Ellie Jo, she took him up on the offer. Confronting her grandmother—asking again about the Joseph family tree—would be easier without distractions.

She was taking Lizzie in to feed her before leaving when David came across the
yard. He wore a ragged tee shirt and shorts,
both liberally spattered with paint.

"We're making Ali's room green," he explained. "She's inside, covered with paint,
but she made me come out as soon as she
saw the car. She ran out of yarn making the
second scarf. The poor doll is so wrapped
up you can barely see her face, but Ali
wants the scarf even longer. She was sure
you'd have more. I'm trying to please her so
she'll please me. She says she's not going
back to New York."

"Mm. She told me that, too," said Dana.

"Did she explain why?" David asked.
"She loves Susan. I don't know what the
problem is."

"Have you asked?"

"Ali? Sure. She says she just wants to live
with me, and then she looks outside and
says it's the ocean, then she looks at your
house and says she likes your baby, then
she looks at me and says she feels bad that
I'm living alone and we'd have so much fun
if she lived here all the time." He ran a hand
over his bald head. It was the only part of
him that wasn't covered with green. "Susan

says Ali was fine when she left New York. The fiancé seems nice enough. Susan says he's good with Ali. She thinks it's just the idea of change."

"Sharing her mom?" Hugh asked.

"And moving. His place is only a couple of blocks away, but he got her into an exclusive new school. It's pretty chi-chi."

"Chi-chi rich?"

"Chi-chi white."

Dana had a thought. "She keeps that doll—the one she calls Cocoa—hidden. Now you're saying she is wrapping her up so you can't see her face. Think she's sending a message?"

David's eyes were worried. "Like she doesn't want to be the only African American at the school?" He put a hand on the top of his head. "Makes sense, doesn't it? Okay. I'll ask Susan." He turned and strode off.

stop & goto bed.

❦

Dana had barely parked in The Stitchery's lot when Tara ran out, wanting to know about Albany. Dana filled her in on the basics, but had no desire to elaborate. She was still on emotional overload where Father Jack was concerned.

Tara didn't press. She had two other more immediate matters to discuss.

The first she pulled from her pocket and passed to Dana. It was a check with the names of Oliver and Corinne James at the top, written two weeks earlier in Corinne's elegant script. The amount was forty-eight dollars and change, payment for one knitting book and the single skein of cashmere Corinne was using to knit her beret.

"I was helping Ellie Jo with the bookkeeping and found this in an envelope from the bank," Tara explained.

"Bounced?" Dana asked in surprise. Corinne was wealthy.

"One of us will have to ask her about it. Coward that I am, I'm leaving that to you. I know how much you love Corinne," she drawled.

"Was she in today?"

"Yeah, but she didn't stay long."

"She never does lately. Something's up with her."

Tara took Dana's hand. "More to the point, something's up with Ellie Jo. She doesn't seem right. I've been content to blame it on her foot, but Saundra noticed it, too. Have you?"

"She seemed distracted?" asked Dana.

"That, too, but I was more concerned by her lack of balance. She was barely over here today. Maybe she's noticing something herself and doesn't want people to see. Or else she really is feeling ill. Saundra's at the house with her now."

Heart pounding, Dana passed back Corinne's check. "I'm there." She half-ran along the stone path, up the back stairs, across the porch, and into the kitchen. The two women were at the table having tea. They seemed perfectly at ease until Ellie Jo asked, "What happened in Albany?"

Dana hesitated. After coming here specifically to report to Ellie Jo, she didn't want to talk about it at all.

Misinterpreting the pause, her grandmother said, "Saundra knows what's going on. You can tell us both."

"There isn't all that much to tell." She slipped into a chair. Veronica was instantly on her lap, staring at her mistress.

Dana briefly described the visit, but that was enough to upset Ellie Jo. "He's hiding something," she said. "Isn't it always the case, the man with the most to hide is the one who turns to God?"

"I don't think it was that way, Gram."

"Of course you don't. You've just found your long-lost father. You want to believe him."

"No," Dana said with some force. "He wasn't there for my mother, and he's never been there for me. That makes me predisposed to distrust him. But Hugh is right. He didn't know we were coming—didn't even know I existed—and his answers still made sense."

Frail hands gripping the table, Ellie Jo pushed herself to her feet. "Men are scoundrels." She turned and nearly fell.

Veronica jumped off Dana's lap.

"Gram—"

"Oprah's on," she said, releasing the edge of the table and hobbling toward the door. "You should watch her, Dana Jo. You'd learn about the lies people tell." Veronica followed her out.

Dana stared after them, before meeting Saundra's gaze. "Is she all right?"

"Touchy," Saundra said gently. "And weak. I've suggested she see her doctor, but she says she saw him for her foot and they didn't find any other problem."

"That was an emergency room visit," Dana remarked. "They didn't look at anything *but* her foot."

"Which begs the question of what caused the fall. It could just be age, Dana. Equilibrium goes the way of flexibility. And now that cast can't be helping any."

"About her general health—do you think there's cause for worry?"

"Yes," Saundra said. Her eyes were sad, her smile kind. "Do I think she'll admit that? No. The best you can do is to have her internist demand a visit when she returns to the orthopedist. Would that work?"

"I'll make it work."

Saundra looked down at the teacups. "And I do agree with you about your daddy. There's always the possibility that he had the story of his sister waiting, if he was trying to conceal his heritage. And it's also possible that his family found the second cousin to donate bone marrow without an extensive search. But he is a priest. I'd be prone to believe him."

Dana was grateful for the support. "That leaves me back at square one."

"Yes, ma'am, it does," Saundra said in a way that made Dana wonder if she knew something Dana didn't.

"I take it this isn't the first time you've had tea with Ellie Jo."

"No, ma'am. We've been doing it most every afternoon since she hurt her foot."

"What do you talk about?"

"Now, if I told you that, I'd be betraying a friend."

"Is it so private?"

"All talk between old ladies is private. Talk is one of the few things left to us as we age. We lose so much else."

"Like?"

"Energy. Strength. Health. Money. Independence."

"You're independent."

"Uh-huh. For now. Another ten years and I might just be needing someone to feed me my oatmeal, or read me my books, or make sure I don't wander out of the house and get lost."

"Exactly," Dana said, reaching across the table to take Saundra's hands. "What if Ellie Jo slides further downhill? What if distraction becomes confusion and she loses her memory? Then I'll never know the truth about Lizzie's roots."

"That's assuming Ellie Jo knows the truth. Are you sure she does?"

"No." Dana sat back. "What do *you* think?"

Saundra was silent for a minute, her eyes troubled. Finally she said, "I think not."

🍃

Hugh called his parents' house, knowing that his mother would answer the phone, and told her what they had learned in Albany.

"A *priest*?" she asked, sounding de-lighted.

"Very Catholic," Hugh reported. "Very Caucasian."

"And you're sure?"

"He was right there in the rectory, wear-ing his collar and called Father Jack by the parish secretary."

"I meant are you sure about the Cau-casian part? If he isn't the source of the baby's color, who is?"

"I don't know. But at least we've ruled out the father's side of Dana's family. More importantly, Dad's spent the last five years assuming the man was a lowlife. Now it turns out he's a priest."

"I'm pleased for Dana. Your father will be, too. Here. Let me get him."

"No, Mom. Just give him the message."

"But this is something you should tell him yourself."

"I don't yet have the answer he wants."

"Hugh."

"Not yet, Mom."

But it was only a few minutes later that the phone rang, and when he picked up, he heard his father's furious voice. But Eaton wasn't ranting about Dana.

"What in the *hell* are you doing to Stan Hutchinson?"

It took Hugh a minute to shift gears. "Drummond called you?"

"Not me," Eaton spit out. "Not first, at least. *First* he called my brother to say that you were harassing the senator and to remind him that there are bills pending in Congress that could directly impact the business. *Then* he called me, but only after *Brad* called to tell me you were out of control and that *I* needed to rein you in. Drummond was more affable, but the bottom line was the same. He said he was calling out of respect for me as a fellow member of the University Club. He wanted me to know that my son was playing with fire."

"Playing with fire? Like I'm a little boy?"

"You have no idea the kind of trouble Hutchinson can cause. The man is powerful, and he's vindictive."

"To hear him speak on the Senate floor, you'd think he's a saint."

"What he says is one thing. What he does is another. He could ruin your uncle, and he could ruin me."

"Ruin you? How?"

"Socially. He could make things uncomfortable for us, both on the Vineyard and here. And he could hurt the publicity on my book."

"You think he has the publishing world in his pocket? You give him too much credit."

"You give him too little," Eaton charged. "What are you doing, Hugh?"

"Apparently, touching a raw nerve."

"By accusing Hutch of fathering some pathetic girl's child?"

"She isn't pathetic," Hugh said firmly. "Nor is the boy. He's a sweet kid who needs help."

"Why from Hutch?"

"Because he's Hutch's son."

"Can you prove that?"

"Circumstantially. I'd need a DNA test to prove it conclusively."

"Like you proved Dana didn't have an affair? Your mother tells me that her father's family is true Irish Catholic. If Ellie Jo has no African heritage, who will you look at next? *Us?*"

Without answering, Hugh hung up the phone.

Chapter 20

Hugh got to his office Friday morning half an hour ahead of Daniel Drummond. Drinking a fresh cup of coffee, he read through the latest evidence Lakey had gathered. By the time Drummond arrived, he was well into his day.

Drummond, on the other hand, looked like he had just rolled out of bed.

"Coffee?" Hugh asked politely.

The other grunted. "Only if it's strong. Cream, three sugars."

Hugh fixed it in a mug decorated with the name of the firm. He gestured Drummond to the sofa. Drummond took the single armchair instead, the one Hugh normally sat in.

In other circumstances, Hugh might have kept it casual, but if Drummond was making a statement, Hugh would, too. Folder in hand, he took the leather chair behind his desk.

"Thanks for coming, Dan. The situation is urgent."

"You keep saying that, but for whom? My client or yours?"

"Given that yours is up for reelection in two months, both."

"The senator has no serious opposition."

"That could change if certain information comes out."

"Is this extortion, then? It's early September. A frivolous charge now would garner publicity that might not be resolved until after the election."

Hugh leaned forward. "The timing has to do with an accident that happened two weeks ago. The child is four. He was playing on his front lawn when a car jumped the curb and hit him. The driver was an elderly man who had a heart attack. He was pronounced dead at the scene. All parties were uninsured. Given a choice, the mother would never be approaching your client. She doesn't want any more to do with him than he does with her. But the injuries aren't minor."

Drummond yawned. "What are they?"

"There's a fracture to the spine between the pelvis and the rib cage. The fracture extends through the growth plates on the right side, which means the child will have asymmetric growth without future surgeries. It's a very specialized field."

Drummond drank more coffee. His voice was flat. "No hospital will deny that kind of surgery to a kid."

"Correct, but they're going to put the mother in debt for the rest of her life. She works as a waitress and falls into that no-man's-land where she earns too much to be covered but not enough to pay the bills. They're already starting to hound her for payment. The boy's about to be discharged, which means she'll have to miss work to take care of him, which means even less money coming in. Add to that the fact that the best doctor to treat his condition is in St. Louis, which means she may have to give up her job."

"This is Boston. We have the best doctors in the country right here."

"Not for this. I've checked it out. The best center for this kind of problem is at Wash U."

Drummond made a face. "Why does she need the best person? Won't the second best do?"

Hugh smiled. "For many people, yes. For a boy whose father is your client, absolutely not. Hutchinson's son deserves nothing less than the best. I'm sure Hutch would agree."

"Oh, he would. *If* this were his son. I'd put money on the fact that it's not."

"You'd lose. The evidence is compelling."

"What evidence?"

"I have six witnesses willing to testify that your man was at the tavern on the night in question and that he was waited on by my client. I have two witnesses, one of them a Ph.D., willing to testify that a car matching the description of your client's was later parked at the motel in question. I have receipts from the car service as well as the motel."

"So she had an affair with the chauffeur."

Hugh shook his head. "There's a surveillance tape." Lakey had done a good job. "Five years back, surveillance tapes weren't as common as they are now, but this particular motel had suffered a rash of thefts, hence the videocam. The tape's grainy, but there's no mistaking the senator."

"Do you know how easily tapes can be altered?"

"Do you know how easily it can be proven that they weren't?"

Drummond let several beats pass. "Is that it?"

Hugh shook his head. He had saved the best for last. "It seems that at the moment of orgasm, the senator shouts a name. I have two women, plus my client, willing to testify to it. That's three women citing the same name."

"*What* women?"

"Nicole Anastasia and Veronica Duncan." Nicole was the actress that Lakey had found first, and though photos of her with the senator remained unpublished, rumors of a liaison continued to surface in the tabloids. Veronica was a lobbyist for the health care industry; she had worked closely with the senator for years.

Understanding the implications of that, Drummond shifted direction. "What *name* do they say he calls?" He was wide awake now.

"Dahlia." Hugh let it sink in. "Not the name of the senator's wife, is it? Nor of his mother."

"Dahlia? Not Dial Ya? Or Dah-ling?"

"Dahlia. Of all the names in the book,

three separate women could not have made up the same one. Who do you think Dahlia is? His first lover? A longtime paramour?"

"I think the name is irrelevant. Do you have direct evidence that your client—what's her name? Crystal Kostas?—was in a motel room with my client?"

"I have no picture of them in bed together."

"What about entering or leaving the room?"

"No."

"Then, my friend, what you have is purely circumstantial."

"But damaging if this goes to trial," Hugh replied without missing a beat, because he worked with circumstantial evidence all the time. Some was flimsy; some, like this, was not.

"You said you didn't want a trial," said Drummond.

"I don't. But if Hutchinson does, I'm ready." Turning a page in the folder, he unclipped a small photo from the next page and passed it across the desk. "Here's the boy."

Drummond looked at the photo. He couldn't quite hide a moment's surprise before he tossed it back to Hugh. "I'll bet I could walk into any school in the country and find a boy who looked like the senator."

"Maybe you could," Hugh granted, "but would any of them be born nine months to the day after the senator was seen in a tavern being served by the mother, a woman who can prove she spent two hours at a motel with him?"

"Prove? You said yourself there are no pictures of them together at that motel. Who's to say they weren't each with other people?"

"There's that," Hugh said, glancing at the photo, which lay halfway between them. He knew it was his ace in the hole. "He's a sweet kid, Dan. His mother says he could kick a ball around pretty good. She was going to start him in peewee soccer next spring. But he may never be able to play now. His whole future's in jeopardy. Given the many pieces of circumstantial evidence that I have, a judge would have trouble looking the other way."

Drummond sighed. "How much does she want?"

"Not want," Hugh corrected him. "Need. And we'd like it in a trust fund. She has no interest in anything from Hutchinson except what her son will require to make sure he can walk. She isn't looking for personal gain."

"So that makes her noble? She still slept with a married man."

"A married man still slept with her. She knew he was a senator, because people at the tavern called him that, but did she know he was married? I doubt it. She isn't exactly a political wonk."

"How much does she want?" Drummond repeated.

"Need," Hugh corrected. "A million."

Drummond stared.

"In trust," Hugh added. "With the option of more if the medical situation warrants."

"Or she'll go public? *That's* blackmail."

"No. It's a medical reality."

Drummond drained his coffee. "A million bucks."

"He has it. He has hundreds of millions."

"And that makes him an easy mark? A million bucks, just on her say-so?"

"If he doesn't trust her word, a DNA test will do."

Drummond laughed in disbelief. "Do you seriously think my client will go for that?"

Hugh shrugged. "We have compelling evidence that'll make for several days' worth of testimony in court. Either a quiet admission or a DNA test will spare everyone involved the time, effort, and humiliation of a hearing. The test is quick. Your client is in Boston a lot." Hugh sensed he was in the driver's seat. He could afford to be agreeable. "I know you can't commit to anything without talking to the senator. Take this folder. It lays out the evidence. At this stage, we'd simply like a written admission of responsibility and the establishment of a preliminary trust so that we can start planning the boy's treatment. I'd just as soon settle this civilly, as I'm sure the senator would." He pushed the boy's picture back toward Drummond. "Take this, too. It may help."

Drummond stared at the picture. "I like your father, Hugh. And I like your uncle. So I just want to be sure you understand that the senator hates being accused of things like this." He held up a hand. "I'm not threatening you, just letting you know that if you go ahead with this accusation and it doesn't pan out, there could be repercussions."

There had been times in his career when

Hugh had sensed that a client was lying to him. Crystal wasn't one of those clients. And he had met the boy.

"It's worth the risk," he said. Rising, he clipped the photo back to the medical report, closed the file, and held it out. "Thanks for coming, Dan. Will I hear from you by the first of the week?"

Drummond took the folder. "Don't push it."

"The senator will be in Boston next Friday for a fund-raiser."

"I didn't know that."

"Then you must not be on his big-donor list. I could arrange for the test at whatever time he wants."

"And if he decides to fight this?"

"Does he want headlines?"

"Does your client?" He gave a man-to-man chuckle. "Hey, any woman who leaves work at a tavern to have a quickie in a local motel isn't a sweet, innocent thing."

"She comes close. She's a good mother, and a good person, and right about now, she's over in that hospital room, beat after working until midnight trying to dress her son over his cast, and wondering what a four-year-old ever did to deserve this. He's being discharged later today, and she has no babysitter who can handle him with his casts, so she's going to have to miss work. That means zero pay. Next Friday will be none too soon."

"Next Friday may not work."

"It has to, Dan. We can't wait. You've saved me the effort of filing papers by meeting with me today, but the more time passes, the more urgent it becomes. If I don't hear from you by Wednesday, I'll call Harkins's clerk to set a hearing for Friday."

"Harkins?" It wasn't a question, more an expression of dismay.

"He's a good judge. This kind of case is right down his alley."

"Yeah, because he has a handicapped child himself."

Hugh nodded. "Right."

There was a long silence, then a short laugh. "You're shrewd."

"Believe it," Hugh said, and showed Drummond out. On the way back to his office, he felt good. He felt effective. He had made the points he needed to make.

Intent on driving to the hospital to share the news with Crystal, he took the elevator to the parking garage and climbed into his car. Once into broad daylight again, though, he glanced at his watch, changed his mind, and headed out of town.

🌿

Strapped in a bouncer on the kitchen floor, Lizzie was contentedly full. She was so intrigued by the play of morning sun on her own hands that Dana decided the bath could wait. An intrigued baby was a happy one, and they weren't due at the pediatrician's until nine. It was only seven-thirty.

Looking at the clock, Dana remembered that this was the time, back when they were close, that Ellie Jo's cousin Emma Young used to call. Emma lived in northern Maine and had been a farm woman for so long that even after the farm was sold and she moved to town, she was up at dawn. Dana would surely find her home now.

She dialed the number she had slipped from her grandmother's dog-eared address book the day before. She had felt guilty then, but there was no helping it. She didn't know where else to turn. As a last resort, she had driven around town and, under the guise of showing Lizzie off, had brought up the question of Ellie Jo's family, to no avail. No one had known her before she moved to town, which was soon after she met Earl. Emma was the only one who had known Ellie Jo back in Maine.

"Hello?" came a scratchy voice. Dana figured the woman was eighty if she was a day.

"Emma? It's Dana Joseph."

"Who?"

Dana spoke louder. "Dana Joseph."

There was a pause, then a cautious "Are you calling about my cousin Eleanor?"

"Yes and no."

"Is she dead?"

"*Lord*, no," Dana cried. "Is that what you thought?"

"What?"

Dana shouted, "My grandmother is fine." There was no point in elaborating.

"When phone calls come after long periods without, they don't always bring good news," said Emma in her broad Maine accent.

"This one does. I have a new baby."

There was another pause, then a scratchier "How new?"

"She's two and a half weeks old."

The woman's voice rose. "And I wasn't called when she was born?"

Dana backpedaled. "I'm sorry. I've been a little overwhelmed. We haven't done anything about birth announcements." Emma had certainly been on Dana's list. But Ellie Jo might have called.

"I was at at your wedding," Emma continued. "Your grandmother needed warm bodies, and I was the token Joseph relative. In every other regard, she shut me out of her life. And do you know why she did that?"

Dana waited. When Emma didn't go on, she said, "Not really." Ellie Jo had simply said that Emma was a crotchety old lady out to hurt anyone whose life she envied.

"Because I dared to say something about her Earl that she didn't like," Emma went on. "The man was not who people thought he was. She didn't want anyone to know."

Dana held her breath, then asked, "In what way was he not who people thought?"

"He was a bigamist."

"A *what?*"

"A *bigamist*—oh, but I shouldn't have said that. Ellie Jo told me I was just jealous because she had married a good man and I hadn't married at all. She said I was an ugly person—that's what she called me, an ugly person—and she slammed down the phone."

"A bigamist," Dana repeated. It was almost ludicrous, given what Dana remembered of her grandfather. He had been devoted to his wife, daughter, and granddaughter, doting even when work took him out of town.

A thin wail came from the other end of the line. "I shouldn't have said that. She'll be even madder at me now."

Dana sensed she was losing the woman. Quickly, she asked, "Was Earl from African-American stock?"

"From *what*?"

"Was his family African American?"

There was a pause. "I *said* he was a *bigamist*."

"What about your father? And your uncle." The uncle would have been Ellie Jo's father. "Did they have African-American blood?"

"Blood *where*?" the elderly woman cried. "What are you *talking* about, Dana?" Her voice left the phone. "*Hello? I'm right here.*" She returned to Dana. "Here's my ride. She takes me in town for my morning tea. Will you tell Ellie Jo that I love her and that I'm sorry if I made her mad and that she's still the only family I have?"

"I will," Dana said, though she doubted the woman heard before she hung up.

She sat a while longer watching Lizzie, thinking she would have better luck with Emma face to face but knowing Ellie Jo would have a stroke if she found out. Besides, Dana had seen pictures of her grandmother's parents and grandparents. They certainly looked Caucasian. If any had looked African American, Emma Young would have known what Dana was talking about.

No, Dana didn't think that the source of Lizzie's looks was Gram Ellie's side of the family. Earl's was another matter, but a bigamist?

Then she spotted the time. Unstrapping Lizzie, she wrapped the warm little bundle in her arms, took her to the open French doors, and held her there in the sun. "Oh, Mom," she murmured, "isn't this the sweetest little girl you have ever seen? Did you feel this way when you had me? Or is it something about Lizzie?"

She was thinking that there were lots of

somethings about Lizzie that made her exquisitely special, when the phone rang. Returning to the sofa, she picked up the cordless, then froze. She recognized the area code: 518. Actually, she recognized the whole number. Father Jack was calling.

With deliberate care, she moved her thumb away from the Talk button and, heart pounding, waited until the ringing stopped. He didn't leave a message.

Coward, she thought.

Tossing the phone aside, she took the baby upstairs. Minutes later, she had her undressed and in the bathroom sink, which, when lined with a facecloth for traction, she found to be easier than the Mercedes of infant bath seats they had bought.

Dana drizzled warm water on the baby's skin. "Ooooh," she cooed, "isn't this lovely?"

Lizzie didn't look so sure of that. Her little body was tense, her dark eyes alarmed.

So Dana kept talking as she bathed her, which was likely why she didn't hear the car. When Hugh suddenly appeared at the bathroom door, she gave a start.

"You frightened me. I didn't expect you home. Aren't you supposed to be at your meeting?"

"I was." Looking pleased, he joined her at the sink as she soaped the baby's hair. Lizzie scrunched up her face. "What's wrong?" he asked.

"I think she doesn't like being bare," Dana said.

"That's good. Think it'll last through her teenage years?"

"Not likely." But she was encouraged by his mood. "How did it go?"

"I said what I had to say."

"Did it register?"

"It did. I gave him till Monday to get back to me. Your appointment's at nine, right?" When Dana nodded, he said, "Mind if I come?"

"Of course not." Any involvement on his part spoke of feeling for Lizzie. "You've never met Dr. Woods." Hugh had done all the research into pediatricians, comparing résumés, recommendations, and group setups, but an emergency had kept him at work on the day Dana interviewed Laura Woods, and when she had showed up at the hospital on the day of Lizzie's birth, Hugh wasn't there.

Dana used a cup to rinse Lizzie's hair. The baby began to cry. "Shhhhh, sweetie, shhhh. Almost done." She finished up as quickly as she could. Hugh had a towel open and wrapped the baby in it, talking softly as he carried her into the nursery.

In that instant, Dana felt completely happy. By the time she cleaned the bathroom and followed them to the baby's room, Hugh had Lizzie dressed. The outfit, another gift, was a little dress with flat pleats at the bodice and matching panties. It was white, with tiny pastel flowers.

"She . . . looks . . . beautiful," Dana breathed.

She wasn't the only one who thought so. From the minute they arrived at the medical building, people remarked on Lizzie's looks. A nurse led them to an examining room and checked her height and weight, before Laura arrived, and examined her with the gentlest of hands, all the while asking routine questions. When she was done, she turned to Dana and Hugh. "Have there been questions about her coloring?"

"Some," Hugh said. "We've been offered a wide range of possible explanations."

"I'm sure," Laura remarked. "For now, Lizzie is oblivious to color, but she won't always be. At some point, you may want to talk with other parents of racially mixed children."

"One half of a pair lives next door. He's been a help."

The doctor had picked up Lizzie's folder and turned the page. "This is from the neonatal tests they did when she was born. The results are all normal. Your daughter is fine for PKU, metabolism, hypothyroidism." She looked up, from Dana to Hugh. "She does test positive as a carrier of the sickle-cell trait."

Dana's heart nearly stopped. "What does that mean?"

"Sickle-cell disease is a red-blood-cell disorder in which normally round red blood cells are sickle-shaped. Because of this shape, the flow of blood in small blood vessels can be impeded. That can cause a low blood count and other problems."

"Sickle-cell anemia," Hugh said, his voice heavy.

"Yes. Most of the people affected are of African descent."

"Lizzie can't be sick," said Dana. "She looks too . . . too robust."

"Oh, she isn't sick," the doctor assured her. "Carrying the trait has nothing to do with having the disease. She should just know that she is a carrier, when she has children of her own. If the father of her child is also a carrier, their child could have the disease."

"How did this happen?" Dana asked.

"It's an inherited trait. One in twelve African Americans carry it."

"That doesn't make me feel better," Hugh remarked. "Could she develop the disease?"

"No, but when infants with the disease are identified early and put on antibiotics, they do better. That's why we do the test on newborns."

Dana was only partly mollified. "So she inherited this along with her brown skin?"

"It would seem so. One of you carries the trait."

Dana swallowed hard. "Without knowing?"

The doctor smiled. "That's what I'm trying to tell you. Being a carrier of the sickle-cell trait has no impact whatsoever on the health of the carrier. It's simply a risk for the next generation."

"So, if we assume I'm the carrier," Dana went on, "and if Hugh were of African descent, Lizzie could have had the actual disease."

"Only if Hugh carried the trait."

"Can Caucasians carry it?"

"Rarely. When we do see it in Caucasians, a closer look usually reveals a person of African descent in the family tree."

"We're Anglo-Saxon," Hugh said. "Norse, on one side way back."

Laura looked at Dana. "You had told me you suspected Lizzie's features to have come through you. The trait goes along with that."

"Then I do carry it."

"Yes."

"No chance it skipped a generation?"

"Not if your daughter has it."

"Then one of my parents had it, too."

"Yes."

Dana glanced at Hugh. "Think my father would take a test?"

"If he's serious about wanting a relationship," Hugh said. He faced the doctor. "What does the test entail?"

"It's a simple blood test. It can be done in any lab. There's one downstairs. Analysis of the sample takes a few minutes."

"I could do it now?" Dana asked, and

looked at Hugh. "How can I ask my father to do it if I don't do it myself first?" She turned to the doctor. "I'd like to do it, please." She wanted to know. It would be the very first concrete bit of proof—the first *conclusive* step in tracing her roots. "Hugh can stay here with the baby."

The doctor wrote the order, and Dana went to the hematology lab. She had no sooner presented the requisition and her insurance card then she was summoned.

The technician drew blood from the crook of her elbow in a way that was painless and fast. The problem came when he said, "We'll have the results to your doctor in a few days."

"Oh no," Dana said quickly, "I need them now." The results wouldn't tell her which of her forebears had passed her the gene, but after hanging in limbo for more than two weeks, she wanted this one hard fact. "Dr. Woods said the analysis wouldn't take long." Her voice became pleading, "Is there no way . . . ?"

The technician winced. "They don't like it when I ask for a rush."

"Dr. Woods said it would only take a couple of minutes." Well, not exactly. But close.

"She's waiting for the results. I can stay here until it's done and take them upstairs myself."

The man seemed resigned. Vial in hand, he said, "Go up. They'll call her as soon as they finish."

Satisfied with that, Dana took the elevator back to the pediatrician's office and found the doctor still with Hugh and Lizzie. They were talking about genetics. Dana bent her head over the baby's, closed her eyes, and concentrated on the sweet scent of her child.

When the phone rang, she quickly looked up. Laura answered, listened, and frowned. When she hung up, she seemed bemused. "The test came back negative."

"Negative?"

"Apparently, you're not the carrier." The meaning of that filled the silence.

Dana broke it. "There must be a mistake. I shouldn't have rushed them."

"You didn't rush anyone. It's only the paperwork that slows things down, not the test."

"Then the reading of it," Dana tried. "Maybe I ought to take it again."

"I have a better idea," the doctor said, and pointed a finger at Hugh.

Dana gasped. "That's ridiculous."

But Hugh said, "It's not. Let's rule it out, at least." He asked Laura, "Are you sure one of us has to be a carrier?"

"I'm sure," she said, already writing up the order.

He left with it, and for the next ten minutes, while Laura saw another patient, Dana was alone. She nursed the baby more for the distraction of it than because Lizzie was hungry. She was burping her when Hugh returned.

Dana raised her brows.

"They'll call," he said.

"While we're here?"

"Yeah. He remembered you."

She rubbed Lizzie's back. "Sickle-cell disease."

"Not disease," Hugh said, leaning against the examining table and crossing his ankles. "Trait."

"I can't imagine walking around for thirty-four years not knowing it."

The door opened and Laura slipped inside. She was looking at Hugh. "Positive."

Dana's eyes flew to Hugh.

He wore a disbelieving half-smile. "That's impossible. Every last member of my family has been accounted for—for *generations*."

"I can only tell you what the test shows," Laura said. "Dana's is negative, yours is positive."

"They must have mixed them up," Dana said, because she agreed with Hugh. "Or misread them."

But Laura was shaking her head. "I asked the head of the lab to take a second look. Hugh's test is definitely positive."

Chapter 21

Hugh wanted to doubt, and it had nothing to do with bigotry. The idea that he was the source of Lizzie's African heritage went against everything he had been taught about his family—everything he had been taught by his *parents* about his family.

But he did believe in science.

The meaning of the test was clear. It shed a whole new light on Lizzie's coloring—and, he realized in a flash of insight, on Eaton's discomfort with it. On the drive home, he was silent, preoccupied gathering bits of evidence that rocked everything he had thought he knew.

As soon as he dropped off Dana and Lizzie, he headed for Old Burgess Way. Fueled by anger, he sped for most of the trip until he swung into his parents' driveway. Within seconds of parking, he was storming up the walk to the big brick house.

He rang the bell. When no one answered,

he used his key. Once inside, he strode through the living room to his father's library. Eaton wasn't there, but his latest book was, sitting smack in the middle of the large oak writing table that had been handed down by Eaton's great-grandfather—Eaton's *alleged* great-grandfather.

Hot off the press, read the handwritten note from Eaton's editor. *Here's to more great reviews.*

Fuming, Hugh went back through the hall to the kitchen. No one was there, but the door to the garden was open. He took the steps in a single stride and, with similar resolve, crossed the pool deck. His parents were with an old friend at a wrought-iron table, shaded by an umbrella, on the far side of the pool. From the looks of their plates, lunch was nearly done.

Dorothy saw him first. Her expression brightened, so that the others looked around.

Hugh looked at his father. "Can we talk?"

"Hugh," his father said in pleased surprise, as though they had talked just the day before and with no dissension at all, "you remember Larry Silverman, don't you? He's just inked a deal to develop the old armory. We're celebrating."

Hugh extended a hand toward the other man. "Tex." He turned back to Eaton. "Can we talk?"

Brightly, Dorothy asked, "Will you have a sandwich, Hugh?"

"No. I just want to borrow Dad for a minute." His eyes turned to his father, who must have seen the passion there, because he rose and took Hugh's arm.

"I'll be back shortly," he said to the others, and, rounding the pool, crossed the deck. At the house, he released Hugh's arm and preceded him into the kitchen. "That was just shy of rude," he said. "I hope this is worth it."

Hugh knew it was—not that he cared how Eaton defined "worth it." He had always respected his father. Despite their disagreements, he had believed his father to be honest. Now he no longer did.

Struggling to keep his voice low, he said, "An interesting thing just happened. Dana and I took Lizzie to see the pediatrician, who was reviewing Lizzie's neonatal tests. My baby carries the sickle-cell trait. Do you know what that is?"

Eaton regarded him warily. "Yes."

"She inherited it from one of her parents," Hugh went on in that same restrained tone, "and, naturally, we assumed it was Dana, because from the start we assumed that the African gene came from her side, since my side of the family is lily-white. Funny thing, though, Dad. Dana tested negative. So I thought to myself, What the hell, I'll take the test myself, because of course it'll come out negative too, then they'll retest Dana. Only my test came back positive."

Eaton's face lost all its color. He didn't speak, just stared at Hugh—which infuriated his son all the more.

"So suddenly," Hugh said, "I started thinking about the way you attacked my wife the day Lizzie was born—the way you were so quick to accuse her of having an affair. I started thinking about the way you didn't want to see my child"—he still smarted from that—"even after I'd demeaned Dana by doing a paternity test to prove to you that this baby *was* mine. So I start wondering why you didn't want to see this innocent brown-skinned baby—you, who have always been respectful of people of color."

Eaton stood rigidly silent.

Hugh braced a shaky hand on the counter. "When I was driving over here, I remembered the last time we talked on the phone. You were fixated on your book, saying that the timing of this was bad, like it was deliberate sabotage on Dana's and my part. Then I thought about the book itself," he continued, "which is nothing if not a testimony to our aristocratic family. I began wondering if you knew your book, your *life* was a fraud."

"I don't know it."

"And the great white liberal your books portray you to be," Hugh raged, "is he real? Or have you been pandering to minorities all these years out of guilt that you were passing for white?"

"I did not write anything with that in mind," Eaton stated.

"Are you truly unprejudiced, or was it all for show?"

"Does it matter?" his father shot back. "Doesn't the end justify the means?"

"No. Motive counts. It's what's here," Hugh said, touching his chest, a gesture Dana had made not so long ago.

"Not always," Eaton argued.

"Even if it makes you a *fraud*?"

Eaton blinked at the word and the fight went out of him. He looked suddenly defenseless. "The sickle-cell business is the first concrete evidence I've heard."

"The first *concrete* evidence? What about *non*-concrete evidence?"

"There was none," Eaton insisted. "No evidence at all."

"But did you know there was a possibility our family isn't what we thought?"

Eaton stared at him. After a long moment, he nodded and looked away.

"When?" Hugh asked. "How far back?"

"Not too far."

"Are we talking Reconstruction?"

"Less. Not even seventy-five years ago." His gaze slid to Hugh's face. "I heard rumor when I was a boy. And again when you and Robert were born. We were spending our summers on the Vineyard." He frowned and pressed his lips together.

"Don't stop now," Hugh warned.

His father looked up. "Hugh. I don't know what I know."

"Start with the rumors." He had never pressed his father this way. He had too much respect. But all that had changed.

Eaton leaned against the sink and looked out over the pool to the wrought-iron table and his wife. He was silent a minute longer. Then he sighed. "Rumor said my mother had an affair with someone on the island."

"An African American."

"Yes. He was a lawyer in D.C., but he summered in Oak Bluffs. My mother used to see him around town."

"See him?"

Eaton's eyes flew to his son—dark eyes, Hugh realized, so like his own, *so like Lizzie's*. "I don't know for sure that there was an affair."

"Dad," Hugh snapped, "I carry the sickle-cell trait. Think I got it from Mom?"

Eaton didn't reply.

"Does she know about any of this?"

"No."

Hugh pressed the throbbing pulse at his brow. "Did your father know that his wife had an affair?"

"I don't know what he knew," Eaton answered.

"Did he ever say anything to you?"

"No."

"What else do you know about the guy? Do you know his name?"

"Yes."

"Is he still alive?"

"No."

"Does he have family?"

"A sister. He was from a racially mixed family—one parent black, one white. He was light-skinned himself."

Hugh focused on the genetics. "So, if he had a child with a white woman, that child stood a chance of being even lighter-skinned."

Eaton hesitated. "Maybe yes, maybe no. I gather that when I was born the rumors died down. They rose again when I turned up on the Vineyard with my pregnant wife. The same gossipmongers began to speculate that my child might resemble its grandfather. When you were born, the rumors died again. Same with Robert."

"Robert," Hugh breathed. This raised another issue. "You stopped after Robert. That's two children. Most Clarkes have three or four. Did you figure you couldn't keep pushing your luck?"

"No. Your mother had a difficult pregnancy with Robert. She was told not to have another child."

Hugh accepted that.

"Robert was proof for me," Eaton said. "When his children were born looking Caucasian, I decided that anything I'd heard at the Vineyard had been idle gossip."

Hugh didn't want excuses. "But you knew the truth the instant you saw Lizzie."

"No. I didn't. Too much time had passed. And there were other possibilities," he said in a reference to Dana's family.

"But this was one of the possibilities," Hugh argued, "and still you didn't say a word. Instead, you accused my wife of cheating on me. How *could* you?"

"It was a possibility."

Hugh was livid. "Like your mother cheating on your father? Did you ever ask her about it?"

"I couldn't do that," Eaton said and started toward the hall.

Hugh raised his voice. "Because it would have been an insult to even *suggest* she'd been unfaithful. Didn't you think the same applied to Dana? She may not have the pedigree we do—" He stopped short with a bitter laugh. "Hah. But we don't have the pedigree we thought, do we?"

Eaton put a hand on the doorjamb. "What

in the hell am I going to do? My book's coming out a week from Tuesday."

"Your book?" Hugh asked. "What about my *wife*?"

Eaton didn't seem to hear. "We have a full tour scheduled. I'm booked for newspaper interviews and TV appearances." He returned haunted eyes to Hugh. "I've presented my life in this book as fact. If it's a lie, I'm done as a writer. Can you imagine the scandal it would cause if this comes out? The tabloids would have a field day." His eyes narrowed. "Forget the tabloids. The *Times* would have a field day. And . . . and my students? How do I explain it to them? Or to the provost?"

Hugh felt no sympathy. "What was it you and Mom always said—don't lie, because it'll come back to haunt you?"

"I didn't knowingly lie."

"But you're a researcher. You know how to dig into the past and get the facts. You've done it for Woodrow Wilson. You've done it for Grover Cleveland. Why couldn't you do it for Eaton Clarke?"

His father drew himself up. "For the same reason you assumed your wife was the source of your daughter's color. I was raised on certain beliefs. It was preferable to cling to those than to entertain other possibilities."

"Preferable," Hugh said.

"Yes, preferable. Don't we all want to think of ourselves as purebred?"

"But we're *not*. And you *knew* that"—he held up a hand when he saw his father preparing to argue—"on some level you did. What ever possessed you to write *One Man's Line*?"

"I'm an historian. *One Man's Line* is history. Clarkes have always played a role in my books."

"Walk-ons. Never the lead before. What were you *thinking*?"

"I was thinking it would *work*," Eaton shot back. "We've been business leaders, politicians, diplomats. We've been at every crossroads in the history of this country, and we've done it through good, honest hard work. I'm proud of my family." He stopped short and put a hand on his chest. "What do I tell my agent? My *publisher*?"

"What do you tell Mom?" Hugh added, knowing the worst of it was right here at home. "What do I tell *my* wife? She'll remember how badly she was treated by this family—by you and Uncle Brad—does *he* know, by the way?" Then it hit Hugh. "Who's *his* father?"

"The man I thought was mine."

- 27 29

Dana tended to Lizzie, trying not to think at all. After she put the baby down, she concentrated on finishing the Faroese shawl. She wanted it done for fall sales.

The shawl took all her attention. Even with the lace pattern done, with selvages on either side, and two main sections divided by a gusset in back, there were stitches to count, markers to move, and a chart to follow over hundreds of stitches. Each row took ten minutes to complete.

She couldn't worry about the call from Albany, couldn't worry about Hugh or Eaton or Ellie Jo. She had to focus on what she was doing. It was therapeutic. She felt relaxed by the time Lizzie woke up to nurse again.

Halfway through the feeding, Ali showed up at the door. She was carrying both of her dolls—Cream, with the red scarf looped once around her neck, and Cocoa, with the dark green one wound so many times that the doll's face was almost completely obscured. When Dana pulled the scarf down, Ali pulled it back up.

"Don't you want to free her nose so she can breathe?" Dana asked.

"She doesn't need to breathe. She likes being covered up."

"Why?"

"This way," Ali explained, "she can see what's happening without people seeing her." Hugging both dolls, she looked up. "Are we going to the shop?"

They were indeed. Ali chatted the entire way about anything that caught her eye, and though Dana wanted to discuss the school issue, she didn't know where to start. Ali was out of the car the minute it stopped, and running into the shop.

Dana followed with Lizzie in her arms. Once inside, she talked with Tara about an order that had been misbilled by the vendor, checked with Olivia about the status of enrollment in fall classes, and questioned Saundra about Ellie Jo's spirits. Hearing that her grandmother was still depressed, she left Lizzie and Ali under Saundra's watchful eye and went back to the house.

Ellie Jo wasn't in the kitchen.

"Gram?" Dana called, and searched the rest of the first floor. *"Gram?"* she called louder, and went up the stairs.

Ellie Jo wasn't in her bedroom or her bathroom, but Dana heard Veronica.

Fearing a repeat of the scene two weeks before, she hurried down the hall to her mother's bedroom. Ellie Jo wasn't there, but the closet door was open and the ladder down, as they had been that other day. Veronica meowed from the attic.

"Gram?" Dana called, and hurriedly climbed up.

She didn't see Ellie Jo at first. It was only when Veronica meowed again that Dana spotted them. They sat together in a low, shadowed corner of the eaves. Ellie Jo's casted foot was stretched out in front. A dislodged piece of pink insulation lay to the right of her hip. Spread on the floor beneath that was a group of papers.

"What are you *doing* here, Gram?" Dana cried, because the stuffy heat had to be bad for the older woman. She scrambled to join her. "What are these?"

When Ellie Jo didn't reply, Dana began gathering the papers. There were several official forms, a newspaper clipping, and a handwritten note.

With a quick, questioning look at Ellie Jo, Dana looked at the clipping. It was dated the day after her grandfather died and described a freak accident in a motel room involving a fall and the discovery of the body twelve hours later. She skimmed the rest. Three words on the last line jumped out: *Long-estranged wife.*

"What is this?" Dana asked, looking at Ellie Jo.

Ellie Jo's eyes were anguished, and something was wrong with her mouth. It was off-kilter, slightly ajar but not moving.

"Gram?"

Her hands hadn't moved, either.

"*Gram*," Dana gasped, and, losing all other thought, rose on one knee and touched her grandmother's face. It was warm, and the pulse at her neck was strong. But Ellie Jo couldn't speak.

Terrified, Dana touched a pocket for her phone and realized she had left it in her bag at the shop.

"Stay here, Gram," she breathed quickly. "I have to get help."

She scrambled down the ladder, grabbed

the cordless phone from the bedroom, and raced back up. First she called the shop. Then she called Hugh.

When she heard his voice, it all came back—the closeness they had once shared, the stability he offered. This was an emergency. She needed him now.

"Yeah," he said in a tone that was oddly restrained.

Dana struggled not to panic. "Where are you?"

"On the highway."

"How far from the yarn shop?"

"Fifteen minutes." He must have sensed her panic, because his voice grew concerned. "What's wrong?"

"It's Ellie Jo," Dana said. She was squatting in front of Ellie Jo, lifting a limp hand and pressing it to her own neck. "They're calling an ambulance, but I may need your help with Lizzie."

"Her foot again?"

"No."

"Heart?"

"I don't think so."

"Stroke?"

"Maybe," she said. "Can you come straight here?"

Hugh arrived at Ellie Jo's just as she was being put into an ambulance. Dana ran toward his car.

"They think it's a stroke, but they don't know," she cried, looking terrified. "I need to be with her, Hugh. Lizzie's over at the shop, and I have no idea how long I'll be. I can't bring her with me. We have those little bottles of ready-mixed formula. All you have to do is open them and screw on a nipple."

"I can do that," Hugh said. Granted, he hadn't done a feeding yet, what with Dana nursing, but he had read all the books.

"Excuse me?" called the EMT.

Dana backed away from Hugh. "Everything you need is in the cabinet to the right of the refrigerator."

"How long do I warm the milk?"

"Just so you can't feel it on your skin," she called, climbing into the ambulance.

"Will you let me know what's happening?"

She nodded. As the ambulance door closed, Tara separated herself from the women who were watching anxiously, and came to his side.

"Thank goodness you're here," she said. "This isn't good. Want me to take the baby, so that you can go to the hospital?"

Hugh trusted Tara, but he wanted to be with Lizzie himself. "Not yet," he said, "but we need a breast pump."

"I'll pick it up. If I run it to the hospital, I can show Dana how to use it and bring you back milk."

"That'd be a help," he said and spotted Lizzie asleep on the shoulder of a woman who was worriedly looking after the ambulance. He had seen her before at the shop and been introduced to her at the hospital two weeks before. "That's . . . Saundra?"

"Saundra Belisle," Tara refreshed his memory. "She's the best."

Saundra met him just inside the shop. She was not much shorter than Hugh, and was stylishly dressed in white slacks and a chocolate-brown blouse. She had short gray hair, light brown skin, and eyes filled with pain. "Did the EMTs say anything?"

"Not that I heard."

Saundra looked distraught. "She hasn't been herself lately. Looking back, I wonder if her first fall was the result of a mini-stroke, a TIA. It could be that she's had several, but she's been adamant about not seeing the doctor. We should have insisted." Easing the baby from her shoulder with hands that were strikingly gentle, Saundra cradled her for a final moment before giving her to Hugh. Lizzie slept blissfully on.

"You're a lucky man," the woman said.

Watching Lizzie, Hugh was hit by a gust of emotion stronger than anything he had ever felt before. She was *his* child. "Thank you for holding her."

"It's my joy."

Something in Saundra's voice made Hugh look at her more closely. He could see that joy and was comforted by it.

"If I can help at all," she instructed, "I live five minutes away. Tara has my number. Please call."

"Thank you," Hugh said, and watched her return to the shop. That was when he spotted Ali Johnson. She was sitting in a big chair at the long table, holding her dolls and regarding him with soulful eyes. "Ali," he approached, "how did you get here?"

"Dana," Ali said in a frightened voice. "What's wrong with Gram Ellie?"

"I'm not sure." He knelt down.

"Is she going to die?"

"I certainly hope not. I need your help, Ali. They're off to the hospital, and here I am alone with Lizzie and not really knowing what to do. It'd be a big help to me if you'd sit in the backseat and keep an eye on her while I drive. Think you could do that?"

Ali nodded.

Hugh smiled. "That's my girl." He stood. "Got a bag for your things?"

❦

A short time later, they pulled up at the house. In the abutting driveway, David was climbing from his car.

Ali was out the door in a flash and running to him. "Daddy, Daddy, something *awful* happened to Gram Ellie. They had to carry her out of the house on a *stretcher*. Isn't that what they do for *dead* people?"

"She's okay," Hugh called over, and took Lizzie from her seat. By the time he straightened, David was there.

"What happened?"

"She had a stroke, I think. The ambulance scared Ali. Is she inside?"

"Yeah."

"Want to know something amazing?" Hugh asked, and what he had learned spilled right out. "My grandfather was half black."

David's face went blank.

Hugh sputtered. "Yeah, I feel the same way. I just found out. This is the first time I've said it aloud."

David frowned. "Say it again."

"My grandfather was half black."

"Which grandfather?" David asked, like it was a joke. *Was it the business mogul, or the ambassador to Iceland?* Hugh could hear him thinking.

"A lawyer my father's mother apparently fell for one summer on the Vineyard."

David was another minute realizing Hugh was serious. Then he was suddenly livid. "You bastard."

"Not me. My father."

"After what you put Dana through? So you're liars, the lot of you, passing for white? Taking every advantage you could all your life. Parading as holier-than-thou, when you were hiding the fact that you were of mixed race."

Hugh didn't argue this time. He figured he

had it coming, figured that he had to let David get it out of his system if they had a prayer of being friends again.

"What do you mean, you just found out?" David asked.

Hugh told him about the sickle-cell tests and his subsequent confrontation with Eaton.

"And he really didn't know?" David asked. "Do you believe that?"

Hugh thought for a minute. "Yeah. I do. I saw his face. I can fault him for not checking it out sooner, but he didn't fake that surprise." He didn't go into Eaton's horror at the thought of his book. It wasn't a flattering picture.

David searched Hugh's face a minute longer, seeming to be waiting for him to laugh and take it all back. But there was nothing to take back. This was for real.

David's eyes lost their anger. He ran a hand over his bald head. "That's actually pretty funny, y'know? Your dad must be in shock. Speaking of shock, I told Susan about Ali's dolls. She flipped out at first, but as soon as she calmed down, she reverted to form. She says I'm imagining things, and that I'm just trying to upset her, and that I've

spoiled Ali so she doesn't want to leave."
He glanced at Lizzie. "Want me to watch the
baby while you go to the hospital?"

"I'll wait to hear from Dana." He held
David's gaze. "Thanks, though. I appreciate
the offer."

"About the other," David said, more quietly now, "it isn't the end of the world."

"No, but it sure changes my *view* of the
world."

"That could be a good thing."

"Maybe. I haven't gotten that far yet. I
only got the news a couple of hours ago."

"I'm glad you told me."

"So am I."

David glanced again at Lizzie. "Do you
know what to do when she cries?"

"I've never fed her before, but we'll manage. If she's hungry enough, she'll eat,
right?"

❦

That was the theory. In practice, it was
harder. He couldn't find the bottle warmer
and, when Lizzie began to cry, had to go
to Plan B, which entailed heating the pre-
bottled formula in a pan of water on the

stove. Unfortunately, the books hadn't warned against overheating the milk. He stood the bottle in the refrigerator for a minute, then, when Lizzie's cries accelerated, in the freezer. He finally took a second bottle, heated it briefly, and screwed on a nipple.

Apparently, Lizzie didn't like that nipple. She continued rooting around for the real thing and grew frantic when she couldn't find it. She finally tried the bottle, promptly gagged, and started crying again.

He checked the discarded package and saw that the nipples were medium flow for bigger babies. Rummaging around in the cabinet, he found a slow-flow package, wrestled one out, and snapped it on the bottle again. When Lizzie continued to fight him, he took a calming breath and tried soothing words. That helped.

Then the phone rang. Lacking a third hand, he tried holding Lizzie and the bottle with a single hand so that he could pick up the receiver, but she started crying again. He propped her safely between pillows on the sofa and held the bottle in her mouth, but even with his arm outstretched, he couldn't grab the phone. When he figured there was only one ring left before it went to voicemail, he took the bottle out of her mouth and lunged for the phone. He was glad he did. It was Dana.

"Hey," he said, "hold on a sec." He picked up Lizzie, quieted her with the bottle, then clamped the phone between shoulder and ear. "How is she?"

"They say she's stable. Why was Lizzie crying?"

"I took the bottle out of her mouth so I could get the phone. What does 'stable' mean?"

"She's breathing on her own, and her heart is okay. The problem is on her right side. They're doing tests to find out the cause."

"What can I do?"

"Stay there with Lizzie. Tara's coming here with a pump. She'll bring you my milk."

"Lizzie seems to be taking the formula okay."

"But I'm ready to burst. And anyway, I need to learn how to do this. Gram will be a while going home, if she does go home."

"She'll go home, Dee. Don't even consider the alternative."

Brokenly, Dana said, "If they find the

cause of the problem, it'll either be surgery or medicine. They don't know if she'll ever regain full mobility."

"If they don't know, it means that she might."

"She'll never be the same, Hugh."

The words touched him. "I'm coming to think that's what life is about, a chronological chain made up of links of change. Each new one aims the whole in a slightly different direction."

"But I want to go back."

"Chains don't have the flexibility to make one-eighties."

"She's my grandmother. She's all I have of the past. She's been my *mother*. That's a special role."

"Yes," he said, suddenly thinking of Eaton. Eaton had been close to his mother. Hugh remembered when the woman died. Eaton had grieved for months.

"I'd better go. I'll call when I know more."

"Please do." He paused. "I love you."

"We'll talk later," she said quietly, and ended the call.

Hugh finished feeding Lizzie, but by the time she had burped, he was focused on what Dana had said. Mothers did play a special role. They were there when no one else was, seemingly bound by an unwritten contract with the child they had nurtured since birth.

Hugh had a mother. If she felt bound to him by such a contract, he needed to know. He picked up the phone.

Chapter 23

Hugh figured that two hours had passed since he had left Old Burgess Way. Lunch would be over. Larry Silverman would have left. Eaton would be in his library brooding, and Dorothy, as always, would answer the phone.

Her hello had none of its normal brightness.

"It's me," he said.

There was a second's pause, then an indignant "What did you say to your father, Hugh?"

"Didn't he tell you?"

"Not one word. He yelled out to us that there was an emergency, and proceeded to shut himself in the library. When I knocked and told him that Larry Silverman was leaving, he said he was on the phone. It was embarrassing, Hugh. Very rude. He answers me each time I call him, but he won't come out. What did you say?"

Hugh couldn't tell her. It wasn't his place. Eaton would have to find a way—have to find the *courage*—to do that. He should have told Dorothy years ago. It boggled Hugh's mind that the man had let his wife go through two pregnancies without alerting her to those rumors. If the lawyer on the island had been one-half black, Eaton was one-quarter so.

That made Hugh one-eighth black. It was surreal.

But he wasn't telling his mother *any* of it. His father would have to do that.

"I have an emergency here, Mom. Dana's grandmother had a stroke." Dorothy gasped. "They're just now at the hospital, trying to figure out what caused it. I really need to be with Dana, but I don't know how long it'll be. I could take the baby with me, but the hospital isn't a good place for an infant. I need someone to stay with her here. Can you?"

"Uh . . ."

"I know you were here before."

"Your father doesn't," Dorothy said, sounding frightened. "What will I say to him?"

"That I need you," he suggested. "That

my baby needs you. I know I'm putting you in a difficult position, but there's no one else I trust." They hadn't hired a baby nurse and didn't yet have a babysitter. He could call a service and hire a stranger. Or call David, or Tara. But Dorothy was his mother, and Lizzie was her flesh and blood. "I need to be there for Dana. The last couple of weeks have been difficult. I haven't been as supportive as I should have been. I owe her."

"Owe her? Is it an obligation?"

"I'll rephrase that. I've behaved badly and need to make amends."

"Badly, how?" Dorothy asked.

"With the race thing. Mom, I can't go into this now, and as for Dad, he and I had a personal disagreement. You'll have to ask him the details."

"He won't tell me. He's angry, and you're putting me in a difficult position. I don't know what to do."

"Tell him about Ellie Jo," Hugh said. "Tell him that Dana's alone. He'll understand."

"I don't think so."

"Trust me. He will."

Dorothy studied the library door. Crafted of solid mahogany, it had eight raised panels, each with a slight variant of grain. She ran her fingers over the texture of one, then knocked. "Eaton? Open the door, please."

His voice was muted. "Not now, Dorothy."

"There's a situation I need to discuss."

"It can't be urgent."

"It is," she called, and flattened her hand on a panel. "Dana's grandmother had a stroke. Dana is with her at the hospital. Hugh wants to join her there, but he doesn't want to take the baby with him. He asked if I'd sit with her while he's gone."

From the other side of the eight-paneled door came silence.

"Eaton?" she called, jiggling the knob. "Please open this door. Please tell me what's wrong." He said nothing. "*Eaton.*"

"Go to Hugh's," he called.

"I told him he was putting me in an untenable position, because you don't want me going there, but I do agree that he should be with his wife."

"Go to Hugh's," Eaton called, more insistent this time.

"Dana must be out of her mind with worry, because her grandmother has been everything to her, so I can understand why Hugh wants to be with her. If they'd known something like this might happen, I'm sure they'd have made other arrangements. It had to have been hard for Hugh to call and ask this favor of me, what with all that's been going on between us. But these things take you off-guard, and I am family, and what with their having a brand-new baby at home—"

"Dorothy! Go!"

"But you're *my* husband," Dorothy said, bracing herself on yet another panel, "and you're upset. I should be with *you*."

There was silence. The door opened so quickly she jerked back in surprise.

"Dorothy." He scowled at her. "I told you to *go*."

Dorothy was not reassured by Eaton's appearance. His hair was rumpled, his face pale, his eyes tired. "Good Lord, you look like death warmed over."

He sighed and pushed a hand through his hair, a gesture Hugh often made. The resemblance between the two had always been marked. "I have things on my mind, Dot."

"What things?"

"I think publication of this book should be postponed."

She was appalled. "But the book is already in print. The tour is set. We have several hundred people coming to a book party in the Sycamore Room at the University Club a week from Tuesday."

"Some of the facts in it may be wrong."

Dorothy let out a small breath. "All right. This is normal. You're having last-minute jitters, like you always do on the eve of a book's publication, but I also know that you don't make mistakes when it comes to facts. You are a *stickler* for facts. Between Mark and you, everything is checked and double-checked."

He seemed all the more weary. "Go help Hugh. He needs to do this for Dana."

"That's what he said," Dorothy remarked, but Eaton's agreement puzzled her all the more. "Something's going on with you."

"I told you. I'm worried about the book."

"You've never cared about Dana before."

"Dorothy."

She figured it was as good a time as any. "I went to see her, you know. Last Tuesday." She waited for Eaton to explode. When he didn't, she said, "I saw the baby. I held her. She's a very sweet child."

"Please, Dot. Just leave."

"I'm taking an overnight bag," she warned. "I may not be back until tomorrow."

He stared at her long and hard.

"Fine," she said. "I'm going."

❦

Eaton left the door open and returned to the large oak writing table that he had inherited from a succession of relatives to whom he was not, apparently, related. He didn't sit, but stood in front of it, head bowed, listening to Dorothy's progress. It was only when he heard the click of the back door and the muted roar of her car that he let out a breath.

Raising his eyes, he ran them over shelf after shelf of books. The same volumes that had brought him comfort in the past now pricked his conscience. The books he had written himself were the worst offenders.

Hugh was right. What had possessed him to write *One Man's Line*? Arrogance? Self-absorption? Complacency?

Dismayed, he wandered out of the library.

The living room, too, was steeped in history, all of the furniture arriving in America soon after the first of the Clarkes. Upholstery had been replaced and wood restored as the pieces had descended the generations, but each piece still bore the personal sign of its maker.

Portraits of the family lined the walls, each signed by the artist who had painted it, all known in their time and some famous still. Miscellaneous relatives, captured in smaller sizes, hung in groups above an engraved chest, a drop-leaf table. Great-grandparents on Eaton's mother's side flanked the hall. To the left of the secretary hung large renditions of his paternal grand-parents. Eaton's own parents, larger yet, had the place of honor over the sofa.

Eaton had idolized his father, had been respectful and agreeable to a fault, des-perate to please the man. His father was named Bradley, as was his first-born son, who favored him both in aptitude and looks. Both of these Bradleys were men of vision, born leaders who relied on employees to see to the vision's daily execution. Con-versely, Eaton was his mother's son, with the same attention to detail, the same creative bent.

Eaton recalled his mother doing the things that women of her class did at the time—sewing and needlepoint and gardening, none of it necessarily practical. It wasn't necessarily creative, either, he realized now.

"God damn it," he swore at the oil rendition of his mother. "Did you truly think I'd never find out? Did it never occur to you that I had a *right* to know? Would it have been *so* difficult to tell me? You had ten years after Dad died to do it." He had a thought. "And what about Thomas Belisle? Were you with him after Dad died? Did he ever know about me, or did you lie to him, too?"

He turned on his father. "And what about *you*, leaving her there summer after summer, did you never imagine—but no, you wouldn't have. You were used to people doing the bidding of the chairman of the board. If you couldn't fathom my becoming a writer, you sure as *hell* wouldn't have fathomed your wife being with another man. *She slept with another man!*" he shouted.

"But maybe you knew. Maybe you knew

and refused to admit it, refused to so much as breathe it aloud lest it hurt your social status. Or maybe you knew and didn't care. Maybe it was like your business, someone else seeing to the details that you didn't have the time or inclination to address. Is that what he did, Mom? Did he know and not care? Did he not care about me, either?"

He took a short breath and said to them both, "There were all those rumors, but you didn't say a goddamned word! I always knew you were cold, but what you did was selfish and—and *shortsighted*. Didn't you think I'd ever have kids? Didn't you think *they* had a right to know? What kind of people are you, to hide something as basic and *consequential* from someone you call your son?"

But they didn't call him son anymore. They had gone to their graves believing their secret was safe.

In the end, Eaton knew that. Blaming his parents was useless, because he wasn't blameless himself. He knew the rumors. Hugh was right. He might have tracked down the truth. He hadn't, because he hadn't wanted to know. It was as simple and shameful as that. He led the life of a Boston Brahmin. Becoming African American meant rocking the boat.

But now he knew. And Hugh knew.

Dorothy had to be told first. He couldn't begin to think of how to tell Brad and Robert, much less his publisher. But he couldn't lie next to Dorothy in bed again until she knew. To perpetuate a lie, now that he knew it as such, would be compounding the wrong his parents had done.

Leaving the living room, he took his keys from the rosewood hall table and, in the process, caught sight of himself in the ornate hall mirror. Dorothy was right. He looked awful. Still, he didn't bother to even comb his hair, didn't want to linger lest he lose his nerve. He went through the kitchen to the garage, started his car, pulled out onto Old Burgess Way, and headed north.

It wasn't an easy drive. More than once, he considered turning back. What Dorothy didn't know wouldn't hurt her, his reasoning went. What Dorothy didn't know, no one *else* had to know—and it wasn't that he feared she would tell. She knew what to say and what not to say.

Once he told her, though, she would be

implicated in any further lie. He wasn't sure that was fair.

Then again, maintaining the lie might be impossible, thanks to the birth of Elizabeth Ames Clarke.

Robert wouldn't be pleased. He joked about being his uncle Bradley's illegitimate son. The truth would be worse in his eyes. Robert was one-eighth African American. His four children were each one-sixteenth.

Robert had to be told. But Dorothy first.

Eaton drove on. He hesitated once more when he left the highway, and again just before Hugh's house came into sight. But his foot stayed on the gas. By the time he pulled into the driveway behind Dorothy's car, he knew there was no turning back.

He went to the front door and rapped lightly. Her face quickly appeared in the side window, puzzled until she saw him, then startled. She pulled the door open.

"Eaton!" she cried in a half-whisper that suggested the baby was asleep.

He nodded. When an explanation seemed called for, he just said, "I thought I'd come."

"Hugh has already left."

"That's okay. Good, actually." He didn't know where to begin.

"What's wrong?"

"Why does something have to be wrong?" he asked softly.

"You haven't been in this house since the baby was born," she said. "And you don't look well."

He sighed. "May I come in?"

She stepped back, scolding quietly, "Of *course*. This is as much your house as it is mine, even though it doesn't belong to us, though we did give Hugh the money he used to buy it."

"Dorothy." He went past her into the hall. "He gets the same dividends we do. And he earns good money. He bought this house on his own."

"Probably, Eaton, but I'm just worried about why you drove all the way up here. Is it something about your health, something you haven't told me?"

"My health is fine." He wandered into the living room, knowing she would follow. He opened his mouth, then closed it and looked around. Hugh's living room was a newer, younger version of their own. He spotted several pieces that had come down through the family, but they were set off cleverly with more modern touches. He stared at the portraits. He wasn't sure he even knew whose face was in each. He sensed they were here more for their artistic value than for any specific sentimental connection.

That was probably good, he realized. Hugh might not be related to any of these forebears.

"Eaton?"

He looked back at Dorothy. "Any word from Hugh?"

"Not yet. He's probably just arrived at the hospital."

Eaton nodded. He wasn't sure exactly how to broach the subject.

Dorothy was watching him, waiting.

"I'm glad Hugh is with Dana," he said. "There may be decisions to make. A husband should be with his wife at times like this."

"Do you have decisions to make with regard to your book?" Dorothy asked directly.

She was a bright woman. She did deserve the truth. "Definitely," he said.

"What kinds of decisions?"

"Whether to go back and correct the things that are wrong."

"But you can't do it, not in this edition. Is the problem so severe that it can't wait for the paperback release?" The phone rang. Frowning in frustration, she held up a finger to say she'd be back, and hurried from the room.

Calling himself every kind of coward, and, in that, more his mother's son than he had ever thought, Eaton followed, but only to the hall. He saw that the bassinet in the family room was empty. Quietly, he climbed the stairs and went down to the baby's room. Hugh and Dana had shown it off the last time he and Dorothy had visited. Typical of children, they had been proud and wanted approval.

Personally, Eaton found the painted meadow cloying. Clean walls with a bright picture or two was more his style.

But then, clean walls with a bright picture or two was the way Dorothy had decorated their children's rooms, and Eaton was a creature of habit.

He wondered if Hugh had a point, that he had deliberately written *One Man's Line* to make real what he most feared was not. He wondered if he had spent a lifetime immersing himself in the protective cloak of ancestry so that he wouldn't have to consider the truth.

He approached the crib. Elizabeth Ames Clarke was asleep on her back. She was wearing a little pink onesie, like those Robert's baby girls had worn, but there the similarity ended. Her arms were bare, and her legs a lovely soft brown. What caught him most, though, was her face. Surrounded by wispy curls that he remembered from the day of her birth, her face was a soft bronze, with the smoothest, most unblemished of cheeks, a tiny bump of a chin, a button nose. Her lashes were dark and long, her eyelids a burnished gold.

She was quite beautiful.

The image blurred. He didn't know whether it was fear of what his granddaughter faced, fear of telling Dorothy, fear of telling Robert, fear of telling friends, fear of losing his public's respect.

But, looking at this child through tears, he didn't see the difference between her skin and his. He only saw her innocence.

Chapter 24

Dana was grateful Hugh was with her. She didn't ask herself why she hadn't called Gillian or Tara. She simply needed Hugh there. He was clearheaded. He listened to the doctor's explanation of what they had found and what they could do. He filled in the blanks for Dana when she was confused, and asked the questions she couldn't. When it came to making decisions, he boiled the choices down to two, explained them both, listened to her thoughts, then supported her conclusion.

Ellie Jo had a blockage in an artery. Her best hope of recovery was surgery, which entailed its own risks. The alternatives, while less risky, raised serious quality of life issues.

It was an awesome responsibility, having to make a choice that could kill someone she loved. Dana hated it.

She held Ellie Jo's hand before they

wheeled her away, told her she loved her, that everything would be fine, and not to worry because she was totally on top of things at the shop. She kissed her grandmother's cheek and lingered for a moment. The scent of apples had been diluted by a medicinal smell, but still she treasured the familiar feel of Ellie Jo's soft skin. When the stretcher finally moved and Hugh drew her back, she pressed a hand to her mouth.

Ellie Jo wasn't young. Dana knew she wouldn't live forever, but she was terrified by the thought of losing her so soon.

❦

Since the hospital cafeteria had closed, Hugh carried coffee from a vending machine back to the room where Dana sat. It was a small room, done in soft grays and mauves that he assumed were meant to be calming. He couldn't say that it worked. He remained nervous.

Ellie Jo had been in surgery for two hours. It could be another two before the surgeon emerged, and still longer before they knew whether the paralysis was permanent, and that was assuming she survived the operation. There was a chance she would not. The doctor had been blunt about that.

Hugh set the coffee on a table to Dana's left, and settled next to her on the sofa. "Doin' okay?"

She shot him a worried look and nodded. After a minute, she said, "Are you?"

"I've been better."

She turned to pick up the coffee and sipped carefully. Then she cradled the cup in both hands and leaned back. Finally she glanced at him. "I didn't know where you'd gone this afternoon. Were you at the office?"

Hugh hadn't thought about the office. He hadn't thought about Stan Hutchinson, Crystal Kostas, or her son. Since late morning, he had thought about nothing but where he'd come from and who he really was.

"I had to talk with my father," he said.

She took that in. Another frown appeared. At length, she asked, "Did you?"

He wasn't sure it was the right time or place. But they were alone in the room, and this discussion would keep her from worry about her grandmother. In any case, he needed to talk. And he had a captive audience. The chance that she would get up and leave if he said something she didn't like was slim.

So he told her about the lawyer on the Vineyard, the rumors Eaton had lived with, the argument they had just had—and though Hugh thought his anger had abated, it revived with the retelling. Sitting forward, elbows on knees, hands clenched increasingly tighter, he was bitter. "He claims he didn't knowingly lie, but couldn't he have checked it out? He's built a career learning intimate details about the subjects of his books. He knows how to dig up dirt."

"He didn't want to dig up this particular dirt."

"Correct. And that would be fine if no one else was affected. But even before Lizzie was born, there was you. He treated you and your family like second-class citizens."

She didn't argue with that.

Hugh stared at the opposite wall. A picture hung there, something in ocean colors, vaguely modern and flowing. He knew the ocean. He looked at it out his window at home. The real thing soothed. This print did not.

"But who am I to criticize?" he asked. "I

was just as bad. I ordered a paternity test."
He looked back at her. "So, okay, I didn't
know about the guy on the Vineyard, and I
bought into the family myth hook, line, and
sinker. That was arrogance, Dana, and
I'm ashamed of it. But I knew you hadn't
cheated on me." He studied his coffee cup
and said in disgust, "This isn't even what I
wanted to discuss."

"What is?" Dana asked.

"Me. What I am."

When she was silent, he glanced at her
and saw she was frowning. It struck him
that frowns clashed with freckles. The latter
were pale against her even paler skin, but
he knew they were there. They were part of
the lighthearted personality he had been
drawn to from the first.

"Do you feel different?" she finally asked.

He wanted to feel different. He thought he
ought to feel different. But he didn't. "No.
Does that mean I'm comfortable passing?"

"Passing."

"That's what I've done."

"Passing has a negative connotation. It
implies you knew the truth and deliberately
paraded as someone else. But where was
the intent? That's what you ask a jury when

you try a case. So did you know you were black and intentionally hide it?"

"No. But I ought to feel different," he reasoned. "Maybe I'm just numb."

"Maybe it isn't that big a thing."

"In my family it is," he warned. "My uncle is apt to accuse my father of deliberately hiding it for the sake of preserving his share in the family business. He'll argue that technically Eaton isn't a Clarke."

"But he is. His mother is a Clarke by marriage. And she was your uncle Brad's mother, too."

A door opened down the hall. In an instant, Dana was on her feet and tensed. When a woman in scrubs appeared and went off in the opposite direction, she made a helpless sound.

Hugh was standing beside her. "She doesn't look rushed," he said. "That's good."

Dana stood for a minute with her head bowed. Taking a breath, she turned and sat. "I wish I had my knitting," she murmured. "How could I be without it, at a time like this?"

"I would have brought some if you'd asked."

"I didn't think. My mind is totally off."

Rejoining her on the sofa, Hugh said, "Ellie Jo will be okay."

Dana shot him a worried look. "What about Robert?"

Hugh had to admire her. He suspected Robert was the last thing on her mind. "Robert won't be happy. He would disown Dad if he felt it would keep him in good standing with Brad."

"That won't change what Robert is."

"Or what I am." Hugh leaned forward again. "Do you care?"

Dana frowned at the floor. "About Robert? No. I'm not sure I'll ever feel as warmly toward him as I used to. I can't trust whose side he's on."

"Are we taking sides?"

Her eyes met his. "Yes."

"What's your side?"

"Lizzie's."

"Am I on that side, too?"

She retrieved her coffee and took a long drink. When she was done, she returned the cup to the table and wiped her upper lip with a finger. Then she looked at him. "I don't know. Are you?"

"Seeing as Lizzie's genetic makeup comes from me, isn't it obvious?"

"No. Skin color is physical. It isn't an emotion."

"I'm on Lizzie's side. Are you on mine?"

"You're my husband."

"A husband's a thing, too." He rephrased the thought. "A while back you asked how I felt being married to a woman of African-American descent. Now I'm asking you. How do you feel being married to a man of African-American descent?"

She didn't blink. "The same way I felt yesterday being married to you. I don't care who your grandfather was. I never *did* care who your grandfather was."

"But back in the pediatrician's office when we got the results of the sickle-cell tests and the meaning of it dawned on you, didn't you feel just that little bit pleased that the snob got his comeuppance?"

She was quiet for a time, studying the carpet. When she looked at him, her expression was gentle. "I felt relieved. This makes you more human. It makes me feel less inferior."

"Inferior?" That surprised him. "Did you really feel that?"

"Yes."

"That was in your own mind," he said. "But weren't you relieved to be proven white?"

"I wasn't found to be white," she said in reproach. "I was simply found not to be carrying the sickle-cell trait. I may have all sorts of traits buried in my family tree. I have no *idea* who my grandfather Earl was."

Hugh tried a final time, half teasing. "But didn't you feel *any* sense of justice?"

"No. I'm sorry, Hugh. I'm not into revenge."

"You're a saint."

She smiled, but sadly. "If I was a saint, I'd understand why you needed to do that DNA test. If I was a saint, I'd have picked up the phone when Jack Kettyle called this morning." She held up a hand. "Don't ask. I didn't pick up. I'm no saint." Her voice softened. "I can understand what you're feeling, because I've been there. But the main pleasure I get from this twist is knowing it guarantees you'll love Lizzie."

"I've always loved Lizzie."

She drew up her knees. "What about me?"

"I do love you," he said. "I need you to love me."

She rested her head on her knees. After a minute, she tipped it sideways to look at him. "Why? Because you're feeling lost and uprooted and need something to cling to? Because you know color doesn't bother me, but you can't say the same for your friends?"

"My friends will be fine."

"Then there's no problem. When'll you tell them?"

She had him. He couldn't answer.

Relenting, she reached out for the first time in seventeen days and wrapped her hand around his arm. "It's what David's been saying. People are fine with minorities until one moves in next door. We know your partners won't be fazed. Work will be fine. The problem may be with some of the people you've known all your life. Like the Cunninghams. By the way, I'm out of the Designers' Showhouse, too."

"Since when?" Hugh asked.

"The beginning of the week."

"Why didn't you tell me?"

"What was the point?" She relented.

"Maybe it's a coincidence, you know, the two jobs."

One job maybe, Hugh conceded. Not two. Dana was exactly the kind of designer the North Shore branch liked to promote. Besides, it strained credibility to talk of co-incidence when the Cunninghams under-wrote the Showhouse each year.

He was furious. "I'll make a call."

Dana took back her hand. "You will not."

"But you wanted those jobs."

She sat straighter. "I've changed my mind. I have a new baby and a grandmother who's not up to running the yarn shop. That shop is as close to a family business as I'll ever have."

"It's not the work itself," Hugh argued. "It's the principle." He studied his hands. It was a while before he said, "What can I do?"

"Nothing. I don't want those jobs."

"I don't want those *friends*," he coun-tered. "If they reject me because my grand-father was part black, that's their choice." He took a quick breath. "But what do I do about the rest? The *being* part black part. Am I supposed to change? Act differently?"

"No," she scolded, but with a smile that

tugged at his gut. "You're still you. You're the product of forty years of a certain upbringing. You can't change that. What changes is what you do with it."

"Like what?"

"I don't know."

"I need help here, Dee."

She seemed almost amused. "If I didn't know what to do when it was me, how can I know what to tell you to do now that it's you?"

Down the hall, a door opened. Ellie Jo's surgeon walked toward them.

❦

Ellie Jo was going to live. The doctors didn't yet know whether she would regain full use of her right side, but they had removed the blockage that had caused the stroke and were confident that medication would minimize the chance of another.

Dana was weak with relief. She wanted to see her grandmother, but was told that she would be in the recovery room until the next morning and, even then, would likely be too groggy to know if Dana was there.

It made no sense to stay now. It was after

one in the morning. With any luck, Dana could be home in time to feed Lizzie. Her breasts were full, and even aside from the physical relief, she wanted the emotional comfort the baby gave.

When they pulled up to the house, they were startled to see Eaton's car in the driveway behind Dorothy's.

Dana's first response was a comforting thought. *This is how it's supposed to be.* Then she remembered the past days' events, and didn't know what to think.

Hugh hadn't moved. He had turned off the engine, but remained in his seat with both hands on the wheel. "I'm too tired for this," he said.

"He's probably asleep with your mom."

"Christ, I hope so," he muttered, and opened his door.

Eaton was asleep, but not with Dorothy. He was neatly arranged on the family room sofa, arms and ankles crossed, loafers side by side on the floor. The television was on, the volume low.

Hugh turned it off, then went for the lights. "I'm leaving him here," he whispered.

"We can't," Dana whispered back. "He won't sleep well here."

Hugh leveled her a look. "Do I care?"

Eaton stirred and opened his eyes. Visibly startled to see where he was, he took in Hugh and sat up. "I must have fallen asleep."

"Go on up with Mom," Hugh said.

Eaton looked at Dana. "How's your grandmother?"

Dana didn't know if he was just being polite. His face said he did care. It held some of the vulnerability she had seen earlier in Hugh.

In Hugh, it had been reassuring. In Eaton, it was oddly disconcerting.

Unsure what to make of that, Dana listened to the reassuring sound of the sea. *Be kind,* her mother whispered in its wake. So she said, "The operation went well. We'll know more tomorrow." She turned to Hugh and added, "I'm going up to feed Lizzie."

❧

Hugh envied her the excuse. Too tired to come up with one himself, he told Eaton, "I'm going to bed. Turn out the lights." He started out of the room.

"Wait, Hugh. I want to talk."

"It's late, Dad."

"Please."

Hugh stood at the door a moment. Then he turned, walked to the armchair, and sat. He didn't say anything. He wasn't the one who wanted to talk.

"I saw the baby," Eaton said. "She's beautiful."

"Her color hasn't changed. That doesn't help the situation."

"Hugh." His father's voice was faint. "I didn't *know*. I should have. But I didn't."

"Is that what you came to say?"

"Actually," Eaton rose from the sofa and went to the French doors. The instant he opened them, the sound of the ocean grew louder. "Actually, I came here to tell your mother."

Hugh looked up. "What did she say?"

"Nothing. I didn't tell her."

"Why not?"

Eaton was quiet. He closed the French doors. With the ocean muted again, his own silence was marked. Finally, he said, "I don't know."

"It won't get any easier."

"Maybe I'll become more comfortable with it."

"The longer you wait, the worse it'll be with Mom. You can say you didn't know before, but now you do. You have to tell her."

Eaton didn't reply.

"What're you afraid of?"

Still Eaton said nothing.

"She won't hate you because your father was half black. She's more open-minded than you are."

"She'll think I knew about it and lied. She'll ask why I didn't track down the rumors. She'll say the same thing you did about the research I do when I write. She'll be angry and hurt." He returned to the sofa and stood there, facing the cushions. "What a mess. I don't know what to do."

Hugh felt his own anger diminish. Eaton looked so defeated.

He remembered what Dana had said about *doing* something. "Tell her. Then investigate him."

"Do I really want to know about him?"

"Yeah, you do," Hugh said. "He's your biological father. Do you think Dana wanted to go looking for hers? We made her do it. What kind of hypocrites are we if we won't do the same?"

"We?"

Hugh hesitated. He tried to sustain some level of anger, but couldn't. Eaton was still his father. "Yes. I'd help. What's his name?"

"Thomas. Thomas Belisle. He summered in Oak Bluffs. He was something of a legend there—a handsome light-skinned black who charmed the pants off many a white woman."

"Eaton?"

Hugh's eyes flew to the door. His mother stood there in a simple white robe. With her hair brushed back and her eyes filled with doubt, she looked every bit her age.

She frowned at Eaton, then turned to Hugh, but what could *he* say? He was only the son. Eaton was the husband. It was *his* job to explain.

She gave neither of them the time. Mouth tightening, she turned and disappeared up the stairs.

Eaton, who had been paralyzed, suddenly came to life. He called her name and started after her, but Hugh caught his arm. "She's going to Dana. Let them talk."

Lizzie was suckling contentedly when Dorothy appeared at the door. She stood there for a second, then slipped in and leaned against the wall.

Between her own exhaustion and Lizzie's suckling, Dana had been almost asleep, but she quickly became alert. "What's wrong?"

"I just heard something strange," Dorothy whispered. "Do you know anything about Eaton's father being African American?"

Dana was trying to decide what to say when Dorothy said, "So it's true. And the wife is the last to know."

"Not the last, Dorothy. Far from it. I know it because of Hugh, but he only learned it today."

"What about Eaton?"

"Learned about it only today." She explained about the baby's sickle-cell test and the subsequent tests she and Hugh had taken. "Didn't he say anything earlier tonight?"

"No. And I don't understand why not."

Dana couldn't read Eaton's mind. But she remembered the disbelief she had felt in the doctor's office, learning that Hugh was the carrier. It was the last thing she had expected. If she was blown away by the news, she couldn't begin to imagine what Dorothy was feeling after more than forty years of marriage.

"I think we have to try to understand what he's feeling," Dana said. "He didn't expect this. He couldn't have dreamed it."

"How can you defend him, after he treated you so badly?"

Dana was too tired to feel anger. Smiling gently, she said, "When you were here Tuesday, you talked about how you grow up in certain social circles and learn to act in certain ways. You don't think about your behavior, because everyone else in the circle does the same things. Eaton wouldn't call it arrogance. He'd call it a way of life."

"They were arrogant. Eaton *and* Hugh!"

"They didn't *know*, Dorothy. Eaton heard rumor, but that was all."

"And he didn't see fit to tell me back then? I bore his children. Shouldn't I have been told?"

"Rumor," Dana reminded her, but Dorothy was past that.

"He prides himself on his intelligence. Did he think I was too stupid to understand—or too indiscreet to keep my mouth shut?"

"No," Eaton said from the door. In the dim

nursery light, he looked beaten. "I didn't tell you because I couldn't tell myself. To tell you would have made it real. I didn't believe that it was."

"It was not," Dorothy argued, "an inconsequential possibility."

"But it was a deeply emotional one for me. To accept the possibility of the rumor would be to accept the fact that my mother had had an affair. That part was just as hard."

"Well, I can understand that," Dorothy remarked with uncharacteristic cynicism. "You have nothing good to say about people who cheat. Tolerant, my foot. You're totally judgmental."

"Yes," Eaton granted. "Sometimes."

"*Sometimes*?" Dorothy echoed.

Hugh appeared. "Sometimes, Mom. He's human, like the rest of us. How much did you hear downstairs?"

"Enough. Will your detective be able to locate Thomas Belisle?"

"He's dead," Eaton said. "His sister may not be."

Dana was rubbing Lizzie's back. "Thomas Belisle?"

"The man who started this all," Hugh said. "Why does that name ring a bell?"

Dana suddenly remembered dark eyes that were riveted on Lizzie, and an expression that was exquisitely tender. In that instant, she understood the love with which certain hands had cradled her child.

Stunned, she whispered, "I know her," and looked up at the others.

Chapter 25

As stunning as the notion was that Saundra Belisle was related to Lizzie, Dana had to wait to pursue it. First came Ellie Jo. Dana drove to the hospital Saturday morning to find that her grandmother had been taken from the recovery room to intensive care. This was standard protocol, no cause for worry, despite the preponderance of machines. But it was hard not to panic seeing Ellie Jo herself. Her head was wrapped in gauze. She looked ashen and frail against the sheets.

Taking a limp hand, Dana kissed it. "Gram?"

Ellie Jo opened her eyes. When she saw Dana, she smiled. It was a little lopsided, but half a smile was better than nothing, Dana thought.

"I didn't die," Ellie Jo murmured. "That's good."

"It's *awesome*," Dana said, relieved that

her grandmother was speaking. "How do you feel?"

"Weak. I can't move much."

"You will. You need to rest and think wonderful thoughts."

"My hair is gone," said Ellie Jo.

"Only the back," Dana reasoned, "and only the lowest part. We're getting into hat season, and you're in the right field. Tell me the kind of hat you want, and we'll have a dozen knitted within the week."

"A wonderful thought," Ellie Jo murmured, and closed her eyes.

Dana wanted to ask what she had been reading in the attic when she had suffered the stroke. But she knew she couldn't upset her. So she sat there for another few minutes, then kissed Ellie Jo's cheek, and slipped out.

Back in her car, she headed for the house by the orchard. She wanted to read those papers in the attic. As she drove, she phoned Hugh to check up on Lizzie, but he was seeing his parents off and couldn't talk for long. When her phone rang shortly afterward, she assumed he was calling back.

"Dana?" came a tentative voice.

Her pulse faltered. She should have looked at the caller ID. Too late now. "Yes?"

"It's Jack Kettyle."

Like she hadn't known. Like she hadn't recognized that voice even after the brief visit they'd had. The tentativeness of his voice alone would have given him away.

"How did you get this number?" she asked. Her home number was one thing. She had told him she was living in the same town where she grew up. He knew what that town was, and he knew her married name. All he had to do was call directory assistance. But her cell phone was unlisted.

"Your mother-in-law gave it to me," he explained. "I'm glad you told her about me."

Dana was not. While she couldn't fault Dorothy—poor Dorothy, who likely thought she was doing the right thing since Jack Kettyle was not only Dana's biological father but a priest—Dana didn't need this call right now. She couldn't handle the emotions involved—couldn't *begin* to think about them. "It's actually a bad time for me to talk," she said. "My grandmother is ill."

"I'm sorry," he said with concern. "Is it serious?"

"Yes. Things are precarious. I can't talk now."

"Another time, then?"

"Yes. Fine. Bye."

"Wait," he said just before she took the phone from her ear. "I've told my family. They'd like to meet you."

Dana's eyes filled with tears. "Uhh, not now. I can't deal with it. I have to go." She ended the call, not caring whether she was cutting him off—and she promptly felt bad for that. What was it she had said to Hugh the night before—that intent was the important thing? If Jack Kettyle hadn't known she existed, could he be blamed for ignoring her for thirty-four years?

The only person to blame for that was her mother, but how could Dana do that? Elizabeth had died too young. Dana didn't want to blame her for anything.

So she focused on Earl. She pulled up at Ellie Jo's house and, ignoring The Stitchery, went inside. Veronica was meowing, trotting in from wherever she had been waiting.

Dana hunkered down. She pulled the tabby up on her thighs and hugged her, which was all Veronica would stand. Jumping off again, she eyed Dana expectantly.

"Ellie Jo's fine," Dana said, stroking the silky fur between the cat's ears. "She'll be in the hospital for a little bit, but it's looking good." Someone was going to have to stop in to take care of Veronica's food, water, and litter. Adding those things to her list, Dana saw to them now, then went up the stairs to her mother's room.

The attic hatch was open, the ladder still down. The papers in the attic lay where they had been left, on the wood planks beside a hanging piece of insulation.

Sitting on the floor, Dana picked up the official forms. The first was from the Illinois state medical examiner's office and listed the cause of Earl's death as blunt trauma to the head following a fall. The second was a copy of the police report stating that the victim had been alone at the time of the fall, and that the fall was judged to be accidental. The third was Ellie Jo's marriage certificate. Its date was the one Dana knew as her grandparents' anniversary, and the year on the form was a full one before Elizabeth's birth.

With nothing jarring here, Dana picked up the newspaper clipping. *Massachusetts Salesman Found Dead in Hotel Room*, read the headline. The opening paragraphs gave details of the discovery of her grandfather's body, details Dana already knew. Then came the phrase she had glimpsed the day before. It was in the last line of the piece.

The victim's long-estranged wife, Miranda Joseph, is a local resident.

Dana read the sentence again, then again. She had never heard of a Miranda Joseph, much less a first marriage for Earl. She had no idea what it meant.

Apparently, neither did Ellie Jo's cousin Emma. A handwritten note from her lay just under the clipping. It was dated several months after Earl's death. "Eleanor, a friend sent me this clipping. Did you KNOW Earl was married before? How could he marry YOU, if he already had a wife? Do you know what this makes EARL?"

Dana set the letter aside and, rocking on her knees there in the shadowy warmth of the attic, wept for the pain her grandmother must have felt. Bad enough, she realized, for Ellie Jo to lose Earl. But the fear of discovery must have made it worse. All those years. And now. Dana could suddenly understand why Ellie Jo had been against the search for Dana's father. One search might lead to another, and Ellie Jo considered bigamy a mortal sin.

Dana wondered whether the stroke had been triggered by fear of discovery. It couldn't have been easy on Ellie Jo, revering Earl in one voice while stifling another that said terrible things.

And Earl? Good, saintly Earl? Like everyone else, Dana had adored the man. A kind, gentle husband, he would have left the details of divorce up to his first wife. But how could he have failed to make sure it was done? Dana would have thought he'd have wanted a divorce decree in his hand before marrying again. She would have *thought* he wouldn't want to die leaving unanswered questions for the woman he claimed was the light of his life.

Dana was oppressively sad. When she felt Veronica rub her side, she wrapped an arm around the cat and buried her face in its fur. Seeming to sense her misery, Veronica allowed it.

Finally, Dana wiped her face and sat up. She gathered up the papers, stuffed them back in the wall where Ellie Jo had kept them hidden, and carefully replaced the pink insulation. No one would find them here unless told where to look, and Dana wouldn't tell. Apparently, Ellie Jo had planned to take Earl's secret to her death. Dana would, too.

Was it right? Dana didn't know. An argument could be made that she was no less certain Earl had committed bigamy than Eaton had been about his mother's affair. The difference, she reasoned, was that Eaton's concealment directly affected others, whereas Earl's—and Ellie Jo's—did not.

❦

Hugh stood at the edge of the patio looking out over the last of the beach roses toward the sea. Behind him, Lizzie slept in her carriage. She was blissfully exhausted after a major crying jag that had had him reaching more than once for the phone to call his mother back to the house.

But Lizzie wasn't Dorothy's responsibility. Hugh was the one who had to learn what to do.

Enjoying the breeze on his face, he thought about that—and then about his heritage. He felt that it ought to affect his work, but as many times as he ran through his roster of cases, he didn't see any reason to change course. He would love to add a discrimination charge to the wrongful termination suit he had filed on behalf of his African-American client—he had wanted to do that before he ever knew about Thomas Belisle—but it simply wasn't legally wise. Should he pervert his best professional judgment just because he had learned something new about himself?

Nor could he see himself sitting his clients down and announcing that he had just discovered he was African American. Not only was it patronizing, but it was irrelevant.

Dana had said something should change. But what?

A murmur came from the sea on a gust of wind, but before he could make out the words, they rolled back out with the surf.

❦

Dana came home to pick up Lizzie, but she didn't stay long. She needed the comfort of the shop. She was trying to be angry at Earl for botching a crucial phase of his life, but Earl was dead. So her anger shifted to Ellie Jo for suffering in silence all those years.

The instant she stepped foot inside The Stitchery, her pulse beat more smoothly. Customers sat at the long table working up gauge swatches or knitting through problems. Others flipped through notebooks filled with patterns, searching for one that they liked. Others were fingering the newest of the yarns, a collection of winter wools, alpaca, mohair, and yak. Some were of solid colors, others were hand-painted and multi-hued.

Corinne James was admiring the latter. She was dressed in navy slacks with a silk camisole. Her hair was pulled back in a carefully placed ponytail. An Hermès scarf hung from the strap of her Ferragamo bag.

She was deliberating over a hand-painted skein that went with her outfit. It was reminiscent of a black watch plaid.

"That's handsome," Dana said as she passed.

Corinne looked up. "Maybe a scarf for Oliver? Or a sweater?"

Dana stopped. "A sweater." She couldn't resist. A sweater would require several hundred dollars' worth of this yarn. But didn't an Hermès scarf deserve fine company? "A sweater. Definitely."

Corinne nodded toward the sleeping Lizzie. "She's very pretty." Her gaze rose. "How's Ellie Jo?"

"Okay, I think."

Corinne nodded. She lifted the sample swatch that Ellie Jo had made just days before. "This is soothing. Traditional."

"I bought some myself," Dana said. She was thinking of making a felted tote.

"Of this? Really?"

"It's so beautiful. I couldn't resist."

Corinne eyed the skein again. She held it in her palm, tested its loft with a squeeze, shifted it in and out of the sun. *Buy it*, Dana nearly said, then thought of the bounced check. She needed to ask about that, but something about Corinne discouraged it. A *fragility*?

Dana had never thought of Corinne as fragile. Fanciful, perhaps. But fragile?

She didn't particularly like Corinne. But Ellie Jo did. So she asked, "Is everything okay with you?"

Corinne looked surprised. "Definitely. Why do you ask?"

"You seem tired." It wasn't tired, really. She

looked tense. "You haven't been around as much."

"Oh, we've had glitches with the museum gala. The people who were supposed to be working on the ad book have one excuse after another for not coming to meetings, and the deadline is next week. I've had to spend extra time on that."

"It'll get done."

"I'm sure." She put the yarn back in its bin. "This'll have to wait. I'm too muddled to be sure this color is right. Besides, I won't have time to work anything up for a while. Please give Ellie Jo my best. If there's anything I can do, let me know."

"I will." Dana watched her leave. She was trying to put her finger on what it was that worried her about Corinne when Saundra Belisle approached—and Dana realized she was talking to Lizzie's great-great-aunt. That made Saundra not only a trusted friend, but, at this moment, the only relative Dana had here in the shop.

Dana didn't hesitate in handing her the child. Nor did she hesitate in giving Saundra a long hug. Saundra seemed to understand it. "Your grandmother will be fine, Dana Jo," she said softly. "This is not her time to go. I feel it strongly. She'll be sitting on that stool again in no time."

Dana drew back to see her face. "Will she be able to function?"

"Maybe not as smoothly as before, but near to it."

"Do I need to make changes in the house?"

"Not yet. Let's wait until we know more."

Saundra was no seer. But Dana clung to her words. She saw to things at the shop, keeping her eye on the cradle. A little later, she nursed Lizzie, then sat beside Saundra to work on the Faroese shawl. She had finished the most laborious part, eight inches of intricate design that circled the wide bottom hem, but there were still decreases to make every other round, markers to move, and a difficult pattern to follow to maintain side selvages and the back gusset.

Saundra fingered the hem of the shawl. "You do a beautiful job. This is a perfect wool."

"It's part alpaca, part silk."

"Alpaca for warmth, silk for strength and sheen—it takes the best from both. There's something to be said for blends, you know?"

Dana smiled and continued to knit. Was there an analogy here? Did Saundra intend it? Of *course* she did.

An easy silence lay between them. It had always been this way with Saundra—this instant rapport. Dana wanted to question her about Hugh's grandfather. But she didn't. She prized the serenity of the moment too much to risk it.

Late in the afternoon, the door dinged. In the seconds following, a brief silence stole over the shop. Curious, Dana looked up. Hugh had come in, with Eaton close behind.

Saundra had risen. Dana realized that she wasn't looking at Hugh, but at his father. Stepping around Hugh, Eaton headed toward their corner, and the pulse of the shop resumed. The register spewed out a credit card slip; the winder cranked; needles began clicking again.

When Eaton reached them, he extended his hand to Saundra. "I'm Eaton Clarke," he said.

The formality was marginally absurd. But Eaton was Eaton. And what else should he do? Dana wondered.

Saundra's eyes were clear. "Saundra Belisle," she answered.

"Is Thomas your brother?"

"He was."

"Did you know that Thomas had a relationship with my mother?"

"I did."

"How?"

Saundra smiled. "One-word answers won't do. Sit with me, please." She returned to the sofa that she and Dana were sharing.

Dana hadn't moved. She wouldn't have chosen this time for Eaton to come. She wanted Saundra to herself a bit longer, wanted more time to gather her resolve before facing Ellie Jo again.

But she could only begin to imagine what Eaton was feeling. He sat bolt upright, crossing one leg over the other and straightening the crease of his pants in a gesture she had seen him make dozens of times.

"How did you know about their relationship?" he asked.

Saundra spoke softly, keeping Eaton's confidence. "My brother was nearly twenty years older than me. I worshipped him. I used to follow him around. I was five when he started meeting with your mother."

Eaton showed no emotion. "Did you ever see them together?"

"Not in bed. But soon after. And once in the backyard. I was too young to understand what it meant when people took their clothing off. When I got older and did, I asked Thomas about it. He admitted to the affair. He was proud of himself. Thomas was incorrigible that way."

"Did he know I was his son?"

"No. To hear Thomas tell it, your mother sweated it out that summer wondering whether her baby would look African American. To hear him tell it, there was a collective sigh when you were born looking like your mother. No, Thomas never knew you were his."

"But you did."

She smiled. "Not until your granddaughter arrived. I always suspected it, so I kept my ear to the ground where you were concerned. You were a good man. I wanted to think you were his son. Then you had your boys, and Hugh looked just like you. When he became a lawyer, I wondered if he had inherited some of Thomas's interests. So I kept my ear to the ground about him, too."

"You followed us?" Eaton asked.

Saundra chuckled. "Nothing as fancy as that. I watched for mention of you in the newspapers. When Hugh has a high-profile trial, I read about it. You write books. I read the reviews and listen to interviews. And I watch television. Hugh was on the news last year when he represented that fellow who shot up the post office. And then there was the *Boston* magazine article on father-son teams. There were pictures of both of you. I hit the jackpot with that one."

Dana smiled at the remark.

Neither of the men did, but Hugh asked, "Did you move here because of us?"

"Not entirely. I had been living on the Vineyard—oh, not that whole time. I lived in Boston when I worked as a nurse. I retired twelve years ago and returned to the island, but it had lost its appeal. The winters were harsh. I felt isolated. The older I got, the more I wanted to be close to friends and to the doctors I trusted. So I picked out several retirement communities and began reading the local papers to learn about each. I used to pore over the listings of real estate transactions." She brightened. "And one day there you were, Hugh, named as the buyer of a piece of land, and I said to myself, 'This town was meant for me.' So I bought my house."

"And The Stitchery?" Hugh asked. "How long have you been coming here?"

Dana answered that. Eyeing Saundra with a blend of amusement and admiration, she said, "Since shortly before my wedding. I remember it. There was so much else going on in my life, but you walked in serenely and bought yarn."

Saundra's dark eyes twinkled. "I'd always been a knitter. There was no way I could resist this place."

"Did you know I was marrying Hugh?"

"Actually," she said, seeming momentarily astonished, "no. That was coincidental. I kept overhearing talk of the upcoming wedding, but it was a little while before anyone actually spoke Hugh's name." She arched a brow. "Apparently I missed the engagement notice. I did see the wedding one. That was a lovely spread in the *Times*." She looked from Hugh to Eaton.

"A mega-jackpot," Dana interpreted. There had been half a dozen pictures in the paper.

"Yes, ma'am."

Eaton uncrossed his legs. "This is going to take some getting used to."

"Me?"

He gestured vaguely. "You. Me. Lizzie. *This*."

"You've just learned about it?"

"Yesterday."

She considered that. "I've had several weeks. That gives me an edge."

"You didn't say anything to anyone," Eaton said.

Dana was trying to decide whether he was asking or warning Saundra when she said, "I don't need to say anything to anyone. The pleasure I get is all my own. I've read every one of your books. I'm proud to be your aunt."

Eaton pressed those thin lips together. Dana had always thought they were a Clarke trait, but it struck her that his mother had had the same mouth. She wondered which of his features came from Thomas Belisle. If she were in Eaton's shoes, she would ask for a picture. She would want to know everything about Thomas, favorite foods and hobbies and interests. She would want to know about the other children Thomas had fathered.

She hadn't asked Jack Kettyle any of

those questions. But the curiosity was there.

Dana turned back to Eaton just as he asked, "What do you need?"

Saundra grew very still. The warmth left her eyes. "Are you trying to buy my silence?" she asked. "There's no cause for that. I don't share personal information with people. Dana, did I say any of this to you before?" Dana had barely shaken her head when Saundra added, "Not even your grandmother knows." She faced Eaton. "My brother had a certain reputation. I can't silence those rumors, but I do have a relationship with his children and their children and now *their* children. They've invited it and welcome it, as I do. I don't have any other family, Mr. Clarke." She looked up at him. "You ask what I need? From you, absolutely nothing."

Eaton scowled. "My apologies. I meant no harm."

"Maybe not," said Saundra, "but I am no charity case. I don't ask for anything I can't pay for myself, and I can pay for quite a bit, thank you."

The look on Eaton's face was one Dana

had never seen before. She could have sworn he was humbled.

"I'm sorry," he said. "I'm trying to figure all this out and clearly said the wrong thing. You're my aunt by blood. If I had another aunt, which I don't, I would have asked her the same question. It had nothing to do with the fact that Thomas was African American."

Saundra relented. "Well then, perhaps I overreacted," she said graciously. "When you've lived my life, it usually does have to do with race. I guess I'm trying to figure all this out, too."

Chapter 26

Hugh wasn't happy when the doorbell rang Sunday morning at eight. Anyone with half a brain had to know that sleep was precious when you had a new baby. More than that, Dana was sleeping next to him for the first time in weeks. Granted, she might have rolled there in her sleep, without conscious intent, but it was the closest that she had come to him since the night before Lizzie was born.

Now she bolted up in alarm. "The doorbell. If it was Gram, they'd phone, wouldn't they?"

"You'd think," Hugh grumbled, freeing himself from the sheets. He pulled on jeans, loped down the stairs, and opened the door, prepared to yell at whoever was outside.

Robert yelled first. He looked like he had just been jolted awake himself. "What the *hell* have you done?"

"Me?"

"Know what Dad's saying now? He's saying *we're* black—he's black, you're black, I'm black. What did you tell him?"

"*Me?*"

"It's your baby that started it all, your wife sleeping with whomever she did—and I don't buy those DNA tests, there's a huge margin of error. Dad showed up at my house an hour ago, saying he was up half the night trying to decide on the best time to tell me, and he just figured it was now. What *is* it with you, Hugh? Brad's in a stew because you're threatening to take Hutch to court—over the paternity of some *kid*? Come on. Affairs happen. Illegitimate children happen. There are only problems when you have a brother like mine who wants everyone else to be as miserable as he is."

Dana appeared at Hugh's side and slipped an arm around his waist. "Robert," she said by way of greeting.

"Dana, can we have a couple minutes?" Robert snapped. "This is between Hugh and me."

Dana didn't budge.

"I'm not miserable," Hugh said. "And what Dad told you? It's the truth."

"Come *on*," Robert shouted. "That is *the*

most absurd thing I've ever heard. You know our family history."

"Affairs happen. You just said it."

"You honestly think Dad's mother had an affair? That icy lady? If she had sex with anyone other than her husband, it was rape."

"It was an ongoing affair. We have proof."

"Oh, yeah. The sister. Dad mentioned her. And you don't think she's after something? You don't think she gets points for saying she's related to Eaton Clarke? Well, I'm not buying it. I'm not telling my kids they're black. I'm not telling the people I work with, and I sure as hell am not telling Brad."

"Dad will."

"Dad is *so* on Brad's shit list right now, it won't make any difference. Brad knows what's up. He's no fool, and neither am I."

"Are you a bigot, Robert?"

"No more than you."

"I am," Hugh confessed, and was instantly ashamed. But he couldn't take the words back. "I am," he repeated quietly. "I wasn't happy when Lizzie was born."

"But y'are now," Robert mocked, "because you're the ultimate progressive who's gonna thump his chest and say, 'Hey, man,

I'm one of you and I'm proud.' And they're gonna laugh, Hugh. Well, I'm not going to be the butt of their jokes." He pointed. "You want to be that? Fine. Not me." He turned and stormed down the walk.

"DNA is DNA," Hugh called after him. "How're you going to fight it?"

Robert turned. "I'll tell anyone who asks that Dad is senile, and that you're trying to cover up for your wife." He glared at Dana. "Your father's a priest? I don't care if he's the *pope*. You're all looking for trouble." He held up both hands and walked away.

Hugh watched until the sleek black BMW disappeared around the bend in the road. "He ignored the DNA part," he murmured. When Dana didn't respond, he looked down at her. She had taken her arm from his waist and tucked her hands in the pockets of her robe.

"Did you mean what you said?" she asked.

"About being a bigot? Yes."

"A bigot is a person who is intolerant of others. You're not like that."

"A bigot is a person who sees other people as inferior to him and hence less desirable."

"You're *not* like that."

"Y'think? I don't know, Dee. I keep going back and forth on it. I'd call that arrogance."

"I'd call it real life. You were already doing everything right where race was concerned."

"Until it came home to roost."

"What're you supposed to *do*?"

He stared off down the road. "Robert thinks we should hide Thomas's connection to our family. He thinks it'll upset his life. He says we're looking for trouble." He looked at his wife. "Are we doing that?"

❦

As Dana drove back to the hospital, she thought about the toll secrets take on those who keep them. She was convinced Ellie Jo's stroke resulted from the tension of keeping Earl's first marriage a secret.

Entering her grandmother's room, she whispered her name. Ellie Jo didn't answer. She was in a private room now, the lone monitor beeping softly.

Pulling up a chair, Dana sat by the side of the bed with her arms braced on the rail.

Though she had put off this visit in the hope of calming down, she was angry still.

"You should have *told* me," she whispered. "You should have brought me into the loop about Grampa Earl. I would have loved him anyway. Did you really think I wouldn't?"

Ellie Jo sighed. Dana didn't know if it was coincidental.

"And didn't you think that keeping this to yourself would make you ill with worry?" Dana asked. "You hid it, and the pressure built and you had a stroke. That was unfair, Gram. The existence of an estranged wife was just a glitch in paperwork. Grampa Earl assumed it was done. When he married you, he acted in good faith."

Ellie Jo's lips parted. "Did he?" she breathed.

Dana sat straighter. "You're awake. How do you feel?"

The older woman didn't open her eyes, but a tiny smile creased the left side of her mouth. "Dopey."

"Good," Dana said crossly. "You *should* feel that way." She wasn't talking about the drugs. "You were wrong to keep this from me. You've made a mountain out of a mole-hill."

"Have I?"

"Grampa Earl did not intend to be married to two women at once. It was an honest mistake."

"Are you sure?"

"Aren't you?"

"No. But tell me you are. I'll feel better."

"Oh, Gram." Dana was dismayed. "Have you been trying to convince yourself of it all these years?" All she could hear were Ellie Jo's comments. Earl was wonderful—Earl was loving—Earl was as good as the day is long. The whole town believed it.

Ellie Jo opened her eyes. "They may send me to rehab." The words were slow, labored. "Will you tend to Veronica?"

Taking a deep breath, Dana reined in her anger. "Of course. And I'll look after the shop."

"About Veronica?" The words were slurred now. "Don't take her anywhere. She likes her own house."

"I'll stop in every day."

"Talk to her." Ellie Jo closed her eyes. "But don't . . . tell her . . . about Earl."

Dana's anger returned. No matter that

they were talking about a cat, she'd had it with lies. "Veronica probably knows. She was right up there in the attic with you while you hid those papers."

"She can't . . . read. Take care of her, Dana Jo. And listen . . . to your mother."

Mention of Elizabeth didn't help. "My mother?" Dana echoed. "My mother, who lied about the man who fathered me? My mother, who kept him from me all these years? My mother is no angel."

"None of us is," Ellie Jo said and let out a breath.

"Rest, Gram," Dana said a bit crossly and rose. "I'll be back tomorrow."

"Don't be angry . . ."

❦

But Dana was. She was even angry at Elizabeth. And that upset her. It put her at odds with *everyone*, which was a lonely place to be. Feeling the brunt of that on the ride home, she put in a call to Father Jack. He was a priest. Priests listened. They gave comfort and advice.

"Hello?" he said.

"Is mass over?"

There was a lengthy pause, then a tentative "Dana?"

"Yes. I don't know when a priest is free."

"Now's a good time."

"Well, that's good then," she said. "I guess."

"Thank you for calling back."

"I was raised well."

Again he was slow in answering. "You sound angry. Is that at me?"

"At you, at my mother. At my grandmother. At my husband. At my father-in-law." She caught a breath. "Should I go on?"

"That depends. Is there anyone left?"

Dana half smiled. "I could be angry at my mother-in-law for behaving like a ditz with her husband sometimes, only she's come through for me in this."

"Are you talking about the issue of the baby's race?"

"Mostly." She couldn't see going into the rest. "And my husband. He's getting better."

"He seemed fine when he was here."

"Like I say, he's getting better. I'm starting to feel like the problem is me. Not only with him but everyone."

"Is the anger justified?"

She gave it a moment's thought. "Well, I think so. Things happen, things you don't expect and you don't understand. So you either deny them, or lie about them, or try to make someone else responsible." She grew plaintive. "Why do people do that?"

"Because they're imperfect."

"But don't they know that it hurts?"

"When they're thinking clearly, they do."

"Well, every one of the people I listed has done something that I think was really selfish."

"Done something that didn't consider your feelings?"

"Yes. That's . . . right." She took a quick breath. "Only now, I'm beginning to think that I'm the one who is selfish. Am I? Is it too much to ask that the people closest to me consider me when they make important decisions?"

"No. You have a right to expect that."

"And when it doesn't happen, what do I do?"

"Talk to them. Explain what you're feeling. Hopefully, they'll act differently in the future, at least where you're concerned."

His voice was soothing. "Did they teach

you this at the seminary?" she asked, and thought she heard a chuckle.

"No. Life taught me this." His voice grew serious. "Dana, I am far from perfect. The good Lord knows the mistakes I've made. You're a leading one—oh, not a mistake in the conception, but in what I did afterward. I should have tracked down your mother. I should have made sure she was all right. I'm sorry that I didn't. I was blinded by my own needs. I apologize to you now for that."

Dana remained silent. She didn't know what to do with the apology. She felt as lost as she had when her mother had died.

"Life is full of should-haves," Father Jack went on. "Only they deal with the past. So we can dwell on them—dwell on the past—or we can move on. I want to move on."

"You've learned to do it. Is it because of your faith?"

"It's mostly common sense. And I don't always succeed. For instance, I don't know how to handle the fact that I have a daughter."

Dana's eyes filled. She drove on without speaking.

"I'd like to get to know you," he said.

"I can't think about that now."

"But you called me."

She had. It was an interesting fact. She reasoned, "You're a priest, and I need help. I'm behaving badly. It doesn't make me proud."

"Acknowledging the problem is the first step. You've done that."

"What's next?"

"Forgive yourself. It's what I said before, Dana. None of us is perfect."

"And what then?"

"Try to get past it. When you're with someone who angers you, force yourself to find three good things about that person."

A huge semi passed Dana on the right. JESUS STEERS ME was painted on the bumper in large letters. "Is that from the Gospel?" she asked Father Jack.

There was a pause, then a quiet "No. It's from me. I always told my children that. It seemed to help."

Chapter 27

Hugh was in his office on Monday, writing an appellate brief and feeling back on solid ground, when he got a frantic call from Crystal. Her voice was as hysterical as it had been that first day in the hospital garden.

"A guy came here and started asking questions about me and Jay. When I asked who he was, he said he was doing a routine investigation, so I asked again who he was, and he wouldn't say. When I told him I wouldn't talk with him, he said I'd be sorry if I didn't. So I asked for identification, and he just pointed a finger at me, like he was warning me, and walked back down the stairs. He knew my name, and he knew Jay's, and he knew where I worked. The senator sent him, I know it."

Hugh pushed back from his computer. "He's trying to intimidate you."

"Yeah, well, he did. I mean, he was this

big guy who could've kicked in my door without breakin' into a sweat. So what am I supposed to do now? Move? I can't afford an alarm, and anyway, it wouldn't help if he decides to burn down the house. *That'd* end my case against the senator."

"He won't burn down the house, Crystal."

"How do you know?"

"Because that's not intimidation, it's murder."

"And Hutchinson won't do that? How can you be sure? Maybe I should just drop the suit."

"If you do, how will you get Jay to St. Louis?" When she didn't answer, he said, "I have to ask you this, Crystal. For the record. Is there any other person, besides the senator, who would want to give you a scare?"

"No."

"What about your mother?"

"My mother?"

"You're not on good terms with her."

"Hey, not on good terms doesn't mean we're enemies. She was here both days this weekend, and she brought food. She doesn't have money to give me, and she can't help me babysitting Jay because she works a twelve-hour shift herself. But she's okay. Besides, I know the people she hangs with, and that guy wasn't one of them."

"He didn't say his name?"

"I told you he didn't. What if he comes back? What do I do?"

"You stay calm and keep your door locked. If he shows up again, call the police. In the meantime, I'll call the senator's lawyer."

It took him five minutes to connect with Dan Drummond—five minutes of Drummond's secretary "looking for him," though Hugh suspected the man was right there all the time. When he finally came on the line, he was genial. "Hey, Hugh. You're early. I thought I had till Wednesday."

"It's the senator who has till Wednesday, Dan, but something else has come up. My client is being harassed."

"What does that mean?"

"She's been visited by a threatening-looking guy who knows more than he should. Tell Hutch to call him off."

"What does Hutch have to do with this?"

Hugh sighed. "Ah, come on, Dan. Let's not play games."

"No games. What does Hutch have to do with some man visiting your client?"

"Maybe nothing. I expected that he would hire a detective to talk with the people she knows, but a good PI would never confront the woman directly. She's a represented party. That makes it an ethical violation. If this happens again, I'll hold a press conference outlining my case. Hutch may have nothing to do with the guy who was banging on my client's door, but the media won't think that way. They love this kind of thing. Tell him to call off his man, unless he wants us to go public. And while you're at it, remind him that I need a commitment by Wednesday—either an acknowledgment of paternity or an agreement to take a DNA test."

"Wednesday's calling it close," Drummond murmured, as if he were consulting his calendar to arrange a lunch date. "The senator has a bill pending—"

"I know about the bill," Hugh interrupted. "It has to do with early education intervention in underprivileged areas. He's getting big exposure as one of its co-sponsors. I'd hate to see his image tarnished because he refuses to take care of his own."

"The senator has a bill pending," Drummond repeated as if Hugh hadn't spoken, "and it'll be close, because the plan costs money. There are those in Congress who don't want to spend for the poor. Hutch is not one of them. He's working his damnedest to line up the votes. I'd say this takes precedence over a trumped-up charge by a woman he doesn't know."

"Wednesday, or I go public."

Minutes after hanging up the phone, Hugh went down the hall to his partner's office. Julian Kohn knew all about the Kostas case. Hugh had kept him in the loop. Now Hugh described the latest twist. "Do you think I'm wrong?" he asked. "She swears there's no reason anyone else would threaten her, and from the digging Lakey did, I'd agree. The woman doesn't gamble, she doesn't do drugs. She pays her rent on time. She juggles three credit cards, but she always pays the minimum balance, and her credit report is otherwise good. Everyone at work likes her."

Julian tossed his glasses aside, leaned back in his chair, and crossed his feet on the desk. "You're not wrong. I'd trust her, too. And, yeah, I'd guess that the senator hired someone. Didn't he do that once before with an aide who quit his staff and went to work for an opponent?"

"Something like that," Hugh said, wandering around the room. Everything was new here—beautifully placed by Dana, who had done most of the offices in the suite. But this office was different from Hugh's. Julian's father had been a butcher, his mother a homemaker. There had been no money to pay for leather-bound books and bronze bookends, much less education. By the time Julian finished law school, he carried nearly a hundred thousand dollars in loans. He'd made a lot of money since then, but he never forgot his roots. The simplicity of the office décor reflected that.

Hugh never forgot his roots, either. Unfortunately, they were bogus. "Want to hear something bizarre?" he said, and told Julian about his grandfather.

Halfway through, Julian dropped his feet to the floor. "That's amazing," he said when Hugh finished. "Your father lived with this?"

"He convinced himself it wasn't so."

"This was his mother, Hugh. His mother. Given who your family is, I can understand why he didn't want those rumors to be true.

His silence may not have been a result of bigotry as much as family loyalty."

"You're a forgiving person."

"Not always. I had a great-aunt who grew up in Eastern Europe. She and her husband denied they were Jewish to escape the Holocaust. Even after they immigrated to New York, they denied it. Their children denied it. My cousins still deny it. I can understand their guilt. The Jews in their town were rounded up and killed."

"They lied to save their lives. I'm not sure I'd condemn them," Hugh said.

"I don't, not for lying. For failing to appreciate life. They complain all the time. To hear them speak, they're always being robbed of something—a job, a house, the golf championship—and all because someone else has a little more money or status. They always come up short. They're never quite good enough. It's guilt. Guilt erodes confidence. But your dad—well, he's lived with the doubt and still made something of his life." He smiled. "African American? That's cool."

His eyes brightened. Swiveling, he opened a cabinet in the credenza behind the desk and took out his camera. "You gotta see this." He began scrolling through shots. "Hold on. Almost there." Another few seconds passed. "Here." He turned the camera for Hugh to see.

Hugh got up for a better look. The picture was one that Julian had taken two weekends before. Hugh remembered the moment. He had felt like a hypocrite, smiling at the camera as the happy new dad, though he and Dana were barely speaking.

But they weren't smiling in this shot. Hugh scrolled back to the picture with the smiles.

"I didn't like that one," Julian said. "The one I showed you is more real."

Hugh looked at it again. The pose was the same—Dana holding Lizzie, Hugh at her side with an arm around them both. But the smiles had faded, and rather than looking at the camera, they were looking at Lizzie.

Yes, it was more real, and quite beautiful.

"E-mail me this?" he asked.

The next day, Hutchinson's bill made headlines. *Hutchinson-Loy Heads to Vote with Surprise Support.* The article detailed

the defection of a major member of the opposition in what was assumed would be a
party-line vote. The defection promised to
swing the vote in favor of the bill's passage.

Dana, who was reading the article as
Hugh did, turned to its continuation on an
inner page.

"Listen to these sound bites," he said
from over her shoulder. " 'The culmination
of Senator Hutchinson's lifelong commitment to the poor.' 'No senator has fought
harder for the underprivileged than Stan
Hutchinson.' 'Perpetuates the legacy of
compassion for the senior senator from
Connecticut.' " Hugh snickered. "If this bill
passes, it'll be because it's an election year,
and the senators who are up for reelection
are running scared."

"But the bill is a good one, isn't it?" Dana
asked.

"Definitely. I can't fault Hutchinson here. I
can't fault him for much of anything he's
done in his twenty years in the Senate. I do
fault him for leaving his morals on Capitol
Hill. What he does on the Senate floor is
very different from what he does in his private life. Has he ever given a penny more
to charity than he thinks his constituents

expect? Has he ever not bedded a woman who is attractive and willing? Has he ever not used strong-arm tactics if he felt someone might thwart him?"

Dana didn't answer. She was reading a small piece tucked just under the fold. *Local Art Dealer Charged with Fraud*. It was only one paragraph, not much information given, but the name of the art dealer shocked her.

She pointed to it in astonishment. "Do you know who this is?"

Hugh skimmed the piece. "Oliver James?"

"His wife is at the yarn shop all the time, or used to be." Dana was stunned. "Lately, she's hardly come in. She must have known this was coming. What do you think he did?"

"Art fraud usually involves passing fakes off as original art." Hugh looked down at Dana. "Have I met the wife?"

"Her name is Corinne. You'd remember her if you had. This is *amazing*," Dana said, but couldn't quite gloat. She remembered thinking Corinne seemed fragile. "Her husband, indicted? She must be dying."

"Will you call her?"

"I don't even know her number. They live over on Greendale."

"Big mansions there," Hugh remarked.

"Uh-huh." Big mansions, big lawns, big cars, which went to show that big money didn't always buy peace of mind. Dana was trying to imagine what Corinne was feeling when there was a knock on the door. Susan Johnson, David's ex-wife, was there.

Susan looked harder than she was. Her hair was long and straight, and she was dressed in black—yoga pants, tank top, cropped hoodie, espadrilles. Back at David's, there would be a large black pouch filled with necessities. By contrast, her smile was light-hearted and bright. She was definitely Ali's mom.

"Susan," Dana said, opening the screen. "I didn't know you were in town."

"Well, David kept saying Ali didn't want to go back to New York, and the situation wasn't getting better. John and I figured we'd drive up to defuse things. I mean, she's supposed to return this week."

"Is she still balking?"

"Not since we figured out the problem."

Hugh had joined them. "The school?"

"Totally. I mean, it's a fabulous school, the

absolute best, which is why I was thrilled when John was able to pull strings and get her in. Then David called, and we decided to get some stats on the place. And, yeah, they're not as heavy on minorities as I'd like. Ali must have felt it when we visited this spring, like, out of place. Someone has to break the color barrier, but maybe my daughter isn't ready. The school she's been at is a good one, too, and she loves it." Susan smiled. "So she's going back there, and is *very* excited about seeing her friends."

"I'm glad," Dana said.

"Me, too. I should have realized there might be a problem. It just didn't occur to me," she said. "Anyway, I wanted to thank you both. You've been good for Ali."

"She's been good for us," Hugh said.

Susan began walking backward, eyes now on Dana. "I need the name of a yarn store in the city. She already told me that."

"I'll get you one." Dana waved. When Susan jogged back toward David's, she turned to Hugh. "*That's* a little scary."

"Susan not anticipating the problem? Very scary. She's smart and she's aware, like we pride ourselves on being, but who's to say we wouldn't make a similar mistake?"

"I guess there are ways to prevent it—do our homework, get all the facts before passing judgment."

"You sound like a lawyer," Hugh remarked, but he wasn't smiling. "It kills me to think of Lizzie on the outside looking in, but it's bound to happen. Some circles are still very closed."

"All kids experience that, Hugh. It's part of growing up."

"But race makes it different. And it involves *my child*."

"We can't protect her all the time. She'll have to learn that prejudice exists."

"Maybe things will be different by the time she's grown up."

If it was a question, Dana didn't know the answer. She did know that she shared Hugh's fear. Wrapping her arms around his waist, she pressed her face to his neck.

Hugh definitely loved Lizzie. This was one good thing.

Eaton was sitting in front of a blank screen when Dorothy appeared at the library door.

"I'm going out," she announced.

"Where to?" he asked, trying to be casual in his curiosity. Lately, she was a loose cannon.

"I don't know. I'll decide when I get there."

Let it go, he told himself. But he couldn't. "That doesn't make sense, you know."

She drew in her chin. "Does it have to?"

"It always did. You're an organized woman."

"That was when I filled my day doing chores for my husband. I don't have to be organized when I'm doing things for myself."

"Which you are now, after finding that your husband has feet of clay."

"If that's a reference to race, I reject it flat out. I'm doing things for me because I'm tired of putting you first. You don't deserve it—and if you think *that's* a reference to color, you're sorely mistaken."

"Dorothy," he said with some pique. She had become an independent-minded woman at a time when he needed his old, familiar wife.

"What?"

He didn't know where to begin. "My book's coming out in a week. And did you know that my brother called earlier?"

That gave her visible pause. "No."

"He told me to keep my mouth shut about what I learned."

"Why does that not surprise me?"

"Do you think I should?"

She opened her mouth to give a quick retort, then closed it again. "Are you asking my opinion?"

"Yes."

She thought for a minute. "Would you please repeat the question?"

He knew enough not to smile, though he came close. His wife was so deep into rebellion that her concentration was shot. It was endearing. "I asked what you thought I ought to do about what I learned about my father."

She considered it. "You have to do what your conscience dictates."

"That tells me nothing."

Her eyes flashed. "Well, I'm just not very smart. If I was, you might have asked my opinion about other things in the last forty years, starting with whether I was worried that those rumors you heard growing up might be true. Honestly, Eaton, you are insufferable. Know what your problem is?"

Eaton could think of a couple, but he said, "No."

"You don't know the difference between docility and stupidity. I may have been docile over the years, because that's what married women my age were expected to be—well, actually not *all* women, only the women in *our* social circle, which is something that is starting to *really* bother me. But I have been docile. That doesn't mean I don't have opinions, and it doesn't mean I'm stupid."

"I just asked for your opinion, and you couldn't give it," he pointed out.

"Couldn't?" she asked, raising a brow. "I certainly could, if I wanted."

He sighed in frustration. "Then please. What am I supposed to do about my less-than-illustrious past?"

Her eyes went wide. "Stop thinking about it as less than illustrious."

"Dot."

"I'm serious, Eaton. Why is this a tragedy? Isn't it an opportunity to learn about yourself? It's not like someone's coming along to call you an impostor and take away your money."

"I'm not worried about my money."

She smiled. "Good. That's progress."

He wanted—*needed*—to get to the other. "But don't you think it's a little shocking that my father isn't who I thought he was?"

"Of course. But is it worth all this brooding? I think not," she said. "Do you want the truth, Eaton? You're interesting because you write about interesting people. Accept who you are, learn a little about your past, maybe alter a little of your future, and you could actually be an interesting person all on your own."

With that, she left.

Chapter 28

Hutchinson-Loy passed by a three-vote margin. This pleased Hugh. If Hutch was feeling victorious, he might be more generous dealing with Crystal Kostas and her son.

Or so his theory went.

Dan Drummond poked a hole in it Wednesday morning, calling soon after Hugh arrived at work. "The senator will fight the allegation," the lawyer said. "He doesn't remember this woman and doesn't believe her son is his."

Hugh was disappointed. He had hoped for a quiet settlement. "Does he deny he was at Mac's Bar and Grille on the night in question?"

"No."

"Will he deny having relationships with the women from whom we have signed affidavits?"

"No. But he'll present the names of other

women who have made claims which were subsequently proven frivolous, like this one is."

Hugh ignored that. "He'll 'present'? You're talking about a hearing. Hearings are public."

"Given the senator's status," Drummond advised, "I think we can get an exception."

"You do that," Hugh said, swiveling to open a file cabinet behind him, "and I hold a press conference."

"We'll get a gag order."

"I'll hold a press conference to denounce the gag order," Hugh countered. He hadn't wanted it this way. But he could play hardball for the sake of the boy.

He pulled out the folder containing the complaint. "I'm ready to go, Dan. I'll be at Probate Court in Lowell at two this afternoon to file an emergency motion for an adjudication of paternity and immediate support, based on the medical needs of a four-year-old child. Good guy that I am, I'll ask for a quick ruling so that the test can be done to accommodate the senator while he's in town Friday."

"You won't get the ruling," Drummond stated.

"Why not?"

"Because you're dealing with a United States senator."

When the call ended, Hugh was uneasy. Dan Drummond was known for being cocky, but there had been a smugness in this interchange that didn't sit right with Hugh. It suggested Drummond knew something Hugh didn't. Someone at the Probate Court must be pulling strings for the senator.

He was wondering if he should call his contact there when the man actually called him.

"Sean Manley is on the line," said his secretary.

Sean Manley was an assistant clerk at the court. Hugh had come to know him several years earlier while representing his father on a vehicular homicide charge. Picking up the phone, he said, "This is mental telepathy, Sean. I was about to call you."

"I owe you, Hugh. You did right by my dad. Word is you're filing a complaint against a certain senator. I think you should know, Quidlark's grabbing the case."

The Honorable Judge Quidlark was old school and misogynistic. He also happened to be a longtime pal of J. Stan Hutchinson, who had, in fact, been the force behind Quidlark's appointment to the bench however many years before.

Hugh smelled a rat. "Thanks, Sean. I appreciate this." Ending the call, he phoned the Probate Court's chief justice. This man's primary job was administrative. Among other things, he saw to court assignments. Hugh had gone to law school with his son.

"Hugh Clarke," the judge said with enthusiasm, "it's been too long since we talked."

"My fault," Hugh replied. "How's Mary?"

"She's fine. And your wife?"

"Great. We have a new baby."

"Well, that's good news. But it isn't why you called."

"No. I hate to hit you with this, but I've gotten word of a possible fix." He outlined his case, stressing the urgent nature of the situation. He didn't reveal his source, and the judge didn't ask. He did ask several questions pertaining to Hugh's evidence, then promised an immediate inquiry.

"I'll be filing an emergency motion at two," Hugh said. "All I ask is a fair hearing."

"Consider it done."

When Dana arrived at the hospital, Ellie Jo was in high spirits. Her thick gray hair was brushed and neatly pulled back so that, as she lay against the pillow, it was hard to see the part that was shaved. Her eyes were bright. "No rehab center," she announced. Her speech wasn't entirely clear, but it was rapidly improving, certainly enough to convey feeling, which, in this instance, was relief. "What I lost is coming back. I can use one stick to crochet," she said, gesturing toward a purple project on the bedside table. "Two sticks is next, knitting. And walking. Another couple of days and they'll send me home."

"That's *good* news, Gram," Dana said, realizing that she couldn't stay angry at Ellie Jo for long.

"I'll need therapy," the older woman went on. "I may have to sleep downstairs. But I'll hold little Lizzie."

Dana smiled. "You will.

"And be at the shop. I miss it, Dana Jo." She took Dana's hand. "Thank you."

"No thanks are necessary. You know how

I feel about the shop. I've loved covering for you."

"Enough to do it forever?"

Dana went still. She knew that look. Something was going on in Ellie Jo's crafty old mind.

"I talked with my lawyer," her grandmother said. "He'll draw up papers. If you want, the shop is yours."

"But it's *yours*."

Ellie Jo's smile was crooked. "Would have been your mother's, if she'd lived. Do you want it?"

"Of course I want it," Dana said excitedly. She was a designer by training, but knitting was in her blood.

Ellie Jo was suddenly serious. "I won't live forever. This stroke may be the start."

"Gram—"

"It's the truth. We need honesty. Don't you think?" Her own eyes answered the question. "I have felt better since we talked about Earl."

Dana nodded.

"Do you hate him?"

Dana shook her head.

"Or me?"

"For doing what you thought was right?"
Dana saw that now.

"He was a good man, and he loved you."

"And you, Gram. He loved you."

❦

Hugh left Boston at noon, though only after a long talk with Crystal. She didn't like the idea of going public. She argued—correctly—that he had promised a private settlement. She was terrified that the media would make a spectacle of her.

He urged her to weigh the benefits against the risks. The benefits were obvious—the finest medical care for Jay. And the risks? Losing monetary support for Jay would be bad enough, but Hutchinson on the offense could be worse. He could attack Crystal's character in the press, calling her immoral, opportunistic, and money-hungry. He could paint her as a schemer and himself as the victim, and he could do it with passion and eloquence.

In the end, it was Crystal's choice. "I can't force you," Hugh said. "I can only advise you. My advice is that going ahead with this now is the right thing to do."

She finally agreed. But she wasn't happy. That raised the personal stakes for Hugh.

He wanted this victory for Crystal and her son, but he wanted it for himself, too. He had taken his ability for granted. Clarkes had the golden touch. Knowing now that he was only part Clarke eroded his confidence.

He needed a win now. That meant he couldn't blink when his bluff was called.

🌿

When Dana left Ellie Jo, she headed for The Stitchery. Once off the highway, though, she turned in the other direction, crossing town to drop in on Corinne. She suspected she was going for her grandmother's sake. After all, Ellie Jo was the one who liked Corinne. Dana did not.

Corinne's property was surrounded by handsome wood fencing that dipped into a low curve on either side of a brick drive. Dana checked the number on the mailbox against the one she had taken from the store's files. Two twenty-nine. This was definitely the right address.

Turning in, Dana started up the drive. The grounds were lavish and well cared for, lawn neatly mowed, flower beds vibrant with the pinks and yellows of fall asters.

The house itself was huge, a stuccoed Tudor with a steeply pitched roof, tall multi-paned windows, numerous side gables, and decorative half-timbering. Pulling up at the arched door, she left the car and rang the bell. A melodious chime was clearly audible.

When no one answered, she peered in. Polished wood floors gleamed; an exquis-itely carved half-round table stood beneath a piece of art in the alcove of a bridal staircase. Sun spilled through the upper balustrade.

There was no sign of life. She rang the bell again.

"Try the cottage," the groundsman hollered, and pointed behind the house.

Dana headed back. Beyond the garage was a miniature of the main house—same stucco, same eaves, same tall, multipaned windows. The shades here were drawn.

She looked for a bell and found none. So she knocked lightly.

No one answered.

She knocked again and was getting ready to leave when she heard footsteps. One of the shades lifted, and Corinne looked out.

At least, Dana thought it was Corinne, though there wasn't much of a swath.

Whoever it was didn't move for a minute or two. Finally the door opened.

It was indeed Corinne, but not the elegantly dressed woman that Dana had known. This one wore no makeup, no diamond studs. Her eyes were hollow, and her auburn hair was scraped back into a messy ponytail. She wore wrinkled jeans and a tee shirt, and looked like she hadn't slept in a while. She was leaning heavily against the door, a hand on the inside knob.

"You shouldn't have come," she said quietly.

"I was worried," Dana replied.

"That's what Lydia Forsythe said when she showed up yesterday morning, but she wasn't worried. She was snooping. She wondered if I actually lived at this address, because I've never had the ladies here, but she *really* wanted to tell me that it would be best if I resigned from the board before anyone suggested I do it. She assured me that they'd be able to manage the gala themselves." Her voice fell. "But of course I knew that. I was their token newcomer. I did the grunt work. I was never one of them."

"Neither am I," Dana remarked, hoping to make Corinne feel better. "I saw the piece in the paper. I wanted to make sure you were okay."

"I'm not," Corinne said sadly.

"What *happened*?" Back at the shop, Dana had wondered if Corinne was too good to be true, but seeing her now was unsettling. "You were always so *confident*."

Corinne rubbed her eyes. When she dropped her hands, it was obvious she had been crying. "The way you saw me was the way I wanted to be."

"Wasn't it true?" Dana asked, actually disappointed. Corinne had added class to the shop. "*None* of it?"

"Oh, some of it was," said Corinne. "I do live at this address, but in the guest cottage, and we rent rather than own. I do drive a Mercedes, though that's a matter of semantics, since it's just been repossessed. I am married to Oliver James, though he's gone so often I sometimes wonder. That'll only get worse now." She meant with Oliver in jail.

"Is the crime he's accused of that bad?"

Corinne hesitated. "I don't know. I worry there's more."

"What do you mean?"

"I worry he's into other things. There was never the money I expected, so I don't think it's drugs. But there were so many phone calls and sudden exits. The police are asking me questions, like I know something, like he confided in me. But he didn't. We had a talk before he was taken into custody, and I asked what was going on. He said I didn't want to know. So was he protecting me? Does keeping me in the dark make me safe?"

Dana tried to think of what Hugh would say. "By law, a wife can't testify against her husband."

"She could be charged as an accomplice."

"But you're not an accomplice."

"Not with regard to what he did. But I'm not innocent," she said in self-reproach. "I wanted the life he offered. I wanted it enough not to ask questions. I didn't ask where he got the jewelry or the cars. I didn't ask why we were still renting the cottage rather than buying the main house, like he said we would. I didn't ask how we were going to pay the bills, and when my credit card charges were denied, he just blamed it on the company, cut up the card in question, and gave me another. And I *used* it."

Dana was mystified. "But how did you do it—like, with the board of the museum?"

"Oliver secured a piece of art that the museum wanted. Maybe it was hot, I don't know. He donated his commission back to the museum, which they loved, so they put me on the board. That's how it works. It's all about money. For us—for me—it was part of the image."

"You carried it off well."

"People see what they want to see. I was an actress once. So I could do it. Only the worry kept growing. We built the proverbial house of cards. One goes and the rest follow."

"I'm sorry, Corinne."

"So am I. I have to be out of here by noon tomorrow. I don't know where to go. If they decide to charge me as an accomplice, I don't know what I'll do."

"You'll call Hugh," Dana decided, "and as for where to go, try my grandmother's house. She'd love to have you there until you figure things out."

Corinne was looking at her strangely.

"Why are you offering this? You don't like me."

Dana felt small. "Did I ever say that?"

"No. But I sensed it. You knew I was a fake."

"I was jealous. I was feeling scattered, and you were together. And about staying at Ellie Jo's—" She had been about to say that Corinne could be a help when Corinne cut her off.

"I can't, Dana. You're sweet to offer, but I can't."

"Why not?"

She smiled sadly. "I can't face those people. It would be too humiliating."

"They're good people. They'd understand."

But Corinne shook her head with conviction and finality. "Thank you. Your offer is kind. But I can't."

Dana was humbled. Nothing she had experienced in the last month—not even the DNA test—came close to Corinne's problems. The self-pity she had felt seemed petty, the anger pure spite. In comparison to Corinne, she had so much.

Driving back to the yarn shop, she remembered her grandmother always saying,

Things happen for a reason. That boy did you a favor by not asking you out, because look at the boy who did. Or, *That college rejected you because this one's far better for your skills.* Or even, *You would not be as independent or strong a woman if your mother hadn't died.*

Dana had lost the Cunningham job and, soon after, a place at the Designers' Showhouse, which meant that other than wrapping up a few last jobs, she had no commitments. Being free, she couldn't think of anything she wanted to do more than run The Stitchery.

She wouldn't change much, but there would always be new yarns to buy, new patterns, notions, and books. She might increase the inventory of decorative buttons for cardigans and specialized ribbons for scarves. She would attend buying shows twice a year, and her shopping sprees with Tara would produce new designs. Dana might even introduce a line of patterns based on things, like the Faroese shawl, that her mother had made.

It was an exciting prospect, a Joseph heritage to pass down to her own child one day.

Later, outside the shop, she found a patch of sun and propped Lizzie on her lap. "This is good, sweet baby."

And it was. Dana was finding herself. She was getting answers to questions that had plagued her for years. She felt more in control of her life. She was continuing to talk to Father Jack, and while she still didn't know if she wanted him in her life, she did know who he was. And his advice wasn't bad.

Lizzie made a cooing sound. She was clearly enjoying the air. Smiling at her daughter, Dana thought of Hugh, who was on his way to Lowell—reluctantly, if she interpreted his message correctly. But he was doing what he believed was right.

So here was another good thing about Hugh. Once he made up his mind, he was committed. Now that he had accepted Lizzie, he would always take care of her.

A breeze rustled the trees, sending out a wave of fragrance. The orchard was ripe with apples, nearly every variety ready for picking. On a screened-in sill of the house, Veronica dozed in the shade.

Dana smiled when Tara's silver van turned off the road. She got up to greet her.

Tara rolled down her window. "You called?"

Dana nodded. It wasn't official yet, but if she was going to own the shop, she wanted Tara on the payroll. That would mean Tara could quit the accounting job that she hated, and though Dana didn't know if she could match the pay, Tara was already spending so much time at The Stitchery that what she netted would come close. Dana wanted to tell her this. But it was too soon to break the news.

So she smiled. "Just wanted you here," she said, and stepped back to let Tara climb out.

❦

The instant Hugh turned the corner and got a view of the courthouse, he spotted the media. He wasn't surprised. He had figured that the press would get wind of the possible lawsuit. The same whispers that had prompted Sean Manley's call would have been buzzing around the courthouse. The senator might not be mentioned by name, but a lot of folks would guess.

Hugh found a space down the street and

parked, but he didn't climb out. It was only one-fifty. He had told Drummond he would file at two.

One-fifty-one. Hugh drummed a finger on the wheel. One-fifty-four. Several more reporters arrived. One-fifty-seven. The hot-dog vendor wheeled his cart closer.

At one-fifty-eight, Hugh grabbed his briefcase and climbed out of the car. He fed the meter and set off.

"Hugh!" came a call.

Ted Heath was a local lawyer with whom Hugh had worked. Hugh put out a hand but didn't stop walking. "How's it going?"

Ted shook his hand and he fell into step. "Can't complain. What brings you here?"

"This 'n' that."

"Hah. Confidential. Must be something big, with the vultures circling over there." He spotted his client, slapped Hugh on the shoulder, and trotted ahead.

Hugh kept walking. He avoided many of the reporters, but two flanked him as he reached the stone steps.

"What's the case, Hugh?"

"Can you confirm that a U.S. senator is involved?"

"Who's your client?"

"What's the complaint?"

Hugh held up a hand and kept walking. He felt the phone in his pocket, but it was silent. Time was running out. Once he entered the courthouse, he wouldn't turn back.

He was nearing the top step when he heard footsteps climbing fast behind him. Someone caught his arm. His own hand was on the door when he looked around.

He didn't recognize the sweating young man, but his worried expression made him an obvious junior associate.

Catching his breath, the associate gasped, "They want me to tell you. We'll do it privately."

"Who's 'we'?" Hugh asked, but he stepped away from the door.

"The senator," the associate said, following when Hugh moved farther from the path of traffic. "I work for Dan Drummond. I just got his call."

Hugh didn't have to ask why the associate was in Lowell. He was there to let Drummond wait until the last minute, hoping Hugh would blink first, before giving in.

In command now, Hugh said, "It has to be done Friday."

"The senator suggests four in the afternoon at his office. If word gets out, the deal is off."

"That goes two ways," Hugh warned. "If he reneges on the deal, I call the press ASAP, and I want this in writing."

"Mr. Drummond is couriering a letter to your office."

"See that Starbucks?" Hugh asked with the hitch of his chin. "I'll be waiting there until my office calls to say it's been received. Either we get it by three or I file."

"I'll let Mr. Drummond know," the lawyer said, and loped back down the steps. Hugh followed, and was immediately surrounded by the press.

"Has there been a postponement?"

"Is it true that a senator is involved?"

Hugh held up a hand. "There's no case. Sorry, folks." Working his way through the group, he crossed the street. He stopped at his car. With his eyes on the grudgingly dispersing crowd, he phoned his office, instructing them to call as soon as the letter arrived. Then he went into Starbucks, ordered a Mocha Frappuccino—*venti*—and finally breathed a sigh of relief.

He would wait for the call, though it was a formality. The letter would come. Dan Drummond was an annoying SOB, but his word was good.

Chapter 29

Eaton had decided to revisit his past. On Wednesday, he drove to Vermont to see towns he had spent time in as a boy. On Thursday, he drove to New Jersey and walked the campus of his prep school. But he knew he was procrastinating. The issue of the blatant inaccuracies in *One Man's Line* had to be dealt with.

On Friday, with four days to go before publication, he spent the morning in his office rereading those parts of the book that involved his parents and himself. The errors were on these pages. If he chose to alter the text for a future edition of the book, it would require research. That would take time. But it could be done.

More pressing, at this moment, was how to promote the current edition.

He didn't doubt that Thomas Belisle was his father. Hugh's daughter provided the missing piece of the puzzle, and Hugh's sickle-cell test confirmed it. Did Eaton want to be tested himself? No. He knew what the result would be.

The question was how much to say and to whom. Once he admitted the truth, there would be no turning back.

When his publicist called first thing that morning to discuss last-minute additions to the tour, he grew more agitated. When Dorothy appeared midmorning with a danish and coffee, he couldn't eat at all. By noon, he was back in the car. He drove past the country club, past the harbor restaurants he and Dorothy frequented, past the marinas that dotted the shore.

Without realizing where he was going, he headed north. Soon after, he found himself at Hugh's office.

Hugh was only marginally more settled than his father, and that simply because he was preoccupied with work. But he was ready for a break when a movement at the door caught his eye.

"I just walked in past your receptionist," Eaton explained, tossing a thumb back toward the lobby. "She must have thought you were expecting me." Tentatively, he came in. "I don't want to interrupt. Finish what you were doing." He took a chair.

Hugh added a final sentence to the memo he was writing and turned to his father. After an awkward silence, he said, "How's Mom?"

Eaton grunted. "Liberated."

Hugh laughed. "Is she still angry?"

"No. But she seems to be withholding judgment. Expecting something more from me."

"Have you heard from Robert?"

Eaton shook his head. "You?"

"No. He's in denial. You've lost weight, Dad."

Eaton shrugged. "I can't seem to eat and readjust to all this at the same time."

"It takes a lot to turn around a lifetime's way of thought." Hugh glanced at his watch. It was one-thirty. "I haven't had lunch. Did you eat?" Of course Eaton hadn't. Hugh rose. "Let's go out. I'm starved."

They went to the University Club, which would be emptying out at this hour. They could talk in private there. It was an easy walk from Hugh's office, and the Elm Room served Eaton's favorite crabmeat salad.

When they were seated, a couple of acquaintances stopped to greet them, but by the time their lunch arrived, they had the wood-paneled room to themselves.

They ate in silence. Hugh bit into his club sandwich, remembering all the times he had eaten this same lunch with Eaton. The University Club, like the country club, was part of his past. He had taken for granted his right to these memberships. Now he regretted that.

With barely half of his salad eaten, Eaton set down his fork. "So would we be here today if I had known the truth growing up?"

Hugh finished chewing. "You might have known the truth about your parentage and still grown up in the same house."

"Or not," Eaton reasoned. "What if my father—Bradley—had divorced my mother?"

"Her family still had a name."

"But no money. I wouldn't have had such a privileged childhood. I keep wondering about what I have now that I might have been denied if, say . . ." He didn't finish.

"If, say, your skin had been brown?"

"Yes."

"You did well in school. You got into college on your own. Same with graduate school. You earned your place at those schools."

"Did I?" Eaton asked quietly. "There were others who were just as qualified as I was, who didn't get in. Was my admission based on merit? Or was it money, or the family name? Same with the books I write. Did the first one sell because I was from an illustrious family? That first one was far from brilliant, but it gave me a foot in the door."

"It was good," Hugh said.

"Good, but not brilliant. There are many good books that never make it into print. My publishers might have given up on me."

"But you were *good*," Hugh argued.

Eaton shook his head. "The image of who I was reinforced the merit of the book. More to the point," he continued, "would we be here now? How many African Americans come to the Elm Room? Not as many as have graduated from the university, I'd warrant."

"They're not comfortable here. It's a bastion of whiteness."

"It's a bastion of *privilege*," Eaton

amended with disdain. "I feel guilty about that. I feel I should have spoken up against the exclusivity here. I always called myself progressive."

"So did I, but here I am," Hugh said. If being two-faced about his liberalism was a crime, he was as guilty as his father. "I spend my days representing minority clients, then go home to a community where there are few minorities. David Johnson is the exception."

"Does that mean you ought to move?"

"Does it mean we should drop our membership here?"

"What *does* it mean?" Eaton asked.

"Beats me," Hugh replied.

A door opened at the far end of the room, and a private party began to disperse. Hugh recognized many of the men. They were prominent members of the business community.

Several stopped at their table, a few dawdled at the door of the private dining room. At the center of that group, one of the last to emerge, was Stan Hutchinson.

Eaton stiffened when he spotted him. "Will this be a problem?"

Hugh shrugged and continued eating.

Hutchinson was halfway through the room when he saw them. Sending the rest of the group ahead, he approached.

Hugh and Eaton rose. Hutchinson shook their hands and gestured toward the bar. "Chivas, neat," he called.

"It's been an interesting week," he said as they sat down. "Your boy played me well, Eaton. Has he told you about that?"

"He certainly did," Eaton replied, fully composed. "He's good at his job."

The senator chuckled and said in the same collegial way, "I'll have to remember that next time some woman hits me with a potentially damaging charge. You know me," he drawled, "I'm a decent guy. I've spent the last thirty years fighting for the poor. I championed raising the minimum wage, I've proposed education incentives and sponsored job-training programs. Hell, know what we were discussing there in the back room just now?" He looked up when the bartender brought his whiskey, and took a healthy gulp. Then he set the glass down and smiled. "That meeting was about getting the leaders of this community involved in hiring teens and raising college scholarships." He thumped his chest. "This is what I stand for."

"No one's denying that, Hutch," Eaton said.

"Your boy is," Hutch argued, still speaking in a good-natured tone. "I stand for decency and honesty and respect."

"And family values," Hugh put in. "Wasn't that your message on *Meet the Press* a couple of Sundays ago?"

"We all know what the truth is here," the senator rumbled on. "We have a girl who has real problems. So she decided to go after me, because she has nothing to lose, not one damn thing. And I'll go along with it, Hugh, because you played your cards right. I gotta hand it to you. You knew I wouldn't want the publicity of even an accusation." He took another drink and set down the glass. "Was it the book, Eaton—because I wouldn't do your fuckin' interview? Or you, Hugh, because I didn't offer you the job as legal counsel for my committee?"

"What job?"

"The one I gave to your law-school pal?" he said, seeming legitimately confused. "What was it? You know me, you know my family. Why'd you pick on *me*?"

Hugh wasn't falling for the act. Stan Hutchinson was a seasoned politician. He might play the part of the bewildered victim, but Hugh knew he must be furious.

"I took the case before I ever knew you were involved," Hugh said.

"Okay," the senator allowed, "but afterward, you could have excused yourself. You could have claimed a conflict of interest."

"There is no conflict of interest. My firm isn't representing anyone else with whom you're involved. I took this case because I believe the woman, and she needs help. And you're right, we all know what you stand for. I figured that you, of all people, would want to make sure a child you fathered would have the best possible care."

The senator made a chiding sound. "Do you *know* how many women try to lay claims on me?"

"He's a sweet boy, Hutch," said Hugh. "He's cute and smart. He's coordinated enough to be a nice little athlete, assuming he gets the medical care he needs."

"He's not my child."

"That's what the test is for."

"Christ, Hugh, do you know the mess this could make? If word gets out—"

"Word won't get out unless you tell someone yourself. Everything will be kept private,
from the test to the settlement. Your family
will never know. You must have investments
your family knows nothing about."

The senator glared at him. "You are a cynical son-of-a-bitch. What if someone did
this to you? What if the tables were turned?
What would you do? Would *you* risk your
family, your job, your image?"

Hugh didn't hesitate. If he believed anything, he believed this. "If it were about doing the right thing, I'd risk it. You have
fought all your life for everything this child
represents. To turn your back on him, when
there's an easy enough solution, would be
the height of hypocrisy. So *do* you believe
what you say in Congress or to Larry King—
or is it all hot air? Does the public voice say
one thing and the private voice another? If
you're a man of honor, you need to show it
now."

Hutchinson stared at him long and hard.
Hugh was bracing himself for another attack when the man made a disparaging
sound, pushed back his chair, and strode
out of the room.

Hugh stared after him.

"That's it," Eaton said, his eyes dark and knowing. "You put it well."

Yes, Hugh realized. He had. And they weren't talking about Hutchinson.

Chapter 30

Dana kept thinking about Corinne. She tried to call her on Thursday, but there was no answer, and when she tried on Friday, a recording said the line was disconnected. She would have driven over to Greendale had she thought Corinne would be there. But she guessed that she was gone. With her real life exposed, her humiliation was real. She would likely be seeking a place where she was unknown. Dana doubted she would see her again.

If things happened for a reason, as Ellie Jo said, Corinne had served a purpose in Dana's life. Dana was more sensitive now to the cost of deception.

That made her even more forgiving of Ellie Jo, who, soon after her return home on Saturday morning, asked about the papers in the attic.

"Hidden again," Dana said with a new patience.

"The clipping and Emma's note—burn them for me?"

"Burn them? Are you sure?"

"Very. You know what they say. I know what they say. Now let's burn them."

Dana set fire to them on the back porch grill and, in so doing, shut one door on the past.

Another door soon opened. She was changing Lizzie after returning home when the doorbell rang. Hugh answered it, and though Dana listened, she couldn't hear more than the occasional murmur. Then she heard two sets of footsteps on the stairs. She recognized Hugh's tread, but had no idea who he was bringing to see her. She had finished snapping Lizzie's onesie and had turned to the door when she gasped in shock.

Despite a slight difference in age, the woman might have been her twin. She had the same blond hair and upturned nose, the same slight frame, the same freckles. And she had the same astonished look in her eyes as Dana had.

For a short time, neither woman spoke. Then the stranger said, "I'm Jennifer Kettyle. My dad wasn't sure you would welcome a visit, but I start fall classes on Monday, so I just got on a plane and took the chance."

"He said you were in San Francisco."

"I will be tomorrow." She grinned. "Today I'm here." Her grin widened. "Is this your baby? She is *beautiful*!"

No, just a few days earlier Dana wouldn't have welcomed this visit. She would have been so angry at what she had missed growing up that she would have missed even more. Now here was her half-sister, the daughter of the man whose identity Dana's mother had hidden, and Dana actually welcomed her into her life.

Things happened for a reason. Dana had much to be grateful for.

And still she wanted more.

❧

The plan was for Dorothy and Eaton to fly to New York late Monday for dinner with Eaton's publisher. Eaton would be interviewed on one of the morning shows early Tuesday. They would fly home in time for the book party Tuesday night at the club, and then begin his tour.

Dorothy packed her bag and then helped Eaton with his. Independence was all well and good, but she had been married to him for over forty years, and continued to take care of him. He was always tense on the eve of a book's publication, but this time there was cause. She tried to get him to talk about it, but he refused.

They were in the plane waiting for takeoff when, finally, he took her hand, threading his fingers through hers.

"How would you feel," he said in a low voice as the plane taxied into position, "if I just went ahead and said nothing about what I've learned?"

Said *nothing*? That wasn't what she had expected. "You have to do what you think is right."

"But how would you feel?"

Dorothy had to think about that—oh, not about her answer but about the wisdom of saying it. If Eaton had his mind made up, the truth might not help. Then again, if this was a test and he really wanted her opinion . . . "I'd feel disappointed. You have an opportunity."

"An opportunity."

"To turn a startling discovery into something positive."

"That 'startling discovery' could discredit every book I've written."

"Because you didn't know the truth? Oh, baloney, Eaton," she chided, albeit gently. "Simply come out and say what you've learned."

"On national TV?"

"Why not? People respect you. You could be a role model."

The plane started down the runway. "I could also permanently alienate our second-born son, not to mention my brother, their families, and a host of people we've called friends all these years."

"You could," Dorothy admitted.

"Would that bother you?"

"Only Robert. He's my son. I would hope that he'd come around."

The plane gathered speed.

"Maybe he needs more time," Eaton said. "Maybe I should give him that."

But Dorothy wasn't so sure. Robert had been under the thumb of his uncle for too long. It wouldn't hurt him to open his eyes and see the broader world. "Maybe he needs a kick in the you-know-what," she said, and repeated, "You have an opportunity, Eaton."

He regarded her fondly, but she saw something beyond mere indulgence. She chose to think it was respect.

He smiled, kissed her hand, and pressed it to his heart as the nose of the plane tipped up and the wheels left the ground.

❦

Monday was an amazing day at the shop. After a cool weekend, knitters who had been lulled up until then by the late-summer warmth suddenly woke up to the approach of fall. Opening the door in a steady stream, they came in search of yarn for scarves, sweaters, and throws. In the midst of it all, Ellie Jo insisted on being helped over from the house to announce Dana's new position as owner.

By noon, just as Dana was feeding Lizzie and realizing she was going to need help, Saundra arrived with her great-niece. Toni Belisle was the daughter of another of Thomas's sons. A fresh-faced young woman, she was taking a semester off from college to earn money for a junior year abroad. She loved children, and was as good with Lizzie as Saundra, or nearly so. Dana hired her before the afternoon was out.

Now Lizzie had a babysitter, which made Dana more relaxed. And the baby had slept for six whole hours Sunday night, so she had renewed energy.

Driving back home, Dana realized her life *was* good. She knew that Hugh did love her. If he had made a single misstep, she couldn't hold that against him forever. There were far more than three good things she could say about him, if she were to follow the directive of Father Jack.

If some of the early excitement of their relationship was missing, well, didn't all new parents lose some of that to the endless chores that parenting entailed?

Hugh was home early. Pulling up behind his car, she had just opened the back door to pick up Lizzie when he came out of the house and jogged barefoot toward the car. He wore jeans and his old navy tee shirt. She hadn't seen it since the morning Lizzie was born.

"Thought you'd never get here," he said, sounding excited.

"Did you make dinner?" she asked. That was always a treat. Hugh was a recipe man, the more ingredients the better, as long as he was told exactly how much of each to use and when.

He unbuckled Lizzie. "Yeah, but that's not it." He turned to Lizzie. "Hi, sweetie. How was *your* day?" He pulled the baby's little sweater—a Tara creation—more closely around her and lifted her out.

"Her day was great," Dana said, falling into step beside him with the diaper bag. "Gram announced that I was taking over the shop, I found a sitter for Lizzie, got Tara to sign on full-time, and ordered an *amaz*ing mohair from a new mill." Her voice softened. "And I called to let Father Jack know Jennifer came."

Holding Lizzie in one arm, Hugh held the door for Dana with the other. She barely had a foot over the threshold when she caught her breath. The front hall was filled with balloons, an endless bouquet of yellows, pinks, greens, blues, whites, peaches, and lilacs. Some were anchored to the floor, others climbed the banisters on each side of the hall, still others clung to the cathedral ceiling high above.

Dana was entranced. "How did you get all these here?" Tulip petals were one thing, easy to transport and strew. Balloons were something else.

Hugh looked proud of himself. "We had three delivery vans outside and had to struggle to get a few of the biggest balloons through the door, but they look pretty good, don't you think?"

"I *do* think," Dana declared. "What's the occasion?"

"We're starting over. It's like Lizzie was just born. But here's the best." With a hand on her back, he guided her through a maze of balloons to the staircase. A box sat two steps up. Perhaps ten inches long, eight wide, six high, it was wrapped in fuchsia foil and decorated with a white satin ribbon.

Dana grinned. "What is it?"

"Open it."

She lifted the box. One pull, and the ribbon was gone. Sliding her finger under a single piece of tape, she removed the wrapping. Recognizing the box underneath, she gave him a curious look. "Stationery?"

"*Open* it."

She raised the lid. There, in two neat stacks, were elegant white birth announcements. Each had a photo on the front and, beneath it, a bold raised script said, *Hugh and Dana Clarke proudly announce the birth of their daughter, Elizabeth Ames Clarke.* Lizzie's birthdate was at the bottom of the card.

"What do you think?" Hugh asked.

Dana couldn't answer at first. Her throat was too tight. The photo was of the three of them, exquisite in every regard—the parents' devoted expressions, the baby's perfect features. Lizzie's pink romper even matched the pink ink of the script.

"Who took this?" she whispered.

"Julian. What do you think?"

There were tears in her eyes when she looked up at Hugh. "I'm stunned."

"Better than the balloons?"

"Omigod."

"It was a rush job. I had to pay double, but worth every cent. There's another box just like this—another hundred. Think we can use them?"

"Omigod."

"Is that a yes or a no?"

Dana's heart was so full she thought she would burst.

"Dana?"

"*Yes.*"

This was what she had wanted—a sign, a gesture, a declaration. She wrapped an arm around Hugh's neck and hugged him, holding on even when the baby rebelled against the crush. She heard the little cry, felt the beat of Hugh's pulse, heard the waves pounding the beach behind the house. "He's proud enough to tell the world," she imagined her mother was saying.

But, of course, the thought was her own.

ACKNOWLEDGMENTS

Prior to writing *Family Tree* I knew precious little about the genetics of race, and while I read a good deal on the subject in preparation for writing this book, I still needed help. For their assistance, I thank Dr. Theodore Kessis and Vivian Weinblatt, as well as Bea Leopold of the National Society of Genetic Counselors. I am especially grateful to Jill Fonda Allen, who put not only her expertise as a genetic counselor to the task but her imagination as well.

My thanks to Martha Raddatz and Shameem Rassam for information on Iraqi life and speech, to Helen Dempsey for helping shape Jack Jones Kettyle, and to my husband's friend, David, for helping conceptualize Jay.

My assistant, Lucy Davis, was as indispensable as ever. I thank her for showing me what real family history is about.

I am particularly grateful to Phyllis Grann

for caring enough to offer me the chance of a lifetime, and to Amy Berkower for making it happen.

And finally, I thank my family for its steadfast support.

#130 5-7-08
379 9-20-08
131 11-5-08
292 3-12-09
281 . 8-6-09
379 10-31-17